King of the Hill

OTHER FICTION BY JOHN MOEHL:

Phobos & Deimos: two moons, two worlds

Closer to God

Ann—a story of intolerance

The Agate Hunter

Waiting—almost there

Son of Paul

Water Striders

King of the Hill

JOHN MOEHL

RESOURCE *Publications* • Eugene, Oregon

KING OF THE HILL

Resource Publications
An Imprint of Wipf and Stock Publishers
199 W. 8th Ave., Suite 3
Eugene, OR 97401

www.wipfandstock.com

PAPERBACK ISBN: 978-1-6667-4307-4
HARDCOVER ISBN: 978-1-6667-4308-1
EBOOK ISBN: 978-1-6667-4309-8

02/17/26

This work is dedicated to Elisabeth who is the king of my hill. She has shown love and courage that would and should be a model for all of the actors in this tale as well as possibly a few outside our story. This is also done, not as a testament to all those who look to find a conspiracy under every stone, but for those who view each day with a practical dose of reality sprinkled with common sense and basic facts.

CONTENTS

AUTHOR'S NOTE

THIS is a history. Through this history, this work sews together many of the activities and actors first presented in *The Agate Hunter*, *Son of Paul*, and *Water Striders*—to a lesser degree, *Waiting—almost there*. The characters in these earlier writings are all linked to the activities that are at the heart of the present tale. While each of these previous efforts is intended to be a stand-alone product, I hope the material presented herewith enriches the preceding stories.

This story is, however, completely a work of fiction. All the characters, locations, sites and events are fictitious. I am unaware of any existing or past companies with the names attributed to various firms and organizations in the text. Any connection to functioning or former firms, businesses, or groups is purely coincidental—all actions and events attributed to groups and enterprises in the following story are fictitious. Equally, all actions or events attributed to any public or private agencies come solely from the imagination and are not based on any facts. This is exemplified by the example of *The Daily News* as a newspaper playing an active part in our story. This paper has no relation with the real-life *Daily News*, the *New York Daily News*, or any other current or previous news organizations. While these characters, institutions, and actions may occur at real places—past and present—these are in no way intended to recount true happenings at these spots. The story is fiction. The themes may, nonetheless, reflect some elements of the human condition. We are all on a voyage that is a learning experience for which there may or may not be a handbook. We may, however, hope for the best.

WARNING

A Word of Caution to the Reader

THE following story may cause vertigo. The upcoming tale is complex, at times convoluted, and always twisted. It contains potentially troubling places and vernacular. It may cause confusion. At times you may feel lost or perturbed. Please rest assured these can be normal side effects that are short-lived. Overall, clinical studies have shown that this product causes no permanent damage although intermittent frustration may be noted.

CAST OF CHARACTERS

In order of their appearance

Shannon Baxter—US Secretary of State
Harold Mitchell—Philip's son
Joe Mitchell—Ukrainian immigrant
Philip Mitchell—Joe's brother
Andriy—Domov co-founder
Lehya—Domov co-founder
Mykola—Andriy's cousin
Yegor—Lehya's son
Taras Kuzmenko—first *Maliar*
Jefet—Domov manager
Heinrich Fuchs—Domov manager
Gershen Van Zyl—Domov manager
Robin McCandless—head of Delpro
Horace Barthley—Robin's brother
Artem—Joe's father
Susan Mitchell—Joe's wife
Anna Mitchell—Joe's daughter
David Mitchell—Joe's son
Vianney Cisse—Ivorian farmer
Antoinette Cisse—Vianney's wife

Marc Cisse—Vianney's son
Luc Cisse—Vianney's son
Abimbola—Vianney's partner
Voldoymyr Rudenko—Artem's nephew
Chantal Silue—Ivorian businesswoman
Tomas Ferreira—Portugese businessman
Florin Enache—head Domov/Romania
Radutu Botezatu—Romanian businessman
Fritz Murphy—Delpro mole in the Department of Defense
Christine Miller—Delpro mole in the Department of State
Florence Gardner—Delpro mole in the Department of Commerce
Lance Newcastle—Delpro mole in the Department of Agriculture
Howard Dunford—Delpro mole in the White House
Orest Savchuk—second *Maliar*
Sophie Arquette—French journalist
Dmytro Savchuk—Orest's father
Fedir Fedorenko—Clan headsman
Rich McKnight—Dakota truck driver
Wyatt & Ida McKnight—Rich's parents
Oriana Arquette—Sophie's daughter
Chakir Awal—Domov specialist
Rodney Mills—DOJ investigator
Hal Schleider—SEC investigator
Eddie Hall—Hal's nephew
Louisa (Lisa)—Eddie's partner
Samantha—Eddie's deceased first wife
Paula Patterson—EHT advisor
Peter Volman—Equatorial Management employee
Evelynn Oppenauer—Peter's partner
Charlie Stancik—Delpro employee

Jo McCormick—Charlie's partner

Cynthia Owens— Özgürlük CEO

Don Drumpfsh—Delpro office manager

Liu Li—Domov board member

Raymond Girard—Domov board member

Janco Momberg—Domov board member

Bohadan Kushnir—Domov board member

Sebastian Carvalho—Domov board member

Jake Sullivan—Senate committee chair Ann Winterbottom—Committee vice-chair

Franklin Brown—Committee vice-chair

Felix Manchester—Leader of Group 8

Blake Samuelson—*The Daily News* correspondent

Evans Parry—*The Daily News* photographer

Awa Konate—Oriana's Ivorian colleague

Koffi Zadi—Cisse manager

Mariama Mbaye—Oriana's Sénégalese colleague

Gage Smith—Domov envoy

Sandra Young— Fordham Business Chair

Claudia De Angelis— Fordham professor

Hans van den Berghe—Domov assistant

Andreea Gheata—Botezatu's assistant

Kyrylo Rudenko—Voldoymyr's son

Minata—Antoinette Cisse's niece

Rebecca Jameson—Senator Sullivan's wife

Drew Sullivan—Senator Sullivan's father

Sheila Ledbetter—Senator Sullivan's mother

Janice Pittman—Senator Sullivan's staffer

Ralph Tave—Kentucky businessman

Mr. Barbaneagra—Rodney's PI

Ted Whether—DOJ forensic accountant Sara McNab—DOJ forensic accountant

Lambert Richardson—Wisconsin businessman

Mercer McMaster—Georgia businessman

Yves Noirot—French businessman

Loretta Williams—Lobbyist IDF

Willy McNaught—*Maliar's* personal medic

Ebikake Dobra—leader NNDLF

Dr. Franz Schmidt—the *Maliar's* physician

Rubén di Paulo—Durango businessman

LIST OF ACRONYMS & OTHER TERMS

AAE—Approvisionnement Alimentaire Européen, a Yves Noirot company

AUCI— American University of Côte d'Ivoire

BAOD—Bank for development in west Africa

BFD—Best Farm Design LLC, Ralph Dave's principal business

Bootstraps Fund—Ralph Tave's foundation

BTF—Bratva Task Force, investigative group under the SEC

CAR—Central African Republic

DCWAS—Development Community of West African States

D-2—the iteration of BTF moved into DOJ

Delpro—a North American-based Domov operation

DOJ—Department of Justice

Domov—international syndicate

EHT—Ecumenical Humanitarian Trust

Energy Elite—David Mitchell's employer

Equatorial Management—a Horace Barthley company

ESGW—an Extraordinary Security Working Group

FLN—Fuerzas de Liberación Nacional, Chiapas militia group

FLS—Fig Leaf Storage, a Mitchell company

Fredericks, Higgins, and Woods—Delpro law firm

General Industrial and Chemical Products—US company linked to Tomas Ferreira

Globalny Fundusz Pomocy—first postwar Domov hub in Poland

Group 8—international organized crime group in DOJ

Gruppirovki—small-scale "traditional" Ukrainian criminal groups

ICDI—International Center for Democratic Ideals

IDF—Investment Defense Fund

INTERPOL—International Criminal Police Organization

J. P. Thorne LLC—a Delpro company

KHHF— Kindred Helping Hands Foundation

Kráľ Hory—King of the Hill

Les Caïds of Le Milieu—the bosses of French organized crime group

Maliar—head of Domov

Matadero Global—Domov hub in Argentinia

NCIIP—Nigeria-Cameroon Infrastructure Investment Project

NNDLF—Niger Delta Liberation Front

NORAD—North American Aerospace Defense Command

NSA—National Security Agency

O*betovať*—Domov "board"

Onyx Associates—Ivoirian-based company established by Chakir Awal

Özgürlük—Cynthia Owens' Turkish-based NGO

Porumbel Albastru—long-term care center in Constanța, Romania

Prestupnaia—mid-level "traditional" Ukrainian criminal groups

RICO—Racketeer Influenced ad Corrupt Organizations Act

RPCV—Returned Peace Corps Volunteer

S&J—S & J Logistics, a Mitchell company

SAMHAFRI—the Samantha and Hal's Friends' Foundation

SEC— Security and Exchange Commission

Section T15-Z—a hybrid special DOJ task force joining Group 8 and D-2

SESB—Special Executive Security Branch

Simpson Investments—US company linked to Tomas Ferreira

Solntsevskaya Bratva—major Russian organized crime group

Soobshckestvo—well-organized, high level "traditional" Ukrainian criminal groups

Southern Continentals—US militia group

Spot On—a Delpro company

Sullivan Committee— a subgroup (not a true committee) of the Senate's Permanent Committee on Homeland Security and Government Affairs

The Farmers' Home—Lambert Richardson's business

USIS—United States Information Service

UNCHANGING CLIMATE

The climate surrounded him,
he could feel the heavy, sometimes wet, sometimes dry, weight.
It was an ample cloak that all too often offered little protection from the elements.

His elements were not the elements of rain or shine, hot or cold.
His elements were not even the elements of good or bad, right or wrong.
His elements were those of life and death, extinction or survival.

His domain was not the forest nor the sea, the mountain nor the *marais*.
He was neither urbane nor mundane, citified nor villatic.
His ecosystem was the globe—he was everywhere and nowhere.

His aim was to resist change; to foster stability—the status quo.
His essence was an immutable climate of consistency;
consistently high profits and persistently in power.

He was one of many, easily lost in the crowd;
a common man with uncommon roots.
He was the *Maliar*—the King of the Hill.

PROLOGUE

THEY didn't know if this was a break-glass-in-case-of-fire moment. Maybe.

They returned to the posh interview room, the centerpiece of an unknown yet sophisticated apartment in an equally unknown but seemingly very unsophisticated and rundown building in the Brentwood neighborhood of DC.

"Thank you very much, Madam Secretary."

The striking yet well-over-middle-age, blue-green-eyed lady stood, arranged her impeccably tailored suit, and left without a word or a handshake.

Before the door could slip closed behind the Secretary's erect frame, one of the team members stuck his head in. "Stu, what do we do with the recordings?" he asked.

"Put them with the rest of the stuff in the evidence room, in lock-stall thirty-nine with all the security cipher notations and tabs, encoded to Section T15-Z."

"OK."

With that, machines were turned off, papers put in briefcases, and the crew exited the building, locking the reinforced steel door behind them. The deck-grey door faintly stenciled with the words GROUP 8.

INTRODUCTION

THE King was Harold. The hill, at least the physical hill, was one that overlooked Cox Rock that overlooked the Pacific Ocean. But the real hill was Domov. And Harold sat on top.

Harold may have been seen by many as having little, even surreptitious regality, but his select group of close confederates knew he was not only the King but also the *Maliar*, the mortician.

This was certainly not a well-known fact. In truth, it was a highly guarded secret that had cost some their lives and many their livelihoods. King of the hill was a serious game. While the costs were high, the returns were higher. This hill was not for the faint of heart nor for the risk adverse—it was a high-stakes poker game where the winner could truly win it all.

Yet, all this required great skill—great power and influence—to pull the necessary strings of a global network while seated in the shadows. It was like tending a garden on a moonless night.

And Domov was as vast as it was complex. Domov's tenacles entangled global politics and economies. Domov may or may not have been a kingdom, but Domov had rightly been called an octopus or a hydra. Others among the few who knew of its existence called it a cancer or a weed—referring to it like crabgrass—once established, it was nearly impossible to get rid of. But Harold and those few insiders of the highest echelons knew it was not a hardy, survive-everything herb. It was, in fact, a delicate bloom that needed to be carefully cultivated on terrain that itself had been carefully prepared. Domov provided bountiful harvests only when it was well cared for and when its roots were deeply planted in fertile soil. In the words of the Japanese philosopher/farmer, Masanobu Fukuoka, "The ultimate goal of farming is not the growing of crops, but the cultivation and perfection of human beings."

BOOK I

Pathways

"The beginning is the most important part of the work."

—PLATO

CHAPTER 1

CULTIVATING OPPORTUNITIES

Now and Then

"Seize the day and put the least possible trust in tomorrow."

— Horace

HAROLD appreciated there was no handbook for his job. But there was a long history. His own roots went back to Schuylkill County, Pennsylvania. From there, his ancestors could be traced all the way back to Kaniv, Ukraine, on the banks of the Dnieper River. From this town with its own rich story reaching into the eleventh century his forefathers had exchanged work in the vegetable fields and dairies for hopes of riches in the growing city of Kyiv, about two and a half hours upriver.

From the earliest family records, it was clear that Harold's forebears had not been members of the *shliakhta*—the nobility. They had been hardworking peasants. And like hardworking peasants of their time, they felt themselves outside the formal economy and laws of those in power—they were the pawns and not the actors. For their own survival, they had adopted a system of governance that viewed the outside world, the world of the rich and powerful, as antagonistic, exploitative, and domineering. This "us-and-them" philosophy led to a romanticizing and even a welcoming of the Robin Hood-like thieves and gangs who preyed on the nobility. With the support of the peasantry, these groups of simple criminals metamorphosed into syndicates of sophisticated operators who provided goods and services to the lower classes who would have otherwise been without. Those engaged in illicit activities were often seen as purveyors of fairness in a society that was otherwise anything but fair.

Once off the farm, Harold's predecessors had started as members of the Gruppirovki in Kyiv—small-time thieves and malefactors just barely surviving on their ill-gotten gains with a meager amount left over to send to family back in Kaniv. But, like Harold, they were good at what they did. Through time his forerunners progressed up the ladder of criminality, becoming members of larger and more recognized mid-level groups called *Prestupnaia*. As success breeds success, successive generations continued the trajectory, becoming key personages in the *Soobshckestvo*—criminal groups whose impact was countrywide with international affiliations including with the Russian Solntsevskaya Bratva. As part of the *Soobshckestvo*, Harold's progenitors had knitted important alliances with powerful political leaders as well as with corrupt factions in law enforcement. They had entered into an integrated web of illegality that was growing in both influence and wealth.

Harold's now urban ancestors, the Myshchenko's, sent a subset of their group to the west of the country, to the Carpathian Mountains, to the small administrative center of Verkhovyna—a long day's travel from the nation's capital. These mountains, cutting through the tri-country intersection of Ukraine, Romania, and Moldova, were rife with smugglers moving all manner of items from cigarettes and brandy to shotgun shells and baby food. Harold's forbearers' crew transferred merchandise smuggled down the Dnieper River from Belarus and Russia to the west to exchange for wares their counterparts brought from Ukraine's southern neighbors.

It was very profitable, and it opened many doors—exposing the family to the intricate commercial and social labyrinths that, in many ways, held things together. However, it took constant care to keep the pathways open. There were numerous and varied participants—both inside and outside officialdom. There were proponents and opponents. The clan was able to bribe or cajole some, but the more recalcitrant often required threats. Vigilance was a constant as was seeking new doors to open.

As alliances were forged and critical players brought into the fold, Harold's clan increased their reach—expanding both geographically and vertically—entwining a growing number of the *shliakhta,* the political and social elite, in their affairs. As the dust from World War II settled and the Iron Curtain clanged shut, Harold's family had the enviable (by some) standing as one of the major criminal groups in Eastern Europe.

Throughout, the family had demonstrated considerable skill—some would call it craftiness, others perhaps mendacity. Whatever its label, the family had learned the hard way to always have options. It was through this strategy of spreading the risk that they decided to send two brothers to the United States.

Just out of their teens, Yosyp and Pylyp Myshchenko, strong young men with what all hoped were agile minds, settled in Pottsville, the county seat of Schuylkill County—two hours north of Philadelphia.

Joseph, or Joe, and Philip Mitchell, as they were now called (they were told their new adopted surname reportedly meant big or someone who is like God—it seemed a good choice), came to the US on visas organized by the Fallon Anthracite Company, based in Pottsville. Some of the world's largest reserves of anthracite coal were in northeastern Pennsylvania. Schuylkill County sat smack-dab in the middle of lots of hard coal and the community started digging it out of the ground at the end of the eighteenth century.

By the time Joe and Philip arrived, the coal industry was already in a decline that was to continue for years. Although production was well off the highs of nearly ten million short tons annually in the early 1900s, coal was still a vitally important product, and the mining industry was in need of hard workers. Here Joe and Philip found their niche—or, at least, their initial slot in the American landscape.

Establishing roots as best they could, both brothers found spouses with whom to share their fifty-hour work weeks. They joined community groups, learned local culture, got calluses on their hands, and had children—Joe two, and Philip three.

The brothers understood the motivation for their transplanting into American soil was twofold. They were anchors for the family in Ukraine. If there were dire events, as the Cold War potentially promised, they offered a possible escape route. Moreover, and of greater importance to the family back home, they were also a seedling that was now growing in the fertile ground of the great and burgeoning economy of the United States. It was anticipated that, as they became integrated into their new community, they would explore options for the family business—seeing where the family's skills from their Ukrainian affairs could be best applied in the New World.

Things generally went to plan. Then things fell apart.

Harold was Philip's youngest son. One day, Harold's mother was picking up his brother and sister from school in the family's DeSoto sedan when the car was flattened by a runaway coal truck. All three passengers were killed instantly. It was terrible.

Philip's soul was shattered.

Philip looked to his extended family. But mostly, Philip looked to a heretofore frequently sidelined God.

Ukraine is considered as a predominantly Christian country—a devout country. While about two-thirds of Ukrainians at home and abroad declare some affiliation with Orthodox theology, and there were Orthodox places of worship including St. Vladimir Ukrainian Orthodox Cathedral in Philadelphia, transplanted folks often found it easier for many reasons to ally themselves with local Roman Catholic parishes. This had been the case for Joe and Philip.

Joe had been pragmatic. He, and later his family, had joined Saint Patrick's Roman Catholic congregation as part of his rites of passage into local society—the church frequented by many of his co-workers. It was a means to an end—and not a religious end.

Philip had started in the same frame of reference as his big brother. He had seen Saint Patrick's as a conduit to his broader assignment of finding inroads for his Ukrainian family. However, much to his own surprise, what he found was a conduit to spirituality—a spirituality he had never known before and a spirituality that helped him deal with the complete wrecking of his life by a runaway coal truck.

As his loss transformed from a seeping open wound into a hard lump in the pit of his stomach, Philip decided he was not cut out to, not able to follow the grand plan laid out by his extended family when he had embarked on his American adventure. No more subterfuge. No more hidden agendas. He was out.

With no real consultation with Harold, Philip arranged for Joe to care for his remaining son—to effectively adopt the young boy. Philip himself entered St. Charles Borromeo Seminary in Philadelphia, determined to give himself to God. As Harold prepared to enter junior high school, Philip, now Father Philip, became the first assistant to the bishop of the Ukrainian Catholic Archdiocese of Philadelphia.

While Joe and his now enlarged American family became part of coal country, the family in Ukraine was hard at work. The family was going through a change in leadership—really a change of life. The family was being flooded with new ideas as to how best to cope as the world responded to the end of two nearly back-to-back devastating overt wars and was then swallowed by a covert Cold War—many of the most recent and precarious forces pushing to and fro in their own backyard.

Nonetheless, the family's Eastern European operations continued to grow in both complexity and scope. The stage was set (or could be set) for them to be top competitors in Ukraine and even move into areas that had traditionally been the territories of opposing forces. The groundwork was being laid, but these were sensitive and frequently dangerous grounds.

Everyone had their own patch, their own space. Everyone had their own specialties, their own standing. It was a balancing act. Grow, engage more, make more money, but step on as few toes as possible.

Initially, it had been finding the equilibrium between the nobility and the peasants. Now it was trying to harmonize, or at least stabilize, relationships between numerous volatile and potentially rival groups of actors.

The family, calling its group the Kaniv Ceață (*ceață* being a word for fog—the fog that would creep up the Dnieper and the obscurity under which they did business), was faced with multiple challenges. They had made their mark in black-marketing—starting small and going big. But they had so far managed to avoid dealing in what they considered as taboo markets: people, drugs, and arms. They were fine with pharmaceuticals—real and pseudo. They were fine with ammunition and even hunting paraphernalia but had tried to draw the line at what they considered military matériel. In a tumultuous world, in a competitive and tumultuous world, it was hard to hold to one's principles.

One of the great and popular thinkers of the day, Albert Einstein was renowned for saying, "In the middle of difficulty lies opportunity." He also said, "We cannot solve our problems with the same thinking we used when we created them."

Whether knowingly or not, Kaniv Ceață took these principles to heart.

Shifting political and economic tempests were changing the topography like the windswept snows drifting across the steppes. At times, new areas would be uncovered and ripe for exploitation—ripe for business. Yet, as with all groundbreaking, these new sites, these new markets, these new arrangements all had to be well prepared—the land well plowed, the soil loose and deep to respond optimally to new opportunities. Furthermore, all these preparations had to be done using the best, most current approaches. Kaniv Ceață could no longer use the same methodologies that had worked well for the disheveled ring of bootleggers in the Carpathian Mountains. New terrain, new clients and partners, and new trades required new and updated dealings. The family had to keep up with the times.

Keeping up with the times was a concern in Schuylkill County as much as in Ukraine. Joe had slowly but surely inveigled himself into the fabric of Pottsville. He was now an accepted member of the mining community as well as the community at large. He was also looking for openings for the family business. He was, however, handicapped by really knowing very little about the status of the family business as it was now functioning. He had only had a cursory view of the inner workings of the family's operations while still at home (Joe continued to think of Ukraine as home—Pottsville seemed more like military service although he did feel real affection for his American family). And, to make things more complicated, unsure of who could actually read what, he could not ask the necessary questions in routine letters home. Definitely, back on the banks of the Dnieper, the government snoops would be looking into people's mail—especially mail from America. There were no easy options. A phone call between Kyiv and Pottsville was out of the question. To get an overseas' connection, he had to drive to Philadelphia and go to the exchange to be able to make a call to Eastern Europe. Then, in spite of the effort, the line did not go through more times than not; when it did, there were likely to be people listening-in.

Although Joe's concerns about being able to achieve his prime objective of bringing the family business to the New World were justified, the fickleness of all their plans intervened. There was ultimately an unexpected but much appreciated alignment, an unplanned common denominator between the activities in Ukraine and Pennsylvania.

While Joe was attempting to see how to hook onto the family's operations, the European family was in the process of overhauling their overall network.

As the family tried to organize in both hemispheres, there was an unappreciated common thread that could possibly help harmonize plans and actions: coal. Not only was Joe in coal country, but the family home territory was also part of the Dnieper Brown Coal Mining Basin. Ukraine was, after all, among the top three or four coal producers in Europe. Although the largest reserves and the highest quality products were in the east of the country in the Donets Basin, there was an existing, if declining market for the lignite mined very near to the family's home turf.

Coal was a community lifeline. Coal was a unique culture. However, declining coal production in both the Dnieper Valley and Schuylkill County meant the lifelines were shriveling and the cultures changing. People were in tough economic times. Whether through fate or divine providence, these tough times provided the opportunities for the family to accumulate both clients and partners while revising efforts as necessary to be able to take maximum advantage of waning economies in both Ukraine and Pennsylvania (and beyond).

Neither common folks in the Ukraine nor Schuylkill County were unaccustomed to tough times. Life was hard. But it was getting harder, and people were looking for ways to make ends meet. Sometimes this meant engaging in alternative, less savory activities. Sometimes this meant changing lifestyles to more affordable models. Sometimes this meant getting rid of obstacles.

Harold's extended family had demonstrated they were up to the task of helping people (or helping people think they were being helped) while they helped themselves. At times, this intervention involved offering substitute (aka, smuggled) merchandise. At times, this involved convincing (applying pressure as necessary) decision-makers to make the right decisions. At times, this involved establishing client relationships with those in need where they made regular payments for necessary or desired services.

In short, through fraud, extortion, trafficking, racketeering, and sundry other actions, the family was able to do good business in coal country (potentially on both sides of the Atlantic).

However, these actions did not erupt spontaneously. They could not be initiated through an open house or a ribbon cutting for a new business. They grew slowly in the shadows. When the terrain was prepared, when the land was cleared and due diligence had been well heeded, these actions could grow and expand, taking root in the community.

Joe thought about his second job, his cloaked assignment, as though it were one of cultivating kudzu—the widely detested plant, weed for most, that slowly but surely covers everything. When the conditions were right, when the conditions were ripe, like kudzu, Joe's projects would spring forth seemingly with an energy of their own. The family was putting down roots in the New World.

Gnarly Beginnings

Looking back, well before Joseph and Philip had gone to America, in fact, not too long after their father had finished secondary school and married this childhood sweetheart, a chance meeting had planted a seed that would affect their lives as well as the lives of many others.

However, even before this groundbreaking meeting had taken place, well in advance of identifying the planting material, the land had to be prepared, the pastures leveled, the fields tilled.

While the ungerminated seed was still an unfulfilled concept, it was a dream sought wholeheartedly by a visionary—a new crop to be cultivated in new ways that would yield new and unimagined harvests.

But, just as the *rol'ník*, the tough and gritty peasants who were the foundation upon which the society was built, had to take risks with every crop, realizing the vision required an acceptance of great risk and more than a little faith in the yet-to-be-fulfilled dream.

Preparing the terrain for this soon-to-come seed, this possibly perilous ambition, was a process predicated by the work of Kaniv Ceață. It was a process whose implementation demanded time (far too much in the eyes of some—the complainers comparing it to the interminable cycle of the thirteen-year cicada). It was an excellent example of the functions, or dysfunctions, of the prevalent Gruppirovki crime groups—not really an organization, more of a disorganization.

The time-honored status quo of these historical groups was unstructured and uncoordinated. It was exemplary of laissez faire small-scale crime. While group members liked to think of themselves as a kind of cooperative in the best of current Bolshevik fashions that were gaining a following at the time, it was more like a youth club than a business. There was no formal leadership although Joseph and Philip's grandfather's second cousin Andriy was, or felt he was, at the very least the group's doyen (some hypothesized this was simply because, as he reminded all, his name meant "warrior").

Andriy the combatant was also a true visionary.

He had long scolded his family. They had chosen a path, but they were unprofessional. They needed what he called îndrăzneală—they needed to be bold. While he wouldn't call it crime, he extolled all to take the family's efforts seriously. This was not a pastime; it was a business. It should be a big profitable business if it was indeed worth doing. The clan was doing alright; they were making more money than they had ever imagined. But they could do better. Andriy had a vision for the family's operations.

Andriy prodded and pulled his clan. They must do better. It wasn't complicated. They simply needed to know their market. Of course, money was in the market and if they supplied the market what the market wanted (or felt it needed), they would get their money. Their work wasn't about vengeance. Their work wasn't about retribution. Their work wasn't about status. Their work wasn't really even about fairness. Their work was all about market share.

Andriy ultimately managed to implant at least some modicum of order into what had been disorder—nearly random activity. The clan began more carefully selecting merchandise moving through their channels. They began to get paid more for what their goods and services were really worth—not with what miserly coins people just happened to have in their pockets at the time. They began to make real money.

⚘⚘⚘⚘⚘⚘⚘

Andriy had been trained as a teacher although it had been a long time since he had set foot in a classroom. Nonetheless, he had been a good mentor to many, and pedagogy was deeply ingrained in his psyche. He was always coaching at best and disciplining at worst. Through his efforts, his family enterprise had bore fruit. In spite of (or perhaps because of) the Great War, Kaiser Wilhelm II, the Versailles Treaty, the pre-war economic growth, and the postwar recession, his family had been able to adapt. His family had been able to do business. His family enterprise had gained traction, market share, and recognition.

Attention was not always a welcome thing when dealing with basically illicit actions. While anonymity was unquestionably the desired state as concerned the authorities and the nobility (often one in the same), a level of notoriety among peers was good for business—clients and partners putting more credence in activities undertaken by a well-known group even if, according to some, a well-known group of bad guys.

As the family began to accumulate some real wealth and slowly move out of the peasantry (as Andriy considered their earlier *ad hoc* methods), Andriy decided he had done his best—the family business was on track. It was time to treat himself for the first time in his life.

He enquired of his competitors—kind of a professional courtesy—where someone from the shadows could have a holiday. Where could someone use to staying in the penumbra go to relax, to be among the nameless, yet be secure, and able to enjoy the modest luxuries of modest sightseeing in the relative undistinguished role of being a tourist among tourists? This was all new to him. He had no idea.

In the end, in consultation with thoughtfully chosen associates, he decided on a sort of working holiday at the small Black Sea town of Serhiivka, fifty miles southwest of Odesa, just south of the Karahvol's'ka Gulf on the Dnister River. This locale was close to major ports as well as numerous holiday destinations. At the harbors, one could check on new avenues for moving old merchandise while enjoying hoped-for invisibility in plain sight.

In Serhiivka, he chose a rather posh and exclusive beach resort unremarkably named Pensiune Lazo after Sergey Lazo, a rather recent local hero. Sergey had been a member of the Moldovan nobility who had exchanged his princely title as a full-fledged boyar to be a cadet in the Imperial Russian Army near the end of World War I. With a bit of a stretch, Sergey, the selfless soldier or wayward aristocrat, might be considered as a local boy as his homeland was just thirty-five miles to the north of Serhiivka—this part of Ukraine tucked under the arm of her much smaller southwestern neighbor, Moldova. Sergey Lazo might even be considered as a provincial, if somewhat veiled, celebrity.

Andriy found it interesting that as he picked up bits and pieces of Sergey's biography, the young cadet, while still at the academy, had changed sides to join the Bolsheviks. Crammed into his few youthful months at war had been battles fighting against the Imperial Army including engaging in Siberia against Imperial allies from America, France, Japan, and Britain. He had ultimately been arrested in Vladivostok by Japanese troops and disappeared thereafter—reportedly killed by the Japanese or White Russians at the age of twenty-six. As a martyr in the prime of his life, his memory and heroic éclat had been spread across a smattering of sites including several street names and epithets at other locales, most notably in the Sikhote-Alin Mountains in extreme southeastern Russia, just across the Sea of Japan from the home of his captors—possibly his murderers. The Lazo name, with much less fanfare, was now also attached to an unassuming hotel where Andriy took his first-ever vacation—a discreet purlieu on the shores of what the ancient Greeks had called the *Euxine Sea*—the hospitable waters.

Andriy had chosen well—perhaps too well. At the same resort, possibly for the same reasons, was one *Gospodin* Lehya Baranov. Andriy and Lehya first met casually at the hotel bar—finding themselves by the grace of the gods on neighboring barstools. After curt introductions, Andriy, ever the erudite schoolteacher, offhandedly commented that his new friend's (or at least his drinking buddy) first and surnames translated (at least in some languages) as lion and lamb—adding that in the Christian Bible in Isaiah 11:6, it was noted that the wolves would dwell with the lambs. He wondered if the same applied to lions.

Gospodin Baranov, Mister Baranov, was taken aback. He didn't know how to react to this oldish, frumpish man nearly his mirror image in form if not in manner. That, by his accent, his new acquaintance was Ukrainian but understood the origins of Russian names was of no surprise. After all, Ukrainians were joined at the hip to Mother Russia—Russian culture and language (and order) were everywhere. But the practically flippant nature of the comment, including the reference to the Christian Bible, was unexpected. Publicly, even at bars, people were predictably seen as being stoic. Cheeky discourse was not normal—especially directed to a man who, if his bar mate ever knew, was one of the czars of Russian syndicates—a leading *vory v zakone* ("thieves-in-law"), a top-level operator in the networks of criminality that arose out of and not in spite of Stalin's Gulag—the anticipated cure creating a more debilitating disease.

But Lehya was on vacation like his uninvited companion. Vodka-induced discourse shouldn't be examined too closely with a microscope. Like his new drinking comrade, he was far from home. He was among strangers. He could afford to relax and just, as his mother had always wanted him to do, "go with the flow."

So it was that two more-than-middle-aged men shared vodka and their stories at a bar in a hotel *cum* resort named after a young Moldovan who was reportedly just as obsessed with what he saw as justice as these senescent men were about what they saw as self-preservation.

It wasn't so much that Andriy and Lehya had a lot in common, although largely in the same sort of business, their personalities were very different—nearly polar opposites. Andriy was intellectual and generally reserved (albeit, at times glib). Lehya was impulsive and boorish (never glib).

Under the present circumstances, it was more their appreciation of good vodka and a priority on invisibility that pushed them to share the same sphere in Serhiivka—to dwell in the same dark shadows. Neither felt threatened by the other. Each was comfortable that, while their paths momentarily crossed, they would ultimately go back to their own families and their own endeavors. Each was comfortable that in old age they shared an understanding of the caprices and indecipherability of their now condensed temporal lives. This led to an unusual level of frankness that verged on unbridled openness when the level of vodka in the ever-present bottle dropped below the midpoint.

Individually, these exchanges impacted on each man differently. Jointly, they impacted on both of the old scoundrels as well as on a covey of their associates. Andriy was beguiled by the scope and depth of Lehya's operations whose tentacles reached the furthest corners of Eastern Europe and, impressively, into Asia. Lehya, for his part, was enthralled at the level of sophistication and detail the old schoolteacher had been able to build into his cartel of erstwhile pirates fleeing the malignity of the Ukrainian *shliakhta*—his own family had felt equally oppressed by the equally malevolent Russian *dvoryanstvo* whose bloodlines he did not share.

On most days, after a filling breakfast of *shkvarky* (dish made from fried pork rinds) and eggs, accompanied by fresh *pampushki* (yeast rolls), Andriy would take a ferry to the barrier island where he could walk along the pristine beach and let his mind soar with the Caspian terns that effortlessly rode the persistent sea breeze. He would think of family, family business, and his own mortality. Andriy was a thinker. On days when he felt he needed more (and this "more" was a lot more, as travel was neither quick nor particularly comfortable), he would hire the hotel carriage to visit local ports—local not being all that close. Odesa was a major port by any standard and before reaching the big city, there was the Port of Chornomorsk—both anchorages important transit points for international freight. When one added to the list harbor space in the Gulf of Karahvol's'ka, there were many suitable maritime passages into and out of the country—passages for Andriy to investigate as his thoughts explored options for his family business to grow further and to have a much larger footprint more commensurate with his dreams—to leave a larger legacy.

While Andriy was wandering about, Lehya, too, left the hotel. He, however, was picked up by a burnished black Russo-Balt C 24, a motorcar still a relatively unique luxury, and taken to unknown points for the bulk of the day. Then, in the evenings, at what the English would call teatime, he would meet Andriy at the hotel bar—the pair having migrated from barstools to a secluded corner table—where a bottle of vodka awaited them.

Over the course of the weeks that constituted their conjunct holidays, the two old men talked of many things—one the astute scholar, the other the audacious criminal mogul. However, drifting above (or under) all was an unspoken tone, a sort of measuring-up—each scrupulously studying the other. As they finished their last bottle of vodka, each going his own way the next day, Lehya offered a toast. "We should meet again. We should do business."

This simple yet direct conclusion surprised Lehya himself who was totally unaccustomed to engaging in any discussions or arrangements with anyone whom he considered to be an equal.

This conclusion was even more surprising to Andriy. Through their nightly bouts of drinking and telling tales, Andriy had come to realize that Lehya was really a prominent person—a prominent person in the same profession as he—a major actor in a whole variety of criminal actions across Eastern Europe and beyond. If Andriy had been younger, he would have been starstruck. As it was, he saw the encounter, the chance meeting, as a quirk of fate. It was good luck to balance all the other happenings that were not always so good. It was a chance to catapult ahead and move his clan to the top of the heap. It was a rare chance to definitely become real players and not just pawns.

Lehya's closing proclamation, his indirect benediction of the newly formed bonds with Andriy, and, by association, with Andriy's clan, had planted a seed. With suitable care and attention, the seed could germinate and, if tended well, produce a bountiful harvest. But the seed was fragile and required diligent nursing.

Both headmen met again several times over the coming months to see how they could craft bilateral arrangements where the whole would be truly greater than the sum of the parts. It was complicated. It required considerable debate. It required considerable introspection.

Then, at about the same time as the Bolsheviks gained a firm foothold in Ukraine, establishing the Union of Soviet Socialist Republics, Andriy and Lehya began to see the structure of their joint effort. Yet, this vulnerable seedling was not in the cleansing light of the sun. It was like the gooseberries Andriy's parents had grown in the shadow of the barn. This new seedling came from the darkness and, for its survival, was necessarily still in the darkness. There was the promise of growth, but roots had to first cling solidly to the shifting soils. Andriy and Lehya hoped the seedling could survive. They could already picture their own union—the recent soviet superstructure actually complementing their plans for a greatly empowered felonious conglomerate.

It was then time to see if the plant would survive the rigors of frigid winters on the savannahs of the steppes or humid summers in the forests of the taiga.

It was complicated.

It was very complicated.

Not only were there legal concerns, but any union between Andriy and Lehya involved different clans, different countries, different norms. Each group wanted to be on top of the heap. Each group wanted its individuality, its status. While the headmen saw many benefits from joining forces, the rank and file would not be easily convinced. For them, sharing was not a priority. Jumping into the fray that was the postwar turmoil and coming out on top was the priority.

These complications made Andriy abandon any thoughts of retirement. While he could and indeed had passed on the routine oversight of family operations to a young nephew with promising attributes, he could not hand over his relationship with Lehya nor the planning underway by these two old strategists.

It became clear that a straight-up partnership between the two groups was a nonstarter. Neither team really intentionally played nicely with others. Still, in spite of the myopic view of most of the troops about collaboration and cooperation, there were, in Andriy and Lehya's eyes, unquestionable advantages to forming a union. Their own exhaustive assessment had highlighted compelling benefits to be gained from joining hands. But the majority of the crew would not see the profit from making a few modest short-term sacrifices for significant long-term gains. For them, the here and now was all that mattered.

In many ways, the traditional nearly tribal groups were quite democratic.

While the aging chieftains would remain central to their respective operations, if they pushed for unpopular integration to form a wider union where each trooper felt he or she would actually lose ground, they would pay a heavy price. Their clans would, as had been done in the past, silently move them to token positions as figureheads while the real command and control shifted to others—likely, others far from their reach or influence. To remain at the heads of their respective organizations, they needed to be clever. They needed to act on parallel tracts. They needed to maintain day-to-day business pretty much as usual while setting the cornerstones for more expansive, combined actions in the future. Only time would tell if they would finally be able to merge into one union or if they would need to maintain the duality of shadows and then shadows within shadows. This could, they agreed, well be the critical factor of their entire strategy.

As could have been, and should have been expected, it was not only complicated, but it also took a lot of time. The fragile seedling was putting down some roots. With luck (maybe no small amount), it would grow into an adult plant, but it would take time. Change was rarely rapid, and behind the veil of crime clans, it could creep painstakingly and haltingly forward—baby steps for giant reforms. Andriy and Lehya, however, did not have unlimited time. As age finally caught up with each venerable warrior—each august lion—hoping they had adequately prepared the terrain for much better harvests to come, realizing they had no choice, they baptized successors; in Andriy's case a much younger cousin,

Mykola, and for Lehya, one of his sons, Yegor (appropriately translated as "a farmer").

As the second pair of strategists took over, the countryside prepared for another world war. Through the vibrations of this war, two new pairs of hands took over the subtle nourishing of the seedling that was still to see the light.

Crafting a Montage

MYKOLA and Yegor assumed not only the responsibilities of their predecessors, including the generous compensation for these responsibilities (in both wealth and status), they also inherited the split personality conventions inherent in roles requiring leadership in the present and vision for the future. In truth, Mykola and Yegor were the chiefs of chiefs for their clans.

Practices set in place by Andriy and Lehya were maintained. Activities that were seen as falling in the traditional bailiwick of the group were, for all intents and purposes, overseen by the headman of the clan. This was a contrived optic. Indeed, as what some might call the operations manager, the headman of time-honored group efforts did run these ordinary actions. In and out of the shadows, this person was the acknowledged public-facing leader of the band.

In a thoroughly cloaked formula established by Andriy and Lehya, these purported leaders functioned within well-defined limits. The ultimate and final authority for ordinary, as well as extraordinary, actions was genuinely bestowed on the two nearly invisible commanders who had replaced Andriy and Lehya—including surreptitiously assuming the continued work at hammering together a much wider and more powerful union. In the parlance of those few select members of both groups who knew of the commander's existence, this overlord was referred to as the *Om Mare*.

Mykola and Yegor were *Om Mares*.

The *Om Mares* had both internal and external challenges—often major dilemmas. These were not only complicated times for the clans, they also were complicated times for Ukraine and Russia—countries with long and often tenuous histories now lambasted by the Bolsheviks.

Before the armistice of the first war, Ukraine declared herself opposed to the Bolshevik uprising while the country itself housed both pro-Soviet and anti-Soviet forces. In the winter of 1917, the Red Army marched against units of the Ukrainian National Republic. Ukraine and Russia were at war.

War can be good for business, especially if you are not one of the warring parties nor one of the target populations. While Mykola and Yegor's clans were not yet properly part of an integrated union as envisioned by Andriy and Lehya, they did consider themselves as elements of the *Soobshckestvo*—members of the broader network in the coexisting economies that embraced all outside the parsimonious and pampered world of the upper crust and the elite. They were not socialists and would have been surprised if some classified them as capitalists. These were practical and pragmatic groups considering themselves as apolitical and agnostic though many kept their ties, overtly or covertly, to the Church—*Ukrayinska Pravoslavna Tserkva*—the Ukrainian Orthodox Church of the Moscow Patriarchate. These were groups able to grasp each and every moment for their own benefit.

By 1921, with the establishment of the Ukrainian Soviet Socialist Republic, the most recent period of open warfare entered a lull. Nevertheless, things were far from peaceful. Nationalist and socialist rifts remained and, in some instances, widened. As always, a prevailing situation of imbalance and uncertainty offered opportunities for those who operated outside the generally accepted norms of good business and good comportment. *Soobshckestvo* groups in general, and Mykola and Yegor's clans in particular, were not only able to profit from these times of turpitude but were also able to look more closely at alliances as both were now generally under the wider soviet umbrella.

However, an all-encompassing union remained elusive. Few saw the advantages of what they perceived as radical change. What had worked before worked now. Why change?

There was already a loose but acknowledged web connecting those operating in the dual economy but operating on the other side of the legal boundaries. The *Soobshckestvo* epithet provided a sort of overarching kinship, a kind of criminal guild that was adopted by many as a badge of honor. It was like being a member of a special secret society—a society that imparted some sort of real or imagined status while not impeding the freedom nor the mobility of the individual.

As the second war that was never to happen gained momentum, the *Soobshckestvo* saw and took opportunities on all sides. There were immense profits to be made on many fronts. From the clans' perspectives, many of the indelicate aspects of their businesses—some would say the most grim and gory actions—were indiscernable during a time of war; it was simply more blood on the ground or more cries in the air.

The cycles continued: war and peace, feast and famine, hope and hopelessness, life and death. A season of stability and tranquility remained a distant dream. There was discord and discontent, and it was good for business. The clans made more money.

However, as the Second World War geared up, Mykola and Yegor realized two things. First, it was highly unlikely there would ever be broad support among their respective bands of libertarian actors for the union—they would need to keep the bimodal structure in place with common activities undertaken in familiar ways while the intricate work of weaving a global tapestry continued in the darkest corners of the shadows. Second, the war was shining a light on the finite nature of the world as well as new technologies that were allowing some (a.k.a. Hitler) to contemplate global action. Nazi international aggression could not go unmet. It was too visible—too blatant. Still, the politics, policies, and economies of world-wide transactions were a phenomenon of the early twentieth century. Communications, transportation, markets, and education all favored widening the playing field. Hegemony was possible, maybe inevitable. Hitler would fail. Mykola and Yegor could succeed.

⚘⚘⚘⚘⚘⚘⚘

Mykola and Yegor had hopes of success, but each group continued to function in different, if frequently overlapping arenas. The Russians did not share their neighbors' principles as to what to do and what not to do. They had few if any taboo areas of activity. Guns, girls, drugs—a dollar was a dollar (or a ruble a ruble). Overall, this difference in business approaches fit well within the bimodal structure the two *Om Mares* had finally chosen to adopt when seeking ways and means to unwind the riddle and establish some sort of broader, more fruitful union.

In the end, different on-the-ground operations and approaches were not a major problem. This had been an issue with which Andriy and

Lehya had struggled. For Mykola and Yegor, after a great deal of thought (probably overthought) and analysis, it seemed obvious they must be commonsensical. There were unquestionably multiple dimensions. Nevertheless, it was the prosaic practices of the clan members on the ground that derived the majority of the clans' profits. Yet, these practices were only profitable due to prevailing policies and processes. As opposed to a yin-yang relationship, it was a macro-micro rapport. The individuals on the ground followed their usual ways. However, the success of these exercises was only partially due to the skills of the operators. A conducive environment was a key to maximum benefits. Pulling the levers at the macro level, therefore, optimized the profit for all.

It was a two-pronged, parallel approach that would best suit a union. The traditional and cautious operatives in the field could work as their predecessors had worked. What had worked before could be maintained. These members, really craftsmen in their own right, could stay in their comfort zone. They would not be encumbered by the need to change to fit into any union mold. Nonetheless, unbeknownst to most, the actions of these local agents would be facilitated and expedited by the intervention of the wider union cloaked in shadows and secrecy.

The *Om Mares* needed to design a concealed yet innovative macro-level superstructure that would add efficiency and lead to greater prosperity for all. There was growing competition and, possibly growing at even a faster rate, expanding opportunities. A marriage of kindred spirits was needed to be able to multiply profits and influence.

Mykola and Yegor strategized, applying many of the axioms of a basic economics class. They looked at the total community within which they worked. They studied the main economic sectors including the industries and institutions that functioned within these sectors. While some firms cut across sectors, the majority occupied a narrower bandwidth. Through one lens, the four major dissectible clusters of the clans' efforts coincided with the major sectors: extraction, including mining, fishing, and agriculture; manufacturing, including utilities; service, including banking and communications; and, knowledge, including education, research, and development.

Looking at the landscapes covered by clan operations, the *Om Mares* developed a blueprint where they charted critical hubs as seen in the general economic grid. It was clear the clans had their fingers in many pots. There was agriculture, covering everything from securing the needed primary resources to supplying the final product to the consumer. They separated out the meat-producing portions, including a particular spot for fishing, where they saw a different set of stakeholders. There was mining. There was forestry. There was banking and finance. There was tourism and entertainment (each interpreted in the largest possible context). There was manufacturing. Then, across this matrix, slicing through these sectoral hubs were core concerns: labor, capital, markets, regulations, transport, and communications. For the nexus of each focal point and each slice there was a unique bracket—a special knot in their tapestry. These knots, these foci, represented critical junctures affecting to a high degree the operating environment, making it more or less conducive. For each knot, they needed to be able to exert influence. To be able to maximize their chances for success for whatever venture was on the table at a given moment in time, they needed some level of control across the grid. Therefore, for each knot, they needed a team—a team headed by a world-class specialist.

Herein the war helped. It was a war of dominance for some, a war of self-preservation for others. It was a time to go all out, seen by many as an existential struggle for humanity. The warring factions were mustering all their fortunes. And these warring factions were inventorying their human resources and identifying those assets that gave them a comparative advantage. It was a great push for great battles and then it was over—only the debris, dust, and graves remaining. As wars ultimately ended (some later than others), the warring parties were inadvertently doing much of the *Om Mares'* work for them. They were highlighting essential human resources who, if they survived, would likely be looking for a job after the war.

The *Om Mares* started by filtering the flow of refugees across Eastern Europe—so many were fleeing so much. From prisons, death camps, destroyed villages, and deserted barracks, people were shaking off the haze of open battle and trying to navigate around the bomb craters to find a new life. Mykola and Yegor, each from their own vantage point, were able to identify key people around whom they could coalesce a team to begin weaving their tapestry.

The first step was the banking and finance hub. Here there was ample local expertise. Among the survivors of Janowska Concentration Camp they found Jefet, originally from Košice. He had managed a local bank before the war and came from a well-off family, practically studying investments before he wore long pants.

Jefet had lost his entire family to the Nazis: parents, wife, children. He had no one and nowhere to go. Mykola and Yegor offered him a destination and a community. It was an easy sale. After an extended period working with the *Om Mares* and then a stint clandestinely linked to both clans, an office was set up in Katowice, Poland, for the newly minted Globalny Fundusz Pomocy (Global Assistance Fund)—the weavers of the tapestry wanting to keep their knots, their hubs, both institutionally and geographically detached.

The same basic approach was used to recruit for other nuclei. The *Om Mares* heard about a former Nazi Colonel, a *Standartenführer* in the Waffen-SS. He had fled to Argentina where he had reshaped his life from being a wartime economist to becoming a polestar in meat-marketing circles with the sobriquet of "*Der Feinschmecker*" (The Gourmet). With similar tactics as those employed with Jefet, Mykola and Yegor were able to recruit the ex-Nazi, Heinrich Fuchs, to head up their meat hub, nominating this knot in their tapestry the freshly minted transnational *Matadero Global* (Global Abattoir).

While in Argentina, in Patagonia, the *Om Mares* discovered Gershen Van Zyl whose Boer family had fled South Africa several decades earlier. When his family was released from the concentration camp in Bloemfontein at the end of what the English called the Second Boer War, they had frantically looked for options to leave their homeland for a new land where they could continue with the family vocation—mining. The answer was the Tierra del Fuego gold rush. They moved to Argentina. Although the family arrived at the tail end of the gold rush, they did manage to establish themselves in the mining industry and over the intervening years had grown their initial grubstake into a family fortune. Yet, in spite of their riches, the family in general and Gershen in particular remained bitter, nearly fixated, on their forced exodus from South Africa—their true homeland, their *echt vaderland*. It was, therefore, no great feat to recruit Gershen to spearhead their mining hub; designated *Wereldwijde Mineralen* (Worldwide Minerals), to be located in the Alberton neighborhood of Johannesburg (Gershen would finally be able to return to his *echt vaderland)*.

The tapestry was taking shape.

Mykola and Yegor began to think they were filtering through the postwar scraps of humanity, almost like grave robbers looking for anything of value, but even grave robbers make prized discoveries.

The *Om Mares* discovered a lot.

One of the key finds, so to speak, was a pair of Romanian refugees. Through a long chain of intermediaries, Mykola and Yegor became aware of the tale of Răzvan and Horațiu. Their parents, suffering from chronic poverty, found they quite simply had too many mouths to feed and sought the assistance of local church leaders to find a way for two of their sons to be adopted, leaving enough food on the table for the remaining family members. Through the miracles of faith (or whatever) the family's priest was able to identify a family in the UK and another in the US who were willing to welcome a new son coming furtively from very unclear origins. Răzvan, now Robin, found himself in Chicago while his younger brother Horațiu, now Horace, ended up in a household in Central London.

Robin's new family provided him with the best of everything. As a relatively young man, Robin, Robin McCandless, took a job at Delaven Professional Industries—Delpro—the former well-known and well-thought-of Midwest Grain and Rail Coop in Delaven, Illinois. The company was run by Roy Franklin, an Army vet fresh from the Western Front. Robin had been brought on board to save the company. After the war, Roy had tried to do too much too fast. He needed capital and had recklessly gone to the mob, Louis "Little New York" Campaga of the Chicago Outfit, for the needed funds. A bad situation turned worse, and Roy could only hope that Robin could turn things around. Then, within two years of assuming his position, Robin had to take over full control of the company now christened "Delpro" as Roy had died from a combination of old war wounds and more recent stressful economic woes.

Robin was initially able to keep the mob at bay by providing them a downpayment using his adopted family's more-than-ample resources. He then reached back into his own past and across the Atlantic to see if he could find some Eastern European groups who could view his company as a way to establish a desirable foothold in the US—the new Slavic mob being able to push the old Italian mob aside.

It was in this way that Robin McCandless and Delpro became known to the *Om Mares.*

Robin was more than amenable to forging new alliances if these would help him shake the Chicago outfit. To this end, Mykola and Yegor had many ways to convince Louis Campaga that Delpro would best be associated with the eastern clans rather than the *Mafioso Italiano*. The outfit was, with some introspection, happy to accept a large lump-sum payment to take Delpro completely off their books.

Delpro now joined the growing population of knots on the *Om Mares'* tapestry, assuming the position of team leader for agriculture and moving its offices to Lake Forest, north of Chicago.

As with all the teams, Mykola and Yegor explained to Robin that his efforts in the future did not need to be limited to agriculture. They were, naturally, all in favor of free enterprise. If Robin and Delpro had additional areas of interest, as long as these did not jeopardize the over-arching plans elaborated with the *Om Mares*, this was fine and to be encouraged. The more diverse and deeply seated the hubs could become, the longer they could be counted upon to contribute to the greater good as seen through the *Om Mares'* lens of a global union.

In support of this union, and through their new ties to Robin McCandless, Mykola and Yegor met his younger brother Horace, Horace Barthley. Robin's sibling was nearly his polar opposite in both form and function. Horace's Cockney upbringing had imparted a sharp edge that pierced most encounters before the interlocutor could fully appreciate its owner's keen mind. Horace, or "Sir Horace" as he preferred to be called, had the mix of churlish bourgeoisie and street smarts, in Mykola and Yegor's eyes, making him a special candidate to be a sort of ambassador at large. Horace became their roving trouble shooter.

Those casually encountering the colorful and acerbic Sir Horace would often consider him as having an unpleasant demeanor, some might even think of him as damn rude. The first impressions of those just crossing the affected aristocrat's path in the name of work frequently concluded the curious chap was simply an arsehole.

With a peripatetic Sir Horace backstopping the scrupulously discerning duo of Mykola and Yegor, the weaving of the tapestry expanded in scope and breadth.

More teams of the union were formed to join Jefet, Heinrich, Greshen, and Robin. But the channels were not directly between the hubs, by design, everything was funneled through the center—through the *Om Mares*. The network for the union was more like the branches of a hydra than the strands of a spider's web.

Each hub was reinforced and insulated (if not isolated). Skill sets within hubs were honed. All were indoctrinated with a sense of common purpose: do more, be more.

New people—team leaders and team members—were identified. Some were quickly discarded (through their own decision or that of the *Om Mares)*, others enthusiastically joined.

Knot by knot, the tapestry grew.

Past Meeting Present

THE tapestry began to flow—to take shape—to have body. Neither Mykola nor Yegor had made great progress, moving from thoughts to deeds. The inscrutable combine now had form and function. It was now time to move from the design phase to the operational phase. And it was now time, these two craftsmen knew, following in the footsteps of Andriy and Lehya, for a change. They realized their time was running out—age was catching up to them.

As Mykola and Yegor prepared to pass on their work, and the work of Andriy and Lehya, to the next generation of overseers, they realized a duo was too unwieldy to be durable. While the two two-man teams had successfully devised and launched what they named Domov, a word for "home" in slavic tongues, the union presently needed (would, in their astute opinions, be best served by) but one overlord—one person ultimately responsible.

In a moment of morbid humor, the *Om Mares* suggested this person sitting at the pinnacle be called the *Maliar*, the mortician. The idea really came from Andriy's grizzled lieutenant Borysko who noted that, while people fought day and night to have a certain appearance, as witnessed by the vast sums floating through the cosmetics industries, it was the *Maliar* who determined the appearance of people before God.

The name stuck.

The *Maliar* would be the ultimate controller, the *Král' Hory* (the King of the Hill).

Managing the intricate pathways and reaping the benefits from the invisible net that was now Domov became the responsibility of the *Maliar*.

After a typically thorough analysis, Mykola and Yegor found the right person to be the first *Maliar*: Taras Kuzmenko.

⚘⚘⚘⚘⚘⚘⚘

Taras had, with severe reservations, accepted an ambitious and grand gift from Mykola and Yegor. He had agreed to, for the first time, don the mantle of the *Maliar* of Domov.

He was the first and, as such, the trailblazer. This was not a task he took lightly. He realized, even if perhaps not full-well, this was a complex and challenging assignment. While he had operated in the margins his entire life, he now had to plunge more deeply into the shadows and spearhead a collection of covert teams that covered the globe and embraced some of the most powerful and most singular people to have walked across its surface. It was nothing short of a mammoth undertaking.

Yet, regardless of the daunting role, it was difficult to comprehend and easy to appreciate the effort and the angst that had been invested to craft Domov. Taras' predecessors had not only been visionary, but they had also been intrepid. They had accomplished what few thought could ever happen. They had built, block by block, a worldwide union that now encompassed unbelievable wealth and influence.

It was incumbent on him to maintain the momentum—to nourish the union.

To succeed, Taras decided he needed to relocate. The *Maliar* was, indeed, a global overseer—the puppet master. The strings and levers he controlled could be operated from anywhere and nowhere. But they could only be operated by the *Maliar*, and then only with the highest level of security and secrecy. Stealth and skill were the key ingredients, not geography.

Taras could work from Moscow, London, or New York. It didn't matter where he was in terms of being able to do his job. He was, after all, invisible and unknown. But it did matter where he was if he had to quickly vanish (realizing the vanishing invisible man made no sense).

Still, it did make sense from some perspectives. Some places were more vulnerable than others. There were places where the political situation was in chaos. There were places, especially with the Cold War, where there were real risks of confrontation. There were places where the culture would make it difficult for an outsider to get lost in the scenery.

For all these reasons, and to put some distance between himself and his clan (for the protection of all), the *Maliar* concluded the best spot for him would be in calm surroundings, not far from a good-sized city where he had access to transport and communications, but in a more bucolic setting where he could easily fade into the background.

He chose Bourg-en-Bresse, France, in the Jura Mountains (reminiscent of home), forty-five miles to the northeast of Lyon and sixty-five miles west of Geneva. Here, or anywhere, he could have built a villa to rival the palaces of European nobility. But conspicuousness was not his aim—quite the opposite. He must blend in, and blend in he did. He moved into a small house on Chemin du Moulin de Noirefontaine, three miles south of the town center and the main administrative offices of the Préfecture of Ain.

He lived alone. The *Maliar* could not have a family. That would open the door to too much potential liability. His papers showed him to be a widower and a veteran (although it was unclear from what army). His university French was still passable as he spoke with few and had no neighbors.

But he was not alone. In town he had a full team of his staff—others located across the macrocosm that was now Domov. The resident team included several bodyguards, a driver, two secretaries and a senior assistant. All told, there were seven people who had come into town over a period of many months, securing various forms of employment or establishing one or another pretext of being able to work from home. This was Taras' hand-picked crew. They were professional. They were watchful. They were dedicated. But they were seldom at their master's side. Only at extraordinary times would they visit the home, and then in the guise of being some sort of worker or deliveryman.

Taras developed a regular routine. It never changed. The Post Office was just a block from the Préfecture. Every day he would drive his Renault-4 into town to pick up his mail and then have a coffee at a small café near Square Lalande. His team, having their own key, was able to add any important documents to his post office box before the pickup and could see him in person, if need be, at the café. More regular meetings were scheduled at the barber shop, the library, the garage, or anywhere where an ordinary inhabitant of Bourg-en-Bresse might go. Meetings with the hub leaders were also organized by his local team. Some of these were periodic and dressed as the meetings of some board of directors or civil society organization (his favorite was Friends of the Planet where he had a role as member of the Board of Directors of this make-believe NGO with the vision of "helping mankind survive hard times"). Other extraordinary meetings were called to address special and often pressing matters; these were held anywhere and anytime.

Still, outside a very exclusive group, no one knew who the *Maliar* was. Few knew the *Maliar* even existed.

The *Maliar* now lived in the Auvergne-Rhône-Alpes région of France. The *Maliar* was now a Frenchman. Among the orchards of Auvergne-Rhône-Alpes, Taras nurtured the seedling that was Domov—the vine, the creeper that was sending shoots across the globe. As the greenery emerged on Domov's stems, a tiny sprout was also growing far away in Pennsylvania coal country.

⚘⚘⚘⚘⚘⚘⚘

Back in Pottsville, Joe never knew of the tapestry. Joe did not know of Taras. Although he had been attempting to grasp the routines of Pottsville at about the same time as two old men—Mykola and Yegor—had been attempting to expand the augustness of the richly woven arras in the hopes of a wider union, Joe had not been high enough in the hierarchy to know of or be engaged in, the actions that were weaving the multitude of threads into Domov.

Joe had never met Mykola nor Yegor, though he had heard of the indomitable Mykola—venerated member of his own clan. He had no idea how complex and intricate the weaving of these revered elders had been.

Joe did know of Kaniv Ceață. He knew his father and grandfather had been involved in many things, but he had had no prior knowledge of the global network that had so dominated the efforts of a select subset of his progenitors.

It was only as Joe attempted to find a Pennsylvania niche for his clan that he began to realize that things were much more complicated than he had imagined. As a raw young immigré he had known so little. He needed to know more. If a new North American holding in coal country was truly to materialize, he had to be better connected with the roots of the organization he represented.

Given the difficulties in communicating meaningfully with his family at home in Ukraine, he arranged to meet his father in Vienna under the pretext of returning to Europe for a family funeral. People in Pottsville were generally unclear or uncaring as to any difference between Vienna and Kyiv. Foreign places were, after all, the same—they were foreign. However, this was happening at the beginning of the Cold War and at the onset of a hot war on the Korean Peninsula. If Joe had traveled any further east, someone somewhere would have noticed. Already, a guy from Schuylkill County going to Austria was strange enough.

Joe's father, Artem, had been a contemporary of Mykola, albeit somewhat his junior. Although Artem's major activities had generally been involved in traditional clan efforts, he had been briefed on the union which had at this time been labeled Domov. Artem had also been briefed by Taras. Artem did not know if Taras was Ukranian or Russian (he didn't even know his surname)—all that mattered was that he was the *Maliar*, the mortician.

The torch that had long lit the shadows of extreme power was passing from the frail and frayed threads of the old cloth of the forbearers to the rich and refined weave of the *Om Mares'*. It then moved again to the shelter of the Auvergne-Rhône-Alpes. The transition to the *Maliar*, to Taras, was underway.

With Taras the *Maliar's* backstopping and blessing, Artem met Joe in Vienna.

When Joe retuned to Pottsville, everything looked different. Everything was different. Joe now had much-needed direction.

While his father was not privy to all the intimacies of Domov, he had known enough to be able to explain in good detail the underlying objectives of the union. Artem had been able to lay out the vision for Domov, underlining the role that was foreseen for Joe's own work in Pottsville and beyond. He had outlined Domov's structure (which was still a work in progress), including the support for another nodule in North America called Delpro—a group that was currently unrelated to Joe's own efforts.

There were many moving parts and many still obscured pieces, but Joe had his own niche in this convoluted landscape.

For the time being, this seemed to be what Joe needed.

The various entities from back home—be they related more to Domov or to the more long-established specialities and proclivities of the clan—were generating large volumes of cash in multiple currencies. They needed an outlet. As land prices in coal country were depreciating, it was a good time to buy and the folks at home in Ukraine had more than enough money to make Joe a major actor in real estate in Pennsylvania.

This could be, however, a problem in and of itself. Joe did not have and should not seek high visibility. Intermediaries needed to be used in all transactions. Stealth and untraceability were required tactics. Within his new plan of action, Joe was also to look into the advisability of opening clandestine market pathways—smuggling in other words. Local folks were in tough times and the clan could offer them bargain-basement prices on things they could not go without—things like tobacco and whisky—things that made the tough times a little less crushing. But opening up new markets required porous borders and adequate market share. Joe had a lot of homework to do.

Still, for the first time in a long time, Joe felt more at ease. The trip to Vienna had been well worthwhile. He now had guidance. He now had a clearer idea of what to do—and what not to do. It was a good, if belated, start.

⚘⚘⚘⚘⚘⚘⚘

Shortly after Joe settled in from Vienna, he was living a double life that took on a new form and vigor. He continued his job at the mine—having been promoted from piloting mine carts to now being a mid-level supervisor. His advancement in the company made it easier to openly have the life he wished for his family and himself. His Kaniv Ceață, now Domov, connections provided him with considerable income. But this had to be kept under covers, with all outward appearances indicating he was living within the means provided by a none-too-generous mining job. At least, now as lower management, he was able to live in a little bigger home, have a little nicer car, and provide better things for his wife and kids—including the now fifth family member, Harold.

It wasn't luxury. It wasn't flamboyant. But it was comfortable, and they could afford to pay their bills (something that eluded many of their neighbors).

Initially, Joe kept all his clan's activities secret. But as these became more complex, more demanding, it became impossible to keep his wife, Susan, in the dark, especially when he was planning a trip to Vienna without her. Finally, if for no other reason than to allay her fears of even more nefarious or adulterous acts that could, in her imagination, be underway, he told her everything.

Susan, a native daughter who, when she'd graduated high school had gone two and a half hours to the south to nursing school at Johns

Hopkins (a fact that added to the mystery that Joe never managed to fully comprehend—how had a wonderful and talented girl like Susan ever agreed to be his wife?), accepted Joe's explanation with surprising aplomb. Unlike many of the homegrown folk, she understood that it was difficult to grasp life's puzzling pathways. Nothing was simple. Joe, a newcomer to this land and this community whom she truly loved, had, as did everyone, his own baggage. At least it wasn't infidelity.

At the time of his epiphany with Susan, their two children, Anna and David (both good Anglo-Ukrainian names although Joe's side of the family would have spelled it "Davyd"), were away at school; one at Shippensburg University and the other at Northampton Community College. Their parents saw no reason to encumber their studies with tales of a long-established family businesses from the old country.

Harold was another story. Younger than his cousins (now his siblings), he was still in high school and really could not be excluded from the lengthy discussions that took place around the hearth.

Joe made a decision. This was one of those dichotomous decisions—potentially life altering. He decided, in consultation with Susan, to bring Harold onboard in spite of his young age.

It wouldn't be possible to exclude his youngest child—he truly felt of Harold as his own (all the more so since contact with Philip had dwindled to nothingness). There was no reason, there were even conceivable risks in bringing his other two children into the mêlee in a half-way fashion. They already had their independent lives, and it was relatively easy to keep them out of any clan-cum-Kaniv Ceață-cum-Domov affairs. Not so with Harold. It was in or out and Harold had to be in.

Thus, as Joe went about his second life when not supervising the extraction of coal, crafting financial channels and exploring trafficking options, little by little he introduced Harold to the heretofore hidden part of his life.

Joe not only explained the activities planned for Pottsville and beyond, he also spent time educating his family consorts on the history behind today's actions. Harold felt as though he was harvesting all the sweat and tears invested by Andriy, Lehya, Mykola, and Yegor. Joe understood. He hoped the harvest would be good.

CHAPTER 2

EXPANDING THE TRADE

"To judge a man by his weakest link or deed is like judging the power of the ocean by one wave."

—Elvis Presley

Capturing the Moment

In August 1944, Vianney Cisse, a thirty-nine-year-old West African from what would become Ivory Coast sixteen years later, sloshed ashore from the Higgins Boat at Cape Negre, fifty miles southwest of Cannes, as part of the half-a-million strong Allied invasion of southern France, Operation Dragoon. A month later, Vianney, still on his feet, was among the Operation Dragoon infantry who reunited with their northern cohorts from Operation Overlord in Dijon to begin the great push of Hitler's armies back into the Fatherland.

Vianney was among thousands of West Africans who had joined the forces of their colonial masters—officially volunteers, but more honestly conscripts. By the end of hostilities, more than seven hundred Africans had died on the battlefields of World War II.

After the armistice, Vianney returned to the French West Africa to his family and home in Man in the west of the country. Prior to becoming the wary warrior, Vianney had, like his father before him, run a small stall in the central market where he sold farming supplies—tools like machetes, hoes, buckets, or wheelbarrows along with consumables like seed and chicken feed.

During his absence, Vianney's shop had been overseen by his wife Antoinette along with their nearly grown sons, Luc and Marc. Vianney's customers were happy to see his return. Of course, they were happy he had been able to survive the terrible war about which they understood so little. Yet mostly, they were happy to have their guide back. Vianney was known as a walking encyclopedia for the use of all the materials he sold as well as for local farming practices in general. Even the district agricultural extension workers would come to him for details about how best to use this or that implement or product.

Whenever a customer left the shop with a new item, Vianney would escort him or her to the entrance with the same advice, "Remember what I've told you. It isn't difficult. Just follow the instructions and don't hurt yourself—farming can be dangerous. Be safe!"

Vianney's admonition for farm safety was based on more than reading farm catalogues and common sense, Vianney was a farmer. Vianney's family had a good-sized cocoa farm outside town.

Unlike many of his neighbors, Vianney was fascinated by cocoa. The French colonial government was insisting that farmers grow cocoa. The natural reaction from the farmers was to refuse if feasible or to be as unenthusiastic as possible if some sort of token compliance was required.

While Vianney (like everyone else) did not like to be obliged to do anything, he had done his homework on cocoa. Information was not easily available nor plentiful, but he had been able to glean a lot from the library at the *Institut d'Agronomie Coloniale* in Abidjan—thanking his mother many times over for pressuring him to go to school in spite of his insistence that it was a total waste of time.

At the *Institut* he had read about the early efforts by the Portuguese to grow cocoa in São Tomé and Principe. In spite of the horrid tales of slavery linked to cocoa farming, it had been a lucrative crop to wash European palates with a sweet drink they had enjoyed since the seventeenth century. As international attention focused on harsh, even inhumane, practices in lusophone Africa, near the end of the nineteenth century in British West Africa, the renowned Tetteh Quarshie brought back from Fernando Po cocoa pods that were to seed an industry not only in his homeland that was to become Ghana, but also next door in the would-be Ivory Coast.

Before the war, Vianney's cocoa farm had been almost a hobby, most of the work done by his sons after school and on weekends. Vianney had realized this was a crop with a unique potential, but it was also intertwined with a lot of local political and cultural issues that made its cultivation limited. Then, about the same time as he returned from the European battlefields, France stopped their policy of forcing people to grow cocoa as well as forcing people to work on cocoa plantations. This completely changed the equation. The door was now open for expansion with the full support of local leaders. And Vianney wanted to be one of the first people through this door.

Vianney really opened the door. He used his meager savings from his military service to buy as much land as possible, preparing it for cocoa farming. He then named his sons, already with considerable practical experience, as the overseers of this new and significantly enlarged cocoa operation. Soon the Cisse Family was the major cocoa producer in the western part of the country.

Vianney refocused the energy that had kept him alive on the front lines in France on keeping him on top of the ranks of the wealthy at home. The family prospered.

⸙⸙⸙⸙⸙⸙⸙

Cocoa was good business in a postwar global economy. Luc and Marc honed their financial management acumen. Soon, with their father's backing and blessing, they were ready to hand off the day-to-day management of the plantations to resident managers while they looked for new investments—new challenges.

As the Cisse Family was getting ready to try new things, the country was making new discoveries. There were diamonds.

Less than four years after Vianney's return, the family had become *actionaires* in the Tortiya diamond mine—the mine 250 miles to the northeast of Man. It was a long way to go, but it was worth it.

If cocoa was good business, diamonds were better business. However, while his sons worked hard to add to the family fortune, Vianney, still manning his farm supply stall, looked for new challenges—perhaps war had changed him.

He had shared a foxhole with someone from the British colonies, Abimbola Agbaje—the good white soldiers always encouraging the Africans to "keep to themselves where they'd be more comfortable."

Maybe they had been right, Vianney thought. When he had finally sailed home from Marseilles, he could think back over at least a dozen really good African friends he'd cultivated through the war—three of whom had survived and shared the steamer with him. On the other hand, he could think of only four European soldiers with whom he had been able to connect—all four making it home after the bloodshed.

Abimbola had been one of his closest comrades at arms. He had told Vianney his name meant "born into wealth" back home in Yurbaland. Vianney had no doubt that his buddy did come from a well-to-do family. As if to confirm this point, over a year after his homecoming, Vianney received a letter from Abimbola, now a flourishing businessman in Lagos where he had his hands in many drawers. He was announcing his marriage to the ravishing beauty whose picture he'd shown Vianney. Life after the war was good.

Vianney sent him a family snapshot and best wishes for his marriage—wishing he could be there to share in the celebration.

It was several years later before Vianney received his second letter from his old mate. Married life was good. Abimbola now needed to build a solid foundation for the big family he was sure he was starting. He thought a good step in this direction would be to see about joint ventures with his good francophone friend. After all, they'd watched each other's backs in France—they could do the same in West Africa.

To begin what Abimbola hoped would be a long and fruitful relationship, he suggested they focus on the bicycle. This was a surprise to Vianney.

As he read further, Vianney realized that, among other things, Abimbola was importing Raleigh bicycles from England into the lushness surrounding the lagoons of Lagos. This was an interesting but still nascent business. People really liked the bikes, but they were expensive, and it was hard for him to justify the inventory of spares he really needed to be able to meet all the various needs of his clients.

His proposed solution was to widen the market. If Vianney were to join in, they could have consignments delivered to both Abidjan and Lagos and then they would have a critical mass of customers that would justify a well-stocked parts depot in Nigeria that could also serve the French-speaking bike-riders.

To make the sale, Abimbola had sent Vianney a bicycle for his inspection. He provided the necessary reference details, assuring his friend that he had paid for all the fees and all his buddy had to do was to go to the port in Abidjan and pick up the bike and see how he liked it.

Vianney did as instructed.

He was surprised how easy it was to get his merchandise out of port—equally surprised it was boxed up and had to be assembled before he could even really see what it looked like.

There was an owner's manual included in the big carton, but it was far from self-explanatory. Yet, Vianney was good with his hands and, working at a filling station across from the small hotel where he had taken a room, he was able to get the shining black bicycle assembled in a matter of hours.

Trying it out in the traffic of Abidjan was no small feat—actually reminiscent of running out of his foxhole to cross a field that was under

German artillery attack. He smiled to himself. In the owner's manual, on the third page there and been a warning: "Riders are warned that falls from the bicycle can result in bodily harm." Indeed, bicycles could be dangerous.

Vianney laughed to himself as he thought of the safety labels inexplicably affixed to some of the wheelbarrows in his stall: "Warning, this product moves when used (*Attention, ce produit bouge lorsqu'il est utilisé*)."

Digging Deeper

THE wheelbarrows from Vianney's stall may have moved, but not as dynamically as the rest of what evolved into his business empire, covering commerce, mining, and agriculture. By independence in 1960, Vianney was a well-seasoned, well-respected, wealthy, and influential businessman with Marc and Luc at his side, sharing the prominence and the profits while Antoinette publicly offered both moral support and the tangible assistance of an agile mind and able hands working on key tasks in the basket of family enterprises. Quietly, Antoinette wondered how they'd got to where they were and where they were going.

And they had gone far.

Although the stall in the market remained the same old stall in the market, the initial hobby cocoa patch had multiplied many times over. The mining activities were lucrative but labyrinthine—there were many parties, local and foreign. The mining ventures were also awash with politics, pushing them about at every level from the village to the globe. On the other hand, the bicycle business was doing well in a very calm and steady way, the stability much appreciated by all.

Yet, while Vianney was happy to watch the pursuits he'd driven forward since the war coast ahead with strong momentum, Luc and Marc were more aggressive. The family was doing a lot, but the brothers felt the family was still not doing enough.

While his sons studiously examined options for adding more blocks to their growing pyramid of investments, Vianney was, equally studiously, examining how they could keep those activities to which they'd already committed operating optimally(optimally, as for everyone, being maximizing profits and minimizing risk).

Farming cocoa, mining, and even assembling bicycles required labor. A post-independence world offered many new opportunities. But it also offered, or imposed, only a nominally freer and more just economy. Vianney understood that, in so many ways, the turning off the switch from colonial to independent rule did little to change the balance of power nor the equity of the vast majority of the population. In the colonial era, ninety-eight percent of the power had been vested in the European masters with a tiny crust of collaborators in-country. At liberation, it was not, however, that the European masters disappeared from the scene. They still controlled the international markets, and colonies had been designed to feed raw materials into the industries of the colonizers. The offshore overlords continued to control imports, and so much of domestic production of anything and everything, especially for any local industry, depended on imported machinery and tools. The absentee overseers never loosened control of the banks, the communications, the shipping lines, and tertiary education systems. In short, the real impact of independence was that the margin of local powerbrokers who shared the control with the Europeans increased from two percent to perhaps twenty-five or thirty percent. There was now a larger (yet still tiny in real terms) domestic elite class who interfaced with and profited from very tight ties with the former colonial commanders.

Vianney was not part of this elite upper echelon. In spite of his wealth, in spite of the size of his varied operations, he still fell far short of being one of the crème de la crème. To use an old WWII term, the *collaborateurs* were really a very select group. Some had French spouses. Most had studied in France. All had residences in Europe. To the complete neglect, overtly the distain of traditional social and cultural structures, Independence had shepherded in a new flock of nobility (frequently referred to by the passerby as *faux noblesse*) that had been forged outside the village *chefferies* and inside the boardrooms of Paris. These African knights honoring European leaders (ironically, Vianney thought, perhaps he had facilitated the situation when, in the fields of France during the war, his and his comrades' prowess in battle had allowed the French potentates to keep control of lands far beyond their own borders) felt no kinship to their Ivorian compatriots. Quite to the contrary, they saw what they perceived as upstarts like Vianney as unwanted competitors. There was no giving of a helping hand—just the reverse, the manicured Ivorian hand, wearing a fine kidskin French glove, was used to push others down.

As Vianney looked for cracks in the artificial walls the *faux noblesse* were imposing to corral his growing family business, affecting their ability to get purchase and rise above the dominant enterprises controlled by the postcolonial powerbrokers, Luc and Marc looked to new frontiers. The brothers built upon their father's strong relationship with Abimbola Agbaje, finding in his sons soulmates in the struggle of new entrepreneurs seeking to find their place at the table. They looked beyond bicycles to find innovative areas of cooperation including forging close ties with burgeoning Asian industries looking for footholds in Africa—fulcrums from where these Eastern executives could exploit the region's vast natural resources while gaining marketshare for imported Asian products.

For the ambitious young African businessmen, domestic interests continued to share the landscape with foreign actions. Cacao prices rose and fell, seemingly driven by engines beyond the ken of the wisest financial soothsayers. Diamonds boomed. However, a dozen years after Independence, the market peaked and eight years later, unable to keep their modest pigeonhole in the world market, the mine was closed. Bicycle imports from Nigeria escalated after formal ties to France were cut. But, in a droll irony given their transcontinental ventures with their Nigerian partners, demand for the relatively expensive Raleigh bike slackened as cheaper Asian models entered the market.

In spite of the vagaries of the market, Luc and Marc were able to bolster the family business—the once smallholder farm and modest market stall becoming Les Entreprises Cisse. To grow, there were some easy steps like expanding the farm supply dealings countrywide. They were also able to procure additional agricultural land, much of this planted with cassava. While cassava, like cacao, had been introduced by the Portuguese centuries ago, it was only recently that improved high-yielding varieties were available from India via their unique Nigerian connection. Cassava was widely used in Ivorian kitchens for, among other things, the favored dish *attiéké*. And, for *attiéké* and other best-liked Ivorian foods, they also developed a thriving export market targeting their countrymen in the diaspora—this population growing as the shrouds of colonialism slowly fell away. One of their pilot outlander markets was the UK. It was through this channel that the irascible Sir Horace Barthley became aware of some ardent West African tradesmen looking for new avenues of investment.

Sir Horace was a pathfinder. Unlike his brother who seemed quite content to sit at home (even if this home was a grand villa) and pull the marionette strings that moved his endeavors ever upward and onward, Horace considered himself a working stiff. He wanted to get his hands dirty. Perhaps it was his youthful connection to the proletariat—feeling no contradiction to this label and his upper middle-class upbringing and his advanced degrees from top universities. Horace was a doer. He was also, though often not recognized, a serious thinker. But he wanted to be considered as just one of the guys—a guy with a lot of influence and no small accumulation of personal wealth.

It was these attributes that had attracted him to Mykola and Yegor. Horace was someone who would get out into the mud, clamor, and the chaos to look for just the right way to do just the right thing to profit from this same mud, clamor, and chaos. He was a pantologist. He was a factotum. He was many things and this made him valuable. His versatility and imagination offset his crude and vulgar demeanor although some had a difficult time accepting this tradeoff.

Horace was a wayfarer who cut a wide swath around the globe. Nonetheless, he maintained his childhood contacts with his old Cockney neighborhood where he could hear the bells of St. Mary-le-Bow church. He also gravitated to activities centered in the African region. Perhaps it was the high return for effort or perhaps the special challengers, but Horace seemed to achieve the most job satisfaction when working on intricate African projects. And, to Horace, job satisfaction was the key. His appetite for riches and power paled in comparison to his contemporaries', including his brother's (his bank account and address book notwithstanding). He felt a good job was a job worth doing. To his credit, and to the gratification of his overlords, he often did a good job. This gratification was transferred from Mykola and Yegor to Taras; Horace was an appreciated fixture, not to mention a flashy personality (in addition to his penchant for splashy clothing, he shared with his older brother a congenital physiognomy that included a thick crop of snowy-white hair that contrasted remarkably with a pink, nearly vermilion, complexion).

Colorful or not, Horace was a useful tool in the toolbox—his suggestions carrying a certain amount of weight for those in the know.

So, it was of little surprise to anyone when Horace informed the *Maliar* of some potentially useful connections to nourish in West Africa (he among the chosen few who knew of the existence of and had access to the leader of Domov).

While Sir Horace was examining how best to solder new joints with a team of energetic wheeler-dealers, another segment of the wider Ukrainian network was also trying to unfold from the humble to the bold. Artem's senior brother's nephew on his wife's side, Voldoymyr Rudenko, lived in Zhdanov—a major city in the southeast of the country on the Sea of Azov named Mariupol prior to 1948 but then renamed in honor of a soviet functionary in the current era. Since the end of the war, the city had nearly tripled in population, surging on massive investments in steel and ironworks as well as tourism along the Azov shoreline. Voldoymyr had a small coffee shop, Kafe Parus, on Prymors'kyi Boulevard that ran parallel to the beachfront. As solid an establishment as it may have been, however, the café was well below Voldoymyr's ambitions. In true family tradition, he knew he was made for greater and grander things. After all, Voldoymyr knew his name meant "of great power." It was his birthright.

Voldoymyr appealed to his uncle to open doors, to do the needful thing so he could live up to his own and his family's expectations. While this task was really outside Artem's remit, and certainly outside his oversight (although he had had contact with the *Maliar*, this was on an exceptional basis and he was truly outside the core that made the sort of sweeping arrangements that could launch Voldoymyr from modest coffee house owner-operator to major actor in the goings-on of Zhdanov and possibly the whole of southeastern Ukraine), he did all he could to flag the young man as a potential resource for bigger and better clan activities.

Artem was respected as a solid soldier. His opinion mattered—all the more so since his own son could possibly be the critical entrée to the much-awaited North American operations.

Then, unsure of why he was the chosen intermediary as well as equally unsure of the origins of the offered suggestion, Artem received a succinct missive to discuss an opportunity with Voldoymyr. This initially had nothing to do with the coffee house, although it could be a good cover for the suggested action. In brief, the upper echelons were proposing that the isolated shores of Kosa Lyapina Island, about ten miles due east of the city, would be a good place to receive all manner of products—products that could then be kept unobtrusively at the coffee house until they were picked up by another operative.

The island was seen as an apt location for a variety of current and planned activities. It was about thirty miles west of the Russian border via the M14 motorway and seventy-five miles south of Donetsk via the H20. Having a base through Zhdanov was seen as a plus. While this was likely not exactly what Voldoymyr had had in mind in terms of "greater and grander things," it moved him from obscurity into a position of relative prominence. With his uncle's prodding, Voldoymyr assumed the proposed duties, becoming the clan's (or Domov's, who knew?) steward of Kosa Lyapina Island.

They say the longest journey begins with the smallest first steps. Voldoymyr's new role was a journey. While the powers-that-be easily saw the advantages of having some sort of presence on a remote and effectively uninhabited island that could serve as a staging-ground and transit point for any variety of goods or people, the practicalities of establishing this presence without attracting undue attention remained to be established. In the end, these practical measures more than the responsibilities of clan purveyor did more in convincing Voldoymyr he was following the right trajectory.

The formula for success as outlined by unseen clan planners involved a major overhaul of Kafe Parus. The coffee house's beachfront location made it a prime property in spite of its unassuming footprint. Almost out of nowhere, Voldoymyr received a substantial line of low-interest credit from the Kyiv branch of Crédit Agricole designated for "enterprise renovations." In private, still in his function as intermediary, Artem was able to explain to Voldoymyr that the clan architects felt it was perfectly logical and unsurprising that the owner of Kafe Parus would want to expand its operations given its choice location and the noticeable growth in the local tourist industry. Thus, to find a novel niche to attract the visitors, the coffee house would be transformed into a small but stylish auberge with a focus on offering residents and tourists day trips to see the splendor of nature in and around the Sea of Azov including, of course, Kosa Lyapina Island.

With remodeled and modern features along with its new and more expansive functions, no one would query why vehicles or staff from Kafe Parus (the name retained to hold onto long-time clients) were scurrying about the hinterland at all times of the day and night. Voldoymyr's world was changing, hopefully advancing—though it often felt now more than ever outside his control.

While the owner of the Zhdanov coffee house, at his own request, reshaped and adjusted his job, Sir Horace reached out to Luc and Marc, offering them a remodeled if not totally transformed life—a life with new features and functions. Although the family had made impressive progress since the end of the war, Horace stressed, without outside assistance, without an outside advantage, it would be hard to maintain their upward trajectory in the face of resistance from the inflexible and territorial forces of the *faux noblesse.* With a *coup de main* it would still be hard but not futile as long as they accepted the helping hand that was being extended to them.

Sir Horace's African actions had often focused on southern Africa. After all, there were diamonds and gold there. Who didn't like diamonds and gold? However, there were diamonds and gold scattered across Africa—including in Ivory Coast.

With this benchmark, Horace had visited Ivory Cost several times before mine-owners Luc and Marc had even popped on his radar. Ever the sleuth, the devious nobleman was always looking for opportunities—be they financial or human. The newly independent sovereign state on the shore of the Gulf of Guinea seemed an apt target.

Abidjan in the post-independence days was exhilarating and dynamic—called "*le petit Paris d'Afrique.*" Farming, fishing, mining, light industry, banking—it had everything. It also had complex and tangled politics. An outsider, even one as conniving as Sir Horace, could easily be swallowed up in the morass that awaited the uninitiated.

On his first visit, leaving the Hôtel Ivoire and taking a bright yellow taxi to the Plateau, the central business district, Horace immediately realized he needed help. The city, throbbing around him, made him feel disoriented, disadvantaged. And, if there was one thing Sir Horace wanted, it was always to be on top of his game when prospecting new terrain for potentially important harvests to reap.

He diverted the driver to Café Sport on Rue du Commerce where he ordered a draft "33" beer and borrowed the phone to call a longtime Greek associate. This was the beginning of the process that led to Chantal.

Horace's Mediterranean associate, now a rather decrepit local trader dealing in nondescript items from nondescript sources, understood. Abidjan was complicated. His visiting comrade—an Ivorian novice—needed help. He recommended a lady named Chantal Silue as a good guide to get to know the inner workings of Abidjan as well as the interior of the country. The old man remarked that the name Chantal apparently meant stone and this woman was definitely as strong and indomitable as the iron ore deposits of Sassandra on the country's southern coastline.

Chantal was a composite of contrasts. Her biography, glued together from many snippets, was memorable if not all that unusual. As a schoolgirl, much to her parents' disappointment and against their wishes, she had determined sex was better than school. After some tumultuous experiences, she met and married a man older than her parents—again, much against her parents' wishes but, seeing things for what they were, with their begrudging consent.

To everyone's surprise, probably her parents too, the rich old man and striking young girl really hit it off. They fell in love and had three children before the old man suddenly dropped dead, leaving his many assets to Chantel and her children as well as his two other wives and their families. A great brawl arose among the grieving families, each sparring for the biggest slice of the pie. In the end, after many hard-fought battles, Chantal secured sizable bequeathments for her children and a nice stipend for herself that allowed her to go back to school and formally learn the business practices that had been central to her life for the past twenty-five years as she had worked side-by-side with her now deceased husband while he had steered his investments to ever-higher levels of wealth.

With her diploma in hand and her personal list of many high-power contacts, Chantal was more than ready to venture out on her own. With her (now married) children's futures assured, Chantel was able to do what she wanted in a way she wanted. She wanted to use her influence, not only to increase her already considerable wealth, but most importantly, to feel the exhilaration of being in control—almost as good as sex.

Chantal became a fixer, an organizer, a liaison. Chantal was a major actor in many ventures. Chantal was in demand.

In spite of this sought-after status, or perhaps because of it, Chantal was happy to meet with this new visitor, Sir Horace. She had no, nor was given any clue of Domov. Yet she sensed that Horace was someone with his own ring of power that could, if adeptly applied, be of benefit to her.

Chantal was unquestionably a benefit to Sir Horace. She had connections and understood how things worked—both how they should work and how they did work. She was more than a guide; she was an advisor. In this role, Horace put her on a generous retainer as he rummaged about for unique opportunities that fit within the singular context of Domov (a structure he had still not mentioned to his new *aide-de-camp* of sorts) as well as his own personal views about how business should be done.

⚘⚘⚘⚘⚘⚘⚘

Chantal was a refreshing respite from many of the toxic personalities with whom Sir Horace routinely dealt in his sojourns across the more opaque corners of the globe. A case in point and a feature of several of Horace's West African travels was Señor Tomas Ferreira. Señor Tomas, a Portuguese national but permanent resident in Guinea Bissau, was about as septic as they come. His principal (and unprincipled) occupation in Bissau was being a pivot point for the transshipment of drugs from South America to Europe—a job that was as enriching as it was dangerous.

Sir Horace in particular and Domov in general tried their best to keep drugs at arm's length. These were no longer taboo as they had once been, but any investments with any sort of drug-related activities had to have layer upon layer of protection to give much more than just plausible deniability. In the specific case of Señor Tomas, Horace and his tenders agreed that the nasty gentleman was simply too flagitious to accept any interactions that could even be associated in the most abstract way with drug trafficking.

This was not to say, however, that Señor Tomas did not have his uses. He did. Dealing with nasty folks was part—a big part—of the job.

Horace and other Domov operatives made good use of Tomas' skills as a totally profligate proctor for all manner of odious acts outside the drug arena—but also as a sometimes surprisingly charismatic delegate or representative to a variety of management entities where Domov wanted to have a surreptitious presence (Señor Tomas himself not initially aware of Domov, its features, nor its functions—thinking he was working with a Ukrainian crime syndicate until Horace had filled in some of the blanks).

Basically, it was concluded after ample observation that Tomas' priorities, even if self-serving (or because they were self-serving), were generally in line with the aims of the organization. He may have been tainted but he was dependable.

Accordingly, at various points in time, the venal but urbane Lusitano was, with Domov's blessing (although, at the onset, he may not have known it), a member of the board of multinationals such as Trusted Industrial Products, Poseidon Consignments, Ace Foods, Farm Services, and Western Farm Supply, including two major US companies, Simpson Investments and General Industrial and Chemical Products.

Señor Tomas was also on the board of a company based in Tanzania, Equatorial Management. Equatorial Management was one of Horace's key surrogates—or, as he saw it, his proxy. Many in Dar es Salaam and probably quite a few up the chain of command would likely not agree. While others saw Horace as a prime paraclete for a whole spectrum of joint company field activities, the cocky Cockney saw things differently, these were his acolytes, and he was the dynamo that drove the processes. For Horace the distinction was not trivial. Either his hand was one of many stanchions or it was the lone controller of the rudder. To the patrician wannabe, there was no question; he held the reins—he was the skipper of many ships.

In the case of Equatorial Management, Sir Horace may not have been far off. He was a chief catalyst for much of what this group did. Equatorial Management frequently attempted to don the cloak of a humanitarian NGO helping rural communities. However, while the most public facing portion of the company generously helped the needy, the more fuliginous forms of their operations were barebones international trade of legal and illegal merchandise.

Whether rationalizing or possibly (doubtfully) apologizing, Sir Horace was fond of saying, "It's all frick'n business"—often recalling the Swahili proverb, *fedha huzaa fedha* (money begets money). Some insiders remarked that the proverb best suited to the would-be nobleman was *hakuna mtu anayezaliwa mkuu—watu wakuu huwa wakuu wakati wengine wamelala* (no one is born great—great people become great while others sleep).

From Bourg-en-Bresse, Taras took it all in: the changing characteristics of an ever-changing program. In Abidjan, Bissau, Zhdanov, and scores of other locales around the globe, Domov was filling voids in the shadows and sometimes planting a flag (generally not its own) in broad daylight.

Leading the Pack

TARAS was the ultimate overseer in both form and function—the overseer of a complex yet intricate structure, an organism really, that required constant care and maintenance. Born on the slippery banks of the Dnieper River, the organism had to be fed and nourished. Like the river, it was a many-faceted ecosystem. The river, nearly fifteen-hundred miles long (Europe's fourth largest) wove its path through Russia, Belarus, and Ukraine before dumping the flotsam and sediments from its almost two-hundred-thousand-square-mile watershed into the depths of the Black Sea. What was to become of Domov as it similarly wove its path from Ukraine and Russia, flooding its banks, meandering far, ultimately ensnaring wide swaths of the forests and fields, towns and villages that circumscribed the planet.

Taras, however, had been unaware of Domov for most of his life. He had not "been born into the job."

Taras had been born in Dnipropetrovsk—a city with many names since its inception as a monastery in the ninth century. The name of the city having been changed in 1926, slightly before his birth, to honor Grigory Ivanovich Petrovsky, the Communist leader in the Ukraine Party. Prior to the Ukrainian Revolution, the city had been named after Catherine the Great, Yekaterinoslav—a name it had boasted since 1787. Even when occupied by the Nazis from 1941 to 1943, Dnipropetrovsk had been an important center growing from a population of approximately two hundred thousand before the war to three times that number by the beginning of the 1950s.

Taras had been born in the *raion* (neighborhood) of Novokodatsky at a time when the city was roughly equally divided among Ukrainians, Russians, and Jews—demographics that changed dramatically in 1942 when the *Einsatzgruppen* (German death squads) reduced the Jewish population by nearly ninety-eight percent in four days. In the postwar period the Russian segment of the population also declined significantly although many families with Russian roots, like Taras', continued to enjoy a comfortable lifestyle in a city that seemed destined for rapid economic expansion.

The city had been a manufacturing and industrial hub since the late 1800s. In 1945, Moscow decided to turn the city into a major producer of military matériel using German POW labor to build a variety of facilities including those working on developing, building, and testing the missiles and rockets of war. At Stalin's request, they developed a secret and shrouded group of enterprises using the technical expertise scoured from the postwar rubble and debris—a group of activities folded into the underground organization simply called "Southern." This combine continued into the 60s when these units built the *Sputniks* that were a key part of the USSR's Space Race.

However, Taras' family had had nothing to do with the overt or covert manufacturing that seemed to drive the city. His father, Matvey, in the tradition of his father and his father's father, decided the nearly slave labor in the factories that was the chief option for the poorly educated was not a route suitable for him nor his family. For generations, the Kuzmenko family had been able to make well more than an average livelihood via a variety of what would best be described as minor criminal activities. As many in the netherworld, they had started as Gruppirovki, basically petty criminals, and slowly evolved to become members in good standing of the more masterly *Soobshckestvo*—topnotch racketeers.

While Taras had been indoctrinated into the family business at an early age, his mother, Anya, had seen far too intimately the price one paid for being inadequately educated. She insisted her son follow his studies even if he followed the family business.

Taras proved himself to be equally adept in and out of the classroom. With high marks and a sharp intellect, he seemed to advance effortlessly through his studies, receiving a master's in business administration from the National University of Kyiv-Mohyla Academy. This three-century-old institution at the nation's capital and on the banks of the Dnieper fine-tuned Taras' skills including his language skills—a quadrilingual graduate (Ukrainian, Russian, English, and French) with exceptional business acumen. Like the two-faced Roman god of beginnings and duality, Janus, Taras, as a young man, demonstrated a unique brace of skills that made him both an adept businessman and an adroit criminal.

Taras' skills did not go unnoticed. It was not, however, Mykola nor Yegor who immediately noticed the potential of the young Taras, he was far too far down the food-chain to be recognizable to the magnates overseeing the vast spaces of Domov.

Kryrylo was a mid-level operator—someone who would be considered a supervisor in most businesses and organizations. He was a contemporary of Artem, though slightly his senior (it was all very entwined—in some cases, nearly incestuous). Kryrylo was the head of the cell in which Matvey worked. Kryrylo had had firsthand and close coverage of Taras' ascension from a rosy-faced boy in patched knickers running clan errands to an erudite yet forbidding young man in a coat and tie.

With the approval of all the entities up the chain, Kryrylo arranged first with Matvey, then with Anya, and finally with Taras that the promising and energetic graduate of Kyiv-Mohyla take over the coordination of activities in Poltava.

This city of about 150,000 inhabitants was roughly equidistant between Kyiv and Dnipropetrovsk. Its history shared many of the elements of Dnipropetrovsk. Its origins, less clear but going back to the twelfth century, were those of a simple and small rural community tugged back and forth by White Russians and Bolsheviks, Ukrainian Socialists and Ukrainian Nationalists. It also shared a Nazi occupation with all its devastation. When it entered into a formal role in the USSR, it was flagged as an education center for, among others, military officers working in communications and missile operations.

Poltava was also an important pivot point for Domov. Transportation, crudely referred to by some as smuggling, was a foundational and important part of Domov activities. Most of this transportation was, to the extent possible, done in obscurity—often under the cover of darkness. Domov's transportation channels, carefully sheltered and maintained through the decades by a variety of "entrepreneurs," were, at any specific point in time, known to but a select few. They embraced land, sea, and air. Often, use of waterways was a method of choice where the potential contraband (animate or inanimate) could be lost in the chaotic flow of humanity up and down the waters.

Poltava was located on the Vorskla River, a tributary of the Dnieper. Cargo could easily be brought up this smaller offshoot of the vast Dnieper system as far as Kobelyaky—approximately fifty miles from Poltava.

From there, for the final part of this leg of the trip, the merchandise could be transferred to trucks or continue on upriver in small skiffs.

In Poltava there was a series of warehouses and other structures that allowed Domov to assemble and store a wide variety and large quantity of products. The smallish city was basically the proverbial fork in the road—the Poltava crew determining the next strategic pathways as all manner of commerce proceeded onward to its final destination. Items going to or coming from Russia would be passed to or received from the east to be dealt with by the cell in Kharkiv while material destined for Ukraine or her neighbors would pass west, through Kyiv.

The switchman at this important crossing was now Taras.

⚘⚘⚘⚘⚘⚘⚘

The custodian, the crossing guard in Poltava, did a good job—a job acknowledged and appreciated by many. In fact, he did such a good job that in a relatively short period he was transferred to Kharkiv to head up the cell there—almost as if he were circling to ultimately land at (at least for Ukraine) the epicenter of Kyiv.

Kharkiv had played a greater part in recent history than Kyiv. A fortress that had been built in 1654 in the land of the Cossacks had become the third largest industrial and scientific hub (including a school for Strategic Rocket Forces) in the USSR with a population approaching a million. Like much of the region, it had suffered tremendously during the Nazi occupation with nearly three-quarters of the city destroyed during back-and-forth battles between the Germans and the Red Army. As much of the eastern portion of the country, the pre-war community had been divided amongst Ukrainians, Russians, and Jews with the Russian culture and language in a dominant role. The postwar city had, as elsewhere, seen a drastic decline in the Jewish population but a rapid expansion in civic and industrial development—much of it aimed at supporting the massive Soviet military complex. This swelling and frequently tumultuous environment offered not only new opportunities for the Soviets—it also set the stage for extensive benefits for Domov.

Kharkiv, roughly one-hundred miles northeast of Poltava and less than thirty miles from the Russian border, was a major piece of the Domov tapestry—practically a manifestation of the Ukraino-Russian dynamism that forged the joints comprising the intricate network.

Kharkiv was a critical concourse for a multitude of activities. Through its portals, merchandise of all sorts streamed in and out of the heartland of the USSR. There were luxury products from the West. There were small arms and the implements of criminality. There was food and drink. There were spare parts and health supplies. There were people fleeing the Stalinist government. There were people other people were slipping into the lands overseen by this very same government.

All this ebb and flow was screened from a government that, while very corrupt internally, brutally sought to seek and destroy any external corruption. The USSR had, in addition to the well-known KGB, all manner of furtive police and security forces whose main goal was to completely stifle just the sort of businesses that were the core of Domov.

The organization's masked channels were essential in avoiding exposure and extinction. These pathways were by necessity carefully guarded and meticulously maintained. They were the arteries that interconnected some of the most important geography wrapped in the Domov web.

These avenues and byways were cared for by Taras.

As had become his trademark, Taras did good work.

The work was hard and complex, providing challenges that honed his intellectual and practical skills. As had been the case in Poltava, as Taras' potential became clear, he was soon moved further up the ladder. Good help was hard to find. Exceptional help was even rarer.

Everyone had expected him to be transferred to Kyiv, perhaps as the second in command. To the surprise of all, including Taras, he was moved to Bucharest where he was the assistant to the head of the Romanian cell.

The head of the Romanian group was one Messr. Florin Enache. As far as his neighbors knew, Florin, a resident of the Ghencea neighborhood in the western part of the city, was part of the groundskeeping crew for the well-known local sports club: *CSA Steaua Bucuresti*. After the 1947 revolution, the People's Army created a sports club which evolved through time to become one of the most successful multi-sport centers in the country. People would have been shocked to realize the mild-mannered Florin was the calculating and implacable principal of an international criminal cartel.

Taras, shunning any obvious public links to his boss, rented a flat in the Tei neighborhood in the northeast quadrant of the city, named after the nearby lake, *Lacul Tei*, and home to the Technical Civil Engineering University of Bucharest where a position had been arranged for him in the office that oversaw the purchasing, distribution, and storage of the multitude of consumables used in the university's day-to-day operations—not only a suitable cover, if modest role, for someone with an MBA, but also possibly a client for some of the cell's merchandise.

Florin and Taras would make biweekly trips on public transport to the city center near the Orthodox cathedral, *Biserica Sfântul Antonie Cel Mare*. This ancient part of the city, called *Lipscani* after the many traders who had occupied the area centuries before, was awash with small cafés and restaurants where the two could meet unnoticed—only additional jetsam in an expanse of humanity coming from the four points of the compass. If urgent matters arose, they would always find a time and place to do what was necessary. However, Taras was now high enough up the ladder that his work chiefly involved careful planning and thorough oversight, leaving the hands-on execution to others who did not know him and whom he scarcely knew.

As was common, as Taras was learning, in a multiplicity of Domov cells, the tapestry had many forms and faces. While the conclusive local decisions were made by Florin with considerable consultation with Taras, there were other actors who were much less in the shadows—much more visible and acknowledged leaders of the business community and upper social circles with the ears and lips of high-level decision-makers at their disposal. One such person was the Romanian-born Radutu Botezatu. His given name meant "happy man." He had been brought up near the Ukrainian border in the middle-sized town of Rădăuţi in Suceava Judet (county) in the historical region of Bukovina. While his early life was largely unplumbed, when he did appear on the Domov dais in his mid-thirties, he was reportedly a much-sought-after member of the upper crust with businesses across the country—economic if not hereditary nobility. While his financial portfolios were thick and diverse, he appeared to have a particular penchant for investments in tourism and the retail trade; in regard to this latter, he owned numerous outlets that sold sports and hunting paraphernalia as well as hardware and building supplies. Mr. Botezatu's interests counted a number of hotels and tourist destinations, including remote mountain-side chateaus. One such palatial structure in the Făgăraş Mountains, smack dab in the middle of the country, was a celebrated getaway for the country's rich, even if not so famous.

This mixture of popular and private (overt and covert) actors and actions was emblematic of Domov. Many of the organization's most important (and sometimes most lucrative if egregious) operations took place in the full light of day, managed and maintained by familiar faces orchestrating seemingly normal events in the public square. Radutu Botezatu was illustrative of the open segment of activities that supplied the client with what he or she wanted, that kept close tabs on the provincial political leadership, and that generated significant wealth for the organization—both locally and globally.

Radutu's businesses were successful in their own right; however, it was a bit challenging determining how much of his business was standalone and how much a Domov outlet. On the retail front, much of his stock came via clandestine channels. Moreover, there were always parallel supply pathways. For every legal hunting rifle sold through a sporting goods store or for every bucket of paint or bag of nails sold through the hardware stores, there was ten times this volume of product moving through under-the-table pathways. Often this underground market dealt with exactly the same material as the retail stores—it was simply procured duty and tax-free with no paper trail to influence Radutu's already (from his perspective) excessive personal tax burden and sold at "special" prices echoing the severely reduced contribution to government coffers. There was, however, a complete menu of illicit items that were offered to Radutu's private customers. These ran the full range of simple yet-to-be-approved black-market products for the builder or homeowner (including such standards as cigarettes and whisky) to much more illegitimate items like guns and ammo, performance-enhancing drugs (the cell shied away from hard drugs on most occasions), stolen and resold appliances and building materials, false documentation, and even reconditioned construction machinery. There was something for everyone.

Now this and much more was all going on under the watchful eyes of Taras—the system carefully cared for and maintained to optimize benefits to the organization up and down the value chain.

Taras' proficiency and finesse at his job had continued to grow. Few, including the man from Dnipropetrovsk himself, had been very perplexed when he had been called to meet with Mykola and Yegor. Everyone, at least all in that tiny group who were in the know, had been perplexed though when it was announced that there was now to be a sole king on the hill. There was to be only one boss: the *Maliar*. And the *Maliar* was the *Kráľ Hory.* And Taras was the *Maliar*.

View from the Top

More than halfway through the twentieth century, Domov, a twentieth-century organization built on much older and deeper roots, was seeping into cracks and crannies around the world. The organization was reaching the most secluded corners of the globe while it was blatantly, and frequently visibly, active on the most populous avenues and street corners.

From Bourg-en-Bresse, the overseer of all this expansive and complex structure was the *Maliar*, and the *Maliar*, Taras, was engrossed in the job twenty-four seven. Today he had driven to Geneva to take one of the company aircraft, a Lockheed Jet Star (even the thoughts of widespread use of jet aircraft were distant in most minds and the idea of private business executive craft even more remote—as usual, Domov was at the forefront), to Marseilles to meet with Les Caïds (the "big shots") of Le Milieu, the kingpins of the local crime families, several still having connections to the Corsican or Sicilian mafia (these villainous groups referred to simply as "the place"). Le Milieu had a high degree of control over the French ports along the Mediterranean—ports that were critical to the movement of Domov's merchandise onto and off of the Continent. As with many potentially competitive or even antagonistic groups around the world, Domov and Le Milieu had long operated through a fragile series of agreements that offered benefits to both sides while effectively keeping each out of the other's way. These arrangements needed to be updated and validated on a regular basis, and this was the objective of this trip from the wintry foothills to the sunny shores.

Taras stared out the square porthole, watching the landscape below stream by as though it were a series of scenes from a flickering 1920s silent movie. Farms and fields, cities and hamlets, petrol stations and grocery stores—they were all there and in one way or another, albeit often totally unbeknownst to it themselves, they were a part of the foundation of the great Domov hierarchy. They ate food coming ultimately from Domov. They put their hard-earned savings in banks allied with Domov. They built homes with materials tied to Domov. They even went to schools and were shepherded by politicians that were influence by Domov.

Domov was now everywhere.

However, there were no guarantees. Domov offered no warranty—neither to those on the inside nor those on the outside. All were exempt from any assurance that benefits or advantages would be as good or better tomorrow than today. It was truly a course that forced one to live in the moment and accept that things could always fall apart. There was no pot of gold at the end of the rainbow, but there was always the potential for great wealth and power—though typically in a position susceptible to any manner of failure or sanction. It was what it was.

This objective assessment of Domov rarely entered into day-to-day decision-making by the majority of actors engaged in the wide variety of Domov-related activities. As had been the case when Andriy and Lehya were first trying to see how to weave their tapestry, most players in the field were interested in short-term returns—quick gratification preferable to waiting for a promise of grander compensation in the future—the opportunity cost of commitment.

Those on the lower rungs of the ladder chose now over later. Those higher up understood the high payoff for patience. Vianney, Chantal, Señor Tomas, Voldoymyr, Radutu Botezatu, and even the puzzling Sir Horace were all patient people.

CHAPTER 3

THE BUSINESS OF BUSINESS

"Business opportunities are like buses,
there's always another one coming."

—Richard Branson

War is Good Business

In 1926 the Great War had reshaped the world that was the key part of Andriy and Lehya's architecture. As described by Illinois economist Simon Litman (*The Effects of the World War on Trade*), the decline of the Austro-Hungarian empire redrew the map of Central and Eastern Europe with many of her neighbors trying to distance themselves from Mother Russia while simultaneously there was a strong and rapidly increasing feeling of nationalism that prompted larger European countries to expand their dominance over smaller nations, some only recently established, to enlarge their resource and power bases.

While this scenario applied to World War I, Taras, having studied it in university, felt it applied in general to the post-WWII phase as well. Russia and the USSR were still central to global strategies and investments—the Cold War a new reality. While they stared with trepidation over the Iron Curtain at their rival to the East, Western European countries were trying to balance the death-throws of colonialism with efforts to establish newer more dissembled forms of hegemony over those countries which could supply the products required to keep the fires burning in European industries.

It was, in fact, these underlying principles that brought Taras to Marseilles and Le Milieu. A significant portion of the raw materials, the machinery, and the labor that stoked western firms traversed the Mediterranean—much of this passing through French, Italian, and Spanish ports as well as, of course, arteries to more distant sister ports in the Aegean and Black Seas and even the Sea of Azov.

Additionally, it was not only supplying time-honored demand. War, even a cold one, was good business—especially for folks like Domov and Le Milieu—folks who operated on the margins. The clamorous politics and policies of a postwar, Cold War, microcosm offered many fissures and gaps where marginal actors could do very well—very well indeed.

Major shifts in the world's geography and economy led to new markets and new prospects as well as new and still incompletely understood risks. These times offered high profit potential but equally high costs of failure. The last thing Taras wanted was to enter into a spat with Le Milieu when there was more than enough on the table to fully occupy the capacities of the two organizations.

It was a time to mobilize. But it was also a time for clear, well-planned action that avoided foreseeable pitfalls while accentuating the comparative advantages for firms operating beyond confines seen as transgressive by many.

France was suffering through what it hoped would be the end of an Indochina War that had come far too quickly after a much-awaited V-E Day. Not long before there had been the Partition of India and the independence of Indonesia after a failed attempt by the Dutch to re-establish their East Indies colony. As Sino-Taiwanese clashes continued, the island once called Formosa entered a period it called "White Terror." Nonetheless, within all this political pother, the Asia Region was undergoing significant changes—changes that opened new doors to Domov if not to Le Milieu.

With the arrival of a new decade, there were energies emanating from the dust of WWII and Asian battlefields while there were other forces igniting flames in small and large countries alike. This was potentially a period with an opening for high growth, and Taras could not allow these opportunities to be derailed by any feuds over trivial matters with Le Milieu. He needed to make sure the French cartel was willing and able to work within the boundaries outlined by their most recent informal yet binding agreements. He needed to be proactive. If there were issues, these needed to be sorted sooner rather than later.

⚓⚓⚓⚓⚓⚓⚓

Discussions with Le Milieu went well and after a recommitment to the status quo, the few pending minor concerns were put to rest promptly. Taras decided to make the most out of his sortie and add a stopover in Granda where Domov had multiple investments before heading back to cooler, more northern climes.

Taras arranged to fly into Málaga Airport where he would be met by a company car to take him the ninety some miles to his destination.

As the plane was landing, it skidded off the runway, tipping up on its right wing in a ball of fire. The crew of three along with Taras and his assistant perished in the crash.

Human Resources

Orest Savchuk became the new *Maliar*. Some of the uninformed claimed this was because his given name meant "he who stands on the mountain." This was certainly not the case, and those few who were truly in the know knew that he had worked his way up the ladder in a way very similar to his predecessor, Taras.

It was not easy. There was no clear process for succession. Taras had been the first *Maliar,* and no one expected his mandate to end so soon nor so tragically. There were no rules—no manual to guide the upper echelons of Domov. They were simply driven by pragmatism and the understanding that every day that went by without stern guidance was potentially a day that could certainly lead to fewer profits and potentially to complete failure. Delay was not an option.

Taras' team in Bourg-en-Bresse kept the torch lit during the transition. They reached out to the heads of all the Domov hubs, informing them of Taras' death and, using protocols they designed and then fine-tuned as they moved forward, asking them to nominate someone to what amounted to a search committee.

When in doubt, fall back on tradition and custom. Most of the hub leadership were businessmen. They understood the process of searching for a suitable candidate for assuming the role of chief executive officer—this was the same thing. The committee was given, by common consensus, a month to nominate a candidate who would in turn be confirmed by a meeting of the hub leadership.

This was what happened, and this was what led to Orest Savchuk's installment as the new *Maliar*.

In point of fact, Orest was nearly a younger carbon copy of Taras. His roots went deep into the Ukrainian clans while he had been fortunate enough to pursue an eduction at the University of Lviv—a school dating back to 1661 when King John II, Casimir of Poland, granted a royal charter to the Jesuits to open an institute of higher learning. Upon graduation, like Taras, he had assumed a variety of roles in a variety of Domov activities.

While many may have had their own personal choice for *Maliar*, none could honestly say that Orest was not qualified.

Orest realized he could not stay in Bourg-en-Bresse; a new *Miliar* required a new centerpiece for Domov. He chose the small village of Holwerd in northern Friesland, one hundred miles northeast of Amsterdam with egress to the North Sea via the Wadden Sea or across the German border seventy miles further east.

There was no axiom that declared the *Maliar* needed to be based in Western Europe. In many ways, this seemed illogical—even to Orest. However, the criteria for a base were essentially ease of transport and communication combined with an ability to be invisible. Holwerd ticked all these boxes.

The immediate and urgent priorities were addressed. Someone, albeit a new and untested man, was at the helm and Domov had a functioning center of operations. The next item on Orest's list, although perhaps not on everyone's, was to thoroughly and quietly investigate the crash in Málaga.

The Spanish government had, of course, made a quick and cursory investigation. The crash of a private jet raised a flag; there were very few of these costly craft visiting the airport and then only for the very rich and well-known. However, Taras was not well-known. He was totally unknown. Thus, the death of an unknown (thereby, unimportant) Frenchman and his crew was far less relevant to the government investigators than wrapping up the inquiry as soon as possible so as not to adversely affect the high-value tourist industry of the Costa del Sol.

Working through the Granada office of Delpro, Orest put a team of fifteen top-notch investigators and analysts in the field. After a week, the team leader reported back that this had been no accident. After three weeks, he presented a detailed and substantiated report laying out how a small explosive and incendiary device had been placed in the wheel well of the front landing gear. This had both a timer and an altimeter trigger—it was very sophisticated. The timer activated the altimeter mid-flight, and the altimeter activated the bomb at an elevation of sixty feet (the elevation of Málaga is thirty-six feet), this then igniting the incendiary portion of the device. The landing gear was destroyed before the plane hit the tarmac and the fire started immediately on contact. There was no chance. There was no margin for error. The elaborated apparatus, undoubtedly installed while in Marseilles, had been a death warrant to all onboard. It was murder.

This added more to the already supercharged workload of the novice *Maliar*. Was this the work of Les Caïds of Le Milieu? That was the easiest conclusion and one that could possibly be backed up by the high-tension competition between Le Milieu and Domov, but Orest was not yet willing to jump to this conclusion. As in Málaga, he fielded a well-funded highly qualified team to look into all options.

Here there was no available hard evidence to examine. Here the research had to start with the soft noises of the street and slowly coalesce into some meaningful messages that could point to areas of culpability. It would be a long process with no guarantees.

There was much else to do.

The routine for Orest in Holwerd was much the same as it had been for Taras in Bourg-en-Bresse—in truth, much the same as routines followed by high-level Domov leaders across the globe.

Although all work and no play may have made Jack a dull boy, all work and no play helped Domov stay on top of the hill. Clinging to the pinnacle was hard work, and the *Maliar* could not do it alone.

Orest had a superb team inconspicuously placed in and around Holwerd—people with simple public-facing jobs and very complex masked assignments in the service of the *Maliar* of Domov. As technology, especially communications technology (an unanticipated benefit of the Cold War) bounded forward, Orest was able to keep in touch with his crew through a variety of indirect methods as well as through a series of orchestrated encounters at any of several cafés, bars, or restaurants in the area or, more often, through walks on the frequently nearly deserted six-mile shoreline from the Ameland Ferry Terminal to Paesens-Moddergat. If more serious or organized meetings were required, these could be held on the island of Ameland where the local team could put a tight cordon around their chief and any prominent visitors needing absolute privacy to settle weighty and highly sensitive issues.

As Orest was getting settled and setting his own priorities, he ran across an obscure article discussing how personnel issues were really matters that regarded human resources. The author was arguing for putting more of a humanistic face on employee management. Orest took this to mean two different things. First, he had to prioritize getting the highest quality staff in key Domov positions. Not an automatic out-with-the-old and -in-with-the-new philosophy, this was an intentional aim to enhance the quality of management at all levels including his own. Second, he needed to focus on the broader subject of human resources—a subject that had been drilled into him early on.

There had always been a basic premise, or he had always assumed there had been such a premise, that the pool of potential employees was nearly bottomless. It was purely a question of over-supply where the employer could dictate the terms because of this endless supply. However, postwar socio-economic adaptations had shown things in a new light. The supply of people from all sources and for all positions was far from boundless. It was easy to foresee many situations where there would be shortages and even more situations where the price point for the needed labor would be so high it would be very difficult to find enough good and affordable candidates. Domov needed to see labor as a commodity—as a target enterprise both internally and externally.

From the Domov summit in Holwerd, there were many priorities, projects, and principles.

Orest knew well, however, that he first had to do his due diligence. He had to understand as completely as possible the organization he headed while establishing the confidence of the people who were wrapped in the massive Domov tapestry that now reached nearly every far corner of every continent. This required pouring over heaps of documentation. This involved detailed discussions. This involved a lot of time.

While Orest was getting up to speed, most of those entwined in the Domov net had no idea there was a new *Maliar*. Truthfully, most had no idea there even was a *Maliar* nor what a *Maliar* would do if there had been one. They most definitely had no clue about specific individuals—especially not about Messr. Taras nor Messr. Orest. While the hierarchy was far-reaching, the nearly universal context was that people only knew about the level immediately above them on the Domov ladder, and even then, only just a few rudimentary fragments, not a real picture of a structure nor an organization. Institutional silos and compartments were built-in by design. The two generations of architects, Andriy and Lehya followed by Mykola and Yegor, had had a clear understanding of the need for plausible deniability. It was often safest and sometimes more profitable if the right hand did not know what the left hand was doing.

Orest's move to the organization's pinnacle was certainly not common knowledge.

Joe heard from his father in a very abstruse communication that apparently there were some changes underway. All other instructions were to carry on as usual—the North American foothold was still a must-do.

Sir Horace was slightly more in the know. He realized there was an on-going change at the very top, but it was outside his remit. As always, he was content to play the hand he was dealt, and while he awaited any special directives, he invariably continued overseeing his carefully chosen favorite personal schemes and tasks.

Radutu Botezatu, Voldoymyr, and Señor Tomas, much like Joe, had heard rumors of adjustments at the very apex of the union. However, this was well above their reach, and they had more than enough to do. They fundamentally understood the old proverb, "shit flows downhill." If there were to be knock-on effects, they would be apprised at some time when it was their time.

Vianney, Chantal, and scores if not hundreds of others were so far down the power scale that they had no knowledge of the goings-on and, had they even been aware, would have likely been happy to remain oblivious and hopefully unaffected. "Ignorance is bliss" rang true to many ears.

While so many knew so little, there was someone who had thought she knew Orest well—one of the few outsiders who had had insight into the man who would become the *Maliar*. This was while he was a rising star. Still, this outsider had absolutely no inkling about Domov nor someone called the *Maliar* who sat at its head.

This person was Sophie Arquette.

Sophie was a graduate of the University of Montpellier—a graduate who as an undergraduate had had a blazing relationship with a young exchange student from Ukraine—a relationship with Orest. Sophie had been born in Avignon at the time when the first FIFA World Cup was taking place in Uruguay.

Sophie's father was a primary school teacher, and her mother was a housewife who raised four children and took in sewing on the side. Her hometown, dating back to 500 B.C. but probably best remembered for becoming the papal residence in the 14th Century as witnessed by the splendid *Palais des Papes* (Palace of the Popes), offered a relatively normal backdrop for her childhood if one excluded the Nazi occupation from November 1942 until August 1944 and the total havoc of battle—with 525 people killed on the 27th of May 1944 alone in Operation Dragoon (ironically, the same operation that had brought Vianney Cisse to France). What may have been special in Sophie's case was her love of learning—probably attributable to her father's deep devotion to pedagogy. Unlike many females of her age in postwar France, she decided she wanted to go as far as she could with her studies, and her nimble mind combined with a potent dose of ambition propelled her far.

In search of her diplomas, she learned of Julie-Victoire Daubié, who, in 1861, was the first French woman to graduate from university. Julie-Victoire also became a respected journalist although she had to work under the cover of an embroidery shop—a more suitable activity for a fine woman of the time. After working through the onerous processes of obtaining a licentiate degree in arts and a master's in literature, Sophie decided to try and walk in Julie-Victoire Daubié's footsteps.

While her academic program was rigorous and often daunting, having few other women with whom to share the road—her leisure time could be called "vigorous." One of the benefits of being one of the few females was that there was a large crop of hormonally active young men from whom to choose when seeking masculine companionship, and Sophie did not lack for masculine companionship.

Although many of these romantic *aventures* were effectively over before they started, her relationship with Orest had been special.

Orest had come to Montpellier through an exchange program that allowed him to take coursework for a *mention droit de l'économie*. When Sophie first saw him walking briskly between buildings on campus, she thought, *voilà quelqu'un agréable aux yeux* (there's someone pleasant to look at).

Orest had arrived in France in what his father would have called "*na vrchole vašej hry*" (on top of his game—some might have called it the arrogance of youth, others the culmination of hard work). Dmytro Savchuk knew the meanings of hard work and hardship. He had been a part-time farmer and part-time member of his clan's Gruppirovki crime group—neither bringing in enough revenue for his large family, including the high maintenance costs for his amazingly prodigious scion Orest. When Dmytro finally moved up in the world of impropriety and became a member of the Prestupnaia, he abandoned farming while adopting a practice of taking his young son along with him when engaged in one or another sort of miscreant mission. He felt the practical on-the-spot education added more value than formal schooling.

It was on one of these misadventures that the young and energetic Orest was noticed by Fedir Fedorenko, a headman of the clan who began to consider Orest as his godchild—the boy, with the full approval of his parents, spending progressively more time with his "Uncle Fedir." Occasionally, Orest would ask his father, "*Chýbam ti* (Do you miss me)?" Dmytro would inevitably reply, "*Samozrejme, si môj chlapec, ale chcem, aby si bol vždy na vrchole svojej hry a nemôžem ti pomôcť dostať sa tam, ako to dokáže strýko Fedir* (Of course, you're my boy—but I want you to always be on top of your game and I can't help you get there like Uncle Fedir can)."

Uncle Fedir helped in many ways, not the least of which was pushing a reluctant Orest to get back into his studies. Older than his classmates, with Fedir's support and guidance, Orest was able to overcome any age stigma and prove himself to be an able student. His good grades and excellent references quickly opened the doors of universities to the young man who once helped his father sell blackmarket cigarettes.

When Orest started his program at Montpellier, he was both physically and mentally fit. However, he was in other ways somewhat socially handicapped. While life may not have been exactly a zero-sum game, when you and all those around you focused totally on building your career, something had to give.

Growing up in Ukraine had been eye-opening in many ways, with everyone from Dmytro to Fedir coercing and prodding Orest in the direction of achieving greater and grander things. But this youthful environment had not provided any insight into the types of interpersonal relationships one encountered at a French university. Fortunately, Sophie materialized to be his life coach.

Among his many proficiencies, like Taras before him, Orest had an ear for languages. Yet, in spite of being a polyglot with French a part of his repertoire, he honestly was not prepared for the rapid-fire slang-laced language of campus.

Orest had been at the counter of the campus post office, unsuccessfully trying to explain to the clerk with a strong Norman accent that he wanted to send some letters to Kyiv. Sophie had been behind him in the queue and had kindly intervened to overcome the apparent linguistic debacle. After his letters were stamped and in the mail bag and Sophie had completed her much simpler task, Orest asked her to join him for a cup of coffee. *La suite est connue* (the rest is history). What began with a cup of very robust coffee ended up with an equally robust bout of lovemaking at Orest's apartment.

While Sophie was not Orest's first love, he lacked by far the experience the girl from Avignon had gained after living years on a male-centered campus. Nonetheless, for both, an unexpected intimacy made what could otherwise have been solely lustful gymnastics a special event. That afternoon after the post office was the beginning of a profound liaison that seemed to drive both young people both in and out of bed.

Sophie and Orest became nearly inseparable. However, each was ambitious and galvanized on getting all the university offered. The goals that had led to their paths crossing at Montpellier were never forgotten—never lost, not even in the fervor of their lasciviousness. They were completely able to compartmentalize profession and passion.

Nevertheless, emotions are hard to constrain—hard to circumscribe with strict limits. When Orest headed back to Ukraine after his year in Mediterranean France, it was with a great lump in his chest—leaving his dear Sophie was almost as physically painful as it was emotionally heart-wrenching. They had clung to each other with intense ardor as they watched their last sunrise together, promising that they would soon be together again and realizing that no one knew tomorrow.

On the train east, Orest, with intense misery, convinced himself he would never see his love again.

Back in her classroom, Sophie knew she would again see her dear Orest.

Returning to the University of Lviv and finishing his studies with honors, Orest left the sheltered corridors of academia and rejoined the real world as seen through the eyes of his mentors such as, among many, Dmytro and Fedir. With significant hands-on practice, an exceptional education, and unsurpassed zeal, Orest moved quickly up the ladder of the Ukrainian criminal clans and up the conduit that he was later to learn was Domov. By organization standards, Orest's rise was meteoric. He was quickly the head of Domov activities in Khmelnytskyi and then transferred to Sofia to oversee the Bulgarian program at the time of Taras' untimely death. Orest may not have known it, but he had been flagged early on as a potentially important resource for the syndicate. Domov as a faceless entity understood it was essential to invest in people. Orest as *Maliar* was beginning to understand that this concept of human capital was at the heart of much of his work—concerning resources both within and without the organization. Staff, from the lowest to the highest echelons, had to be carefully selected, to be nourished, and to be cared for. People were the springboard for profits and power. The old adage "the customer is king" had waned in general over recent years; nevertheless, the organization had to have a good relationship with its clients if it was to succeed.

People, broadly and narrowly speaking, had become a foundational principle for Orest Savchuk, the new *Maliar*. It wasn't because he was a people person nor that he felt an inherent link to the society that had led him to the peaks of power. It was much simpler. Though an unavoidable necessity, people were always the weakest link. Though whimsical, they needed to be carefully nourished. Though erratic, they needed to be carefully shepherded. And, above all, they needed to be carefully watched. It was the people principle.

Following this principle, the *Maliar* and his entourage, at least at the higher levels, understood their organization's profitability if not its survival depended upon its human holdings more than its financial assets. Not only were sustainable operations dependent upon good staff and good networks, but they also depended even more on favorable markets. It was all, as always, about supply and demand, and theirs was the supply side of the equation. Yet, if the demand side was not there, it was for naught. If the human dimensions of demand were not addressed, it was all for naught.

Most of their customers and clients had no idea what Domov even was. They were a cross-section of global society that was fulfilling their needs from the marketplace—consuming goods and services that, knowingly or unknowingly, came from a worldwide web that was Domov.

As Orest saw every day, the market was capricious.

⚘⚘⚘⚘⚘⚘⚘

Everyone knew markets were capricious or at least felt the effects of their fickle behavior. For the majority, it was a struggle.

Wyatt and Ida McKnight understood the struggle; as faithful Presbyterians who went to church almost every Sunday, they knew they were lucky as so many others had a much more difficult time just making ends meet.

The McKnights lived in Minot, North Dakota. Ida was a third-grade teacher at Roosevelt Elementary, and Wyatt was an insurance agent with his own independent agency including two employees, an assistant, and a secretary. He knew Minot had been called the "Magic City" back in the late 1880s when it was founded—the magic being the speed with which the community had grown. More contemporarily, Wyatt had seen this growth continue up to the present, with the city nearly doubling over the time he had been trying to provide it with the best possible insurance coverage; this was a good thing for him as even the current population of 40,000 was not a big market for a tough sell like insurance.

Wyatt and Ida had tried and tried to have children but were finally unable to deny the apparent truth; they could have none. They adopted Richie, and they thanked God. Richard Wayne McKnight brought an entire new sense of meaning to their lives. He was a good kid. He wasn't a star athlete nor a top student, but he was definitely a good kid. He passed his exams, even if with difficulty. He helped his father clean the office every week. And he loved the great outdoors that surrounded Minot. The town was an hour north of Lake Sakakawea and the headwaters of the great Missouri River as well as being surrounded by a plethora of small lakes and ponds. It was no wonder that Richie's extracurricular passion was fishing—but not regular fishing, ice fishing. Unlike many who lived in the shadow of the Canadian border, he was anxious for the temperatures to plummet, the snow to fall, and the waters to freeze rock hard. Summer was just that trying period one had to wait through to be able to get out on the ice and absorb the true pleasures of frigid fishing.

Over those could-have-been-boring summers, when he was old enough, Richie worked on his Uncle Warner's ranch—the 42,000-acre R-X Ranch near Bowman, about four hours to the southwest. Uncle Warner, Wyatt's younger brother, had married Sally Offhauser (originally *Aufhauser*)—daughter of one of the state's richest families. The R-X had been a wedding present to Sally from her baron-like father, Rutger.

Richie proved himself to be a good ranch hand and was offered a permanent mid-level position by his uncle and aunt. However, to respect his father and mother's wishes, he decided to take a shot at college although this was far from a personal priority. He enrolled at Turtle Mountain Community College, two hours to the northeast of Minot, spitting distance from the border.

Midway through his sophomore year, Richie's (Rich as he now preferred to be called with no reference at all to the synonym for wealth) stars realigned. College, as he had imagined, was not a good fit. As usual, he was a persistent if mediocre student, but there was no fire. There was no *joie de vivre*. As he was planning how to let his parents know college was not for him, he received the sad news that Uncle Warner had unexpectedly passed away after a massive heart attack. The ranch, of course, stayed with, as it had always been, Sally. However, Warner had startlingly made a special accommodation for his much-admired nephew Richard; he bequeathed him the sum of $200,000.

This was a windfall and a bit embarrassing since his parents had received nothing from Warner except mention in a dry and scripted farewell to all the family in the closing paragraph of his will. Nonetheless, Wyatt and Ida were thrilled and the shock of this fluke of fate, as they saw it, dampened their sadness at their son's leaving school.

Wyatt wanted his boy to come by the office, and they would develop an investment plan for his inheritance.

Rich had another idea.

When he did belatedly visit his father's office, he had a clear idea of his next steps. Tactfully, he explained to his father how he had split the unexpected bonanza into two equal parts. One half, hopefully as an acceptable concession, would be invested following to his father's guidance and his father knew his stuff. But the other half would be used to purchase an R series Mack truck with some money set aside for fuel and maintenance. After a lot of digging, Rich explained to Wyatt, he had decided upon a pathway that he thought would give him the best of several worlds. From spring through early fall, he would travel about with his truck taking loads of cargo to any points scattered about the four corners of this vast country. Then in the fall, he would return to Minot, park the truck, and spend the winter ice fishing. It ticked all the boxes. There was a potential for some pretty good if not super income. There was a chance to see the world which heretofore had been hidden behind the prairies of North Dakota. And, critically, there was a chance to ice fish to his heart's content.

Once again, Wyatt and Ida were taken aback by their son's suggestions. Still, these were not bad ideas, and the entire strategy was flexible and could easily be amended if his infatuation with trucks or ice changed. Accordingly, with reservations, his parents blessed his intentions, and Rich was soon the owner of a bright red Mack truck that would hit the road as soon as he got his Class C commercial driver's license.

Rich the novice teamster was filled with great expectations; he had managed to land a dream job that allowed him to fish in ice holes from the first freeze to the first thaw. At the same time, he was seeing marvelous new landscapes through the windshield of his shiny Mack R series. At the same time, he was learning that people were the constant ingredient. Although alone in his cab most of the time, he still had never-ending encounters with a rainbow of people—some like those at the R-X Ranch or Turtle Mountain Community College and others oh so different. People were always part of the equation. There were his clients, there were the freight agents, there were the folks at the truck stops and the diners. There was no avoiding it. While Rich cruised the country, he cruised a most varied slice of humanity.

Rich himself was now part of the landscape and part of its ever-changing community.

As Rich the new community member drove down the highways crisscrossing the States, he had no idea he was among the millions who were, in one way or another, clients or customers of an unknown and unseen Domov. For him, each day on the road offered a new horizon and a new experience. It was all good and it was all exciting. He was unaware of the days flying by just like the mileposts.

Globalization

As Orest (and Rich, for that matter) was quickly learning, people led to places. This was the essence of Domov. Sometimes brashly in the full light of day, other times buried under layer upon layer of dissimulation, Domov was everywhere and did everything. Nonetheless, it was the people that formed the organization's map and not the places—as people changed, so did the map.

While some tried to grasp walking in space, others were simply trying to gain a foothold on individual liberties and freedom. Meanwhile, blood shed continued in Viet Nam accompanied by additional hotspots such as the China-Taiwan conflict, the India-Pakistan border, and the Angolan civil war. At the same time, old colonies were becoming newly independent nations while those in the seats of power on both sides of the Cold War tried to persuade the newcomers to come to their side of the wall. Things were, as always, messy. Messy things offered unique opportunities for Domov.

In Holwerd, Orest was physically far removed from most of the action on the ground. At the top of the imaginary hill, Orest was hierarchically and operationally far from this action as well. While he was the ultimate commander—the paramount chief—he relied implicitly on those below him to provide factual and meaningful information and to engage actively in the needed debate to be able to guide corporate decisions that would lead to even more power and wealth.

To a large extent, this process was serendipitous. The messy and fluid world affairs meant that most often the critical decisions were made spontaneously on the spot to take advantage of specific, perhaps fleeting circumstances.

Thus, the ground troops were not just "grunts." The ground troops were frequently the ones who opened the doors to future engagement by

Domov. The vertical movement of information and instructions up and down the hierarchical ladder, therefore, had to be very efficient and very rapid. The heads of Domov silos needed to have considerable autonomy as did others in specific decision-making roles across the breadth of the cartel.

A big part of the job was knowing when to intervene and when to let those in place take the key decisions. The questions of where and when nearly universally were left to those further down the ladder, Orest monitoring closely but to a great degree keeping his hands off and his mouth shut.

One of the topics most closely monitored and most difficult to keep hands off was the project to get a toehold in North America. This was more than finding access to potentially highly profitable markets. This was establishing a base or bases of strategic importance. Joe, following tactics worked out under Taras' leadership, was making good progress, but it was a delicate dance and one that could easily falter. It required considerable self-control on Orest's part to observe from the sandy shores of the North Sea without getting much more actively engaged. It was hard to let slow processes take effect and, hopefully yet unassuredly, lead to the outcomes so important to the *Maliar* and Domov.

Fedir had told Orest tales from ancient Greek mythology. He had spoken of Argus Panoptes, the all-seeing guardian who was rumored to have had one hundred eyes to be able to see all he needed to see. Orest felt he needed at least a hundred eyes to scrutinize all the places where Domov was cultivating the land—both literally and figuratively.

Orest was not alone in his thoughts about how to leverage places into power. Domov had always been and continued to be very discerning in regard to its people. These people, at all levels, were devoted to the cause—the cause of self-enrichment through more and more power and more and more market share.

Greater holdings required greater dominion. More was always needed—more land, more resources, more luck. It was as much a grab bag as a land grab.

In West Africa, with the tutelage of Chantal and the ever-present desire to have more, Sir Horace left few stones unturned. He was captivated by a kind of a gentleman's competition with his big brother, a competition not only about wealth and power, but about methodology.

Robin was building an empire—the Delpro Empire. It was most often public and prosperous; branch offices scattered about the globe but solidly welded to the master's domain on the shores of Lake Michigan. Delpro was, thanks to Robin's direction, like Ford Motor Company or American Express—you were never surprised to see its spoor anywhere—even in the most remote portions of the planet. It was widely familiar if not iconic. If it had ever really come out of the closet and operated totally aboveboard, Delpro would likely have been a Fortune 500 company.

Horace had taken a different tack. He wasn't much one to build monuments nor big flashy offices with multinational staff, which he saw as one in the same. He did have close ties to special companies that were more or less established in short order to deal with unique sets of opportunities and that regularly disappeared when these opportunities had been tapped. He was, nevertheless, closely tied to some more permanent fixtures, among others, Equatorial Management (based in Tanzania but Africa-wide in scope) and Southwest African Beef Company (home offices in Namibia but activities covering much of southern Africa and into Europe). Yet, typically, Sir Horace followed his gypsy spirit and had done pretty well in so doing.

He felt lucky to have been able to build a relationship with Chantal. In Ivory Coast (now called Côte d'Ivoire by all) and the wider coastal portions of West Africa, things were indeed complex. Vianney Cisse had been an excellent entrée into multiple operations. Although Vianney was getting a little long in the tooth (as were they all), Marc and Luc had proven themselves to be more than capable of taking up their father's mantle. They understood the culture, had good practical skills, and considerable business-oriented vision. They lacked ample funds and the specialized expertise, however, to be able to maximize their efforts. Sir Horace was sure he could provide the necessary additions to make these good opportunities truly exceptional, but he needed Chantal's help.

As a foursome, they were planning to go where few had gone before, and Sir Horace hoped, places where his big brother would never think of going.

One of these places was the public square. Horace and his entire cohort realized knowledge was power and that timing was everything. As the Africa region was rapidly metamorphosing into a continent of awakening and at times booming economies, money from many sources was flowing—all too often with only modest oversight. Much of the targeting and distribution of these monies was taken care of by public agencies—a large share moving through multinational economic communities that were being set up across the numerous newly independent countries. Advance knowledge of sums and sources was a boon.

With some well-planned and well-oiled gymnastics, Horace was able to secure a high-level position in the Development Community of West African States for Chantal. DCWAS had recently been established, with expansive headquarters in Nigeria, to facilitate and coordinate economic development efforts across their ten-country zone. With the tug of the Cold War and the exultation over the ending of colonialism, both the direct funding (or redirection of funding) and the medium-term financial prospects were significant. Chantal, as an insider, would be able to provide Horace with invaluable insight.

Expanding domestic economies and newly savored independence did not, however, stifle the desires of many seeking kinder and gentler places—each also looking for his or her own pot of gold at the end of the rainbow. Emigration, both official and unofficial, remained a problem. Some called it a "brain drain" as the better-educated found much improved working conditions in the thriving and expanding prosperity of Western Europe and North America. Yet it was not only the elite who found a high external demand for their services accompanied by a growing thirst to taste the good life. After all, even those in remote colonial schools had been bathed in the allure of European civilizations as though they were in spitting distance of Big Ben or the Champs-Élysées.

Common labor was in demand in these times of blossoming investment. While the under-educated could not afford costly air fare nor a new suitcase filled with warmer clothes for colder climates, they could do as they always had done—they could improvise. A variety of overland routes developed to shepherd, for a fee, those who wanted to get their piece of the good times of the mid twentieth century.

Countries tried to counter this outflow by imposing exit visas and attempting to strictly control borders. Countries tried to do all they could to keep their needed human resources in place. It was difficult. Underpaid immigration officials more times than not opened the gate for the price of a beer.

The overland pilgrimage was difficult beyond imagination. Many turned back. Some fell by the wayside. Only the most hardy reached the shores of the Mediterranean, and even these survivors were ultimately confronted by the dilemma of piercing the European barriers to be able to live and work in their desired destination.

These conditions led to another sort of improvisation. Like the jackals that followed the big game herds as they moved across the East African savannas, there were scavengers who realized the opportunities in following this stream of sufferers desperately seeking better times and better places. The followers picked up the stragglers, nursed the weakened, and offered solutions to the courageous who had reached the sea's shore. The followers corralled and blandished this mix of humanity in search of Arcadia.

However, these were not humanitarian workers trying to bind the wounds of their fellow men. These were true scavengers—buzzards who took advantage of the lost, the frail, and the powerless. They would ferry their prey via carefully constructed covert byways to the secluded factories, farms, and homesteads in need of cheap or even slave labor.

Sir Horace understood more than most the need for affordable labor and the gnarled pathways bootleggers had devised to meet the demand. He understood, but he was not supportive. He wanted no part of this subset of flagitious actions that occupied his world. This was not because he was empathetic to the sufferings of the victims. He was not. This was because he understood caprice and the most capricious thing of all: human beings. Trafficking in "produce" that had families, that had roots, that had a homeland was risky. It was more. It was dangerous. In his own youth he had seen firsthand how capricious life was when he was able to reconnect with his big brother. When it came to people, no one knew what could happen. Moving thousands about against their will may have been good business and may even have been necessary for some businesses, but he did not want this to be part of his business—at least not directly. His own chosen assignments had to pass the white-glove test—his own fine linen gloves not to be sullied by this distasteful task even if many of his investments ultimately relied upon forced labor.

Nevertheless, this assertion of taking the moral high ground (as hypocritical as it was) did not truly prove to be an obstacle to the wary Sir Horace. As with all complications, there was an answer, even if imperfect. As Marc and Luc were expanding and going to new places that required more and more labor, Sir Horace subrogated all his labor affairs to the brothers. Any inputs or requests were passed through Chantal—the old man keeping his gloves snowy white.

Scores left the home and hearth in search of the Elysian Fields. They traveled and they suffered. They reached new places. Unfortunately, often they found themselves in circumstances they could never have imagined—not streets paved with gold, but days drenched in sweat and nights filled with pain and nothingness.

At the same time that Chantal was building a solid base of influence, Marc and Luc were exploring new places for new investments while Sir Horace struggled (or maybe not) with some of the broader implications of his opprobrious actions. Over 6,500 miles to the northeast, Voldoymyr Rudenko's sphere began to swell wider and wider. Over and beyond Kafe Parus, Kosa Lyapina Island proved to be a reactant for actions in new and unexpected places.

All manner of material flowed through the island nexus. Outgoing products, Voldoymyr supposed, moved through the Black and Mediterranean Seas to ports around the world—to places far outside the scope of his base in Mariupol. Incoming wares seemed to multiply month by month. These typically appeared to fall into two baskets. There were covered baskets—materials Voldoymyr never saw. Materials of which Voldoymyr was totally unaware other than the fact that they transited through Kosa Lyapina Island. This untouchable merchandise arrived and left tightly wrapped, unknown.

Most of the material, however, fell in the other basket. Here there was a preponderance of what could generally be called black-market items—everything from perfume and champagne to socks and sneakers. Most of these products continued on into the interior, destined for markets in the Ukrainian and Russian heartlands. However, a portion of these goods remained with Voldoymyr for his own use—either marketed through Kafe Parus and his tourism businesses or through totally new enterprises that he was establishing in the city and along the southern coast as far as Berdyans'k.

Berdyans'k boasted a population of nearly 100,000, a noteworthy commercial fishery that provided delicacies for the café's tables, and shrouded distribution routes to provide more products to more people in more communities. Voldoymyr and his patchwork of agents and agencies did all they could to provision the residents, long- and short-term, of the shores of the Sea of Azov with all manner of items to complement their lives while they looked for new places yet to benefit from the organization's opulence.

⚓⚓⚓⚓⚓⚓⚓

One person who was not looking for new places was Sophie. She was pregnant. Orest did not know. Now Sophie did not know how nor when she might see the father of her child again, and she did not know if Orest would ever find out he was a father. What she did know was that she needed to be in the security and comfort of a well-known place to have her baby.

Fortunately, her pending motherhood came at the very end of her master's program. She was able to fully complete her studies before returning to Avignon and, after an initial shock and awe from her parents, settle into her home nest to prepare to become a mother.

Sophie welcomed her daughter, Oriana (named after the sun rays from that last sun rise she and her beloved Orest had witnessed together), and quickly set about all the tasks of a single mother while simultaneously building her new career in Avignon as a reporter for *Le Parisien Libéré*, a national newspaper that had started as an arm of the French resistance during the war and continued as an important portal into national and international news during the period of prosperousness in postwar France. Sophie knew Orest would have been proud.

Business Savvy

In Charles Dickens' *Christmas Carol,* Jacob Marley reminded his old business partner:

> *"Mankind was my business. The common welfare was my business; charity, mercy, forbearance, and benevolence were, all, my business. The dealings of my trade were but a drop of water in the comprehensive ocean of my business!"*

Orest had not read Dickens' 1843 novella (nor seen the 1938 American film directed by Edwin L. Marin featuring Leo G. Carroll as Marley), but he likely would have agreed with Marley with a rather dramatic different twist. Domov was global and certainly, from the highest vantage point, mankind was their clientele—their business. Furthermore, in doing this business, Orest and Domov realized that the appearances of charity, mercy, forbearance, and benevolence were necessary facades—not only to engender public support but also actions in and of themselves that offered considerable leverage to power and wealth when managed correctly.

Domov was certainly in the business of doing business—a wide and varied assortment of most often questionable if not downright illicit businesses. The *Maliar* was the CEO. Orest was the *Maliar.*

While he could not ponder Marley's words, having not heard the story, he often did ponder a proverb from his childhood that was reported to have come from across the Mongolian steppes: *Ostricž vidí iba červa a nie hák - človek vidí len ruble a nie nebezpečenstvo* (A perch only sees the worm and not the hook—a man only sees the rubles and not the jeopardy). His role, naturally enough, was maximizing the profits while minimizing the risk, but it was not a simple equation where the end justified the means. It was complex. While profits and power were the principal objectives, so was sustainability. Domov the institution took precedence over any one member of the institution—even the *Maliar* himself.

It was true that only a very, very few even knew of the existence of Domov, let alone the *Maliar*. To this select group, by design, the *Maliar* was seen as all-powerful—the ultimate arbitrator and decider. It was understood that there was no structure that superseded the absolute authority of the *Maliar*.

But this was not the case. There was another level.

Very similar to situations in some traditional societies in Africa, there was an invisible and undisclosed group with license approximating a board of directors—a check and balance put in place to act early if concerns arose about the possibility of a totally uncurbed autocratic leader. This board could, in spite of the CEOs refusal, remove the *Maliar*—this only possible by removing him from his earthly domain. Or, if the *Maliar* had to unexpectedly disappear on his own volition, they could name a temporary successor to bridge the gap until the normal processes could be undertaken to put on seat new leadership. They were the hidden force of communalism.

The board was called the *obetovať* from the Slovak word for sacrifice. This was a double entendre—perhaps a pun slipped into the arcane Domov vocabulary by one of the pioneering felonious šéfovia (bosses or chiefs)—referring to both the personal sacrifice the *Maliar* must make to satisfactorily fulfill his responsibilities and the personal and permanent sacrifice he would make if he failed in this effort.

The mechanism to activate this masked group, the *obetovať*, remained the same since the inception of Domov. In the case of the *Maliar* needing to vanish, it was initiated by the leader himself. In the case of needing to change the leadership against the leader's will, the action was started by unseen hands. Yet in both cases, it was a simple act.

In the case of a failed leader, in the personal sections of *The Times* of London, *The New York Times*, the *Tokyo Yomiuri Shimbun*, and *Le Figaro* in Paris, a short ad was posted: "Road blocked, classes at Svesa closed, please assist."

Svesa had been the small village where Andriy had had his first job as a teacher. The proscribed message in the papers had not changed since that time.

According to the foreseen process, within days of the publishing of the message announcing the cancellation of classes, the *Maliar* vanished.

In cases where it was the Maliar himself initiating the process, it was nearly the same—the posted text reading: "Referring to blocked road and cancelled classes at Svesa, be advised road opening soon."

So far, neither message had ever been posted.

While the *Maliar* knew of the *obetovať* and the messaging process, neither he nor anyone else in the acknowledged Domov web knew the identities of the members of the group who activated and who were activated by the message. They remained concealed and, if the processes would be implemented, the small portion of the outside world that witnessed the management of the highest levels of Domov would only see a new leader appear and assume duties. What was hidden remained hidden.

For now, the hidden change agents were nowhere to be seen and Orest was confident in his position—both politically and practically as he began to accumulate many months of service which had made the previously implausible now possible. His team worked smoothly and overall, the immense amoeba that was Domov seemed to thrive.

At any point in time, a snapshot of the whole operation would have shown a different configuration and different allocations of resources. Yet overall, the trends were positive. The hubs as charted years ago by the *Om Mares* continued to be the foci and the largest portion of the organization's footprint. However, this tread was composed of many parts including semi-independent groups of financiers and entrepreneurs. There were also diminutive bits that could only be traced back to individuals linked to Domov with the greatest of difficulty and no small dose of good luck. It was understood that those with very modest roles were often key pieces to the puzzle. This engagement of a wide swath of highly varied individuals had been encouraged by Taras. He saw a large and variegated crew from paupers to kings as one of the best defenses against Domov's enemies; you snipped one arm and in its place two new arms appeared like starfish autotomy on steroids. Lots of moving parts leading to a more powerful and wealthier whole. Taras had highlighted the principle by citing the French proverb: *Les petits profits sont bons s'ils viennent souvent* (Small profits are good if they come often).

Orest wondered at times why there seemed to be so many references to proverbs—maybe it was their Ukrainian roots?

Regardless of the proverbial anchors, Domov remained a vast and highly disaggregated organization that reaped large profits from many sources in many ways. It took a watchful eye and careful coordination, but it seemed to be working.

Communications, rapid communications, were critical. Orest's team in Holwerd included several communications, what would later be called "IT" specialists. One of these technicians was a young Syrian named Chakir Awal. He once told Orest his name meant "the chosen one," so the *Maliar* hoped this choice included the fact that he had chosen a top expert in the communications field.

Chakir, who was based in the town of Leeuwarwden, eighteen miles to the south of Holwerd (the practice being to not put everyone in the same place so as not to call attention to too many outsiders), assured his boss that he was up to the job. In fact, he was more than up to the job, and he wanted his boss's blessing to get involved in local agricultural businesses where he thought there might even be a future for expanded Domov investment sometime in the future.

Orest appreciated Chakir's enthusiasm and his thoughts about building to an even brighter future. He also knew the Netherlands offered many good examples of modern agribusiness. The country was highly advanced in many forms of agriculture as land was at such a premium the harvests had to be good and the profits large to be able to keep farming. Thus, he encouraged his young assistant to go ahead.

The *Maliar* followed up and found that Chakir had invested through a cousin in several highly intensive farms: Lowland Fish Farms producing an imported African catfish as well as Holland Valley Flowers and Dutch Blooms—the latter two farms growing in massive greenhouses high quality flowers for year-round export.

It all seemed good, and it all seemed emblematic. Domov needed to provide what the consumer wanted. Domov needed, at the same time, to attract young blood (Orest himself still easily classified as "young") and diversify while still jealously guarding their traditions and their history. As this somehow appeared to be a time of proverbs, the *Maliar* found it all summed up nicely if somehow inadequately in a proverb Chakir shared from his homeland: *Shit may stink, but better to make a profit out of shit than to have losses with perfume.*

CHAPTER 4

TUG OF WAR

"Success is not final; failure is not fatal:
it is the courage to continue that counts."

—**Winston Churchill**

The Protectors

WHILE to some it all may have seemed good, appearances could be deceiving, especially when viewed from totally different vantage points. As a DOJ investigator who had spent years investigating irregularities that seemingly tied to a major criminal organization some called Domov, Rodney Mills understood he saw only fragment of the full frame. He knew that reading those few available reports about Domov was like taking a freshman history class—like Western Civ he had taken way back when. The material covered a vast landscape over a long period of time, showing many shapes with little definition. It was like watching a fleet of sailing ships moving in a dense fog—all your senses had to be alert.

Yet, in spite of the obtuseness, Domov had progressively become the heart of his professional and possibly private life for far too long, dominating all.

As small portions of the fog slowly lifted, Rodney began to realize that Domov was possibly so huge as to almost defy description. At the same time, Domov was still so cloud-covered that it was hard to objectively assess its scope or impacts. It was, Rodney thought, like those little white pills some people touted that they claimed cured everything—a scam or a miracle, proof was needed. However, if the proof about the little pill was hard to come by, the proof about Domov was nearly impossible to uncover after having been carefully camouflaged for years by scores of criminally minded people.

Nevertheless, Rodney doggedly dug for the facts. He understood all too well the need for persistent digging. After all, it was not that long ago that the existence of Domov was not even known—all had felt the eventful uncovering of Delpro was a major breakthrough and that Delpro was about as big as it could get. Nevertheless, excavating more and more layers eventually revealed scraps of Domov that dwarfed the proportions of the impressive Delpro.

Rodney knew one always had to keep digging.

DC resident Rodney Mills was an Ivy-League-trained lawyer. With the bearing of an erudite urbanite, Rodney's roots went back to Chippewa Falls, Wisconsin—a small railroad town that had probably hit its zenith at the end of the nineteenth century when the Eau Claire and Chippewa Falls Railway took flatcar-loads of logs off to nearby sawmills. As much as Rodney's father had wanted him to stay and manage the hardware store built by his grandfather, Rodney, a good student with a scholarship, insisted on going east to Georgetown where he had a free ride to a bachelor's in economics. This proved to be the springboard to Harvard Law which, in turn, led to a position with the Division of Enforcement of the Security and Exchange Commission as a member of a task force team headed up by chief investigator (the agency called them analysts) Hal Schleider.

Hal was already a legend when Rodney had joined the team. He had been with Special Forces in Viet Nam and then migrated to the CIA in the Central Highlands before moving to Cambodia as part of the Studies and Observation Group. Having carried out the rites of passage, Hal was recognized as an experienced and talented senior operative, taking on assignments across the world before finally settling down with the SEC where he was the focal point for high-level international corporate criminality with an assignment to identify leading offenders of the Commission's federal security laws on the global stage. The team was to do all possible to limit if not eliminate these rapscallions.

A major threshold in terms of the team's work came, surprisingly and nearly completely by chance, from Hal's nephew, Eddie Hall. Eddie, a surveyor taking on all sorts of odd jobs, had worked for a company called Delpro in Spain and then in southern Africa. In undertaking his contractual duties for the company, he had uncovered information that began to portray highly corrupt actions—misappropriation of land, falsification of agricultural products, and more, including kidnapping people and forcing them into slavery. While Eddie had been trying to get a better picture of the potentially foul goings-on, devastatingly, his wife Samantha was killed in an accident that Hal, upon hearing the story, felt was almost surely a murderous act to drive Eddie away from Delpro's sphere. And it had worked. Eddie returned to the US where, in spite of his best efforts to do otherwise, he found more acts of corruption and venality tied to

Delpro. At this point, he joined hands with his uncle to try to dissever the horrifying riddle that was coming into their lives as Delpro. However, before completing their work, Hal suffered a fatal heart attack. A heart attack that Rodney was later able to prove was not a heart attack at all but another murder to again remove a threat to Delpro's clandestine operations.

When Rodney had joined Hal's team in DC, they had worked in the same nondescript office building among a row of 1950s brick apartments along Blue Plains Drive, not far from the Potomac Job Corps Center, which was the head office of the SEC Division of Enforcement. The structure's stodgy exterior belied a modern and bustling interior filled with state-of-the-art communications and analytical equipment.

Over the years Hal and Rodney worked well together. They did more than just get along—they developed a special relationship. Ultimately, though kept as a carefully guarded secret, Hal and Rodney became a couple. When Hal died—been murdered—Rodney was shattered.

Hal was gone but he had left a spoor—many breadcrumbs to follow based on his years of assiduously studying Delpro and its affiliates. When Rodney was named as Hal's successor (the upper echelon having no idea of their personal relationship), he began to follow the trails laid out by his beloved and now departed partner. These trails led far and wide to numerous other entities including such well-known commercial actors as General Industrial and Chemical Products, Ace Foods, and Farm Services. These firms, among others, had investments in Africa, Asia, and Latin America to produce foods to supply lucrative markets in Europe and North America.

Hal had also identified two brothers as key players in the Delpro drama: Robin McCandless and Horace Barthley. Romanian by birth, they had been adopted by families in the US and the UK. Robin, the older US-raised sibling, seemed to be one of the main people in Delpro. The younger Horace remained more of a riddle—not to say Robin was not a puzzlement. The UK-raised Horace, now using the sobriquet "Sir Horace," seemed to appear and then disappear all across the globe.

Hal's work became the core of Rodney's investigations. He reached out to all of Hal's sources, and he reignited a good relationship with Eddie. He contacted numerous sources highlighted by Hal including Paula Patterson who had worked in Geneva for the Ecumenical Humanitarian Trust—EHT. In the course of her normal work, Paula had discovered close links between EHT and the International Center for Democratic

Ideals (ICDI). Rodney's team then found that ICDI belonged to Delpro; it was one of their outreach arms. Through Paula, Rodney got to know about an EHT intern from Tanzania, Evelynn. Evelynn's boyfriend was Peter Volman. He worked for a company based in Dar es Salaam called Equatorial Management. This firm was involved in shady affairs throughout the continent and was closely tied to Sir Horace Barthley. Through intense analysis of Peter's life, they flagged his close associate, Charlie Stancik. Peeling off layer upon layer of detritus from Charlie's variegated professional trajectory, they found strong ties to Delpro.

It became clear to Rodney that Delpro was an essential portal to bigger and even more dramatic activities. A much larger investigation was needed. He made the sale to his overlords and was able to get the required additional resources to target the full array (as he now saw it) of global Delpro interventions. Thinking back to the Russian mafia, the Solntsevskaya Bratva crime group, Rodney recalled the word "*bratva*" could be translated as meaning "lads." Thus, he baptized his newly reinforced team of Delpro investigators the *bratva*—the lads. Soon it became simply BTF— the Bratva Task Force. Separate BTF groups probed every available aspect of Robin's and Horace's lives. Other staff explored sites and businesses crisscrossing multiple continents. It was a major undertaking.

BTF was not only able to undertake extensive criminal investigations, it was also able to document Delpro's history. This was the first time a comprehensive set of verified information had been available about an organization that had frequently operated in the open all the while dealing in some of the most unimaginable covert affairs. This biography, so to speak, of Delpro was able to separate fact from fiction.

For example, at one point it was thought that Robin McCandless' ability to establish Delpro had been due to his marriage to Maribel Dubois, a very wealthy heiress who had married Robin shortly after her father Wilson's unexplained death. Maribel had also died mysteriously five years after her marriage, and all her considerable assets passed to Robin. Rodney's team was able to verify that, while Wilson and Maribel's deaths appeared to be the result of treachery, and while the Dubois family wealth had unquestionably added to McCandless' net worth, these events ultimately, in spite of being surrounded by unrevealed impropriety, did not appear to be related to Delpro. Robin's ties to Delpro seemed to, as reported, date back to his first job when he worked for Roy Franklin and Midwest Grain and Rail Coop in Delaven, Illinois. The Coop and not the Dubois' treasure had been the embryo that had grown into Delpro. Slowly, some of the clouds cleared.

As the fingerprints of a higher entity began to appear in Delpro dossiers, an even grander superstructure began to be seen in the haze. The big became bigger. The menacing became even more threatening. Rodney's team scaled up. BTF became D-2, the two D's for Delpro and Domov (recognizing the name if not the meaning and history of this latter group that was now rising from the fog as they were able to conclusively tie Delpro to the overarching heretofore unknown organization—Delpro operating under the Domov umbrella which seemed to have its epicenter in Eastern Europe).

More pieces were added to the puzzle.

After exhaustive examinations, the team unearthed the names of several mid- and high-level civil servants at the Pentagon and the Departments of State, Commerce, and Agriculture who were clandestine Delpro agents. The most glaring included an adjunct second deputy for advanced capabilities at the Department of Defense, Lieutenant Colonel Fritz Murphy, a deputy secretary for business affairs at the Department of State, Dr. Christine Miller, an assistant secretary for international trade at the Department of Commerce, Ms. Florence Gardner, and an assistant secretary in foreign trade at the Department of Agriculture, Dr. Lance Newcastle. Joining the list was the name of an advisor at the White House: Dr. Howard Dunford.

McCandless' personal files, made available by Charlie as part of a plea deal, revealed another important asset: Cynthia Owens. She was the CEO of a Turkish-based NGO called Özgürlük (Freedom). Özgürlük targeted refugees, professing to be able to relocate them to Europe, but actually assigning them to slavery in Delpro-related industries on three continents.

Although all these targets had fled, Rodney's team prepared a full set of grand jury documents charging Robin McCandless, Cynthia Owens, Fritz Murphy, Christine Miller, Florence Gardner, Lance Newcastle, and Howard Dunford in absentia. They were confident they had solid lawsuits and should move ahead with the legal processes while they tried to locate the subjects of their litigation.

Robin McCandless was reported to have died in a boating accident as he was trying to evade prosecution. However, thanks again to documents provided by Charlie, Rodney's team was able to prove that the corpse identified as Robin's was in fact that of an unknown person and the big boss of Delpro had apparently successfully avoided arrest. The team then set about finding Robin, concentrating on his still-under-surveillance younger brother. By following the good Sir Horace on his trips away from his base in Namibia, the team was ultimately able to track the aging Cockney to Romania where it appeared the brothers had returned to their roots. McCandless had settled into another luxurious villa in the small town of Vama Veche, near the Bulgarian border on the Black Sea. Although still receiving visits from the criminal element including Cynthia Owens, McCandless seemed to be in semi-retirement.

While the team kept a close watch on McCandless, they continued to build a formal legal case against him in the hopes of a possible extradition, acknowledging the legal prerequisites were not truly in place as regarded Romania (as McCandless undoubtedly knew). As the scale of activities became clearer, the team looked beyond the brothers—finding probable culpability in the furthest corners of the macrocosm that was the world economy.

They continued to find new threads to pull, all the while still dissecting and decoding the reams of material already exposed through the work of BTF and now D-2.

Rodney went back to the large volume of documentation provided by Charlie and was able to locate a company called Inter-Act in Kansas City. When Robin McCandless had moved from his long-time center near Chicago to the shores of Chesapeake Bay when he had first begun to sense an expanding Delpro investigation by the Feds, he had transferred most of his administrative activities to Inter-Act under the management of Mr. Don Drumpfsh. Rodney questioned Dumpfsh and then sent a crew to comb through the big office's stacks and stacks of files. Although some supporting information was gleaned from the work, there were few new revelations and energies were refocused elsewhere with a pin stuck in the Inter-Act name for a possible revisitation.

Rodney also tracked down and then interrogated Heinrich Fuchs. The ex-Nazi who had relocated to the *República Argentina* and reportedly headed up another group similar to Delpro linked to Domov, had disappeared for decades before resurfacing in Kenya. He had resettled in Malindi, a coastal tourist town with a relatively large German population.

As an old man not wishing to spend his remaining days in a courtroom, or worse, a jail cell, Fuchs collaborated fully with Rodney and his team after a non-prosecution agreement had been signed.

The research continued.

Charlie and Peter, along with Eddie and at times Paula remained key witnesses, providing pieces of the puzzle. Following arrangements with various agencies that agreed not to move forward on any formal legal charges, the quartet, with varying past links to Delpro and other arms of Domov, committed to remain available to testify along with other identified frontline actors whenever firsthand information was necessary.

Slowly, far too slowly for Rodney, an important foundation of critical evidence was building.

With great difficulty, Rodney's team even unveiled details of important global planning sessions organized by Mr. Radutu Botezatu at his mountain-side chateau in the Făgăraş Mountains—exclusive meetings that took place on Easter weekend each year. In addition to Radutu Botezatu, core of the invitees included Liu Li from Singapore, Raymond Girard from Canada, Janco Momberg from South Africa, Bohadan Kushnir from Ukraine, and Sebastian Carvalho from Brazil—some of the most powerful people in the world. The D-2 team developed biographies for the sextet, realizing these individuals were higher up in the hierarchy than either Robin McCandless or Horace Barthley.

While some pieces fell into place, in the aggregate it appeared they were uncovering more questions than answers.

⚓⚓⚓⚓⚓⚓⚓

It was a chess board with a hundred times the normal number of pieces. Rodney often felt overwhelmed. Then he thought of Hal—brutally killed—ripped away from him in the worst way at the worst time. He thought of Samantha—like Hal, a life lost because of Delpro and ultimately Domov. Of course, there were Charlie, Peter, Paula, Eddie, and scores—probably hundreds, maybe thousands of others—lives irrevocably changed while people like McCandless and Barthley unabashedly enjoyed their ill-gotten gains. And the two brothers, as Rodney now knew, were far from the top of the food chain. There were layers—perhaps many—above them that led to even more ruthless and dangerous people. Rodney felt overwhelmed.

Yet, overwhelmed or not, it was necessary that the truth come out. The nearly omnipotent (as Rodney saw it) structure that was Domov needed to be exposed. The oozing and purulent wound that was Domov needed to be excised. The truth would not redress all wrongs, but, moving forward, it would hopefully minimize the vulnerability and jeopardy of the innocent and the unaware.

Forces of Order

THE SEC was an independent federal agency with a big job. D-2 made the agency's job harder and more costly; chasing villains around the globe was very expensive and time consuming. Finally, D-2 had simply outgrown their home bureau, and they were adversely affecting other critical commission actions (or at least seen as such by senior management). They had to be let go. If they couldn't find another home, being let go meant shutting down in spite of the acknowledged and serious threats coming from the two Ds.

While one might have thought the SEC leadership or other high-level folks would have been actively looking at ways to resolve this situation—searching for a new place to house the essential work of D-2—this didn't seem to be the case. The prevailing mentality seemed to be: Delpro and Domov are bad, but there are lots of bad things out there.

As so often, Rodney realized that if it was to get done, he would have to do it himself.

Fortunately, Rodney had been able to link into Hal's extensive good-ol'-boy network and now knew a lot of people who knew people. After a great deal of effort, much wasted, with Hal's good name as leverage, Rodney was able to connect with some senators, including the Honorable Jacob Sullivan of Virginia, who somewhat begrudgingly agreed to look for a remedy to this problem that jeopardized their constituents' livelihoods. With politics able to go where logic could not, the complete D-2 dossier was transferred from the SEC to the Office of International Affairs in the Department of Justice.

It was a good move even if Rodney's own future engagement in the work was uncertain.

When the paperwork came through, there was a big surprise. Not only were the label, D-2, and the mandate retained, the upper ranks of the team, including Rodney, his assistants, and the senior analysts, would be detached to the Department of Justice for the duration of the investigation. Furthermore, Rodney would be the activity coordinator. The one new and possibly intriguing piece was that D-2 management, through DOJ, was now required to report semiannually to a legislative group, in-house generically referred to as "the Special Senate Committee." The chair of this formal coterie was the same somewhat reluctant Senator of Virginia, Jake Sullivan. He was joined by Senators Ann Winterbottom of Arizona and Franklin Brown of Alabama as vice chairs and four other members from both sides of the aisle. The new dossier from this Senatorial group included an invitation (more of an edict) to the first committee meeting in six months' time.

As the unavoidable paperwork accumulated describing D-2's new slot in the overall hierarchy, a rather loose channel of command and control appeared, flowing down from the Assistant Attorney General of the Criminal Division to the head of the Human Rights and Special Prosecutions Section, through an Investigative Analyses Office to D-2.

The position of D-2 in this otherwise tortuous hierarchy seemed loose since Rodney had basically a free hand for all activities sanctioned and funded by the Senate. He had nearly the autonomy of a special council as long as he had the Senate's blessings.

This critical legislative oversight and budgetary authority was assigned to the Honorable Jacob Sullivan of Virginia through a specially minted body that was informally christened a committee, although it wasn't a true committee at all. The Sullivan group was part of the fourteen-member-strong Permanent Committee on Homeland Security and Government Affairs, under the Subcommittee on Emerging Threats and Spending Oversight with ten Senate members. Nearly hidden under this powerful subcommittee with its far-reaching mandate was a small seven-member group simply entitled "Action Items."

It was this group that through the mysteries of governmental procedures had somehow ended up having oversight for D-2. It was this group that insiders in DOJ simply called, be it ever so erroneous, "the Sullivan Committee." Maybe some midlevel administrator hoped this appellation would add gravitas to the management requirements and encourage staff like Rodney to submit their reports on time.

Rodney assumed the new reporting requirements were due in part to these senators' support of the transfer to DOJ. Things changed and things stayed the same. Rodney prepared for a new address, a new office, a new boss, and an old challenge.

What Rodney initially did not know—what many if not most did not know—was that D-2 was not alone on the field. The National Clandestine Service, NCS, of the Central Intelligence Agency had been quietly and methodically exploring first Delpro and then Domov, working completely independently and in parallel with the SEC and now DOJ teams. For all intents and purposes by design, the two groups appeared to be completely unaware of each other. At times, such bureaucratic walling off was intentional to allow higher-ups to compare data from two independent sources; at times, it was simply bureaucratic inefficiency. For whatever reason, two groups were now chasing the same bone. The NCS work was undertaken by a branch unintelligibly called Group 8.

Group 8 was a hybrid. While it was administratively led by NCS, it had members representing the Criminal Investigative Division, CID, of the FBI and the Echelon Program of the National Security Agency. This consortium was chiefly focusing on organized crime and its possible links to the Russian or Chinese mafias, mainly the Solntsevskaya Bratva and the Triads, respectively. Group 8 was mostly involved in monitoring operations, eavesdropping, surveilling, and using physical assets to follow activities of foreign criminal elements while assessing how these racketeers might be connected to activities of criminal syndicates in the US as well as the wider ecosphere of organized crime worldwide.

Of the tiny group that knew of the existence of Group 8, most were confused as to its name; in fact, most were confused about its overall *raisin d'être*. The name, to those in the know, was an obtuse Biblical reference that the namer thought captured the work of the group. The name came from the Second Epistle of Peter in the New Testament which was often seen as a warning against corruption. The verse stated: "*For if God spared not the angels that sinned, but cast them down to hell, and delivered them into chains of darkness, to be reserved unto judgment; and spared not the old world, but saved Noah the eighth person.*"

The namer and the leader of Group 8, Felix Manchester, was a religious man, devoted to the principles that good would thwart evil—even if it often needed a push. He saw his work, his mission, as part of the push, accelerating good's battle over the darkest parts of humankind. He saw his mission as delivering the wicked unto justice while upholding the "good" even if the good were only every eighth person. Indeed, Felix thought, if twelve percent of the world's peoples were honestly good, God-fearing folk, this would likely be a great improvement.

Felix was on a crusade.

However, just as Group 8 was complicated, Felix was a complicated man. He understood his fervor for pursuing goodness had to be measured and laser focused. For, as much as Felix was a zealot, he was also an ambitious civil servant. There was a tug-of-war between his zealotry and his professional aspirations. He realized the riddle. To be able to accomplish what he wanted, he had to be in positions of authority, he had to professionally and privately comport himself in ways that met with the fickle consent of his overlords.

Felix had to throttle back. Although the head of Group 8, the interagency structure of this unusual assemblage made any unilateral management difficult and open to criticism from many fronts. He had to craft operational strategies that assured the buy-in from all the partners, that allowed each entity to shine in its own way, and that produced results that would be applauded by those up the hierarchy. It was a very ordinary situation for a very extraordinary group.

In the end, as much as Felix wanted desperately to rush onto the battlefield with his God's ensign held on high, he was forced to modulate. Group 8 was an information-gathering body.

It was in this function that the squad had initially become aware of Delpro and Domov.

The first substantive indications had come from overseas—the breadcrumbs there on the path for the keen observer to see.

When Andriy and Lehya had begun actively collaborating and communicating, the Echelon Program had intercepted some of the missives and highlighted this link between Ukrainian and Russian crime syndicates as potentially worrisome. They had continued to watch conscientiously but had only been able to capture snippets—enough to know there were changes underway but not enough to know exactly what was happening. It was frustrating.

Later, domestic members of the surveillance Group had raised a flag when their sources indicated a certain Mr. Robin McCandless had entered into discussions with Louis "Little New York" Campaga of the Chicago Outfit about the future of the Midwest Grain and Rail Co-op. Again, few specifics but enough to keep the flag planted.

At the onset, there were no connections between Robin McCandless nor (what they would later unveil as) Delpro and what European colleagues were ultimately able to identify as Domov. Group 8 had its own tentacles across the globe, collecting, collating, and analyzing massive quantities of data—much of it discarded after analysis. There were so many false leads that one of their biggest concerns was throwing out the good data with the bad. While they were very talented at their jobs, it was obviously hard to look at tidbits collected today and predict how these would influence tomorrow. It was nearly an impossible task.

As much as the juggling of the Group's cohesive management was a challenge, so was grappling with the subjects that were main objective. Their scope was worldwide. Their focus was organized crime. Whether the Japanese Yakuza, the Primeiro Comando Capital in Brazil, the 'Ndrangheta in southern Italy, mafia groups in such disparate spots as India and Nigeria, or scores of other criminal organizations; they all fell into Group 8's mandate in one way or another.

This global monitoring mandate was critical. They could not sacrifice one part for another; they had to address the whole. This meant that, in normal circumstances, they could not disproportionally devote more resources to one actor than another. This was a core precept.

Then the status quo was altered.

Senior agents from Felix's team, at the White House's request, met with Secretary of State Shannon Baxter in the Brentwood neighborhood of DC. The striking blue-green-eyed chief diplomat was interviewed by the agents for several hours. She was very concerned. Among other stories, she recounted how she had been briefed by her staff from the embassy in Maputo about reports of a large facility that had been built in northern Mozambique—basically a warehouse for slaves. She did not have independent confirmation, but the initial indications were that, amazingly, this was being done by a US company—a company called Delpro. Moreover, and equally amazingly, it was rumored that former high-level government staff, Howard Dunford from the White House, Florence Gardner from the Department of Agriculture, and Christine Miller from her own department, were involved and perhaps others. It was unbelievable. It was unacceptable. It was shameful. But it seemed to be true: US slavers!

She had spoken with the President. This could not go unpunished. The White House was reaching out to other agencies as they spoke, but Group 8, with its organized crime mandate and its inter-agency structure, seemed to them—the President and herself, she reminded her interviewers—to be a good starting point to try and rectify this horrid situation.

The Secretary's recorded comments, encoded with the most advanced cryptanalytic tools available, were the first entries into a new White-House-endorsed red-flag program of the greatest secrecy and of paramount status; in the strange bureaucracy of complex entities, this new epicenter enigmaticly labeled Section T15-Z, adopted the file stamp used for the original Brentwood interview with the Secretary of State to designate the entire new transnational program.

Section T15-Z became the magnetic pole for Group 8.

The dense fog was still there, but additional portions of the cloaked landscape began to emerge from the mist. Then, with a clearer perspective and as endorsed by the highest levels of government, Section T15-Z became the unifying framework of D-2 and Group 8 to jointly combat a new, or at least previously underestimated, and veiled threat to the country and the greater good.

The scales were tipped. Felix shifted priorities, concentrating in areas more directly complementary to Rodney's long-time crusade. Delpro and its partners would be a centerpiece of their work moving forward.

Felix promptly set about making the needed adjustments to more fully focus on Delpro. Group 8 did not immediately connect the dots between Delpro and the collaborating syndicates in Ukraine and Russia that were part of Domov. However, the groundwork was well laid for these pieces to fall into place.

What Rodney and Felix were slowly realizing, in their own spheres, was that there was no safe haven. As they were able to pull back the curtains, with apprehension they began to better appreciate the full scope of the amoeba that was Domov although they intuitively understood they were only seeing a few disaggregated slices of a much larger whole. First impressions were daunting. Domov was everywhere. Domov could affect anyone anywhere.

While each government group mounted an offensive from different vantage points—each unaware of the other before their unexpected union—the hoped-for result was the same. Prior to being sewn together in the sack curiously stamped Section T15-Z, each group independently realized Domov as a threat. Now, as a merged body with significant impact, they realized that while eliminating or severely curtailing Domov was a good thing, it could not be further delayed; it was an essential action, an existential action, that must happen promptly and that had fallen into their hands to make sure it did happen.

Choices

NEITHER Rodney, Felix, nor the *Maliar*, for that matter, had ever visited Samui Island in Thailand. In a country renowned for its cuisine, Samui was known for producing unique and sophisticated curries composed of scores of piquant dishes with rare ingredients ranging from fiery chilies to pungent fermented fish. For those in the know, the highly diverse and complex ingredients of Samui curries were the holy grail of exotic fare—for the epicurean, the pinnacle of gourmet sensations for the palate. The uninitiated could, however, only indiscriminately shovel a few random samples at a time onto their plate, hoping to discover the perfect mix, but more times than not finding mediocrity. Those wishing to control (or eradicate) Domov, as well as those attempting to expand the organization's horizons, were like folks dining on a Samui curry. The table was full of choices, many excellent, but some not-so-good; it was all about knowing the backstory. Looks could be deceiving. The ultimate conclusion was not only how the food tasted on the tongue but how it rested in the stomach. A meal in Samui just like associating with Domov could be a lottery, all hoping they had the winning number.

But control was difficult.

Self-control was famously hard and that involved only oneself. Control of one's destiny was equally well-known in terms of its difficulty. Then, when one opened the door and expanded beyond the individual shell, control issues amplified by orders of magnitude. Controlling an empire from inside, to maximize its effects, or from the outside, to minimize its effects, was more than challenging—it was a major task subject to lottery-like chances for success.

In many ways, Felix, Rodney, and the *Maliar* were facing similar dilemmas. While Felix would see it as the brightness of yang juxtaposed with the darkness of yin, an outside observer would likely see it as driven people wading through the muck of a morass that would likely suck them under.

It wasn't so much about controlling the price as it was about controlling the cost. For all the actors, from all camps, at all levels, it was all about cost. What were the financial and political costs? What were the costs versus the benefits?

Rodney and Felix, although allocated comparatively generous budgets, had to be parsimonious as there were always strings (visible or invisible) attached to public funds. Similarly, from the *Maliar* down to the grassroots Domov overseers, there was an acute understanding that higher costs meant smaller profits, and this was antithetical to the founding principles of the organization.

Nowhere were these issues more keenly felt than at the ground floor. Unlike those seated at the apogee of the great organism that was Domov, actors like the Cisse family and Voldoymyr operated on relatively small margins. Regulations, competition, bad weather, and much more were among the multitude of reasons that costs could soar and profits plummet. This required a high degree of adaptability—abilities to rapidly close one venture and open another—often totally unrelated.

Survival necessitated control—either direct control of events or control of the consequences of uncontrollable acts.

Control was at the forefront of efforts undertaken by Chantal and Sir Horace (though age was pulling on his shirt tails) while Horace's big brother still feigned a high degree of disengagement that made some feel he might have truly entered a sort of sedentary retirement.

Basically, all clinging to the Domov ladder, at whatever rung, or in its shadow, were fixated on controlling their realms, be they big or small.

For some, the question was profit or loss. For some, the question could be as grave as life or death. For many, including, among a horde of others, Senators Sullivan, Winterbottom, and Brown, it was about pure raw power (which, of course, sated their other carnal needs). Although few had probably read the works of Abraham Lincoln, they probably should have when he wrote: "Nearly all men can stand adversity, but if you want to test a man's character, give him power."

Joe felt as though his character was being tested daily. For him it was certainly not a question of getting control—it was all about getting traction. As a dedicated and hardworking employee, he continued to receive welcomed promotions in the coal business. The "real" (as he saw it) business, however, of opening clandestine market pathways, in spite of all the homework already undertaken, was proving to be harder than anticipated. Relatively speaking, borders were not porous. Relatively speaking, there was considerable market oversight. It wasn't easy. Indeed, local folks were in tough times and these times presented multiple opportunities. But finding the right formula was more than a little tricky; he even had Harold working on trying to untangle some of the less felonious issues on the margins of the larger challenge of getting a good grip on market share. He now reported his less-than-sparkling results up the ladder to Orest rather than Taras. Yet, other than a new person sitting on the *Maliar's* seat, things did not seem to have changed much. Rather than opening vast new horizons, he sensed he had only been able to slightly crack the window open—his window to the horizon being an old wooden single-hung opaque aperture with a broken sash lock and paint-pealing frames like so many of the coalminers' homes around Pottsville.

Among the uninitiated, Sophie was as far outside this quest for control as possible, or at least she thought of herself as a typical and unaligned resident of Avignon. Single mother and neophyte journalist, her hands were full. Some quiet moments between sunset and sunrise, she would wonder about Orest. Where was he? What was he doing? Did he think of her? However, most of the time she was running just to keep up. Oriana and *Le Parisien Libéré* were the marrow of her days and she loved them both. She gave each her all and each reciprocated. Oriana was a smart (brilliant, Sophie thought) and responsible child who grew into a resourceful and astute young woman who was a good student and (somewhat surprisingly, Sophie thought, given the not infrequent chaos of her daughter's environment) a warmhearted human being. Alongside her dear girl, *Le Parisien Libéré* was not the least bit warmhearted, but it was responsible and resourceful. It was also (as was Oriana) appreciative. Sophie demonstrated a keen aptitude for journalism and the paper rewarded this with promotions and assignments to top-tier stories. Sophie quickly metamorphosed from neophyte into an accomplished and artful journalist—some called her a columnist. She had truly managed to follow the trail of Julie-Victoire Daubié.

Yet, in spite of offers to move to Paris, Sophie stayed in Avignon. First it was because of Oriana's schooling, and then it was because she needed to take care of her aging parents. Finally, she had to accept that she simply liked the place. She was *chez elle*.

Orest had been her true love. While she finally gave up on ever seeing him again, she would not give up her memories—now embellished through years of fantasizing. Nonetheless, she was not celibate, she was simply a single mother. She was a single mother who enjoyed a glass of good wine (or two, or more) at a familiar local bistro and could find herself going home with someone if the stars aligned. She was not celibate.

As Sophie tried to blend the present with the past, and as she came to terms with the realities of never seeing the father of her child again, she decided she should, in her view, protect Oriana. Declaring, she thought, her enduring love for Orest and describing to her daughter a father she would never see, seemed unfair. When Oriana grew and asked those typical questions of her mother, Sophie replied with a bland and laconic tale of student life with many friends and too many forgotten evenings—the fable soon became the fact.

As Oriana moved quickly through her studies, unlike her mother, she saw Avignon as a point of departure and not a destination. She dearly loved her mother. She greatly respected her mother—she did a wonderful job as a journalist. In fact, her mother was such a polished and professional journalist that she herself wanted to follow in her footsteps as her mother had followed Julie-Victoire's. The thing was, she wanted to do this somewhere else. Somewhere outside Avignon and outside France.

After graduating with a bachelor's from the School of International and Political Studies in Paris, with excellent grades and recommendations as well as ample financial support from a now senior journalist, Oriana was able to gain admittance into a masters' program in New York City at Columbia University's Journalism School.

Mother and daughter knew they were each where they should be. The challenges of past years, difficult though they may have been, had built a strong foundation for the future. The cost may have been significant, but each of their lives seemed to be bearing fruit. Good education, strong work ethics, and an inherent generosity of spirit had led both ladies to places where they could be at peace, if not utterly content. They had, in their own view, each found an acceptable degree of serenity and satisfaction.

Totally unaware he was a father, Orest would never have described his status as serene nor satisfied. Radiating out from Holwerd like a seismic wave flowing from its epicenter, Orest, the *Maliar*, was pulling levers connected to the planet's greatest economic centers as well as its most remote and forgotten corners.

Still, this power and this influence were well hidden in a man often seen as only a silhouette, wrapped in a mackintosh, slowly walking along the margins of the *Wattenmeer* (Wadden Sea)—protected from much of the North Sea's wrath by the Frisian Islands and from human wrath by his attentive guardians—invisible but always there.

There were formal meetings, business travel, and unannounced missions. However, much of the life of the *Maliar* was a life of solitude. Ironically, he seemed to spend considerable time with Chakir, exploring how to use the latest communications technologies to reduce further the away time and, most importantly, expand the *Maliar's* reach—expand the *Maliar's* power.

Orest was informed about everything—everything except Sophie. He might have been surprised to know that like he himself, she thought of their union and their passion during those darkest hours of the night. Orest never forgot. He carried her as part of his soul. He understood his life was not the life of a family man nor a married man. Loved ones were a threat—a threat to the job. Dear family members became hostages. Dear family members disagreed with fundamental objective decision-making. Family members were a distraction. Orest yearned for family but knew it could not be. Life at the summit was not wine and roses. It was hard work. It was solitude.

Orest had not read Abraham Lincoln's words. But if he had, he would have found them wise—even if the price was high.

CHAPTER 5

LEARNING LESSONS

"The roots of education are bitter, but the fruit is sweet."

—Aristotle

The Three R's

ALTHOUGH she had lived in the big city—lived in Paris—New York City was a shock. It seemed to be the city by which all other cities were gauged. It was throbbing. It was pulsing. It was intimidating.

Oriana, the new student at Columbia, heard that Americans had referred to schooling as learning the 3 R's: reading, "riting," and "rithmetic." She decided, to survive—no, to succeed—she needed her own 3 R's. She needed to be resilient, ready (for anything), and regardful. Every day, as she set off for class, she ticked-off her R's.

Every day she marveled.

Every day offered new challenges.

Every day she was reminded how far she was from family.

Sure, New York City was different from Paris—in some ways, very different. Yet very quickly she realized the biggest adjustment was being away from her mother. The two had always been together. Even when Oriana had been studying in Paris, Sophie had frequently been by her side—the now well-known journalist spending just as much time in the capital as in the provinces. This was the real change. She missed her mother.

It wasn't so much a cultural adaptation—New York was nothing if not boisterously multicultural. It was an emotional adaptation. It was learning to compartmentalize her deepest feelings and to move forward, understanding there was really no one there to catch her if she fell.

Move forward she did. It was honestly easier than she had first imagined.

Oriana's English was good; technically, it was very good. She had a melodic accent and an expansive vocabulary. However, she would sometimes translate too literally from her Gallic lexicon, inventing English phrases that were hard for her contemporaries to understand. Nonetheless, overall, language was not a barrier.

There really were not any real barriers.

Sooner than she had thought possible, she felt part of the Big Apple, with only fragments of nostalgia for the subtle and calmer ways of Avignon (if she excluded her mother from the flashbacks). She became part of the ever-present throng that flowed through the city, feeling an indistinguishable member of the masses.

Her studies were interesting—at times enthralling—but not demanding. Perhaps, she thought, she had inherited her mother's ability to effortlessly traverse academia, earning high marks with minimal exertion. Scholastics for Sophie had been a breeze. Oriana kept her fingers crossed.

After two years, she not only felt herself to be a New Yorker—a New Yorker with a master's degree—but she also was grateful, as much as she still missed her mother, that she had indeed apparently acquired her mother's academic acumen.

Oriana's optimism about life in general and her current circumstances in particular was reinforced when, almost immediately after receiving her diploma, she got a job as a stringer for *The Daily News*.

This proved to be both a benefit and a revelation.

Although a stringer, she was fully occupied—nearly seven days a week—and well paid. It was always different and exciting, but it was also always an eye-opener. Much of what she saw—the material upon which she reported—was from a segment of society with which she had, heretofore, had no contact. A segment of society with which she had no experience nor any deep understanding about the how's and why's life functioned as it did.

It was a baptism by fire. On a routine basis she saw and wrote about the unthinkable: murder, rape, battery, violent deaths. Deaths or assaults on prostitutes and addicts. Deaths and assaults on ordinary people. Deaths and assaults on women and children. It was, she was certain, as far away as one could get from her sheltered childhood byways of Avignon.

Still, like her mother before her, Oriana proved to be an above-average—possibly even an exceptional—reporter. Those same eyes that were opened by the daily carnage were amazingly vigilant and perceptive. She was able to capture the nuances of events in her soul and in her writing. Whether a relatively minor story about a child separated from her mother on the MTA (a subject that hit home in many ways to Oriana) or the murder of an entire family on the Upper West Side, she treated all aspects of her work thoroughly and with compassion.

It was not all work and blood 'n gore. She forced herself to take time off. She went to some plays on Off Broadway. She visited the Museum of the City of New York and similar galleries. Of course, she went to the top of the Empire State Building. She enjoyed the seemingly endless array of culinary delights and quaint bistros. She even hooked up with the occasional appealing male patron to appease underserved hormones (perhaps for both—who knew). Nonetheless, none of these *aventures* led to meaningful relationships—not even to relationships that lasted more than a few days.

Oriana was, she knew, still on a steep learning curve and she could only push the great stone up the hill so fast.

Then things changed demonstrably.

As a fluently bilingual journalist, Oriana was a bit of a rarity—especially since the non-English language in question was French. There were a variety of skirmishes—some reportedly considerably more than a skirmish—across Africa. *The Daily News* asked her to be their person on the Continent—their agent in Africa.

Oriana was again going to cross the Atlantic.

Spare the Rod

THE *Daily News* focused principally on local news—the gods knew there was certainly an ample quantity of hometown chaos for them to cover. However, one old-time reporter on the national desk was charged with scanning the international scene to pick up any pieces that might be of particular interest to their readership. The seasoned reporter loosely overseeing international affairs was Blake Samuelson.

Once overseas, Blake Samuelson would be Oriana's conduit back to *The Daily News*—her interlocutor to her New York readers.

Blake Samuelson was not only a weathered correspondent, he was also a veteran old-school evangelical conservative who believed we all reaped what we had sewn. He felt, he would admit, the unfortunate ills befalling people—homelessness, poverty, illness, and worse—were a result of a lack of discipline. It was the old adage: "pull yourselves up by your bootstraps." People with real discipline—with moxie—would not fall into the pit, or, if they did, they would claw their way out. It was the weak, the heartless, the obstreperous, and the intemperate who suffered the ills of their lack of self-control and determination. It was survival of the fittest (or the richest or maybe the most Godly or maybe all three).

Blake Samuelson would not wince when challenged that he lacked humanity. He would reply, "It is God's way," citing the Old Testament's Book of Proverbs 13, versus 18, 23-25:

> *"Whoever disregards discipline comes to poverty and shame, but whoever heeds correction is honored . . . An unplowed field produces food for the poor, but injustice sweeps it away. Whoever spares the rod hates their children,*
>
> *but the one who loves their children is careful to discipline them. The righteous eat to their hearts' content, but the stomach of the wicked goes hungry."*

In spite of his, what many would call harsh outlook on life, Blake Samuelson was a professional. He was a good columnist in terms of being able to take complex issues and distill them into straightforward text that effectively communicated with the reader. Whether or not they aligned with his view of the human condition, nearly everyone at the paper admired his ability to feed the presses succinct high-quality (technically, if not always thematically correct) products.

Oriana counted herself as lucky. Although her overseas assignments fell under Samuelson's purview, distance and geography superseded doctrine. The grim newspaperman would not filter nor alter Oriana's work. He would edit it. He would make it sharp, but he would not modify the message. She had the best of both worlds—the ability to tell stories in her own words but, at the same time, benefitting from the decades of writing savvy of a stern old journalist and going to press with truly first-rate copy. Just possibly her movement up that learning curve was accelerating.

Oriana's first assignment put a new perspective on one of her earlier assessments. She'd thought she was about as far as she could be from Avignon when she was in the concrete jungle that was New York City, but she now found herself in a real nearly impenetrable jungle in eastern Zaïre, not far from the shores of Lake Kivu.

When two local chiefs began a spat over adjoining fields, everyone thought it would quickly blow over. It would undoubtedly be the type of dispute that, through centuries, could be promptly settled by the traditional leadership. However, rather than tamping down the discord, one of the chiefs, a young man from Kinshasa who had forcibly been brought back to the village to sit on his now deceased father's throne, possibly to demonstrate his dissatisfaction with his present circumstances, threw petrol on the flame to the point that there were soon real flames engulfing homes and fields.

Politics in the region of Kivu were already stressed, and the central government could not allow a relatively minor issue to balloon into a major clash that could ignite much more than a few villages. The President recalled his elite forces, commandos called the Cobras, who had been firefighting in Chad. The Cobras were dispatched to Kivu to keep the peace (the caveat "at any cost" was understood). Larger conflict may well have been avoided, but the heavy hand of the Cobras called unwelcome, worldwide attention to the problems of the area and the repressive measures put in place to avoid potentially a much greater loss of life.

Third- or fourth-tier international press was soon snooping about to see if there was meat on the bones.

The government did all it could to dissuade the journalists, but they stuck like barnacles on a ship's hull.

Oriana's task was to join the unwanted pack of reporters.

She flew to Brussels to connect with a flight to Bujumbura from where she hired a car and local driver-cum-guide—driving the three hours to Bukavu and transiting through Rwanda before reaching Lake Kivu.

Bukavu had been the site of a battle in 1967 between Congolese forces and Belgian and Katanganese mercenaries headed by Jean "Black Jack" Schramme. It had been bloody and destructive. Structures in the city still showed the pockmarks of bullets and mortar rounds. Bukavu was taking a long time to recover and now again possibly staring into the darkness of more strife.

The affray over land proved more to be an entrée to other stories than a centerpiece in and of itself. While the land issues were not easily nor quickly reconciled, the Cobras effectively put a lid on the overt magnification of this discord. The story of disputed land tenure ended up being more of a stimulus to look into the wider governance issues of the area.

It quickly became obvious that the immense size of the country and the almost insurmountable logistics and communications concerns combined to establish a situation where eastern Zaïre was effectively cut-off from the capital and much of central government—even the quickest way to reach this part of the territory was via Burundi. It was practically an island unto itself with very complex political issues—many boiling just under the surface.

The isolation seemed to exacerbate the chronic ills that floated among the islands of crisis. Poverty, illness, and corruption added to civic turmoil to create an environment where the tiny minority of rich got richer, and the vast majority of poor got poorer—a scenario not all unique to eastern Zaïre.

To what was often referred to as "the outside world," there was often a framing of—a paternalistic if not colonialistic reaction to—these activities similar to Blake Samuelson's take on life: these were impoverished and undisciplined third-world countries who brought on most of the problems themselves by being so underdeveloped and so far away from accepted "Western Ways."

Overall, it was great fodder for Oriana's reporting. There was a litany of tales to tell—stories that were novel and even fantastic to most NYC readers of *The Daily News*. Although these were unquestionably not front-page material, there was a subtle but positive reaction from the readership and Oriana was given the green light to continue—to dig deeper and to look for new accounts to weave.

She spent over six months in Bukavu, crafting reports on everything from military suppression to barriers to coffee exports. She interviewed hundreds. She talked to local leaders, farmers and fishers, wives and mothers. Finally, she felt she had scoured the ground for most of what could be vacuumed up and, at the same time, was beginning to wear her welcome thin.

She returned to Bujumbura and took a room at the Burundi Palace to see what news she could uncover on the shores of Lake Tanganyika. With a new appreciation for vastness and inaccessibility, Oriana began slowly to try and understand even a small slice of the mosaic that dotted the shores of the great Lake.

She moved slowly around the shore, going north to the Rusizi Delta Game Reserve where the numbers of crocodiles and hippos was truly impressive. She ventured out on the Lake with fishermen of Greek origin who spent their nights trying to capture the small sardines of the Lake's cool waters that were an integral part of many local plates. She then took a ferry across the lake to the Zaïre town of Uvira—the Zaïre lands along the lakeshore some of the most remote corners of the globe.

Finally, she took a ferry fifty miles down the lakeside—the water route much less arduous than the parallel land route; although, on the map, this path was the National Highway No. 5—to Baraka, the *chef-lieu* of the Fizi Territory, a center for political opposition to the leadership in the very far off national capital of Kinshasa.

After these very insightful lakeshore visits, each producing several top-drawer articles to send back to New York, Oriana concentrated on the Burundi hinterland. This was no easy task. While politics and political upheavals in Zaïre were exacerbated by a sweeping ethnic, cultural, economic, and geographic landscape, the undulating topography of Burundi was much more uniform and the country much, much smaller—a more homogenous nation that would seemingly facilitate her reporting.

Yet the politics were daunting.

There were but two major ethnic groups sharing a common language, broadly a common religion, and many common customs albeit very dissimilar origins—one being Bantu and the other Nilotic. This superficial homogeneity had proven time and again to be a flammable and deadly imbroglio. The origins of these entanglements had, in fact, made long-term stability a goal that could only be achieved through major sacrifice—a condition that was still an aspiration and not an actuality.

Each major ethnic group was an émigré—the Bantus coming from the northwest through the Congo Basin and the Nilotics coming from the north, up the Nile. Once *in situ*, there developed a feudal monarchical social structure where the warrior Nilotics, the nobles, headed by a king called the *Mwami*, overlorded Bantu serfs. It was a bimodal community with very different liberties based on social status. These inequities combined with the brutal reign of the nobility led to periodic conflicts—conflicts that were bloody and costly not only in human life but also in terms of national development.

This history, these problems, though well-known, were not openly discussed. There was a story, many stories, for the perceptive journalist to tease from the annals of this area that some called, "the land of eternal spring." However, these tales were covered with layer upon layer of secrecy and taboo. Journalistically, each story came at a high price.

Blake Samuelson undauntedly would have attributed all the misfortunes to a lack of discipline, but it was much more complex. These were generational tribulations which Oriana was trying so hard to unravel and then blend again into stories that attracted her readership's attention while, hopefully, offering a lesson in the planetary fight for human survival. These were ancient narratives that were difficult if not impossible for the outsider to interpret. Nevertheless, Oriana did her best.

After three months, Oriana had combed through the *colines et marais* (hills and valleys) of the country, writing a collection of articles on a variety of topics running the gauntlet from political and humanitarian analyses to assessments of deforestation and erosion in the mountainous and densely populated nation. Then, before things could become monotonous for her or her hosts, she received word from New York to quickly get to Angola to cover the growing civil unrest.

As often the case, it was easier said than done. She would have to fly to Nairobi and spend a week there to get an Angolan visa and make her onward travel arrangements. She would then fly to Johannesburg, connecting for Luanda. All in, "quickly" was ten days.

Luanda was a city—a big city—at the edge of war. The *Movimento Popular de Libertação de Angola* (MPLA: People's Movement for the Liberation of Angola) and the *União Nacional para a Independência Total de Angola* (UNITA: National Union for the Total Independence of Angola) had been at odds since before independence. While they had both fought hard—often hand-in-hand—to shatter the colonial yoke, they each reflected different elements of the wider political tide that was sweeping across the region. MPLA was aligned with communist supporters. As a Lucophone country, ties with Hispanophones were linguistically easier—the MPLA having many Cuban advisors. The antithesis for those with more of a socialist bend was, following the trending global dichotomy, capitalism. Yet, in spite of this trend, UNITA professed itself to be more democratic in focus than capitalistic and was aligned with South Africa, and through South Africa, with several Western supporters. The Cold War entered markedly into local politics in Angola.

Local politics in Angola were often abstruse. While there was no love lost for the colonial powers, the Portuguese had been in Angola a very long time—much longer than most European colonialists. They reportedly built a colony in Luanda in 1575. They had left an indelible footprint. Unlike many other European colonies across the Continent, this Portuguese footprint reached to the furthest village after centuries of indoctrination.

This latticework of history, culture, and politics permeated every inch of Luanda. Luanda Province itself was outside of the heated fighting that erupted across the other seventeen provinces. Because of this, the capital was inundated with internally displaced persons fleeing the carnage of war. The city was engulfed—there were people everywhere. The homeless went to any cranny for shelter including unfinished high-rises where the inebriated and toddlers not infrequently fell to their deaths as they tripped out of wall-less rooms. The destitute covered the city, their offal fouling sidewalks, and their debris pushed about by the Atlantic winds. Oriana found Luanda and Bujumbura to occupy opposite ends of a spectrum of nice places to visit.

Not only was the environment less than pleasant, but also the job was often impractical. Oriana was not able to travel outside Luanda Province. The warring parties had placed mine fields throughout the interior and these had proven to be the weapon that kept on performing. People were, of course, killed and maimed when encountering the original field. But more devastatingly, in the heavy rains that irrigated the country, the light plastic mines moved with the water and mud flow, relocating the field to kill and maim again.

Both practically and philosophically, the job in Angola was very different from her previous assignments. Here it was much more geopolitical. Russia, France, the US, and the UK all had their fingers in the pie, but the pieces were hard to define. The working conditions made site visits and village-level interviews impossible. Oriana had to rely on second- and third-hand information, using an ample dose of imagination to interpret what turned out to be her version of the news.

Nonetheless, she was able to file multiple stories over the fortnight she worked out of the Casa Ilhmanne—the small auberge on Ilha Do Cabo (Cape Island), the narrow peninsula that separated Luanda Bay from the Atlantic Ocean. Although literally a stone's throw from ocean beaches, she was also five miles or less from most of the offices and places she needed to visit—a distance easy to walk on most occasions but here requiring a taxi as the streets were all too often unsafe.

When word from New York came that she seemed to be in diminishing returns in her reporting on the chaos of Angola, and that she should go to Guinea to follow another hotspot, Oriana happily went to the Guinea Embassy for a visa—for her, saying goodbye to Angola would not be hard.

Getting the visa, it turned out, was easier than getting to Conakry, the capital of Guinea. She had to first fly back to Johannesburg and then wait twelve hours for a connection for Accra. Once in Ghana, she had to queue for four hours for a transit visa to get to a hotel (not paid for by the airlines) for the twenty-four layover for the flight to Freetown from where she had a final connection to Ahmed Sékou Touré International Airport in the Republic of Guinea.

Her final destination was town of Nzérékoré in the *Guinée forestière* region in the southeast of the country. This was an area called by some "the parrot's beak." It was a crossroads where Guinea met Liberia and Côte d'Ivoire (and less than 150 miles from Sierra Leone). It was an area rich in resources including diamonds. It was also an area rich in conflict.

Upon arrival in Conakry, Oriana was met by a freelance agent who had been hired by *The Daily News* as her chaperon and assistant. This fact alone signaled to Oriana that the upper echelon at the paper considered this assignment either very important or very dangerous or both. Ali, her new escort, helped her get situated in the New Atlantic Hotel (again, she thought, right on the beach—same ocean, very different country) while they, as Ali called it, "took care of formalities."

Nzérékoré was five-hundred-fifty miles from Conakry. If they went by road, it would take a full day if things went well. The quickest route was actually to cut across Sierra Leone, but this was out of the question. By whatever means, prior to any departure from the capital, they had to register with the authorities and make sure all their press credentials were approved and up to date.

Once the paperwork had been taken care of, they decided to travel by air, Ali already having arranged for a Land Rover once they got to the forest zone. Flying was more involved than Oriana had imagined. The air service was undertaken with a Soviet-built Antonov An-12 which was out of order about as often as it flew.

They were lucky and the plane did fly on their chosen date. However, as the passenger cabin filled with dripping humidity and the windows fogged over (from the inside!), Oriana wondered if flying had been such a good idea. After two hours and twenty minutes, partially bathed in the water dripping from the overhead vents, they arrived in an equally hot and damp Nzérékoré.

Oriana had made the questionably imprudent flight to Nzérékoré with Ali to examine reports highlighted by her paper's editor. According to international news releases filtered in New York, armed gangs were moving through the forest, more or less redrawing momentarily national boundaries while they vacuumed up what they thought were (or what were) diamonds before vanishing behind accepted international borders. Armed bands from Sierra Leone, Liberia, Côte d'Ivoire, or Guinea, almost like in a choreographed ballet, danced into a cluster of villages, declared this to be the land of their native country, killed any opponents, and then undertook a massive treasure hunt before vaporizing and leaving a space for the next group of hoodlums to do the same. It was like an Olympic relay race where the baton was a bag of would-be diamonds that was not handed over to the next runner but to the powerbrokers back home.

This truly was the forest zone. It made Oriana again reassess her benchmarks, the imposing boscage making the forests on the shores of Kivu seem like backyard woods. She was thankful for Ali's insight in securing a Land Rover for their on-the-ground work—without such a workhorse, they would have been totally foiled.

As previously, Oriana divided the territory that was the object of her scrutiny into blocks. She started in Nzérékoré town where she met and interviewed local leaders and common folk. This was her first time working in a predominantly Muslim culture and she relied heavily on Ali for guidance and on-the-spot cross-cultural training.

When she felt adequately educated about her new surroundings, Oriana took on the next block—the nearby communities of Nzao and Kapaya where there were refugee camps. When the marauding gangs attacked villages, the villagers fled for their lives—many making their way to the environs of Nzérékoré where UN agencies and NGOs had established camps for their, hopefully temporary, accommodation.

This portion of her work proved to be a real revelation. While all the citizenry condemned the terrible acts attributed to the roving gangs, and all were sympathetic toward the villages attacked, there was an unexpected effect—growing jealousy for the refugees. Nzérékoré was generally a poor community. Many had inadequate nutrition, poor access to health and education services, and often not even a dry place to pass the night. However, with support from donors, the camps for refugees had ample food, warm places to sleep, built-in schools and clinics. In short, the refugees often lived in better conditions than the folks outside the wire fences that enclosed the camps. Those offering shelter to despite folks fleeing for their lives were ultimately envious of these same displaced people. It would have been ironic if not so sad and so true.

Taking this lesson to heed, Oriana then decided to visit some of the villages that had been directly affected by the diamond hunters. They were skirting the Diécké Forest Reserve on their way to Pela, twenty-six miles west of Nzérékoré when a World-War-II-vintage GMC CCKW 6X6 army lorry came barreling down the road, pushing the Land Rover off the shoulder and over a steep embankment where it rolled four times before stopping with its mud-encrusted tires spinning aimlessly in the air—like a tortoise trying to forlornly upright itself.

Although the army lorry that had driven them off the road never stopped, a taxi minibus had not been far behind them on the throughway to Pela. When the taxi driver came across the overturned Land Rover, he immediately loaded the two unconscious passengers into the taxi, leaving his original passengers to hitchhike the rest of the way to Pela, while he headed quickly back to Nzérékoré. With the two injured persons still unresponsive, authorities at the local hospital decided to send them by ambulance to the hospital in Man, Côte d'Ivoire, which was reportedly much better equipped—it was nearly four hours away but offered greater chances for full recovery (or so the Nzérékoré doctors hoped). On arrival in Man, Ali was regaining consciousness and was admitted into the local hospital. However, his female companion, his white French-national female companion, was still unconscious. Under the circumstances, the doctors in Man wanted to pass the buck and called for a helicopter to medevac the unknown French woman to Abidjan where she would get the best care the country had to offer.

It was only during the admittance process in Abidjan that, in going through the woman's pockets, they discovered her journalist credentials and contacted *The Daily News*.

Oriana had a concussion, a fractured left humerus, sprained ankle, and severely bruised back and neck muscles. It wasn't good but she had been extremely lucky. Fortunately, both she and Ali had been wearing their seatbelts. They had also been going very slowly. Even though the Land Rover's chassis was hardened, the roll down the hill had been destructive, totaling the vehicle. Yet, the gods had smiled, and the two passengers had not been permanently injured. Still and all, Oriana was in store for an extended period of rehabilitation. The paper had offered her a ticket home as soon as the doctors said she could travel. However, she had proposed, and it had been accepted, that she stay in Abidjan and hobble around to ferret out any stories of interest. Healing was going to be painful anywhere and she felt she'd rather be somewhere where she could hunt for stories rather than be confined to a couch in front of a TV in a New York apartment.

⚘⚘⚘⚘⚘⚘⚘

Oriana decided to make lemonade. This was an opportunity to follow-up on some things that had popped-up during her recent assignments—things she had not been able to explore as they had really been outside her core mandate of reporting on civil strife—outside then, but not now as she recuperated.

One of the key issues in altercations she had covered was who supplied the arms? Obviously, guns were big business. Merchants were everywhere. However, the pathways this weaponry took were often stories in and of themselves. In the case of Angola, there was a clear east-west Cold War divide at the geopolitical level. Yet, at the village level, things were less clearcut. UN agents, in collaboration with some of Oriana's international press colleagues, had identified a lusophone arms ring fluctuating back and forth between Brazil and Angola; this was a possible ganglion for the wider continental dissemination of weapons to the highest bider regardless of political bend or affiliation. In digging deeply into this transatlantic mostly illegal trafficking of weaponry that wound its way up the Eastern Atlantic from South Africa to Portugal, sister war correspondents had uncovered a number of other potentially unusual market channels—but channels that were beyond their remit.

Confederates had apprised Oriana of these interesting and obscure trade routes, most seemingly involving agricultural products interwoven with munitions. Angola, for example, had an unquestionable arms market. It also had a countrywide program to expand cassava production. Cassava, an export crop, was noteworthily marketed through both formal and informal avenues. A Portuguese company, Alimento Atlântico shipped cassava products from Luanda to the Portuguese port of Faro. Surprisingly or not, it was reported that Angolan cassava was used as a filler for bogus medications that were flooding the Costa de Sol and moving into the Côte d'Azur. These investigations also indicated that Alimento Atlântico shipped Botswana beef into the EU via Faro, foregoing most if not all required inspections. To complete the circuit, Alimento Atlântico often transported soy from the Brazilian port of Porto de Victória where UN investigators had reported still-to-be-confirmed possibilities that Alimento Atlântico vessels were also carrying arms, some reaching rebellious groups on the Pacific side of the Continent. It was all complicated and very murky. Part of the bigger picture was a possible organized ring of illicit traders working along the West Coast of Africa—a story yet to be corroborated.

As Oriana was now more-or-less confined to a rehabilitation mode—confined in West Africa—this seemed to be a good object of her attention.

She had taken a long-term room at Hôtel Résidence le Vasseau; roughly equidistant between Chu Cocody Hospital where she had been transferred to receive her follow-up treatments and American Univeristy of Côte d'Ivoire where, with the help of *The Daily News* and Blake Samuelson's personal support (Samuelson, to her surprise, proving to be one of her staunchest proponents in contrast to their drastically different views of the human condition), she had arranged with the administration to have access to the library and some additional research facilities. With bright orange city taxis in abundance, logistics were not a concern. She could shuffle to the hotel's *porte cochere* where she would slide unaided into an awaiting taxi that dropped her at the front door of the university.

At AUCI, thanks to the paper's intervention, she had an extra benefit. A student specializing in business communication had volunteered to be Orianìa's temporary assistance with a modest stipend from *The Daily News* as well as (an anticipated) sterling letter of recommendation. If first impressions were any indication, Awa Konate would get very good marks. She was enthusiastic to the point of being somewhat in awe of Oriana. She was, as her specialization perhaps reflected, a good communicator and, importantly, she was not a clock-watcher. Whatever, whenever, however Oriana suggested something, Awa was ready and able.

From her own perspective, Oriana was also enthusiastic about her present work; in spite of being handicapped and often in pain. Albeit her main task was mending, it was good to feel as though, at the same time, she could finally take a breath and rest after her pilgrimage through areas so hard-hit by conflict. She was ready to change gears. She was looking for calmer waters to explore.

Nonetheless, as Oriana and Awa probed into their subject, as they tried to build on reports of agricultural trafficking along the African Atlantic Seaboard, they quickly realized these would not be calmer waters—in truth, they would possibly be abyssal in both shape and form. The fact was trafficking was routine and omnipresent. When the purchase prices for cash crops like coffee or cacao varied from one country to the next, there was a flow of product from outside to the highest payer. When there was an influx of humanitarian aid (including US Title XII foodstuffs clearly labeled "Not for Sale"), there was a flow of these products from areas of dire need to areas of the highest bidder. Clearly, agricultural product distribution was market-driven and did not adhere to national borders. What to some, especially the authorities, was "trafficking," to many others was simply the regular supply of goods to local markets. Twentieth-century political lines drawn by outsiders on an unwanted piece of paper could not superseded centuries-old trade and commercial routes.

The trick was to dissect the local, more "traditional," conduits from those where there was a high level of international engagement. The unusual and obscure tracks pointed out by Oriana's colleagues were all of a certain scale; they all offered the makings of profits for big multinational actors. In all likelihood, Ivorian investors involved in these more felonious business opportunities would already have a certain standing—they would already be entrepreneurs of note within the hierarchy of national executives and financiers.

This was where Oriana and Awa started their search.

The list of candidates was long. There were many wealthy and powerful businessmen and women. There were many with extended international ties—especially with the former colonial master, France. There were many with anonymous and unexplained investments. There were many where there was no information where there should have been some, if not a lot. There was even a not-very-small number of folks who had already seen various agents of justice in regard to smuggling or other illicit business affairs.

However, when filters were applied, the list shortened. Referring to her notes, although in a francophone country with no strong links to lusophone areas, Oriana decided to look for businesses that used the port of Faro and those exporting cassava—also an important crop in Côte d'Ivoire.

Here, one business stood out: Les Entreprises Cisse.

Awa set about trying to undo the shroud that seemed to wrap around the diverse Cisse ventures.

It was easier to get biographical details about the individuals than about the business or businesses. The Cisse Family—Vianney, Antoinette, Luc, and Marc—was widely lauded. Not only was the father a war hero from humble roots who had become part of the country's economic aristocracy, but the family was also supported by farmers who were the grassroots members of the proletariat with a long history of helping develop the country's cacao industry. It was a family of innovation and generosity where accolades from the citizenry abounded. It was a proud public tale that overshadowed a very private and prosperous family business.

Les Entreprises Cisse had an office in Abidjan, so Oriana and Awa decided to pay them a visit.

This initial contact was easily covered by the simple truth of Oriana's work: she, an international journalist, was examining the agricultural export markets of the country, potentially as part of a transnational study to compare this status across the region (this latter bit perhaps a stretch of the current assignment, but who knew?).

At the unimpressive but functional Cisse offices, the two ladies were met by the manager, Monsieur Koffi Zadi, an almost overly affable if markedly overweight gentleman who offered monosyllabic replies to all their questions and then referred his visitors to a colleague who he assured them, "had all the answers."

The associate, it turned out, one Monsieur Camara, was effectively the office gofer (Oriana would have called him a "*planton*") who really accomplished very little other than getting the two women out of Monsieur Zadi's hair (had he had any). They would have to try another tactic.

On the way out of the office, looking for another orange taxi for the ride back to AUCI, Oriana noticed an enlarged picture near the reception of two youngish men with a slightly older woman in front of a very modern building of the sort not often seen in Abidjan. The caption of the picture read, "Messrs. Luc and Marc Cisse with Mme. Chantal Silue at the offices of Development Community of West African States." Next to this rather underwhelming photograph was another that stood out because of its gaudy colors. The same lady from the first snapshot was in the second, this time not in a conservative skirt and blouse but in a vibrant traditional dress of brilliant yellow and green with a matching head-tie. She was bracketed by two men. On her left was an oldish gentleman, wearing a traditional Dozo outfit with both the pants and the top made from fabric interwoven with contrasting strands of rich dark green and bright sky blue. To the woman's right was an older white man with a glistening pink complexion and snowy white hair wearing a maroon blazer with oversized brass buttons over a gold turtleneck and navy slacks with white loafers peeking out from under the cuffs. The caption read, "Our founder Monsieur Vianney Cisse with colleagues Madame Chantal Silue and Sir Horace Barthley."

Once seated in the taxi, Oriana wrote in her note pad: "Chantal Silue and Sir Horace Bartley."

They hadn't succeeded, but they weren't sure they expected to. This had been a test run and as a test maybe it had been OK. They shouldn't expect to simply knock on the door and have someone welcome them, readily offering up all their deepest secrets that had been long hidden in dark cracks beneath the woodwork. Big business meant big secrets.

The experience with Monsieur Zadi allowed them to strategize the best methods to achieve their aims. First and foremost, as they scraped their way through the postmortem, it was clear that, overall, this was not to be a quick and easy venture. Its time requirements far exceeded the time Oriana had remaining on her recuperation calendar.

The first step was to get the thoughts of *The Daily News* on her (so far, chosen solely by herself) assignment. Oriana managed to arrange with Awa's advisor a call to Blake Samuelson through the AUCI's switchboard after having earlier dispatched with urgency a brief on the matter to Samuelson and the editor.

The call went well, but perhaps not for the reasons Oriana had initially surmised.

Oriana had proven herself to be a talented and energetic reporter. Not something or someone to treat lightly. With her bilingualism and world view, she was an asset to the paper. Not an asset they wanted running around war zones where she could vanish in the blink of an eye. They wanted her in what they felt was the safer and more controlled environment of greater New York (a point with which she would respectively disagree). However, they still wanted her to keep her international activities current—possibly even expanding these to become a more prominent part of the paper's global offerings to the public. Ultimately coming back to NYC but still working on this non-battlefield African-centric criminal-involved theme seemed to be a perfect fit. She was heartily given the green light (with conditions, of course).

Blake Samuelson and his higher-ups agreed to give Oriana another six weeks in Abidjan to get all the pieces in place—her corporeal and professional pieces. This included making Awa's role more permanent and more financially rewarding (to the young lady's delight). Oriana would then come back to New York and resume a more diversified dossier with the African trafficking component as a centerpiece. If the work expanded, they would hire other local talent like Awa with the overall coordination from Oriana in New York—going into the field only as absolutely necessary (this latter point stressed).

It was a plan.

Oriana and Awa carefully outlined their work for the coming weeks.

There was work to do at multiple levels.

Before she left, Oriana needed to work with Awa to find a friendly face in the ministries of agriculture and commerce and if possible, finance, too. Reasonable monetary incentives could be covered by the paper through a budget category (used more often than one might imagine) entitled "expediting." As long as the sums were not outrageous, no one would complain, and, if they got the products they hoped for, all would applaud.

They needed to put together portfolios that documented major agricultural exports to Europe, especially Portugal. As these government-collected, publicly-available data would specifically be for formally acknowledged official exports, they also needed to understand what informal pathways were known for informal and parallel markets and how to assess these.

This should better clarify the place in the bigger picture of Les Entreprises Cisse while shining a light on other actors still to be identified. This should also be indicative of how difficult this task would be and how far down the rabbit hole they could go before they hit a dead-end.

At the same time, both Oriana and Awa, in their respective venues, needed to develop biographical profiles of the Cisse family plus Chantal Silue and Sir Horace Bartley. What might not be able to be mined from public records and the civil service might be found in the vaults where these individuals kept their secrets.

It was evident that this was not going to be a quick endeavor. They were poking about where few chose to prod—either due to significant negative incentives or due to ignorance. Now, Oriana and Awa were prying—many might say meddling. They could not blame ignorance, only possibly the exuberance of the naive. Bulging notebooks of battlefield notes perhaps had not prepared Oriana for the even more sinister and covert battles that could be, and likely were being waged for the almighty dollar in the farms and businesses that dotted Côte d'Ivoire as elsewhere across the globe. What negative incentives—what barriers— would arise to hinder their progress?

Continuing Education

What barriers? Oriana did not know the answer to the question. It was unclear if she even knew the full implications of the question. Yet, acknowledged or not, fully understood or not, many of their subjects would happily and aggressively throw up impediments to hinder the work of an upstart journalist and her big-boy American newspaper backers who were daring to illuminate in the full light of day their organizations and arrangements that, from the darkness of years of political and financial subterfuge, had provided harvests of wealth and power for years.

Unenlightened or not about the path she was now trodding, she was moving with much more ease as her painful injuries from the Land Rover accident were all but healed—the remnants now more a matter of painful memories from her work across what some still called "the Dark Continent" and her latent desire to remain on the "Old World" side of the Atlantic and not among the masses of traffic, tumult, and throngs that were New York City.

Her personal desires aside, in line with the expectations of the paper, with a solid base now laid in Côte d'Ivoire and feelers out across much of West Africa, it was time to move on, plowing into the morass of traffic, tumult, and throngs.

Her departure from Awa and Abidjan had been bittersweet. A new assignment and improving health were real pluses, but leaving was not easy. She had grown attached to the adept and energetic girl from AUCI just as she had grown attached to the city that some called (maybe the same who spoke of an adumbral continent) "the Paris of Africa." Still, she saw little comparison, simply two enjoyable cities, each in their own right.

Back in the city that was somehow (inexplicably, to her) equated with an apple although it was a colossal slab of concrete and steel, she was able to reinsert herself nearly effortlessly. In fact, some of the staff of the paper, folks she rarely saw, asked, "Where ya been? Haven't seen ya in a while!"

The paper had generously paid the rent on her apartment while she had been on assignment, so it was only a question of turning on the lights and pulling off the old sheets that covered everything against the surprising amount of dust the filtered in from who knew where in the paved-over megalopolis.

Her experiences over the past months were, of course, her touchstone for her planned activities. One of the lessons learnt from her stay in Abidjan and her forays into the more abstruse and unrevealed elements of international businesses, as foiled as many may have been, was the advantage she had gained from her liaison with AUCI. Now, back in New York, she needed to go back to school.

This was not as a student. It was to try and develop relationships as she had had in Abidjan where she could use the school resources and possibly students themselves to try to better pull back the veils on her subjects.

Her subjects were, after all, actors, probably important actors, on the world stage. They were hidden and worked hard at staying hidden. However, it was like a brontosaurus going past your bathroom window. You caught just a glimpse. Even if you weren't sure exactly what you were seeing, you knew it was big. Oriana was seeing almost random slices of very large, well-orchestrated, and impactful actions. The entirety was not visible, but even the slices were impressive—foreboding and (at least intended to be) intimidating.

With the already formidable backing of the paper added to the talent and capabilities of a university, Oriana felt she could gain traction and bore into the hidden world of her subjects.

Blake Samuelson, once again, surprised all. He had close personal ties with one Dr. Sandra Young, Chair of the Business Economics Program at Fordham University and head of the professional MBA project. Fordham was a highly esteemed institution with a large campus at Rose Hill in the Bronx and an equally large business and finance faculty. It was (but not really) practically Oriana's neighbor. The MBA project, moreover, targeted individuals who were already working in the business community but who wanted to enhance their CV with a graduate degree. These were people with one foot in the office and one foot in the classroom—the perfect choice for someone to work on Oriana's assignment, that, for internal consumption she had dubbed the "manioc mess." Cassava, one of the assignment's early linchpins, was manioc in French. Much to her chagrin, Oriana considered the whole affair so far to be just one big mess.

With Blake's leverage, one of Oriana's first jobs after getting clean sheets on her bed was to visit Fordham and try to find a local equivalent of Awa while exploring options for collaboration on the manioc idea.

For the first part, it was all much too easy. She could only think it was due to her links to Blake, but in one morning she was able to lay the foundation she sought—it was too easy. Through Dr. Young, she was introduced to Dr. Claudia De Angelis, who the Chair felt was a talented resource to assist Oriana with her assignment with more of a global vision as her grandparents had immigrated to the New World from the Lazio area of Italy in advance of the pending war. Claudia had been part of the transformative generation that still felt the tug of the old country but whose roots were firmly planted in American soil.

Before assuming a professorial position at Fordham, Claudia had worked at the UN and at the Fiat headquarters in the city. She had broad international political and business experience.

After a very relaxed but cogent chat with Oriana, Claudia suggested that it would be best she personally take a supportive role but that one of her students could get more directly involved in "the guts of the matter" (as she called it). She specifically proposed one of her grad students, Mariama Mbaye, as the ideal person to engage in the project. Mariama, a Sénégalese, worked for Eastern Atlantic Imports while also pursuing an MBA in international business. New York City had a number of Sénégalese restaurants as well as a notable portion of the West African diaspora. Eastern Atlantic Imports supplied these clients with Sénégalese foodstuffs ranging from fresh fish to manioc. She was indeed the perfect fit.

For the second part, the nuts-and-bolts collaboration, this was less matter-of-fact. Through Mariama's work, Claudia De Angelis would be able to keep a professional and a scholastic eye on the efforts underway—Sandra Young could be brought in if and when needed. This, the "manioc mess," could be classified as an add-on student project that was linked to Mariama's thesis. However, this was very much an informal arrangement. For university staff to get involved formally, to be able to produce work that carried the university's imprimatur, would require official links to Fordham and this would require what they didn't have: some sort of substantial extra-budgetary funding to entice the academy to put its high-powered savants to the task.

As Claudia summarized, "Such is academia."

Before leaving campus, Oriana briefed Sandra knowing that this would complete the circle, word getting back to Blake—knowing his services had been well rendered.

Sandra was relatively noncommittal, recognizing that the real interface would be between Oriana and Claudia. Nonetheless, as her guest got up to leave, the Chair of the Business Economics Program offered a parting admonition, "Careful, as they say *chez toi*, not to *avoir les yeux plus gros que le ventre*—don't bite off more than you can chew."

Oriana understood, but for her it was good start.

It all went well. There was now a francophone triad turning over stones, backed up by a well-known academician (who also spoke French). Claudia had an impressive address book that she generously opened often to guide the searchers. Additionally, the university's Walsh Library at Rose Hill had an impressive collection of material on international trade and commerce as well as the latest data-gathering tools. Oriana found herself in the hallways of Fordham so often that she really felt as though she had gone back to school.

It would have been very easy for Oriana to have been swallowed whole by the project, but Blake Samuelson, still her immediate boss, would have none of it. The hunt for international intrigue and shady business deals may have become, with the blessing from on high, the centerpiece of Oriana's day-to-day work, but there was a lot more. She was, after all, a journalist and not a university researcher nor a soothsayer.

With long days and tremendous support from "her ladies," Oriana somehow managed to make considerable progress amassing information about potential business deals which merited more in-depth probing while keeping her overlords happy with regular contributions to columns, ranging from accounts of new violent outbursts in the Sudan to updates on the city's Haitian community.

⚘⚘⚘⚘⚘⚘⚘

It was a new old life. Back in *The* City. Far, far away from the cries and chaos of the battlefields. Back to a life of medallion taxis, slices of pizza, and workouts in an upstairs gym reached via creaking stairs that felt as though they would crumble under each step. It was all the same, yet it was all different.

It was the work, it had always been so, that was insatiably driving her. The whole package enthralled her—she wondered when she would stop wondering. While the dissecting of commerce up the African Atlantic Coast was still a major focus, as she slipped back into the city, she was infected by the contagion of the intense vitality that seemed to seep from every corner of the metropolis. There was always something. Given her language and cultural skills, she generally was assigned more offbeat stories. Here she was not just part of a gaggle—she was, more times than not, pursuing a story in which no one else seemed interested. Time and again she was handed a lump of clay and asked to sculpt a pot.

It all came together.

What did not come together was a life outside the paper. There was none.

When her hormones appeared to take control and she needed release or rupture, she would go to any of the profusion of bistros that populated her neighborhood and (intentionally) have one too many. About half the time this ended up being many too many and the other half she ended up having someone go home with her or she going home with someone (awakening with a start in totally unknown environs). But, in her view, it was all transitory—simply biological and not emotional.

There was only so much space in her life and, with the exception of regular phone calls with her mother, this was occupied by *The Daily News*. It was not because of the salary nor opportunities for career advancement. It was devotion to a profession, devotion to people and places otherwise unseen. It was possibly an obsession.

⚘⚘⚘⚘⚘⚘⚘

A piece of her offbeat beat was to filter-out local activities organized by ethnic subsets of the hodgepodge that was the city (obviously a proficiency much better honed in a European, or so most at the paper seemed to think). If some special events were deemed to have adequate importance to appeal to enough readers, Oriana would be dispatched to try and translate these ethnic specialities into Americanized versions that would pique the interest of an average subscriber to *The Daily News*—converting the *coq au vin* into fried chicken.

It was in this category of her broader reporting work that she found herself at Saint Nicholas Russian Orthodox Cathedral in Manhattan for the September Eighth celebration of the *Nativity of the Theotokos* (*Theotokos* from the Greek *Theos* meaning God and *Tiktein* meaning giving birth). Mary, the mother of Jesus, was the *Theotokos* and the celebration was the celebration of Mary's birth.

In reading-up on her subject before going to the celebration, being no expert on religion in general not to mention issues regarding the Orthodox Churches, Oriana felt again like she was back in school. It was complicated. Unlike Catholics and similar "Western" religions, the orthodox creed apparently did not believe in the Immaculate Conception but rather that Mary was the natural born daughter of Joachim and Anna—born on September the eighth. The historical background for this version of Christianity was attributed to the *Protoevangelium* writings ascribed to James the Lesser, the cousin of Jesus, describing, among others, the life of Mary including her birth and childhood.

The truisms of events several millennia earlier aside, this celebration on this day at this time was majestic. Built in the opening days of the twentieth century, the imposing cathedral itself was splendid—primmed and polished. With space for nearly a thousand of the faithful, the Russian Baroque architecture transported one from the restless horde outside into the cool inner shadows that were insulating even if somewhat oppressive. The rich red tapestry behind the impressive golden crucifix in the chancel was set off by graceful murals proudly disclosing the colors of a spring bouquet. Woven into all this history and art was a festive congregation attired in their best to wish their *Theotokos* the very best birthday.

Oriana had fortunately come with Evans Parry, one of the paper's top-notch photographers as this was an event that would be best appreciated through photographs rather than words. She would be able to add a few carefully crafted paragraphs, not going off into too much religious detail (where she was woefully ignorant), that should be just the thing to appeal to the paying customers Blake and his higher-ups were courting.

Reviewing her thoughts and plans for this assignment, Oriana realized, possibly with some surprise, that for her this was all transactional. She had no religious connection to the goings-on. She felt in no way celebratory. Honestly, although appreciative of the work, she felt no sense of awe for the magnificent edifice nor its story. She felt no real link to the Eastern Europeans who sought solace under Saint Nicholas' sculpted roof. She was just doing her job.

After scribbling a few pages of notes, she looked for a spot where she could wait for Evans—a spot where she could be invisible yet still regard the proceedings like a raptor perched above its prey. Then wondering, did she really think of herself as some sort of detached spectator, maybe even a predatory one, that was removed from its surroundings—just doing a job? Maybe?

She found her refuge to the left of the transept where there was a large space carved out of the naive for the confessionals—no one confessing during Mary's birthday party. Here there was a short hardwood bench set against the wall, just the sort of place for which she was looking—a place to rest and look and see.

Here, in the protection of obscurity, Oriana's psyche drifted. This was that kind of etherial space where she felt her spirit float to the high ceiling, marveling that somehow today had actually happened. Startled, she felt her spirit flee back to its corporeal confines as someone sat down the bench beside her.

Back in the here and now, she saw a young man—she had to admit, a handsome young man—about her age who had simply plopped down beside her.

"Sorry," the unexpected person said softly. Oriana imagined that if the light had been brighter, she might have seen him blushing (and liking the thought). "I didn't mean to disturb you—just needed a dark corner to change the film in my camera."

This, Oriana thought, was possibly a ham-handed excuse for crushing her reverie or possibly an entrée for more conversation. She didn't know which, but regardless of the interloper's reasons, her contemplation was lost.

"Oh, OK," Oriana offered, equally softly and equally inelegantly.

"These things can get pretty heavy," the young man countered.

Feeling she was just doing her job, or should be, and not seeing how this intruder related to her work, Oriana felt it was time to be dismissive, even if perceived as supercilious. "Well, we are all here for our own reasons and I'm here for work, so I'd best get back at it."

Her unwanted companion appeared oblivious to her condescension, continuing as though she had said nothing. "My ancestors go way back into the depths of Orthodoxy, but this is pretty strange stuff to me."

"Yeah." She felt obliged to say something else, "to us all."

"Maybe some more than others?"

"Huh?'

"Oh, I've got a pretty good ear for languages. Like I said, my folks and their folks go back to the old country, back to Ukraine. I can easily pick up an adopted accent, even when one speaks English so perfectly as you do. I'd guess your origins take you back to France."

Oriana was taken aback. She was not looking for conversation. If anyone was going to be patronizing, it would be she. Yet here was this interrupter still sitting on a bench next to her in the shadows of the cathedral—and showing no signs of leaving. Still, feeling the need to maintain a modicum of civility, she tried to close with, "Great—your ears are correct—*je suis française*—but my colleague is waiting, nice to have seen you."

"Wait," the now irritating young man seemed to shout softly, "I noticed you in the naive before you came over to the corner. I noticed you taking some notes and I noticed your colleague has a camera as do I. I assume this all means that you are a local. I am, probably obviously, not. And, while I'm here for a short time, I really need advice. Sorry, but could you please help me? I need to know which is the best play on Broadway to see if I can only see one!"

That was Oriana's introduction to David Mitchell.

David, Joseph Mitchell's (a.k.a. Yosyp Myshchenko) second child had transferred from Northampton Community College where he had pursued a curriculum in electromechanical technologies to Thomas Jefferson University in Philadelphia where he had been awarded a scholarship to continue his studies to achieve a degree in engineering.

With a diploma in-hand, and the self-satisfaction of having finished third in his class, David got a job at Energy Elite, a company in Reading that helped small manufacturers automate. Reading was about fifty miles south of Pottsville on Highway 183, just about the midpoint between Pottsville and Philadelphia. Looking at it from another angle, David had never been too far from home. He was still a regular guest at his parent's home where his mother continued to serve his childhood favorites and remind him that he was doing well. His father enjoyed his son's visits and was happy for the fine fare Susan prepared in his honor. However, though he knew his son had done and was doing well, he wished he would be more adventurous and see more of the world.

Then David went to New York and met Oriana.

Power is Knowledge

THE awkward moments at Saint Nicholas between the gawky guests to the cathedral had led to a cup of coffee that had led to a show on Broadway that had ultimately led to Oriana's bed. Not in a matter of days, not even a matter of weeks, but in a matter of months the two were often wrapped around each other's minds and bodies. The fire had been slow to ignite but had grown into a hot ember if not an inferno.

Oriana now had more things to juggle. She had her infatuation (and maybe more, she didn't know) with David (her beau), her tasks for Blake (her boss), and her own high priority work with Awa and Mariama (her ladies, including often but not always Claudia). With little apparent overlap, it was really living and juggling three lives—trying to live each with as few slips as possible. She remembered, as a child in Avignon, seeing a *jongleur* in the circus (*Cirque Medrano* making a rare *tournée* south) with three spinning plates—one on each hand and one on a foot. This was now her model. She had three separate spinning dynamos amongst which she had to divide her efforts and her energies.

Yet, finally having what some might call "a social life" seemed to energize the other components of her daily activities; she wryly imagined it was because, for the first time in a long time (possibly for the first time ever) her hormones might be under control. She was certainly not an experienced lover and David apparently had an even thinner track record. But together they seemed to do just fine. There was an intensity with which she was only now becoming familiar. There were heightened senses and calmer interludes—there was almost, as foreign as it felt, a feeling of serenity. Always attempting to be forearmed, she warned herself not to let the serenity transform into lethargy or indifference. She had important aims, and she could not let herself be dissuaded or redirected. David was great. Blake's work was fine. But her true mission was the work with her two ladies—the work that was still not revealing itself.

⚘⚘⚘⚘⚘⚘⚘

David was less conflicted. This was wonderful! For the first time, he actually had someone else in his life—someone beyond his mother and father. He had someplace else outside the ellipse circumscribed by Pottsville and Philadelphia. Now he made regular trips into the city and even considered looking for a job there. Broadway and the blare of the metropole were no longer strangers. He was at home wherever he was as long as he was with Oriana.

Fulfilling his expectations was less challenging for him than his amour. He had an eight-to-five, forty-hour-week job that paid well and allowed him both the time and the resources to travel to the city on a regular basis—weekly if possible.

There were a number of travel options. They all seemed to entail up to three hours on the road—but well worth it.

In three hours, with a bit of luck encountering metro traffic, he could be at Oriana's apartment. If they decided to get out of the city, in the same amount of time, for each of them, they could be at their favorite retreat—Hawley, PA, in the Poconos.

Ironically, to David, Hawley was named after Irad Hawley, the first president of the Pennsylvania Coal Company. This was a stark reminder to David of his coal-dusted childhood—his father still investing long hours in an industry considered a dinosaur by some and a beast by others.

But David did not come to Hawley for coal. He came for Oriana.

In addition to the natural beauty of the Poconos, Hawley sported two unique historical landmarks: the Bellemonte Silk Mill and American Glass Works—both built near the end of the nineteenth century. The latter castle-like structure located near the confluence of Wallenpaupack Creek and the Lackawaxen River had been converted into a rather luxurious hotel where Oriana and David had "their" room that overlooked the falls on the creek that had once been the source of the power for the old glass factory. With the door to the small veranda open, the thundering of the falls seemed suitable accompaniment to their vigorous yet tender lovemaking—the same throbbing power being a somnolent to the spent couple now wrapped languidly in each other's arms.

Whether in the Poconos or the city, David brushed off and forgot the coal dust and reveled in his love of Oriana. He loved her and he loved getting to know her (and there was a lot to get to know).

⚘⚘⚘⚘⚘⚘⚘

This was all well and good.

Oriana relished the attention and the intimacy. She now had a much-needed emotional and social counterbalance to what had been a totally work-dominated life.

She was happy to share her life and her life's story. It was cathartic. It was supportive. It was invigorating. She felt exhilarated. She felt an inner power.

But it was only half of the larger tale. It was share and share alike.

David, however, appeared to feel somewhat overshadowed or minimized. What had he done? Where had he been? Before meeting Oriana his life had been defined by a home range that touched on four (of the sixty-seven) Pennsylvania counties.

Before meeting Oriana his life, covered in coal dust, had not even managed to be a smudge on the wall of his community. He had been part of the nameless and easily forgotten majority whose chief accomplishments may have been a college diploma and a job with a pension.

Nonetheless, it was what it was.

If he didn't have a soaring tale of his own accomplishments to share with his lover, he could share his family's story. That, after all, was a real story and, as a European-based chronicle, it was something with which Oriana could quickly relate.

Truth be known, David did not really know all that much about the backstories behind the accounts he shared with Oriana—it was more fable than fact. Still, he did his best to tell the tale of his roots and his origins.

For better or worse, this was pretty skeletal. Oriana learned that David's father, Joseph Mitchell, had come to America after the war with his brother Philip to seek the promises offered by "the land of the free." His Ukrainian ancestors had always been ready to follow their stars and their hopes. Looking for greener pastures, they had moved from Kaniv to Kyiv to Verkhovyna in the Carpathian Mountains. It was only natural to expect them to wander further and further, finally ending up in coal country in Schuylkill County, Pennsylvania.

David was not clear on all the details, but his uncle, Philip, had not been able to handle well the hard work of the coal business nor the hard life of mining communities. To seek refuge, he had ultimately felt the tug of the strings of his forebears and joined the church, becoming the first assistant to the bishop of the Ukrainian Catholic Archdiocese of Philadelphia.

David, of course, was much more up to speed about his mother. Susan was a native of Pottsville and a now sought-after nurse. She was also a loving wife and not only an equally loving mother of her two children with Joseph, Anna and David, but also the adoptive mother of Harold. Harold was Uncle Philip's youngest son. One sad day, Philip's wife and first two children had been killed in a terrible accident. This evidently had pushed Philip into the church's open arms with the inevitable result that he had had to give up his family—Harold all that remained. Joe and Susan had agreed to adopt Harold and Philip had vanished from the scene.

That was pretty much the tale. There was also a shred of the story that regarded Artem, David's paternal grandfather. While David had never met the old man whom he assumed still lived in Ukraine, he knew his father had met with him and continued to be in frequent contact with the aging gentleman and, through him, undoubtedly the rest of the family on the other side of the Atlantic.

Oriana enjoyed the family history; her journalistic antennae telling her that if she scratched the surface deeply enough, she would find even more interesting details. But this was play, not work.

And Oriana and David did play—raucously and hungrily.

On whichever side of the state line and in whatever spot (or position), they took pleasure in each other and in their being together. The physical pleasures mixed easily with the mutual pleasures of sharing space and time.

The months turned into years, and their relationship grew and strengthened. They became comfortable with each other even if they were not as comfortable with thoughts of how to classify or (dare they say it) formalize their relationship. There was a commitment. There was a deep affection—real love. There was patience, acceptance, and the never-ending desire to do more together. However, there was no discussion of marriage, children, visiting parents, or dealing with their union through any of the more typical institutions. They were satisfied with taking things one day at a time—some would say, fearing to look beyond tomorrow.

Looking too far ahead can, of course, lead to surprises. Yet one must keep one's eyes on the road.

Among the things that perhaps made David the same but also made him different was his choice to combine transport and exercise in the form of his bike which he took from home to office on all days that offered a relatively open and dry road. He did not consider himself a cyclist and was certainly not addicted to two-wheeled means of conveyance. He enjoyed the open air and the thought that he was getting a good workout—that was it.

One day, kind of a weepy day when he probably should have taken his car, he had nearly made it home when a student driver from the nearby high school wiped him out with a Toyota Camry. The almost dew-like coating on the road added to the mishap—effectively destroying the bicycle and leaving David with a badly bruised hip, three broken fingers, and a dislocated shoulder.

Thankfully, David had good insurance and a good employer. His medical expenses were fully covered, and he was given a generous three-month break to recover. His mother kindly offered him his old bedroom back for his period of recuperation. However, Oriana, knowing all too well the ins and outs of getting over an accident, quite easily convinced him that he would do well to accept her own invitation to move into her place in the city—at least until he was well healed.

His mother understood (and was silently grateful). With Oriana's help, David moved to New York City for convalescence.

In moving to the city, David had had to make a number of adjustments—now facing fully conjoint lives and spaces in a city that covered all in a bubble of boisterous chaos. One seemingly simple relocation task was to deal with his personal mail. This was straightforward for the correspondences—and this was most of his mail—that came to his home address in Reading. The post office just forwarded the lot to Oriana's address. However, there were still some rare communications that continued to come to his folks' home—things for which he should've long ago updated the address. His negligence notwithstanding, his mother happily arranged to send a weekly 9x12 catalogue envelope to NYC with all his Pottsville mail. After all, she reminded her beloved son, he was laid up and out of action (this being the nurse speaking) and his girlfriend was at work. What else did he have to do other than go over the mail?

Cohabitation had begun.

Oriana had readily shared her bed. In spite of his mother's observations, to Oriana's profound gratifications and satisfaction, David was not "out of action." She was more than happy to be in bed with him.

Sharing her desk was another matter. This was her domain and the place where she did a lot of her best work (in her humble opinion), but concessions had to be made. Reluctantly, she offered David one small corner of her over-sized old-fashioned oak teacher's desk. After all, he was logically only a minor user in the best of cases. He only had some mail to sort, some insurance claims to file, and a few letters to write. Nothing compared to her high use of this valuable space. So here too they shared, just not equally.

One afternoon when she had told Blake she'd be working from home, Oriana was sorting through some documents uncovered by Awa when she noticed a neat pile of letters in David's space. She knew he had just received a big envelope from his mother, so she guessed this stack was the recent forwarding from Pottsville. As David was out for physical therapy (his shoulder healing more slowly than initially hoped), convincing herself she was NOT snooping, only organizing the pile, she thumbed through the half dozen correspondences from his other home.

One thing stood out. There was a rather rumpled letter addressed to Yosyp Myshchenko in care of Harold Mitchell with a postmark from Málaga, Spain. To say it was eye-catching was to fail to grasp how unusual such a correspondence was. This was, at least through her reporter's lens, strange if not bizarre.

She assumed Susan had accidentally included some mail other than David's in the envelope—easy enough to do when the ever-busy (according to David) nurse and mother was covering a lot of bases. Again, convincing herself she was not going behind her lover's back, not encroaching on his private life, with long experience gleaned from her field work, Oriana managed to open the envelope in question without physically damaging the paper.

Inside was a neatly penned letter on rather soiled notebook paper written in, she supposed, either Russian or Ukrainian. Now her curiosity had truly taken over. She knew, or thought she knew, that David did not speak nor understand Russian nor Ukrainian. She knew, although she had never met him, that Harold was David's adopted brother-cum-cousin. She had no idea about Yosyp Myshchenko.

Her investigative journalistic instincts took control. She went out to a nearby convenience store that had a photocopier and made two copies of the missive. Back in her apartment, uncomfortably feeling even the walls were watching, she carefully resealed the original letter in the envelop, insuring there were no outward signs of tampering. She then called Blake and made up some story about an article she was preparing about Eastern European immigrants and that she now needed the services of a good and discrete translator. With the address of a suitable linguist in hand and the new destination not too far away, Oriana was able to get one of the copies to the translator and still get back before David returned from PT.

She made no confession. She asked no probing questions. She told herself the letter had arrived *chez elle* purely by accident—could happen to anyone—serendipity. Although, she told herself, this was really none of her business, still, she rationalized, she needed to make sure her lover was not in any sort of danger. She further told herself that she would never divulge her in-house espionage. This was Oriana being Oriana, but it should not, it could not, become a spark that could ignite some sort of ill-feeling between them. She had to keep her silence—at least to her housemate.

Nonetheless, when she got the translation, she read with great trepidation and no small dose of anxiety:

> *Dear Son: It is not safe to mail letters to the States from Ukraine, so I have given this to a colleague who is accompanying a shipment from Czechia through southern Romania, ultimately landing in Málaga before reaching the destination of the port of Faro. I trust mail from Spain to the US is a common enough thing so as not to stand out. We certainly did not want to call attention to ourselves and staying in touch has always proven to be a difficult task. Basically, you have done well taking care of nearly everything yourself. Nevertheless, I wanted to take this opportunity to*

send a message and to make sure we were still on the same page. Radutu Botezatu is organizing his normal Easter weekend meeting at his mountain-side chateau in the Făgăraş Mountains. After discussing with the mortician (the Maliar), we feel it is important you do all you can to attend and to be ready to brief all about the progress made on your various fronts. As the date is fixed, this makes the planning easy. You may not be aware, but you have a cousin, Petruso, who lives in Paris. I trust you will be able to find a reason to visit France the week before Easter and Cousin Petruso will help you with all the other arrangements. You should organize for a two-week absence from home. With business done, we all send our greetings and hope you and all your American family are doing fine. Artem.

She didn't know if it was a bombshell. It certainly, on the surface, didn't seem to be anything that could be bad for David. It really appeared to have nothing at all to do with him. It seemed to simply be a misguided letter between David's father and grandfather—proposing a trip by the former to attend an event that was apparently a regular activity of which Joseph ("Yosyp" she now understood) was already aware. It was almost certainly matter-of-fact regular stuff—a simple misdirected family exchange.

But there was something there.

She used the paper's resources to look into Radutu Botezatu. It turned out this was one very important person indeed. Joseph or Yosyp would not be going at his father's behest to meet such a man for an Easter egg hunt nor even to celebrate what the Orthodox called "*Pascha.*" Radutu Botezatu had large investments in tourism and the retail trade. He owned numerous retail outlets and building supply centers along with hotels and tourist attractions. Radutu Botezatu was a major financier in several Eastern European economies if not a much larger region.

Although, even after digging a bit, it looked like all of this was completely outside David's ken, there were definitely some questions about his father's connections. Her correspondent's senses began to get traction. What would a mid-level coal company manager who had worked his way up from the bottom as per David's biography be doing with people who were potentially global economic leaders? There was much more here. Knowing this, understanding this, put Oriana in a powerful position—especially if she could somehow link this to the work of Awa and Mariama. Hadn't Artem mentioned the port of Faro? This was a pivot point in her ladies' work. Was the group of Radutu Botezatu, Artem, the *Maliar*, *et al* somehow related to the ladies' investigations of illicit trafficking up the West Coast of Africa? Who was the *Maliar* or the mortician (the translator Oriana had used apparently unsure if the original word should be maintained as written as a proper noun, which he had put in parentheses, or translated into its more commonly used form)? So many questions. Too many questions. But now more information, more knowledge—potentially more power.

Knowledge was power but power was also knowledge, and both needed to be used judiciously.

This was all well and good, she mused, but her personal search, which she now had to admit was a potent, at times a consuming, driving force, was not for power. It was not even for knowledge in the absolute sense. Knowledge and the power it derived were vehicles. Vehicles for her search. This search was for truth.

There were many truths. One, she felt that was still a work in progress, was the possible truth that David was her soulmate and partner—an amazing and rare relationship that should not be put at risk and certainly not sacrificed to the abstract truths of shining a light on illicit affairs or widespread injustices.

She was still the *jongleur* and she had a lot to juggle.

If some had known the whole story, and no one did, they might have been prompted to say Oriana had inherited, at least in part (her mother was pretty good at balancing acts herself), her juggling skills from her father. By definition, the job of *Maliar* was multi-tasking to the highest degree.

Yet, on those still evenings when he needed a change from the energy-charged atmosphere of the throne-room of Domov, Orest would walk along the shoreline from the Ameland Ferry Terminal to Paesens-Moddergat, feeling alone with himself but realizing he was never out of the line of sight of his protectors who were always in the shadows—always there.

These private moments were times to think and rethink problems of the day. These moments were also times of rare introspection. Orest was, if he were honest with himself, as surprised as anyone to find himself seated on the immensely powerful cathedra of the *Maliar* of Domov. He was actually shocked to be where he was.

Orest was aware of the fact that he was not an ambitious person—certainly not someone who had had ambitions of great power. Many were. He was not among them. He had always been someone who took satisfaction in doing a good job—be it ever so menial or mighty. Ironically, it was perhaps this attribute that had pushed him ahead of other seemingly more qualified contenders into the seat of power for the hydroid organization that was Domov.

Orest brought this ethic with him to Holwerd, but it was unclear how it fit—how quality could take precedence over quantity when working on a global scale.

Thus far, in his private thoughts, he remained uncertain if his being the chosen one had been the right choice—the best choice.

He was no longer a novice. He had proven himself, under fire as it were, to his colleagues and to himself. He was respected and even feared.

However, he was not able to assure the overall quality of results that he was wont to do. It was simply too much. It was unrealistic. If he let it, it could become overpowering. And he was alone.

It demanded great finesse, audacity, and self-control to keep all the parts moving—to be a skillful juggler.

BOOK II

Aspirations

"Use your weaknesses; aspire to the strength."

—Sir Laurence Olivier

CHAPTER 6

DEFYING GRAVITY

"Power is given only to those who dare to lower themselves and pick it up. Only one thing matters, one thing; to be able to dare!"

—Fydor Dostoevsky

Imperfect Balance

JUGGLING was a skill needed by many.

Some would argue all life was a balancing act—that even the simplest jobs were complex (the most basic assignments only done well with good training and technique). Whether farming cacao or sitting on the pinnacle of power, from the glittering palace to the hamlet pasture, life was a tour de force. Life was complicated. Tangled and intricate actions were often required from actors at all levels of the hierarchy—actions that could be truly dumbfounding to both the leaders and those being led. Actions that could be, intentionally or not, influenced and even hijacked by others.

Life was a riddle. Yet, the actions often seemed far from the answers. The juggler had many items spinning at once.

As technologies and communications spiraled up to never-seen-before levels, many found it hard to keep up—many felt overwhelmed. There was too much to juggle. Yet those among the leaders and the led who navigated the latest tools in the toolbox were able to use the feelings of imbalance of others to their advantage. There were always opportunities, even if these sometimes came at high costs.

The epicenter was the marketplace. In this arena, the most insipid commoner could overshadow the brash elite. In the marketplace, rules of étiquette were displaced, even if done behind closed doors. Public protocols and societal norms could well fall into the sordid drains that evacuated the market's offal. The grizzled mossback wrapped in squalid clothes in a dark cranny of a market stall could well be more influential than the shiny blueblood adorned in silks and sapphires strutting about the square.

Margaret Mead had said, "Never doubt a small group of thoughtful, committed people can change the world. Indeed, it is the only thing that ever has." The market kings and queens, the market vendors and conscripts, were committed, either individually or in concert, to change the world, or at least their corner of it, into their vision of substance and success—whether good or bad, whether true or false.

Oriana had devoted considerable effort to juggling—to trying to keep all the moving parts moving to better understand the heretofore unknown. Had Artem's letter to his son (David's father) been revelatory or just family prattle? She didn't know. Had that possibly unwittingly found letter been a key or a lock, opening new doors on her search or a snare, locking her out of a much-needed relationship? She didn't know.

Nonetheless, like the juggler, once set in motion, one needed to keep the motion going. One needed to move forward.

Without engaging David (not because she felt he was culpable but because she did not want her exploration, that could turn into a fool's errand, to weaken the growing bond between them), she had done her own research and reached out to her colleagues, Mariama and Awa (holding off on reaching out to Claudia for the time being). These early stages of scrutiny involved more the individuals than the institutions. She had names and places, and she was trying to connect the dots.

While Oriana was just beginning to get some traction in her digging, Joe, having finally received his misplaced missive, was, at his father's request (insistence) leaving Paris for an Easter weekend in the Făgăraş Mountains. Cousin Petruso had been very helpful, even providing the twenty-five-cent tour of the City of Light while they were making the onward travel arrangements. Joe had known the trip would be complicated, traveling from the States on Holy Monday to make sure all the pieces could be put in place. But what had started out as complicated turned into, from Joe's seat (literally), a mess.

The general consensus had been that trains were the best choice of travel once "on the Continent." This turned into a classic case of easier to say than to do. The nearly twelve-hundred-mile trip just to Bucharest took over thirty hours. There was the ten-plus hour trip from Paris to Vienna with train changes in Stuttgart and Munich. Then after much too long a delay, there was a three-hour trip to Budapest and then another train change for the almost sixteen-hour slog to the Romanian capital. Joe had traveled across amazing countryside rich in history and culture not to mention at times breathtaking natural beauty. Yet, the sad reality was that this had all blended into a blur moving across the windows of his train compartment—the unnoticed and overlooked riches had merged into a sort of deeply detached kaleidoscope overshadowed by travel fatigue.

It was already Good Friday eve when Joe pulled his rented car into the parking of the mountain-side chateau after the four-hour drive up from the city. As he got out of his car, through the lethargy of far too-little-sleep, he realized (but could not understand why he had had this realization) that his trip from Paris had been nearly the same length as Charles Lindberg's flight into that same city in 1927.

Joe was efficiently if a bit dispassionately greeted at Botezatu Chateau's main entrance by liveried staff and promptly shown to a large and stately room that he barely noticed as be made a beeline for the bed. Although he had had the benefit of a *couchette* on the longer legs of his journey, with the change in time and the hours on the rails, he was exhausted. He fell asleep quickly, his ears still ringing with the hum of the train.

Stiff and groggy, Joe found his way to a capacious dining area that the butler (or whatever he was) politely informed him was the breakfast alcove and not the real dining room which was in another wing of the chateau. The brightly appointed room, set off from the hallway with mitered-glass French doors, had a variety of conformable-looking chairs scattered about the spaces not consumed by the center of attention, a highly polished large rosewood table that extended well into the space created by oversized bay windows that overlooked splendid gardens. Seated around the table was a covey of men who, by the look of the empty plates on the linen placemats in front of them, had finished their repast and were enjoying a cup of coffee, hopefully not waiting for him to join them. Men, Joe thought, who looked like they could well be part of a photo gallery from the Yacht Club de Monaco.

"Well, our voyager has come to our table," announced the fit and more-than-middle-age well-dressed man at the head of the table, continuing as he gestured to Joe to take an empty chair, "welcome to our humble mountain homestead."

As Joe took his seat, he remarked that his apparent host had been speaking in English, fluent if rather heavily accented. Sliding onto the embroidered chair cushion, his mind somehow (he really didn't know how as he wasn't sure he had been aware of such trivia—maybe it was delayed jet lag) quickly recalled that this probably made sense as his ancestral Ukrainian was an East Slavic language using the Cyrillic alphabet while Romanian was a Romance language with a variant of the Latin alphabet—very different vernaculars with few cognates. Even here in the old Eastern Bloc, English, as in so many places and settings, was the default *lingua franca*.

Fidgeting with the silverware (real silver silverware) precisely positioned on his placemat, Joe could only offer, "Thanks for inviting me, it's a long way from Pottsville."

As he spoke, Joe looked around the room. In addition to the host, there were seven people seated around the table—none of whom he knew. His father, as expected, was not there to chaperon. Joe had never met Orest, the *Maliar.* However, he would not have expected him to attend such a reunion. Given his cloaked, hopefully unrevealed to the majority of the population, role as a global puppet master, he could rarely afford to attend organized get-togethers but could appear spontaneously any time, any place.

"OK," the chateau's master continued, "we all know you as Artem's American son, so before we given you a chance to update us on all your exciting work in the Land of the Free, let me introduce you to your colleagues. We have Mr. Liu Li from Singapore, Mr. Raymond Girard from Canada, Mr. Janco Momberg from South Africa, Mr. Bohadan Kushnir from Ukraine, Mr. Sebastian Carvalho from Brazil, Mr. Hans van den Berghe from Holwerd, the Netherlands, and finally, Mr. Gage Smith, a Yank like yourself but apparently living in London."

Joe smiled and made a slight bow of his head to acknowledge each man as he was introduced. He recognized the first five men by name only as key high-level pillars in the Organization and, as his father had told it, regular attendees of the Easter meetings in the Făgăraș Mountains. Again, based on confidential information gained through his father, he understood the *Maliar* was now based in Holland and assumed van den Berghe was somehow connected to the *Maliar's* nerve center. He had, however, never heard of Gage Smith, had no idea of how he was connected, but knew he had to have some clout if he were among those assembled in this very surreptitious and powerful group (his main takeaway from the otherwise nondescript Mr. Smith was his husky voice that he had heard when he had entered the room and that, when he wanted to emphasize a point, became so harsh as to rankle the nerves like fingernails scratching a blackboard—realizing that such an observation dated him terribly).

With the formalities accomplished, the group's chairperson and host continued, "Before I ask Joe to brief us, let me set the stage or at least a small corner of the stage as we are all, or so it seems, so often awash in the theater or theatrics.

"No one need to tell you, you are, to say the least, an influential group. You are also interconnected and interdependent if not one big family.

"You are all industrialists, investors, powerbrokers. You are all kings in your own right—each with his own kingdom and own community of wisemen and knaves.

"Bohadan's products from the Carpathian Mountains make their way under our watchful eyes all the way to the jungles of Sebastian's western neighbors. Raw materials from Janco's operations on the margins of the Sahel make their way to Raymond's northern factories traveling in our lorries and our ships.

"As you know, there are a multitude of examples. Incidental details which you did not come all this way to discuss. But these actions and the myriad of others that join them are emblematic of our work and of our priorities as well of our risks and the need for us to successfully meet at times like this Easter rendezvous.

"We are pieces of the great Domov puzzle. By that select few who know of our activities here in Romania, this work is called the "*lucru*"—the thing. You see, we are part of concentric rings. Domov may be the largest, the most Delphian, and the most potent—even the most nefarious, but all the interlocked rings are important—all must talk to each other, and all must work to make the whole greater than the sum of the parts. This is why we're here.

"These meetings, or ones like them, have been taking place for decades. Today with modern and rapid communications, some might think that taking the time to travel to far-off places and meet face-to-face is a waste of time—time better spent making profits and gaining leverage.

"Yes, it is true. Today, by several means, we can communicate nearly instantaneously. But I warn you all. Beware of these seeming state-of-the-art marvels. As easily as they facilitate your communications, they also facilitate others eavesdropping on your conversations. Stay in the shadows. Do not be baited with new technologies that seem to add value but only add risk.

"We have time-honored methods that have served us well. We should continue with what we know best—in both business and politics as well as communications.

"Mr. van den Berghe has joined us to both ensure that the results of our discussions make it to the highest echelons and also to reinforce the admonition that we must all be careful—doubly careful. We have always been the object of examination—usually the targets—for agents of law enforcement and all manner of agencies wishing to control or confine us—or even abolish us. But these efforts are magnifying. More are seeking our downfall. More are digging into our secret places. We are under threat.

"Need I say more?"

There were scowls but nods around the table.

"Fine." Radutu Botezatu concluded his keynote address. "Let me hand over to Joe to give us an update about what's happening in the US."

Joe wasn't sure he really had much to say. After all, he had started work as a Ukrainian kid in the Pennsylvania coal fields—what did he know of the tortuous universe of power and finance that occupied the efforts of those seated around the table? He had followed his father's instructions—orders really—as all good sons were urged to do. He had left the home of his birth and established a new home and a new family in the New World. He had experienced what so many young men experience, happiness and sadness, joy and pain, grief and guilt. Was this to be the subject of his presentation to the august group assembled?

He thought not.

He sparingly recounted how he had come to where he was and then described with hopefully ample specificity this current situation. There really wasn't that much to go over, he felt, as he was still laying a foundation for potential opportunities but so far, his efforts were pretty much limited to coal country (where there certainly were favorable conditions for growth and, as he noted, perhaps there were similar promising mining areas elsewhere). Overall, he was confident, he assured his audience, that this fledging work in what some called Appalachia or the Mid-Atlantic region, would ultimately become a strong contributor to *lucru*. He concluded by mentioning that he was working closely with his adopted son, Harold (he did not mention that he shared some of his Domov secrets with his wife Susan).

As he sat back down, he felt he had said a lot about what were truly, on-the-ground, presently only very modest accomplishments.

"Excellent," Radutu Botezatu complimented his special guest, "do colleagues have any questions?"

There was a short period when most of those assembled asked sometimes banal, sometimes piercing questions about everything from supply channels to local and state regulations as well as banking arrangements. Most of the issues were focused and fortunately Joe was able to answer them with the succinctness anticipated.

When the questions had run their course, coffee was served. Joe stretched his legs and was admiring the garden through the cathedral-style bay windows when he felt a solid tap open his shoulder. Radutu Botezatu was at his side, coffee in hand.

"Good job, son. I know your father is proud—*Mi se pare că semeni cu tatăl tău* (it seems you're a chip off the old block)." The chateau's keeper continued, "We've still got a bunch of boring things to cover, but I don't think we need to tire you with all the monotony. I hope you won't mind; I made some arrangements for you to get a good rest before you start the arduous journey back?"

Joe could only nod—somehow seeing himself as irresolutely jiggling his crown like one of those bobblehead dolls the miners had on their dashboards.

Apparently unfazed by the almost imperceptible reaction, the Romanian mogul continued, "One of my assistants will accompany you through some beautiful mountain backroads to a place near the little dorp of Buda, on the shores of Lake Vidraru, called Complex Turistic Cumpăna. This is a tranquil spot where you can enjoy our beautiful country for a few days before departing. I hope these arrangements are suitable."

"I am honored," Joe inadequately offered, thinking he had not come on holiday and wondering if his terse discussion had been worth the travel; of course, as in the coal mines, he worked and traveled at the pleasure of his masters.

"Fine." The organizer raised a finger, and a striking young lady appeared at their sides. "May I present my assistant Mademoiselle Andreea Gheata? She'll help you with all the needful and then accompany you to the shores of our beautiful lake tucked away in our spectacular mountains . . . I wish I were able to go along with you.

"But," the manor's master wrapped up his pleasantries (heartfelt or cosmetic), "like all of us, I've got a job to do so I can only wish you a good rest, then a good return to the warm embrace of your dear family in the US—Adieu."

⚘⚘⚘⚘⚘⚘⚘

Andreea proved to be a knowledgeable and cordial traveling companion.

At first, when she told Joe her name meant "Ice Warrior," he was unsure how to relate to his imposed guide. However, her jovial nature and in-depth insight into the backstories of the forests and glens through which they traveled quickly won him over (making him appreciate, at the same time, that he had unfortunately, blindly, taken such a long journey across such rich terrain from which he had gained so little).

Reaching their destination, as they checked into chalets, it was subtly clear that she was available to share his bed if he so wished. Joe was tempted but was first and foremost committed to Susan—he was also committed to his independence and saw any tryst with one of Radutu Botezatu's insiders as an unwanted high-risk complexity to be avoided.

Andreea seemed indifferent to Joe's decision and maintained her convivial air as they had evening drinks while she described the Poenari Castle whose ruins they planned to visit on the morrow. The castle had been built on a strategic site in the thirteenth century to be occupied by various local rulers only to ultimately be abandoned and then renovated in the fifteenth century by Vlad the Impaler: *Vlad Drăculea*—known to many as *Dracula*. In spite of several relatively recent earthquakes, the keep's walls and towers remained more-or-less intact and, as they mounted the steep trail to the castle ramparts, Andreea, with a picnic lunch prepared by the resort in her knapsack, regaled Joe with stories of Wallachia, this region of Romania which was flush with tales of great battles—great victories and great losses.

After two nights and a significantly enhanced understanding of Romania's past, with some insight into her present, Joe headed south for the one-hundred-and-twenty-five mile trip to Bucharest where he would spend one more night in the country whose national bird was the great white pelican and whose national patron saint was Saint Andrew (who reportedly was the first to convert the people of the region to Christianity).

It was then back to the rails. However, this time he only went as far as Vienna from where he had a flight to Heathrow with a connection to Philadelphia. After two sleepless nights en route, he found himself snuggly in his own bed, awash with the afterglow of lovemaking with Susan.

The next morning, surrounded by the coal fields, the Făgăraş Mountains seemed as a dream—maybe it was a movie he and Susan has seen. The routine became routine surprisingly quickly.

⚘⚘⚘⚘⚘⚘⚘

While Joe was getting used to coal dust after the brisk and pristine air of the Făgăraş, it was not only the group who had spent Easter in these mountains who were interested in the progress being made in getting a high-level toehold in the US. The *Maliar* and his closest advisors were often analyzing this topic in minute detail—as always, looking closely at the past to plan for the future.

In recent history, the States had never been exempt from, free from Domov's influence, investments, and programming. Mykola and Yegor, who had accepted the reins of power from Andriy and Lehya, had made the first more or less permanent investments in the US through the Romanian refugee with the adopted name Robin McCandless. While these were not the first activities to take place in the US, interventions and relationships going back beyond to the early Gruppirovki crime groups, this was the first time there had truly been a discernible footprint traceable to the homeland. Delpro, through McCandless' skillful management, had developed into a sort of empire on its own and an excellent emissary of and conduit for Domov, but still seen as a cloistered American venture with international investments—not the reverse.

However, actions in the shadows are often precarious and even fugitive. With all the layers of governance and public control in the country, some said McCandless had done an impressive job hanging on as long as he had. Perhaps the ultimate desistance of Delpro was a foregone conclusion from the onset.

Previous missteps or weaknesses, if diagnosed, should certainly be avoided.

Whatever the diagnosis, Domov high-level leadership had long since ceased to rely on crystal balls as they had also learned not to brood too long over unwelcome changes that were probably inevitable and irreversible. McCandless was ultimately able to flee back to Romania and set up house in Vama Veche; his role, never at the topmost levels, had now become that of a pensioner who comes in part-time to help out.

The collapse of Delpro in the US under a full barrage of investigative challenges from various powerful agencies was not totally unexpected and the practical matters—as they related to the hole in the Domov network—were quickly corrected, adjustments made, and the actions of the former Delpro assumed in short order by other Domov hubs. While ground-level activities did not suffer too much, there was still little in terms of a physical coordinating presence for the Domov group in the States—a situation that was less than desirable. The preeminent leadership, therefore, looked to Joe to be able to rectify this obstacle by finding a pathway for a more enduring if also more invisible mechanism for Domov to have the presence it desired and it needed in the US.

Although Joe was not implicitly aware of this broader context for his efforts, it had been clear for a long time and was recently reiterated by his trip to the Botezatu Chateau, that his mission was seen as one of the utmost importance. He hoped he could deliver.

Oriana—now Joe's son's best buddy—wanted to deliver too. As a juggler, she had many delivery points. She wanted to deliver herself to David. She wanted to deliver good copy for *The Daily News*. She wanted to deliver a good project working with her colleagues at Fordham. She wanted to deliver with Awa and Mariama and produce an earth-shattering revelation that would skyrocket their careers .

It was a lot.

It was at times both frustrating and enervating.

Oriana remembered her mother's (perhaps a bit crude) saying, "*on ne peut pas avoir le cul entre deux chaises*" (don't get caught sitting between two chairs). She felt like she was balancing between four chairs, not just two.

But reality is a tough master. Regardless of what she wanted to deliver, there were externalities that really controlled the situation. As Sandra Young had warned, she had been too ambitious in outlining her plans (more hopes) with Fordham. The university had limited capacity and not enough time. Hence, her project christened the "manioc mess" had to be truncated and streamlined. At the end of the day, it was little more than an analysis of the future of the cassava industry in West

Africa. A topic of interest and even potential value but far less than she had initially imagined.

Similarly, her groundbreaking work with Awa and Mariama had to be reframed in more realistic terms. They were still moving ahead and still trying to take a broad look into their chosen subject, but things were going much more slowly than Oriana had hoped at the beginning. Instead of a major plunge, it turned out to be a modest leap of faith. Like Oriana, Mariama had to contend with the realities and requirements of her academic program. Awa, moreover, in spite of her diligent efforts, did not have the necessary resources to make big steps forward. Everything slowed down.

The upside of all this was that Oriana had more time for David and for this she was most grateful. She still hadn't been able to unravel all her questions emanating from the letter she never should have seen. She still hadn't discussed this with David. However, as she was rethinking her ability to deliver, she began to think all these questions about David's family didn't matter. David mattered.

Oriana thought back to her childhood in Avignon. It had already been quite a journey, and she was far from her final destination.

Dropping the Ball

Mr. Robin McCandless was neither a banker nor a beggar, though he knew both (and might have been overheard remarking that he often could not tell which was which). For Domov and through Delpro, McCandless had been a groundbreaker. But the Feds and others had now pulled the curtain way too far back and the formerly hidden empire of McCandless ceased to exist—in many cases, evaporating almost overnight.

Robin had staged a theatrical departure from his realm and then haltingly found his way back to his native Romania, at times joined by his younger brother Horace (when he could be wrenched away from his Namibian sanctuary). While Horace, Sir Horace to the outside world, continued to wander and wrangle "once-in-a-lifetime" deals, Robin was generally content to adopt (as he really always had had) a more sessile life. He would make regular sorties to banks in Bucharest where he would assist in a number of ongoing activities—usually at the bidding of others. He would also receive houseguests from "the network" seeking details of his past operations or advice on strategic approaches to grasping more wealth and power. It was a routine that suited him and, with a well-prepared bolthole through Bulgaria if needed, he was satisfied to enjoy the seashore and the crumbs of Domov, apparently not overly concerned about possible pending legal jeopardy from any of a variety of sources. He seemed to be guided by the oft-quoted passage attributed to Mae West: "You only live once, but if you do it right, once is enough."

Robin McCandless may have moved to the margins, but obviously Domov was an entrenched amoeboid and perennial organization that saw actors at all levels come and go—the actors vanished but the play went on. In many ways, Domov imitated life (some might have said life imitated Domov).

Unfamiliar with Robin McCandless, but well-versed in the persona of his brother Horace, Luc and Marc Cisse continued expanding their businesses, largely unaware (or indifferent to the fact) they were indeed part of an overarching global structure known as Domov. The Cisse company maintained a remarkable growth rate even if the investments that comprised their portfolio at any point in time were consistently changing. With insight from Chantal, they were able to stay ahead of the curve and shift assets to be able to take advantage of rare one-of-a-kind opportunities. Unlike the early days with their father at the helm, now they were not undercapitalized—not beholding to the bankers. But they were often understaffed.

With improved economic development across the African region and expanding educational opportunities for many, the company was able to find ample supplies of well-qualified mid-level personnel. It was the basement-level worker who was surprisingly in short supply. It wasn't an absolute shortage of available labor—it was a shortage of labor willing to work for the pittance the company was willing to pay; every franc in a labor's pocket was one less in Luc and Marc's—a reality they felt painfully.

Whether cacao farms in the lush hills of western Côte d'Ivoire, fish processing facilities on the arid shores of Mauritania, or bauxite mines in the Savannah's of Guinea, wherever they were working and whatever they were doing, these were labor-intensive undertakings requiring large teams of unskilled but hardworking laborers—teams that were progressively harder to assemble as better-informed townsfolk and rural dwellers insisted on better wages for increasingly expensive modern lifestyles.

From the brothers' perspective, economic development had spoiled the market.

The problem was partially addressed thanks to the seemingly ever-present strife in the region—whether at the village or the country level. Muslim-Christian, Northerner-Southerner, Francophone-Anglophone, farmer-herdsman, coastal dweller-fisher—there was no shortage of schisms that could send one group or another fleeing—sometimes to the nearby brush, sometimes to the far-off city.

What was surprising to some was that these problems did not happen even more frequently. Nonetheless, whether a hand-full or an entire village, there were generally people uprooted and looking for a better tomorrow.

These displaced people were vulnerable. These displaced people were potential laborers taken-on (voluntarily or not) for less-than-subsistence compensation. Once these truculent if lucrative mechanisms were in place to fill their own labor needs, with the tacit approval of the good Sir Horace and using up-to-date insider information from Chantal, the Cisse brothers decided to enlarge their abduction and coercion operations to do their best to fill the omnipresent clandestine labor demand in the region and moving into the states across the Mediterranean Sea. Les Entreprises Cisse further diversified. Animal, vegetable, mineral—they did it all as long as there was a good percentage to be had.

Voldoymyr Rudenko was following a trajectory very similar to the Cisse's. His transit business through Kosa Lyapina Island proliferated. He was savvy enough not to mess with the inviolable packages that passed through his portals, but for the everyday items for everyday people there seemed to be a bottomless market. Contraband and over-priced luxury merchandise were sought by many thinking material goods could sooth the rigors and adversities of a challenging if not punishing life.

The future was looking bright and Voldoymyr decided to bring his first-born, Kyrylo, into the business. His son had attended Pryazovskyi State Technical University (Voldoymyr himself not making it past secondary school), an institution with its origins in the once flowering steel industry of the 1930s and an institution that still provided a practical hands-on education. Kyrylo proved himself to be a smart kid with a very pragmatic head on his shoulders. As the increasingly diverse business interests expanded, Voldoymyr turned more and more over to his son. Soon the son was the driving force with his father, still a keen operator, more in a role of navigator than pilot.

Voldoymyr, like Artem and certainly Andriy, was a traditionalist in the tradition of the clan's moral guidelines as outlined by the work of the postwar (World War I) *Soobshckestvo.* There was good business and there was bad business. This had nothing to do with legality nor criminality. This had everything to do with the clan's view of the world and its moral stance on issues—there was honor among thieves (at least within the context of the early clan societies).

It was a complicated, at times contradictory, code where norms were almost tribal customs. There were formal taboo activities such as human trafficking or bootlegging military weaponry. Yet for every interdiction there were exceptions. Despite bans, blind eyes were often turned to forbidden topics if these impacted significantly on the bottom line.

While the older generation seemed content with this Kabuki theater, their follow-backs had no patience for such, as they saw it, double entendre. For them it was simple. It was clear-cut. If it made money with an acceptable risk, do it. The younger generation was ready to do it all. Luc, Marc, and Kyrylo were emblematic of their contemporaries. They were intelligent and aggressive businessmen. They saw themselves as the wave of the future (the unsaid part being the older folk being a hindrance or possibly a barrier to this wave).

Although none of the young men from Ukraine or Côte d'Ivoire knew of Cynthia Owens or Özgürlük, there were common forces moving through the global marketplace—often common problems that benefited from common solutions. While Cynthia may have begun ahead of time, the opportunities to supply a demanding labor market were apparent to many. The fact that this labor was forced was a detail that received little attention. There was the market. There was demand. At the onset, Cynthia, then Luc and Marc, and finally Kyrylo found ways to supply products to meet this demand—the fact that these products were in more than a few instances human beings was of little importance. The groups of neophyte operators, whether on the fringes or mainstream Domov, had very different views than their predecessors regarding the market and their role in profiting from the labor value chain. Whether acting as monarchs or knaves, those riding the new wave were generally acting in self-interest.

Orest was probably the closest of any at the higher Domov echelon when it came to being a banker—he certainly had control of a lot of purse strings and budgets albeit he considered himself a businessman more than a financier. He realized, however, that most looked to him as a visionary as opposed to an entrepreneur—Moses-like leading all to the promised land of never-ending profits and power (recognizing that this required no small dose of knavish behavior).

Yet, Orest too was a traditionalist. He was also a pragmatist. From the mountain top, the work in the valley fields was far off, viewed as though looking through the wrong end of binoculars—the workers seen as ants on a distant mound. He was the king of the monarchs and the leader of the leaders, but he was also distant and sadly often too disconnected from day-to-day routines to feel he could really monitor the pulse of the on-the-ground activities.

Much of what happened on his watch involved actions with which he morally disagreed but with which he practically or politically had to agree—such was the cost of being the paramount leader. Sacrificing what he wanted to do for what he felt he must do was all the more difficult because he believed in repercussions; there were no free lunches. He knew there were always costs and he believed in the inevitability of unpredicted and unwanted aftermaths. He was all too familiar with the 1800 writings of Johann Gottlieb Fichte in *The Vocation of Man* where he wrote, "*You could not remove a single grain of sand from its place without thereby ... changing something throughout all parts of the immeasurable whole.*" Else ways, Orest knew Fichte's hypotheses had been called "the butterfly effect" by others. To him, it was the law of unexpected consequences. It was to be avoided but it was unavoidable.

Cops and Robbers

Казаки-Разбойники—Cossacks and Robbers—was the equivalent of the western children's game "Cops and Robbers." It's played like a criminalized version of hide-and-seek The robbers go and hide and the Cossacks *cum* police try and find them. A good reflection, Rodney thought, of reality—or at least his reality. And there were many places and ways to hide.

Rodney was preparing his report to the Jake Sullivan's Committee and a great deal appeared to be hiding. After all these years trying to uncover what he felt was in plain view, Rodney had really only been able to bring to light a few shards in the mosaic—the key pieces remaining hidden and veiled.

He asked himself what he really knew—that, after all, was what the committee wanted to know. He had unearthed a fair amount about Delpro and Robin McCandless—most of the hard evidence thanks to Charlie Stancik. Much of this had been corroborated by Peter Volman whose inputs had also helped Rodney's crew glean more about McCandless' brother Horace. Here, with testimony from the two young men, there was a lot of hard data—data that was now unfortunately marginalized with McCandless' staged death and subsequent resurfacing in Romania. All of this good to know, but not the sort of material that Rodney could take to DOJ as the crux of a major case against organized crime in the form of (as he had learned through his investigations) Domov.

Rodney and his team had an eye on McCandless and followed Horace—the former, from all indications, quasi-retired and the latter still piddling around in this and that but no longer a major actor. They had also discovered links to other probable felons such as Cynthia Owens, the Easter Group in Romania, and the former Delpro agents entrenched in government (at least some of them). The intervention of and headlining by the Secretary of State had called attention to Delpro and, through subsequent intelligence and analysis, to the Domov group in a pivotal way as well as shining a light on the important part this scandalous throng likely played in present-day slavery. All activities of the once proud US company Delpro were now classified as entities of the cloaked and dangerous global Domov; this situation became a chief reason for convening the Sullivan Committee.

This had, as well, been instrumental in the (forced) forged alliance with Felix Manchester and Group 8. With pressure from the very top, a red flag operation through Section T15-Z had been mandated to regroup D-2 and Group 8. While, at field level, each entity would retain its functional integrity and independence and receive their own budget allocation through the Sullivan Committee. At the utmost levels of planning and coordination they would link through Section T15-Z—a temporary and exclusive emergency management structure (an ESGW—an Extraordinary Security Working Group) that reported directly to the White House and that was composed of a senior staffer to be named by the President, a key analyst from NSIE (the Network Security Information Exchange), Senator Sullivan or his representative, along with the chiefs of the D-2 and Group 8 teams including any aids and assistants as required. By its highly confidential sanction, this was not a group to finesse issues but one intended to rapidly and with surgical precision find solutions to critical problems, be these ever so harsh—even distressing (the repercussions to be dealt with post factum). The top-secret decisions of T15-Z, including all relevant communications and background, would be the doctrine guiding the fight against the miscreant named as Domov—a serious threat to homeland security not to mention global governance.

For Rodney, this imposed a new set of operational protocols that was a blessing and a bane—likely more of the latter. The liaison effectively spread the blame which was surely to come at one point or another; it limited the individual liability, but it also significantly encumbered what had heretofore been streamlined and limber operations. Rodney greatly preferred to work alone with his handpicked group of field-tested professionals (and he was truly uncertain as to the under-fire professionalism of Group 8). However, he was wise enough to realize that the association of the two agencies could be the means to saving his career if things went sideways. Government survived on scapegoating and the more top-level agencies involved the less likely that only one component would be crucified for the greater good; ironically, in the political arena if not in the on-the-ground battlefield, he had Felix's back and Felix had his.

Under the new structure, like it or not (and the private, introspective Mr. Mills had a hard time adjusting), Rodney was the point of the spear. He was not only the chief presenter to the Sullivan Committee, but he was also the formal congressional focal point for Section T15-Z joint activities, representing both Group 8 and D-2 (though one of the Ds was now passé, no one seemed to notice or care).

⚘⚘⚘⚘⚘⚘⚘

As Rodney tried to craft his committee presentation, making sure it was all blessed with ESWG approvals and saying enough to keep the critical group's support but not so much as to create over expectations or open unwanted doorways, Senator Sullivan looked at his calendar and regretted his chairmanship of this unavoidable committee. Domov and all that went with it was a no-win situation for him—for any public politician. It was a poisoned fruit that should have been passed to his adversaries long ago and not left on his plate to suffer the inevitable unpleasant and possibly damaging repercussions. If the veil held, he could be judged as incompetent—impotent. If the veil fell, he could find himself in prison.

While he ruminated, his phone rang. It was Gage Smith. The husky voice, not a whisper today, seemed to pierce his eardrums.

"Jake," Gage began, "been a long time."

The unwanted caller grated on the Senator's senses, making his head throb, but he could not be ignored nor put-off—power came at a high cost.

The would-be Virginia gentleman, attempting to insert a bit of a drawl into his inherited "yinz-ish" dialect, tried to open with an air of convivial bonhomie, "Well *Surh*, so good to hear from you."

"Senator," the unwelcome caller replied, the tone hardening to almost a rasp lacking all cordiality, "somehow I feel as though you've been avoiding me."

"Absolutely not, I assure you," the fidgety functionary continued as the political rhetoric began. "You know I'm just flooded these days—my schedule chucked-full of duties to meet my constituents' needs. Sadly, sometimes things fall through the cracks."

"Well, we're no crack, if you know what I mean."

"Oh, no offense intended. Of course . . ."

"Indeed, you're a busy man—an important man—if, in no small part, due to your strong friendships with folks like us."

"Truly, you know in what great esteem I hold you and your illustrious colleagues"

"Naturally, Senator—not certain that 'illustrious' is a good choice of words—you know we're not really seeking fame nor glory—kinda shun the limelight, if you know what I mean. Yet, even in the background, we have a role. It's the hand that feeds you, huh? And we know you won't bite, but we just want to make sure that you'll keep those pesky—honestly troublesome—DOJ dogs at bay. After all, if they start digging up bones, who knows whose those will be."

"My dear friend . . ."

"Please, Senator, do not conflate work and friendship—I am a messenger, not a 'mate' nor a 'buddy'—hell, I don't even vote."

"Of course." Years in the arena allowed the time-tested politician to continue without missing a beat. "And I appreciate your efforts as emissary as well as all the support from your associates."

"Sure. As much as this has been a wonderful pleasure chatting with your august self, I have to get back to work. Just remember, we are counting on you."

"Of course . . ."

The line was dead.

⚘⚘⚘⚘⚘⚘⚘

Totally unaware of the Honorable Senator Sullivan and continuously baffled by what the international press described as the "American political system," Marc and Luc had been getting to work. With the intelligence provided by Chantal and no small dose of encouragement from the good Sir Horace, the brothers had begun acting on, not only thinking about, a significant upscaling of their organization. They had suppliers, they had contacts, they had distribution networks. Why limit themselves to West Africa or even to Africa? This was a time of globalization, and the market was truly global. Les Entreprises Cisse blossomed.

A normal avenue for this expansion was to follow the pathway once tread by Vianney Cisse—to begin operations on the shores of their former colonial master (neither brother missing the irony). Europe was a massive market and there were more than a few Ivorian contacts with whom to establish supply chains across the Continent. There were also more than a few pathways to this market, both covert and overt. The immediate choice based on advice from both Chantal and Horace was the maritime commercial channel going on the seaward side of Îles du Frioul (site of the Château d'If, setting for Dumas' tale of *The Count of Monte-Cristo)* and entering the congestion that was the Port of Marseilles—from there spreading like a spring shower into the hinterland.

While the Ivorian diaspora was a resource, the brothers wanted a reliable anchor of their own *sur place.* Antoinette's niece, Minata, was the perfect choice. She was family and an excellent cook. It was a relatively simple matter to get her set up in a small but suitably chic restaurant, Maquis Maman Afrique on Rue d'Aubagne, just off the main avenue Rue de Rome and only a few blocks from the Vieux-Port de Marseille—the backdoor to the massive Marseille harbor system. It was all flawless—or so it seemed.

It took some time, as all good things do, but soon Maman Afrique was doing excellent business serving a diverse clientele including the nouveau riche of the city as well as West African newcomers—all wanting a taste of the truly superb plates prepared under Minata's discerning eyes (and more discerning palate). The Maquis was not only a place to sample savory dishes, it was also a rendezvous where business could be done in a quite corner surrounded by the tantalizing aromas of simmering vegetables and roasting meats.

As the restaurant's bank account grew, so did the parallel businesses that allowed the brothers to recruit an entire crew of Ivorian immigrants to work the streets and byways of the port, moving all manner of merchandise, some alive and kicking, to disparate destinations across the region.

Just as the Maquis' reputation and standing grew with its bank account, unavoidably, so did the reputations and standing of the brothers' other ventures. More quickly than imagined, La Famille Ivoirienne (as they were soon baptized) became known as a supplier of many of the most-difficult-to-obtain but in-high-demand items the market sought.

Although the brothers had been forewarned that they needed to tread softly, they had assumed their startup would be slow and they would initially be able to operate under everyone's radar—the everyone being both the authorities and more critically, the Marseille Mafia. The long-established and very powerful crime families, known jointly as Le Milieu, controlled much in the city and the country through *les beaux voyous*, the "goodfellas," who engaged in everything from bank robberies to extortion and oversaw all activities including counterfeiting, prostitution, and drug trafficking. If Marc and Luc had seen *The French Connection,* they might have had a better idea of upon whose territory they were trespassing; unfortunately, they had never seen the 1971 Academy-Award-winning film (nor read the book).

Le Milieu did not tolerate trespassers. However, there were encroachers on all sides. They had to prioritize—protecting their territory could not be allowed to become so all-consuming as to adversely affect profits. They carefully picked their fights.

Les Caïds of Le Milieu were initially more irritated than threatened by La Famille Ivoirienne—the bothersome brothers were like a mosquito buzzing in their ear, keeping them from getting a good night's sleep but not worth getting out of bed to try and hunt down. There were bigger intruders.

Les Caïds were up until now not completely clear about Domov, and they were certainly unaware of any possible links between this amorphous khokhol group and those they had nicknamed *Les Cosaques Africain Menaçants* (the Threatening African Cossacks), the annoying Ivorians. They knew of the Eastern European Cartel as either a competitor or a collaborator or both. They had witnessed the rhizopodan-like expansion of Domov as it seemed to seep and creep into each crevice and crack from the Côte d'Azur to the banks of the Rhine in Alsace. Friend or foe practically did not matter. Control was necessary. They had arranged for Taras' elimination in the hopes that cutting off the head would make the body wither. The man from Bourg-en-Bresse had been more than a little troublesome, not to mention the foreboding of the ill-understood organization of which he had been the leader. But his removal had not stilled the organization. Everywhere there remained clear and current signs of Domov's presence. Les Caïds were still deciding what to do—there was little time left over for these African mosquitoes.

When the vexing Ivorian network grew and began to flex its muscles, Les Caïds decided they had to do something. Nonetheless, they did not want to engage in drastic measures as they had with Taras. First, in their assessment, the competition from the unfortunate Africans was still minor. Second, and of greater consideration, *en gros* the African community was large and potentially volatile; Le Milieu did not want to make unnecessary waves to alienate a population who in other terms was occasionally a client but, in most cases, an indifferent observer.

The easiest solution appeared to be to let the system take care of itself. Through their multitude of channels, they shared bits and pieces of information about La Famille Ivoirienne with INTERPOL—let the police police the situation.

⚘⚘⚘⚘⚘⚘⚘

While Maman Afrique dished out delicious servings of piquant *attiéké* as well as other likely less-appetizing but much-sought-after illicit African delicacies, Voldoymyr Rudenko was looking upward and onward. More and more was happening beyond Kafe Parus and Kosa Lyapina Island. More and more was happening under Kyrylo's management.

As in France, bank accounts swelled as did (wanted or not) visibility. Voldoymyr and Kyrylo were in an unusual and possibly an unenviable situation. They had one foot inside and one foot outside. They were part of Domov, yet they weren't.

Voldoymyr's position was honestly a hybrid—a "tribrid," he thought. He was master of some of his affairs, but he had two other masters—the organization and the clan.

Most ominously and most imperatively, there was Domov. He appreciated that he was a functional tool for the organization's work albeit not totally clear on all the functions he served, but he was a minor player with no real standing. He played exclusively defense so as not to commit a serious *faux pas*, offense was for those players much higher up the pecking order.

Voldoymyr was a distant relative literally and figuratively.

He had been able to get into the business because of his family ties and also because of his existing assets. Kafe Parus (not unlike Maquis Maman Afrique) was a purlieu for a cross-section of individuals linked in any of multitude of ways to Domov. It was a transaction hub.

Some of the interactions taking place at the *Kafe* involved the complex movement of items through Kosa Lyapina Island—only part of this falling completely within Voldoymyr's purview. This in-and-out of Domov (what Voldoymyr drolly occasionally thought of as multiple personality syndrome) was a main principle of the trifecta that had become the set of enterprises established by Artem's senior brother's nephew and now run by his son Kyrylo.

The third leg of the stool involved work done for the clan independent of that involving the organization. True to its origins, the clan continued to traffic in a wide selection of material, and Kosa Lyapina Island was an important node in their network.

This triad had been a juggling act— Voldoymyr developing finely tuned skills to balance action so as to benefit his own family without aggravating or irritating any of the other essential actors. It was yet to be seen if Kyrylo could find the same equilibrium.

Nevertheless, perhaps a bit naively, Kyrylo relished his new responsibilities. For years he had been at his father's side—feeling he was more in his shadow. Now, as Voldoymyr, the deft juggler, settled into the back row to be more of an observer than a driver, Kyrylo energetically grabbed the reins.

Less traditional, less constrained, Kyrylo felt a need to prove his worth—to make a show of his taking the helm. He expanded his father's networks to include more younger folk such as himself. He explored new options and new markets. Then, feeling no license from anywhere was needed, he set about remodeling things into what he considered to be a modern and more profitable structure.

The first piece of this new architecture was weapons. The Ukraine-Russian zone was rife with weaponry. Others in sister subsets of the various organizations, clans, or Domov, such as Radutu Botezatu, as Kyrylo knew well, had already set in place channels for arms movements following the sea lanes across the Tahanroz'ka Gulf and all the way to the port of Faro and thence to the four points of the compass. With his enlarged network, it was a relatively simple matter for Kyrylo to make the arrangements to insert his own merchandise into this conduit—arrangements that made complete business sense to the new Chief of Kosa Lyapina but arrangements made without bringing on board or even seeking consensus from the Rudenko family's traditional partners.

Soon all manner of weapon was moving out of the island for the world's hotspots while Kyrylo reveled in his swelling bank accounts—accounts that his father had long since ceased to follow. However, others were following from afar and, as Kyrylo made more and more single-handed agreements, he appeared oblivious of his observers.

⚘⚘⚘⚘⚘⚘⚘

Rodney, understandably, had no firsthand knowledge of the goings-on in Kosa Lyapina Island, the Tahanroz'ka Gulf of the Sea of Azov, the Îles du Frioul that announced the *Feu de la digue Sainte Marie* at the entry to the Port of Marseille, nor the Canal de Vridi leading to the Port of Abidjan—he was now far removed from the field. He had little direct experience dealing with the multitude of convoluted trade routes that crisscrossed the seas. But he had detailed and personal experience with the impact of the products—chiefly illicit products—that were traded across these routes.

His beloved Hal had given his life to try to stamp out these ruinous yet immensely profitable pathways and markets. His own niece, Denice, had died of an overdose that was traced back to opium from Afghanistan.

The traders and despots using these avenues and trafficking in this merchandise represented a serious assault on everyone's health and well-being.

Rodney understood all too well the stakes and understood, whatever the odds, his team must win this battle.

Rodney did not share the religious zeal of Felix. Rodney was a pragmatist.

Rodney knew Group 8 and D-2 had to continue and continue with a high-level of support—even if this was clandestine (quiet undisclosed advocacy often more impactful than blaring political prattle). He knew he had to have the support of Sullivan's Committee, and he knew his presentation was likely a pivot point as to whether or not this group of time-hardened politicians would want to invest not only the proceeds of the people's purse but (critically) their own political futures on the success or failure of DOJ when confronting a massive transglobal criminal conglomerate.

The pressure, therefore, was high when Rodney delivered his presentation to Sullivan and his committee. In the end, it was a perfunctory exchange, Rodney sketching the status with simply the slightest background (assuming, he knew probably incorrectly, the senators already had a good foundation on the topic), the panel only asking a few essential yet easy-to-answer operational questions (possibly the ignorance-is-bliss syndrome in play). Then, with convoluted promises (empty or not) for eventual full budgetary support and an equal dose of political backing, the congressional hearing was over and Rodney was back at his desk, as always, trying to filter fact from fiction.

As Rodney briefed Felix and tried to forecast an unforecastable future, INTERPOL liaison agents for both Group 8 and D-2 received tips from their contacts within the global agency advising of a significant uptick in trafficking of all nature of products from people to pot. Some of this was attributed to the intensification of Domov activities—a group they too were closely watching, yet a group with which they too were more times than not baffled and feeling inept—a somewhat known entity. But where there were now also signs of new offshoots that were entering into new markets with new actors. It was troubling.

The INTERPOL contacts were able to offer two specific examples of this amplification: a group from the West Coast of Africa now moving into Europe engaged, among others, in human trafficking; and an additional flow of weapons out of the Sea of Azov, further contributing to the already flourishing arms trade in that area, that also appeared to be supplying markets as far away as Peru.

Rodney and Felix assigned agents to dig deeper into these tips.

They hoped for actionable intelligence. Yet, so often, they felt like they were chasing their own tail, spinning into vertigo.

CHAPTER 7

PUSHING AHEAD

"Success usually comes to those who are too busy to be looking for it."

—Henry David Thoreau

Useful Disorder

OREST was unclear about criminality and being a criminal.

If someone had asked him about being a lawbreaker (and no one ever would), and if he had been familiar with Nelson Mandela (which he wasn't), he might have answered using Mandela's words: "When a man is denied the right to live the life he believes in, he has no choice but to become an outlaw."

Going back to the roots of the Gruppirovki crime groups and the ill-matched tug-of-war between the *shliakhta* and the common folk, Orest would defend the past and support the present by reciting the family adage that they had done what they had needed to do to be able to survive—survive poverty, cruel nobility, two world wars, and a heartless communist system.

This is not to say Orest spent a lot of time on introspection. He did not.

Things were as they were and there was no shortage of daily emergencies with which to deal.

As was the case for all in Domov (or at least as was the prevailing fundamental management assumption which was an all-encompassing priority affecting all), Orest was keenly aware that all in the complex coalition were very much the objects of the agents of law enforcement, regulators, and other forces of order across six continents. This was, of course, an omnipresent concern. It was a threat.

However, in his eyes, and the eyes of most of the senior leadership, this threat was eclipsed by the threat from competitors—visible and invisible.

The Russian Vorovskoy Mir along with its extralegal cousins and clones had been active in Russian criminality since the Imperial period. Of late, however, these groups with similar histories to the Gruppirovki were overshadowed by the even more dramatic and enigmatic Solntsevskaya Bratva—all the Russian cartels consistently sparing with Domov over the years. Naturally, this was not just an Eastern European affair. There were crime families and syndicates everywhere.

However, unlike in the time of Andriy when gentlemen's agreements were respected and people were satisfied with their slice of the pie, now there were immense, unimaginable profits at stake and the aim of global hegemony a true possibility. The same ever-changing technologies that made it increasingly easier for constabularies around the world to track and even capture ill-doers also made it easier for these very ill-doers to gain more and more terrain and attain more and more power. From this voracious new playing field, there was no retirement nor amicable merger—you fought and survived, or you were gone.

This battle was growing more complex, more difficult to oversee. As Domov developed tertiary and, in some cases, quadrivial layers of actors, close centralized command and control was fast slipping away. Diversification and siloing were good for business and good to enhance the organization's cloaking efforts, but they had drawbacks. Compartmentalization was frequently necessary, but it absolutely hindered the heightened degree of global oversight that had heretofore helped Domov imperceptibly seep into the furthest corners of the world's economy.

In the daily chaos and disorder that seemed to entangle the globe, Orest attempted to outcompete his rivals in plain sight. After all, directly or indirectly, Domov (and its challengers) aimed to provide products and support to the average citizen as they slogged ahead through their everyday struggles. Orest thought of his business as a great emporium that was everywhere and so commonplace that it completely blended into its surroundings, attracting the needed clients without calling attention of the unwanted regulators and adversaries.

Yet, in spite of his best efforts, things were slipping away—or so it seemed.

Although, under Orest's watchful eye, Domov had escalated its activities significantly, had this growth come at too high a cost? Had the *Maliar* miscalculated? Had he misled?

Holwerd as the nub of a global hydra had met expectations—at the same time being invisible yet well-connected. But the shores of the North Sea were far from the Domov epicenters that required most of the *Maliar's* attention. Although information technology was improving at an unbelievably fast rate, Orest was of the opinion that the more one relied on long-distance reporting the more one risked being told what he or she wanted to hear rather than what reflected the on-the-ground reality. Nonetheless, the facts were what they were. When one sat at the pinnacle, there was only so much direct oversight that could be expected. The base of the pyramid that supported this apogee was no longer the Dnieper Basin, it now circumscribed much of the known regions of the planet. The *Maliar*, though far from a figurehead, could not exert, could not be expected to apply, direct operational management. There was a hierarchy, and it had to work—it had to support the base and bring the power and the treasure back to the vertex, even if this fastigium was on the damp and weathered beaches of the North Sea.

The often windy and raw seashore was, at least psychologically, closer to the North American portion of the hierarchy than those parts situated in the distant corners of an atlas. It's often cloudy and grey maritime umbrella was a stark reminder to Orest of the need for Domov to be tightly cloaked in spite of the never-ending efforts of so many to pull back the curtain—to shine light into the shadows. It was a constant and nearly overwhelming challenge requiring the support of many.

Hans van den Berghe had, of course, reported back to the *Maliar* after his visit to the Făgăraș Mountains. Orest was aware, as he had been since assuming his duties, of the potentially critical role Joe played—fascinated by the insight of his predecessors to transplant two young men into coal country—reminiscent of the rumored "illegals program" of sleeper child spies planted in the US by the Russian Directorate S within the Foreign Intelligence Service.

For his part, Joe increasingly appreciated how he was a segment, a crucial segment, of a greater whole. He accepted his responsibilities and understood his assignment had been planned and undertaken to reap important harvests. He realized his participation in the Easter meeting and discussions with that core group headed by Radutu Botezatu had been part theater and part a directive: he had to expand.

More was needed.

He considered he had a mandate that would translate into the needed support and resources to do the necessary. Establishing a bigger but unseen footprint required a major adjustment from the low level of engagement that had so far been the focus of his efforts, supplying hard-pressed mining communities with their needs by whatever means possible.

This ramping up would require a total realignment of his life, but he had been sent to do whatever was necessary to implement the steps as designed by the organization and he was there to do just that.

He and Susan strategized—she had been a valued partner throughout the voyage. They would stay in Pottsville; they now had roots and a history that would hopefully deflect any unwanted attention. However, Joe would resign from Fallon Anthracite Company, saying he wanted to get into private business. As his parallel and more clandestine work had heretofore been supplying the community with all manner of items, it was rather an open secret that he had been a conduit for a variety of goods and services. Therefore, it made sense, he posited, to start a company: S&J Logistics. This would not be their entire American operation, just an initial move in that direction.

Susan, though a prized advisor, would stay in the background and carry on with her life as usual. Harold, however, would be formally and openly brought in as a key executive of S&J—the story being he was taking up the slack because Joe was not as young as he used to be (believable and to a large degree true).

From the onset, S&J significantly increased the variety and volume of products they supplied to coal country vendors—mostly buying in bulk from major East Coast suppliers and distributing to small local retailers. In this scenario, it also made sense that they needed warehouse space. They devised a design where they would build facilities that were two-thirds public mini storage units and one-third commercial storage. Ballooning materialism translated into a reality whereby even depressed miners found they had more stuff than they could accommodate, and they needed to rent affordable extra storage. Small- and medium-sized bargain-basement-priced units for home overflow were in high demand.

When Harold had been in seventh grade, Joe had taken him on a trip to Philadelphia to visit the Philadelphia Art Museum (not visiting Father Philip, by then first assistant to the bishop of the Ukrainian Catholic Archdiocese of Philadelphia. Philip's contact with his blood family as opposed to his now much closer religious family was generally limited to a perfunctory annual post-Easter visit to Pottsville).

Joe was certainly no art connoisseur, but he had felt a visit to a prominent museum was good exposure for a kid otherwise living in a rather cloistered mining community with much shallower cultural roots than many of their European counterparts. On the day of their visit, there was an exposition of statuary on loan from the Vatican. Looking up at a statue of Apollo with his genitalia covered by a fig leaf, Harold asked Joe, "What's the leaf for?"

"It covers natural things that some people don't want to be seen," Joe's reply.

"If it's natural," Harold continued, "why don't folks want it seen?"

"That's how it is," Joe responded. "Natural or not, sometimes people just prefer to keep things hidden although a lotta folks still know what's hidden. People can be funny that way."

Remembering this exchange, Joe decided they would start a second business that would focus on the warehousing facilities: Fig Leaf Storage. Harold shortened it to just FLS.

Joe and Harold smiled to themselves at their insiders' joke. Just as patrons of the museum might wish to lift Apollo's fig leaf, but could not, some might wish to uncover the inner works of FLS. The Mitchell's hoped their own leaf was just as immutable as was Apollo's stone covering.

The basic architecture of a post-Delpro North American operation began taking shape. While different cells or components would need supervisors vetted by Domov at the highest levels, there was a real need for foot-soldiers who would concentrate on the routine daily work that would be the difference between success and failure.

It was Susan who had a novel approach for the people needed to make the machinery function: foreign students. She suggested they identify foreign students on an education visa that would expire at the end of their studies but who wanted to stay in the States. There were a lot of folks in this category. Yet, changing the student visa to a work visa was difficult. Numerous of these now unregistered hangers-on quietly just ended-up persisting and finding a job. Many employers did not ask about immigration status and rarely were there identity checks for the citizenry that would uncover individuals in-country under expired visas. They simply stayed.

These people, Susan opined, would be motivated to work hard, would accept lower wages, and, if things did not work out, were basically disposable (a quick call to INS could make them disappear).

It worked.

They did not want to connect with students too close to home. Harold (who was proving himself to be a very smooth operator) developed a spiel that he would spin with the International Students Office or the equivalent at campuses across the country. He professed to represent a charity that was interested in linking foreign students coming from the same endemic areas, so they did not feel so cutoff from their homeland and their culture. With few further questions, most of these offices promptly mailed a list of their international student body with some general details about date of arrival and anticipated departure as well as area of study.

They had all they needed.

As the pieces slowly began falling into place, it became obvious that the new operations would be very different from Delpro. The former McCandless firms had been principally focused overseas with limited on-the-ground activities and investments in the US. This was not to say they had not done business (and maneuvered transactions) in the States—they had—they were wont never to let a good opportunity slip away. But their main targets had been offshore as a way of distancing the precise locales of the most ignominious misdeeds from those pulling the strings from afar—a literal extension of keeping things at arm's length.

Unlike Robin, Joe's concerns were fully focused on North America, principally the US. Each region had its own specificity. Joe now understood that the US liked to think of itself as being more in control without the heavy-handedness it criticized in other quarters—having the needed authority without hindering the much-valued perception of liberty. This almost paradoxical philosophy left lots of holes and gaps to exploit if one had the time to uncover the weaknesses that were often camouflaged by a patina of self-righteousness

It was like finding the right foot to fit Cinderella's slipper. As Joe, Susan, and Harold methodically developed a bare-bones blend of enterprises that just maybe could effectively deliver goods and services from coast to coast. They knew they needed to carefully strategize, and they needed to scrupulously identify those goods and services to deliver and to whom.

They were designing and building a foundation that had to be able to bear the weight of major renovations and expansion.

It was more than structure and function. Joe recalled Radutu Botezatu's admonition as they parted, quoting Tolstoy, "The two most powerful warriors are patience and time...so remember, great achievements take time, there is no overnight success."

Still, success was the aim, and it seemed attainable.

Joe and Susan had come a long way from when they had had to collect Green and Gold Bond Stamps to be able to get a new electric frying pan.

Much like his Big Boss, Joe did not spend much time thinking about whether or not his planned (assigned) activities were legal or illegal, moral or immoral. As he told Susan and Harold, "We've got a helluva job ahead of us. Let's not get bogged down by worrying a lot about tomorrow's possibilities—good or bad—but concentrate one hundred percent on today's tasks just to reach tomorrow."

Joe, along with Susan and Harold, did spend a lot of time planning. They created a sort of war room in the basement. They knew where they needed to go, they just didn't know exactly how to get there.

The skeleton began putting on muscle.

After weeks of examination and exploration, they had a blueprint.

As the endgame was a countrywide diversified and discretely shrouded operation, they decided to start in two zones that could be springboards for a national or even transnational scheme. The first zone, based in Pottsville and overseen by Joe, would cover the Mid-Atlantic, going west into Ohio and south into Kentucky, but avoiding the chaos of New York City at the onset. The second, headed up by Harold, would be based in Durango, Colorado, and cover the Southeast as well as Utah, Kansas, and Oklahoma, and much of Texas—skirting the metropoles of Dallas and Houston for the moment.

These zones covered a large part of the American demographic and would provide insight as to which products were the most appropriate, where there could be pushback, and what level of control could be anticipated. These would be action zones for S&J Logistics, initially looking at institutional clients and using these to get an open and solid foothold in various wholesale markets while they closely studied the parallel clandestine market channels.

Once there was a modicum of business established in a specific community, they would begin the process of diversifying by preparing buildings for FLS. The ties between S&J and FLS would be public—both entities being set-up in concurrence with relevant local codes, regulations, and policies. Everything would be above board.

They would offer support positions at S&J and FLS to selected ex-students with Joe and Harold assuming direct management of all operations while Susan would find time in her already busy schedule to keep a common set of books to coordinate between the two zones.

This required, obviously, a lot of capital—far more than the rather paltry assets to which the Mitchell family currently had access. But this was not a problem.

The entire project had the ardent support of Orest and the senior leadership. Money was not an issue—getting the funds into Joe's hands unnoticed could be a challenge. Large sums were required to simultaneously support all the foreseen actions.

This required a multi-pronged approach.

Domov fully bought a bank in Kentucky (Cumberland Savings) and another in Kansas (Great Plains and Western Bank) to channel a portion of the needed resources with an eye to buy more investment firms if need be. They also guaranteed loans to S&J and FLS through other banks where they had no direct control but some political influence. Finally, they created the Kindred Helping Hands Foundation in Arkansas, ostensibly as a charitable organization to assist the needy but in reality, yet another pathway to expand their geographic imprint and surreptitiously disseminate important levels of funding.

The soon-to-be nationally recognized foundation was built on a completely contrived story crafted late one night by Susan. Augustus Hill Garland had been an Arkansas governor and senator before becoming US attorney general under Grover Cleveland in 1885—his memory still fondly cherished across the state. With this historical base, they invented a Garland cousin named Avery Abercrombie, according to the tale they spun, a rich businessman who passed a fortune to several generations of Abercrombies before the final sole spinster survivor donated all her wealth to helping the poor through the new Kindred Helping Hands Foundation.

With the foundation, labeled KHHF by Harold with his penchant for shorthand, there was a trio of operations plus two satellite banks to begin reestablishing a repurposed Domov labyrinth in the United States.

Practically, it was decided to put most immediate effort in the western zone. While the fact that they were established community members in Pottsville helped the family shift from being seen as part of the mining industry to being private entrepreneurs, this transition had to be slow and follow tracts they had already hone into the local landscape over the years. Change had to be deliberate and modulated so as not to attract too much of the wrong type of attention.

In Durango, the slate was clean—they could build exactly what they wanted without needing to protect any past efforts or old contacts. This was Harold's job, and he was more than a little anxious to get it underway.

The new Domov skein being imagined by Joe, Susan, and Harold did not include all the Mitchell family. As throughout, by design Anna and David were not part of the team. This was not to exclude them but to protect them. Joe and Susan knew their covert activities posed real risks and even possible dangers. While Harold seemed strangely adept at these subrosa exercises, Anna and David had studiously carved out relatively normal lives for themselves and the rest of the family did not want to put these in jeopardy. The entire family understood the juggling act and the don't-ask-don't-tell philosophy. There were curtains that were never drawn back.

After graduating from Shippensburg University with a degree in economics and a concentration in political science, Anna had taken a job as an assistant city manager for the City of Sacramento, heading up the Office of Innovation and Economic Development. In all senses of the word, she was far from Pottsville.

David had stayed closer to home. His job at Energy Elite had been his centerpiece until he had met Oriana and until he had fallen off his bike. His extended recuperation and his moving into his lover's apartment had changed everything. As his bruised and abraded body began to heal, his soul became affixed to Oriana. She was his new epicenter.

The gods, however, seemed to smile on this union. Energy Elite proved to be an accommodating employer in many ways. They had an office in Elizabeth, New Jersey—a half-hour train ride from Penn Station. Once back to full form, therefore, David transferred from Reading to Elizabeth. Thereafter, when Oriana went off to the paper, David took the train to New Jersey—both of them completely unaware of the plans of Joe, Susan, and Harold.

Though no one who knew was surprised, Robin McCandless would have been surprised—probably livid—if he had known that a new American network was being set-up with absolutely no regard for, nor seemingly any lessons learnt from, in his view, a very successful and profitable network he had established and run for years.

Though withdrawn from nearly all routine activities and responsibilities, Robin considered himself as an emeritus officer. He considered himself as being on standby when needed. In spite of being contacted less and less by former colleagues, he kept in regular contact with his brother Horace and his long-time protégée Cynthia Owens. He felt he still had his fingers on the pulse of Domov as had been clearly demonstrated by the unquestionable significant accomplishments of Delpro thanks to his tireless leadership. He had been a skilled skipper at the helm of a complex and high-spirited ship. He had been a valued actor then and should be a valued resource now that he was a man of leisure in his most comfortable villa on the shores of the Black Sea at Vama Veche.

This villa welcomed both Horace and Cynthia—sometimes at the same time. The *anciens combattants* would enjoy stiff drinks and soft cushions as they looked out across the sandy beaches, turquoise shoreline, and diminutive breakers to a blue-black sea that seemed as unfathomable as their daily existence. As much as they wanted to look to the future—a bright and rewarding future—they felt they were only hanging on in the present and were forced to relish the past if they were to find any tranquil moments as they sipped their biting highballs and nibbled on savory plates of grilled Rapana—a local much-appreciated seafood—a predatory whelk.

At one such session with both his guests present, Robin explained the irony of their snack. The Rapana fed principally on clams. The snail would literally smother its prey with its large and fluid body. So, Robin observed, did Domov try to smother its clients and competitors, even its employees—wrapping them up so tightly they had few choices, all of which benefited the massive if enigmatic conglomerate. When the whelk had sucked its dinner dry, it would cast away the shells much as, after taking its pound of flesh, Domov cast away the dried-up husks of those antagonists with whom it came into contact.

Yet, none of them, McCandless observed, would have been able to enjoy this tasty treat and the delightful sea-breeze without the generosity of a hardened and often heartless Domov. Had they not fallen into the

Domov net, who knew where they would be and what they would be doing?

Many, truly many had been swept up in the Domov net. Some, like Eddie Hall, never really recognizing it, had their lives severely shaken by the ignoble, and at that time unknown, organization. Others, such as Peter Volman, seemed to have had some cursory knowledge of the organization but appeared to have been unwittingly fully caught up in the net as their life was in free fall. Another group, including Charlie Stancik, had seen the transnational cartel as their pathway to achieving their own life goals.

The organization—"the outfit," to use the epithet coined for Al Capone and the Chicago mob in the early twentieth century—was indeed omnipresent if one knew where to look.

The Cisses had found Domov (or, probably more correctly, the organization had found them) while Voldoymyr Rudenko had grown up knowing that Domov or some iteration thereof would be there to help him push his aspirations forward.

This was the advantage of Domov and the genius of its founders. Unlike many competing syndicates, it could be anything to anyone or all things to all takers. It was a true functioning example of mimicry—the biological definition and not the theatrical one—a planned close resemblance to something else in order to gain advantage. On most fronts, Domov went to great efforts to seem, at first glance, like a regular and respectable international corporation. In reality, of course, it was much, much more.

It was this riddle, albeit not yet understanding the full context, that had hooked Oriana. Although righting wrongs was important, it was really solving the puzzle of the mimic versus the mimiced that drove her forward.

Rodney was also driven, but his aims were retribution and justice—in that order.

Droits de l'Homme

ALTHOUGH many were in favor of human rights—in favor of justice—there were not many who knew of the existence of Domov. This was not a terrorist bombing nor a grade school shooting where one could rely on the press to shine a bright light (all too often, a glaring light) on the crimes. These were actions that took place in the darkest, most secluded and cloaked corners of the country. These were actions, in spite of significant negative impacts that touched many, that took place with no one seeing—no one knowing. The press rarely had an opportunity to flash even the tiniest beams into these shrouded spaces. This was about human rights, but the rights of the unseen and the unnamed—the faceless and the forgotten.

The pursuit of justice was not as straightforward as many might have hoped, however. As with nearly any and all topics, it was subject to politicization. Even when supported by fickle politicians, it was subject to budgetary and administrative limitations and regulations. It frequently appeared to be too damn hard to do what was patently the right thing.

This was a frustration common to those engaged in what was broadly categorized as law enforcement. It had certainly been a frustration for Rodney.

In the present case, however, it was thought (hoped) by the powers that be that high-priority action would be expedited, whether by design or default, by the tactics chosen perhaps more by compromise than by cunning. It was a gambit involving a loose administrative structure within DOJ at field level combined with close links to a compact and focused Senate group all overseen by Section T15-Z, avoiding some of the bureaucratic moras that seemed to suck so many into the muddy margins of functionality. D-2 was now perceived as being streamlined and fast-tracked.

However, from Rodney's vantage point, it all appeared to rely on the waffling whims of a detached leadership. It all appeared to depend upon the tenuous ties to Sullivan's group—both in terms of their direct support and in regard to their role in T15-Z and its planned links to the executive branch.

To complicate matters, at least in Rodney's humble opinion, although he was the focal point to the committee, he still had to work with Group 8 and Felix Manchester—both of them thoroughly interwoven into T15-Z. This included double duty while stroking Felix's sometimes tender ego. It required getting the Sullivan Committee's concurrence and capitalization for their joint operations while providing the necessary feedback to Section T15-Z.

These complications were multiplied when there was some backsliding on the original arrangements. Although the ultimate oversight and decision-making was initially planned to be provided by ESGW, a new exclusive emergency management structure that reported directly to the White House with a senior staffer to be named by the president along with an analyst from NSIE, the best intentions often do not materialize. ESGW had apparently been such a good idea that a multifaceted spat between the executive and legislative branches developed—each claiming the other was smashing their toes through an overt abuse of power. The chain of authority and responsibility became a highly disputed grey area. Finally, under pressure and in spite of the Secretary of State's great displeasure, the White House turned over full control of Section T15-Z to the Sullivan Committee as a show of its respect for congressional authority on matters of vital national security (or so the spiel went).

Whether political brinkmanship or good planning, it didn't matter in practical terms. The functions of Section T15-Z were now totally at the mercy of Sullivan and his committee.

It remained to be seen, moreover, if what was being instituted as expeditious and efficient was really an asset or that, in fact, the new protocols were simply adding more unnecessary layers and personalities to a structure that was already cumbersome to say the very least.

Rodney was a traditionalist (his liberal views notwithstanding), ascribing to the "if it ain't broke, don't fix it" ideology. The old crew under his beloved Hal, that very effective team that had torn into Delpro, had been known as BTF— the Bratva Task Force (this before they even knew of the existence of Domov and were considering Delpro as a US subsidiary of

Solntsevskaya Bratva). BTF had had a lot of autonomy, ample resources, and had got the job done. Not a bad model, Rodney thought.

But there was no going back.

His present team was seasoned and competent. As everyone transitioned to the new way of doing business, Rodney felt D-2 could move forward in the immediate on their own inertia; there were a lot of leads to follow and cases to build. At the same time, he needed to partially pull back from his direct supervisory responsibilities, shifting effort to assessing and building a workable and positive relationship with his operational linchpin (or contender): Senator Sullivan.

While he had already taken a perfunctory look into the honorable senator's background earlier when first enjoined to connect to the committee, he now, in the relative security and tranquility of his office, took a deep dive into the man who could determine to a large extent how successful their efforts would be to corral Domov.

As stated in his official congressional bio, Senator Jacob Sullivan had supposedly been brought up in Culpeper County, Virginia, and was in his fourth term as a senator representing the good people of Culpeper and Virginians in general. Jacob Sullivan happily portrayed himself as a man of the people and a history buff to boot—consistently reminding constituents that he was well-placed; after all, the town of Culpeper had first been surveyed by a seventeen-year-old George Washington (unclear as to the exact relationship between Washington's surveying skills and Sullivan's political craftsmanship—but no one ever asked).

According to public records, the senator had been married to the former Rebecca Jameson, a Culpeper native, for over thirty years; the couple had two grown children—a son who was a dentist in Wayne, Oklahoma, and a daughter who was a high school chemistry teacher in Detroit. Rebecca was a distant relative of Captain John Jameson who had commanded the Culpeper Minutemen in the Revolutionary War and had continued on to become a major Virginia landowner with political leverage that corresponded with his real estate holdings. As far as anyone knew, this leverage had filtered down to Rebecca's family and her storybook marriage to the Honorable Senator Sullivan.

Personal accounts often used by the Sullivan political machine indicated that the senator's father, Drew, had moved south from Stockerton, Pennsylvania, as a young man—in true American fashion, seeking his fortune and his legacy. The original family home from which young Drew had migrated was reputably somehow linked to the Sullivan Trail which traversed the Wyoming Valley and passed through the town of Stockerton. The trail was named after General John Sullivan, a thirty-nine-year-old, New Hampshire-born lawyer, who, in late 1779 under George Washington—at that time an older and wiser man—had led a campaign against Iroquois Indians and the British fortresses in Oswego and Niagara. Although there was no substantive proof of the Pennsylvania Sullivans being related to the New Hampshire Sullivans, the senator was known to connect these dots on more than a few occasions.

In point of fact, the legislator's statements to the contrary, as Rodney dug through the archives, there was no evidence tying Jacob Sullivan to any family named Sullivan ever having lived in Stockerton (or New Hampshire for that matter).

Unable to find any spore of the popularly proposed lineage of Virginia's senior senator, Rodney widened his lens and focused on Drew. With access to a trove of data, the ardent investigator swept the broader geography assumed to the home range for Sullivan or his ancestors, looking particularly at a swath of counties that covered much of Appalachia from southern Pennsylvania, through West Virginia, Virginia, and Kentucky. He found records that a coal miner named Conor Sullivan, a locally known union organizer, had had a son named Drew. The family had lived in Johnson County Kentucky, in the town of Van Lear, named for Van Lear Black, a coal company executive.

Conor had died of unknown circumstances when his son was sixteen; this unexplained death was formally logged as unexpected and suspicious, the reason for the murky record that Rodney was later able to uncover. At the time of his death, in addition to Drew, Conor left five fatherless children.

Rodney then found court records from Prestonsburg in Floyd County for multiple cases of breaking and entering charged against Drew Sullivan. He had ultimately been found guilty of all charges but in a plea to the court, citing his responsibilities to provide food for his mother's table now that his father had passed, he had been given a reduced sentence of three years' incarceration with five years' probation thereafter. During this probationary period, with the help of his probation officer, Drew got a job as a groundskeeper at the city park behind the Prestonsburg post office. His probation file showed he married a widow, Sheila Ledbetter who had two children. Drew and Shiela then had another child together and named him Jacob. As rather an afterthought, the reporting officer added that Shiela, a devout Baptist, fondly remembered Genesis 28 from

Sunday School: "God promised Jacob lands and numerous offspring that would prove to be the blessing of the entire Earth" (as she recalled her teacher's interpretation). In honor of this passage, as she herself had told the officer, she had named her son Jacob (thereafter keeping her fingers crossed, Rodney imagined, smiling to himself).

It seemed the blessings of God for Drew and Shiela were fleeting if not imaginary. Rodney found death certificates for the couple, killed at a railroad crossing near Eriline in Clay County by a westbound freight.

In Rodney's current harvest of documents, the last set focused on Jacob himself. He had been ten at the time of his parents' death. Apparently, there were no adult family members to raise the young boy; his two half-siblings old enough to strike out on their own and apparently chosing to do so. By unclear means, Jacob ended up in with a foster family in the community of California, Pennsylvania, outside Pittsburg. He attended California Area Elementary School after which there were no records until he and Rebecca applied for a marriage license.

It looked as if the good senator's backstory was quite different from the biography spelled out in flowery prose on the fliers that were disseminated in advance of every election. Still, Rodney knew this was a delicate and potentially risky subject. Records went missing. Not everyone, thankfully, had a complete paper trail. While it appeared the gentleman had misrepresented his early years, this was not in and of itself a crime and perhaps the would-be politician saw his youth and family as unseemly and detrimental to his political ambitions. He certainly would not be the first public figure to polish his life's story and bend the facts to paint a picture more in line with what one deemed to be acceptable to the population upon which one depended for one's livelihood, standing, and prestige. Wasn't the first rule of politics telling people what they want to hear?

The descendent of a valiant Indian fighter was much more impressive than the offspring of a burglar who was raised in foster care.

Rodney had to be careful.

⚘⚘⚘⚘⚘⚘⚘

Jacob Sullivan (Jake to his friends, and he hoped everyone was his friend) was, naturally, totally unaware of Rodney's conundrum. He had his own conundrum: Gage Smith—so far only a curt (he would actually call it "rude"), faceless voice. Shortly after his recent phone call with this inscrutable and inescapable pain in his side, he had received an invitation for an exclusive fundraising event at the Mount Vernon Yacht Club, just across Dogue Creek from the cyclopean Fort Belvoir—the US Army facility housing nearly a dozen military agencies and centers with more employees than the Pentagon and, in the mid-eighteenth century, home to the powerful Fairfax family and former site of the 2,200-acre Belvoir Plantation.

Events such as this fundraiser were not infrequent. They were, however, generally muted, with little fanfare as some of the participants would rather remain anonymous in terms of their political support. The more elitist the venue, the more laconic and hushed the event. In this case, it was very top-drawer and very aphonic.

The senator expected this to involve meeting a number of the rich and powerful, those considered as the captains of industry and finance in the country—from his funders' perspective, an opportunity for a sort of stealthy reality check to make sure their man was on the same page with them on all the key issues of the day. As anticipated, the influential and the puissant were gathered at the Yacht Club—so was Gage Smith.

There was the requisite brief status report from the lectern where the senator slowly, with an accented drawl, verbalized all the wonderful things he had done since their last meeting—things which were, of course, no news to those assembled. This was all show and no tell. The critical portion of the occasion was the Q&A session that followed the formal banal production. The questions and the questioners were of the utmost importance to the senator and a measure of his ability to keep his high-roller coalition squarely behind him. He and his staffers carefully recorded who said what. While his public replies were rather mundane, the senator or one of his chief staffers would reach out personally and attentively to the individuals in question during the cocktail period that followed the humdrum public performance. It was there and then that the core concerns were dissected—hopefully to the mutual satisfaction of both parties.

As Jake Sullivan was preparing to engage his crucial backers with a mint julep in one hand, a firm handshake ready in the other, and a beaming smile on his face, he felt the slightest tap on his shoulder. Turning, he saw a lanky nondescript gentleman.

"Senator Sullivan, sir, do you have a minute?" asked an unsmiling, nattily dressed, middle-aged man, who could have been anyone anywhere.

"Of course, sir."

Silence.

"Ah, Mister?" the senator enquired.

"Gage Smith, sir."

The polished politician tried to keep his face expressionless as he followed this interloper away from the pack of supporters and sponsors.

The two strolled to the large balcony overlooking the boat basin connected to Dogue Creek, the crooked marina channel that joined the streambed reminding the senator for no apparent reason of the neck of a Chesapeake Bay quahog clam. The men feigned interest in the wide assortment of rich-men's toys that bobbed softly in the oil-stained waters as the uninvited Gage Smith quickly drove his point home.

"Senator," Smith began in a gruff voice that he was obviously trying hard to sweeten. "My friends and I wish you success at today's event."

"Why, thank you . . ."

"Of course, whatever windfalls you reap will be modest compared to the reliable and regular support you receive from my colleagues."

"Indeed." Sullivan felt the less said the better, as he was not sure where this was heading nor who exactly were the unpleasant man's colleagues.

"Yes, indeed," Smith said, his tone deepening a bit, "these monies are seen as a wise investment in what is best for all."

"Naturally."

"Well, maybe not so naturally, but in whatever way possible we all understand that there is a quid pro quo. My colleagues and I are, as you know so well, investors—we make what we hope are good investments."

"Certainly."

"We agree, the investments are considerable?"

"Yes, very much so."

"And we all understand that my colleagues and I have very extensive portfolios—many, many things can affect our investments."

"Absolutely."

"We understand from our confederates that you are in a unique position. You are heading up a group that has tremendous influence over some very high-level investigations—investigations that possibly could get a wee bit too close to some of our more sensitive affairs—affairs that we might call 'works in progress'—affairs we really would not want interrupted, sidetracked, or examined too fully. This could truly develop into a problem. We clearly would not want this to happen, would we?"

"Definitely not."

"Definitely not—positively 'definitely not.' Some of my colleagues are not as polite nor as patient as I. They wanted me to be very insistent. However, I assured them that you were a very savvy gentleman who would quickly grasp the imperatives in front of us. I guaranteed my colleagues your cooperation would be immediately forthcoming. I hope I wasn't wrong?"

"Surely sir, you have correctly reflected the situation to your colleague."

"Good to know, Senator." The emissary seemed to carefully weigh his next statement, "Ya see, some of my colleagues think we never should have come here—invested so much in a tattered—their words, not mine— Appalachian politician. They said to me, 'Ya'd think a guy like good ol' Jake with all that baggage would be more careful, not wanting to get involved in stuff like this and be able to keep us all outta the mud—seeing he's supposed to be such an astute politician and all . . . '"

Gage's stare captured the legislator. Jake Sullivan said nothing.

"These folks I work with, you know, they can be kinda a tough bunch. They keep saying unseemly, kinda uncouth actually, things about having you by the testicles and it only taking a few more missteps—the rougher chaps among them calling 'em 'fuck-ups'—for you to feel the snip."

Another uncomfortable moment of silence.

"I've assured my somewhat choleric colleagues that no one is better placed than you, what with your long and glorious career and all, to make sure things don't get out of hand and to button-up this unwanted investigation quickly, with no mess. I hope I have not misled my colleagues?"

"You have not, *sir*."

"Wonderful. With that, I'll leave you to your harvesting that I know you do so well as I have other affairs awaiting my attention."

"I bid you a good day, *sir* ."

"Back at ya."

As Gage Smith left the deck, Senator Jake Sullivan exhaled a great hot breath of uneasiness. In what bed had he lain?

The good Senator Sullivan, Jacob on his birth certificate, remembered what his mother used to say, "Boy you're in a pickle now." Indeed, he was—stuck in the middle of the chicken coop between the fox and the hens. It was not too hard to connect the dots. Gage represented Domov and the Section T15-Z team was dead-set on bringing Domov to heel.

For the Senator in the middle, this had all the signs of a potentially ruinous situation—both Gage Smith and Rodney Mills were determined to be undeterred.

⚘⚘⚘⚘⚘⚘⚘

Orest had no direct knowledge of Gage Smith's day-to-day efforts, nor should he have had. He was only personally involved—only personally participated in discussions with parties outside his core Holwerd team—when there were very special circumstances that necessitated the *Maliar* himself to engage. These were rare.

The chain of command was, candidly, imperfect. Nonetheless, it generally worked well enough. There was a rather rigid hierarchy and expectedly well-defined designations of roles, relationships, and responsibilities. All of this was encompassed in a philosophical if not a strategic consensus as to the best means to achieve their common ends—the ends being the continued accumulation of as close to unrestricted power and wealth as possible—the means being to do whatever was necessary.

Early in Orest's tenure there had been extraordinary meetings, mostly in Holwerd, with senior staff and devoted advisors about the situation in North America in general and the US in particular. From the original plans of Mykola and Yegor, even going back to Andriy and Lehya, this area had been a pivotal piece of the structure that was to become the Domov mosaic. Delpro had been a highlight but, given this region's global economic and political status, there had been a wide variety of other actions that had all been affected by the vanishing of Delpro. Now everything relied on their relatively new implants in the US. Everything relied on Joe—there were no real contingency plans. This was why Joe had been invited to the Easter meeting. This was why Orest had relied on Radutu Botezatu to impress on Joe the essential nature of his work.

Hopefully, Joe understood well, that the American presence crucially needed to be firmly reestablished—expanded. Domov's American footprint needed to be greatly enlarged since, as the saying went, they "covered the world" (and it was not an advertisement for paint).

Nonetheless, this was but one part, albeit a critical part, of the mosaic.

Orest had to be (as a presence if not in-person) everywhere all the time. Omnipresence was difficult, of course—verging on the impossible.

An essential component of the *Maliar's* work was prioritizing—the priorities often changing in the blink of an eye.

His direct attention was immediately focused on hoped-for once-in-a-lifetime opportunities in West Africa identified (hopefully correctly) some time back by Sir Horace. The old incorrigible would-be nobleman still cavorted around, mostly in Africa, but was spending increasingly more time with his brother on the seashore. Even though generally fading from the field, the aging rogue was as clever as any and could ferret out a deal after capturing just the faintest scent on the wind.

Horace had emphasized a project years in the making—a very large roads and bridges project joining Nigeria and Cameroon. A major infrastructure project skirting some of the richest oil fields anywhere around. There was a multiplicity of opportunities from getting involved in the construction itself to being principals in setting up new markets opened due to the roadwork, not to mention the expanded black-market trade that would inevitably bloom with new access to this heretofore remote and rich region. It was not the proverbial goldmine, but it was seemingly a real chance to make significant profits.

This project did not fit nicely into one of the Domov silos—at least, not yet. Orest decided to take the exceptional steps of assigning someone from his own team to the initial explorative work. Chakir Awal had, from the time he joined the family, been someone who thought outside the box. His early investments in agriculture in the Netherlands had developed models for highly profitable integrated farming that could be and were replicated around the world—especially in the Middle East and the southern parts of Eastern Europe. These activities had, furthermore, been examples of how Domov could benefit from both ends of the supply chain—they controlled the inputs and marketed the products.

Chakir Awal would be a good person to assess the realistic expectations from this new potential action in West Africa.

For his part, Chakir was most pleased (his reserved personality precluded him saying something like "really excited"). This was an opportunity to get out of the more or less routine work of Holwerd and plunge into a project where he had professional freedom (and responsibility) and where he could, he was sure, really have an impact.

Chakir recruited some contacts with known capabilities and set up a shell company in Abidjan called Onyx Associates—an inscrutable appellation named curiously after the blood-red stone found near his ancestral home in the area of Hama.

Orest and the senior management group had felt it was prudent to have an open-to-the-public base of operations outside the target area. Abidjan was far enough away as to be able to totally divorce themselves from actions in Nigeria and Cameroon if they so wished. Abidjan was also cosmopolitan and international enough where a small, ill-defined company would go unnoticed.

Chakir left, therefore, the cool and clammy dampness of the Wadden Sea for the steamy humidity of the lagoons of the "*gemme d'Afrique*."

Chakir's reassignment to Abidjan benefited unexpectedly from his Syrian roots.

Much like the English *colonnes*, who often brought a Southern Asian "B-Team" to help administer their colonies, the French often brought a Lebanese team to assist with critical functions of colonial management. While these Middle Eastern accomplices were frequently from Christian groups, there were no small number of Muslims, many of whom Chakir met on his first day at mosque. Across much of West Africa there was a North-South, Muslim-Christian rift. These colonial period outside managers and entrepreneurs from a country itself often split apart by sectarian violence did not want to bring this factional baggage to their jobs. They separated their public and private lives. Socially, they generally chose to stay within their rather small ethnic and theistic communities—communities which welcomed Chakir as a fellow outsider of shared faith.

With these inroads, he was quickly able to put together a small local squad of seasoned bureaucrats and find some perfunctory work for Onyx Associates in assuming spill-over secretarial and bookkeeping services to bolster several Lebanese-owned businesses and Lebanese-managed services. It was real work, but it was also an effective smokescreen for their manifest *raison d'être*.

This entwining of mandates and activities and weaving together of staff, funds, and facilities was emblematic of how Domov organized itself in the furthest enclaves of the world economy. Here Chakir was putting in practice the strategies and tactics he had overseen so effectively from his perch in Holwerd. It was complex, it could be painstaking, but if often gave good results—at least as far as he had been able to observe from his far-off corner of the arena. Now he himself was centerstage.

⚘⚘⚘⚘⚘⚘⚘

Whether in West Africa, Western Europe, Western US, or anywhere on the globe, it was all about appearances—showing people what they wanted to see. If there was a patina of correctness, of respect for others, it was enough—be it ever so contrived and even flat-out false. In the words of Americana economist and astute political observer Thomas Sowell, "When you want to help people, you tell them the truth. When you want to help yourself, you tell them what they want to hear."

A Bird in the Bush

To a certain extent, of course, everyone wanted to help themselves—it was generally a question of by what means and at what cost.

Gage Smith knew he wanted to and should be able to help himself. He was, after all, allied with a powerful cartel, if not the most powerful cartel to be found. He was, thankfully, in their good graces and had exceptional access to their highest levels—even the *Maliar* under extraordinary situations (a liberty or a responsibility not offered to many).

It would have surprised anyone who had known a young Gage Darius Smith that at some point in his life he would be positioned near any seat of power.

He had started off far from the centers of influence and authority.

He had been born eight years after the end of the Second World War in Alma, Harlan County, Nebraska. He had been born to a single mother although it was well known that his father had been an ex-German POW who, during the war, had been remanded to Camp Atlanta in neighboring Phelps County from where the unfortunate detainee had worked as laborer on a Harlan County corn and soy farm. He had continued to work on this same farm after the war and had fleetingly met Rachael, Gage's mother, who had briefly taken care of the farm's small dairy herd.

The former Third Reich warrior had ultimately drifted away to be absorbed into the chaos of a postwar booming US economy. Rachael had become a housekeeper for one of Alma's grand old families who had grabbed land when the Union Pacific first came through in the 1870s. Gage struggled on, having to suffer, as he saw it, the indignities of the working poor until he would be able to flee with an education and a small grubstake.

Young Gage had learned early on that the path of least resistance was frequently telling people what they wanted to hear. You could be materially poor but rich in spirit.

Gage had always been able to control his emotions—turning off and on nearly at will vicious anger or loving tenderness. He had been a good student, in the top ten percent of his classes at Alma public schools. As a teenager he had been willing to do almost anything if the pay was right. After school, he had quickly found work at a nearby cattle ranch and everyone, including Rachael, figured he'd end up a cowhand like so many local boys (not all that different from Richard Wayne McKnight who was to confront similar options a few years later).

While he hid his feelings well, Gage had had no intention to stick around. He hated cows. He was going on to much grander things, though no one could have detected this ambition from the serious, hard-working kid who diligently helped his mother and never got into serious trouble.

When Gage had turned sixteen, knowing her beloved son had had a scuffle or two on the playground due to his unusual first name (kids can be cruel), Rachael had told him she had given him his name because it was from the French meaning oath—she'd read about it in the public library. She wanted him to know and always to remember that when he had been born, she had taken an oath that her son would do better than she had—her son would be a success.

Gage never forgot.

He took his own oath that he wouldn't end up sweeping up the messes of rich folk.

However, he continued herding cows. He was good at it in spite of his feelings toward the, as he saw them, smelly and noisy critters. It was the environment and not the job itself. The open spaces felt good.

Then, all outward signs notwithstanding, after two years as a ranch hand, Gage took those same rails that had opened up the county years ago and went as far east as he could. After a number of intermediary stops, he ended up in New York City where he was easily able to demonstrate an unscrupulous determination that quickly allowed him to integrate into the unseemlier portions of the socio-economy and endear himself to key personalities in the city's complex criminal hierarchy.

As an outsider in more ways than one, Gage was able and willing to take on unpleasant tasks that could have been problematic if done directly by the major crime families. He was sort of a freelance mobster, and he was good at his work.

The Genovese family increasingly sought his services and valued his professionalism to the point they arranged and paid for him to go to an evening law program at Fordham University. After passing the New York bar, he became a de facto member of the Genovese.

While Gage had had a very diverse portfolio covering an impressive variety of white-collar and not-so-white-collar crimes, in the lead up to the Yugoslav Wars he found his assignments focusing more and more on the Balkans. Relationships between the six republics comprising Yugoslavia declined precipitously after Tito's death in 1980. Things began to fall apart. Gage's adopted family saw opportunities. As patience waned and anger rose, there was high demand for black-market munitions. Then the panic caused by the civil disorder made people consider abandoning homes they never thought they would leave. Amongst the refugees were young women from whom the family could pick and choose the most outstanding and offer them modeling opportunities—modeling a more palatable and even tempting substitute for the true pathway that provided a major influx of new bodies into the family's prostitution businesses.

Gage had his first major encounter with human trafficking.

He did well.

It turned out that he was very adept at strategic thinking. He seemed to be able to undertake an almost 3-D analysis that allowed him to simultaneously plan multiple options and maintain forward momentum in spite of rapidly changing obstacles. It was nearly as though he were clairvoyant.

Gage was a real asset. While assets were advantageous to their owners in their own right, they were also valuable stock in trade.

Gage was never sure of the details, but, to his consternation, he was literally traded to the McGraw Firm in Glasgow, run by Thomas "Tam" McGraw—a heavyweight UK gangster who had reportedly started out as a shoplifter. Obviously, the McGraw's had something the Genovese's wanted, and Gage was the price.

Still, it all worked out in the end.

While tackling a grab bag of tasks for the firm, not all that dissimilar from those he had done on the other side of the Atlantic, he crossed paths with several operators who were also moving pawns on the panEuropean stage—operators who, as it turned out, were part of Domov. In as much as the more classical hoodlums seemed to concentrate on either moving youthful candidates for their bordellos or smuggling in or out high-paying business or political aristocrats, the Domov malefactors dealt with what was left over. They dealt with human displacement purely (and dispassionately) as an economic product—an input for industry and business. Both factions were, in the simplest evaluation, human traffickers. Furthermore, Gage's skills in these areas did not go unnoticed by the full array of actors.

For a second time, again without knowing the details, Gage was traded—this time to Domov, or more precisely, to Delpro on behalf of Domov—a connection he did not fully appreciate until sometime later. Each transaction had required considerable effort, but each change had also produced a significant increase in Gage's standard of living. After the conclusion of the most recent arrangements and a "training" stint in the US, Gage found himself living in a sumptuous home in London with a more-than-ample salary as well as a generous expense account. After his stateside internship, his job description, as best he could discern (of course, it was never written down—there was no contract), was to be an emissary of the Domov leadership through Delpro. He was to do whatever they asked wherever they needed it done and with a high degree of individual interpretation as to how the job actually got done. He was expected to deliver results. He did so.

Now, back in the US, after the dissolution of Delpro but still with the Domov flag flying, Gage was becoming Senator Sullivan's best friend.

If anyone, especially anyone from Harlan County, had known of Gage's activities, and no one outside a very tight circle did, they might have said he had seemed like a wild bird, a raptor, fidgeting in the hands of an overprotective aviculturist, unable to stretch its wings. Gage knew how these folks from home would think (although he certainly had no homesickness for Harlan County). Gage also knew these thoughts were yet another misrepresentation of his core—his being. He was not hemmed in by anything. He was free in his own sphere—master of his destiny as he had hoped all those years ago when being a cowboy seemed like the best option available to him. He was no cowboy.

Jake Sullivan definitely did not think of Gage Smith as an ensnared creature (although he probably would've agreed with the appellative of raptor)—he rather thought of himself as ensnared by Gage Smith.

Gage's message had been clear. There were forces at hand that wanted anything and everything remotely touching Domov to be permanently suspended—forces that knew things they should not—things that could disrupt Jake's planned upward trajectory in the DC game of money and influence.

However, it was not as easy as just closing a door. The DOJ staff and their colleagues were dogged. They had been on the scene of major, and on some cases horrific, crimes for some time and were now totally committed to bringing the guilty to justice.

These champions of due process, seemingly all now united in Section T15-Z, were as determined as they were capable. Jake's only advantage, it appeared, was that his newly earmarked adversaries were indeed all united in one, be it ever so fragile, group that relied on Jake's committee for its very essence—a group, moreover, that had all its interactions with the Sullivan Committee funneled through one man—Rodney Mills.

Were all the eggs in one basket and easier to smash or at least derail?

Rodney was too sharp and had been at it too long to simply be stonewalled. Jake had to have a strategy that would either completely divert Rodney or at least hold him at bay for an extended period while the good senator could find a more long-term solution.

Jake decided the best tactic was to open a trail that led away from DC—far away. The Secretary of State's concerns had been fundamental in getting this whole issue brought to the White House. And the Secretary of State's concerns had been founded on reports from Africa.

What better aberration than something lotsa folks had heard about but didn't know about? Something like Africa!

Jake needed to throw the investigators a bone—along with some financial support from the committee of course—that would lead to long forays in Africa and keep the DOJ out of the hallways of DC.

The anxious statesman also needed tangible action to be able to report back to Gage Smith if their paths crossed again (and Jake knew they would).

Jake needed a diversion—a serious deflection even if completely bogus.

He needed a ploy that led all the way back to Africa and would keep that damn Secretary of State quiet.

A plan was taking shape.

One of his staffers had been in Peace Corps in Africa (Jake couldn't recall where—it didn't matter as it was all probably the same). He remembered Janice Pittman (Jan was indeed something to remember if he only had had the courage to risk his wife's ire to entice the young lady into more than a professional relationship).

Jan, a most attractive thirty-something overachiever who had gone on for a master's at Columbia after leaving Peace Corps, came to Jake's office at his request.

Forcing himself to keep things low-keyed and strictly business, Jake shared with Jan the story he had just concocted: some Virginia businessmen, some very prominent Virginia businessmen, had contacted the senator enquiring about investing in Africa—seeking his office's advice as to the best opportunities. While the senator had had to confess little direct knowledge on the subject, he had promised to follow up. He had then recalled that he had one of his own staffers in the person of Jan her good self who had firsthand experience with that massive and complex Continent.

A flattered Janice Pittman confirmed she had been a Volunteer in Sénégal for three years, serving as a math-science teacher. She did speak French and had traveled a bit through some other countries in West Africa, but she cautioned she should in no way be considered as an African expert.

With a great smile, Senator Jake Sullivan assured his aide she unquestionably had a sterling background and just the right skills to assist these important constituents. The assignment was hers. If somehow things got complicated in any way, not to worry, she would, as always, receive all necessary support from his office and as needed, even additional resources from the wider congressional community as he was the head of several important committees and would make sure she had everything she required. He knew, without a shadow of a doubt, she was the right person for the job, and he would instruct his chief of staff to develop a budget for Jan's work as well as assign her a small team of part-time support staff. Everything would be taken care of—she could start immediately.

Janice Pittman was breathless as she went back to the cubbyhole that she shared with three other low-level staffers. How had this happened?

Jan was, pretty much as far as she could tell, just like everyone else. She had been born and raised on Foxboro Drive in Dayton, Ohio. She had gone to Meadowdale High School. She had always liked people, so she had pursued a bachelor's in sociology at Ohio University in Athens—150 miles east of home and close enough to get home for weekends when campus life got overloaded. After graduation she had worked at a Kroger near her home for almost two years trying to decide her next steps. Then, still feeling unsettled as to the arch of her future, virtually on an impulse, she had joined the Peace Corps.

As should have been expected, this had been a life changer. It reshaped completely her views of everything including such fraught topics as the social fabric of human communities. After three years, amid feelings she should stay longer and do more, she tore herself away to do bigger and better things, starting with graduate school at Columbia. Once she had finished a masters in comparative politics, she went back to Peace Corps to work as a desk officer in the DC headquarters. She found herself part of an active Returned Peace Corps Volunteer—RPCV—alliance that was very politically engaged and, through this group, getting to know people working for the charismatic Senator Sullivan—ultimately, thanks to these contacts, landing a position with the good senator herself.

Now, low and behold, she was somehow his envoy to Africa.

She wasn't sure how to start.

She knew, however, she had the time and energy to get the job done.

There were few competing forces. She was not in a steady relationship. She tended to move in and out of terse libidinous affairs with suitable specimens from the large crop of single males that flowed about the city.

Her father had passed away several years ago and the house on Foxboro Drive sold; her mother moved to California to be closer to her younger sister—the more stable, some would say "sane" sibling who was an orthopedist in San Bernardino.

In the final analysis, it seemed she had no life outside the senator's office so, with his promised support, she felt she should be able to make a go of her new African assignment.

She was excited.

With surprising rapidity, Jan was soon working with a team of support staff, putting together a detailed plan to present to Senator Sullivan. Jan didn't really know where or how to start and her boss seemed somewhat indifferent as long as there were highly visible activities in Africa that could soon be seen as pathways to business opportunities for his supporters (undoubtedly, given the level of special attention, big-dollar supporters—real big).

Jan did not want to go back to Dakar where she still had lots of Peace Corps memories and some old connections she did not want to intermingle with this new assignment, so the next best choice seemed to be Abidjan—a big city with lots of global connections that should appeal to an American investor.

Looking more closely at Côte d'Ivoire's profile, aside from an environment that was friendly to a wide variety of developmental, financial, and civic institutions, agriculture was a key part of the country's economic foundation. Jan decided, with assent from her team, they should focus on agribusinesses in Côte d'Ivoire that could attract Virginian entrepreneurs—either exporting agricultural inputs to West Africa or importing West African produce into the US or both. Whatever the structure, the details would not be forthcoming from DC. Jan needed to go to Abidjan and the senator was more than happy to approve the travel including a special stipend so she could stay at the Hôtel Ivoire—reportedly *the* place to be seen in the local investment community.

With what seemed like incredible speed, Jan had, to her dismay, traded the antiseptic and polished corridors of DC for the crowded and dusty sidewalks of Abidjan—causeways filled with colors, aromas, noises, and a clamor that stretched the imagination—even for an RPCV.

There was an awe of life and she welcomed it.

Meanwhile, Senator Jake Sullivan was in awe of his nemesis Mister Gage Smith's obduracy with his now regular phone calls reminding the gentleman from Virginia in no uncertain terms of Smith's colleagues' concerns. Gage professed and then redoubled his assertion that the senator was easily the best-placed person to be able to make sure the overzealous DOJ investigators did not overreach and impede the vital economic activities of his partners who were, as the lawmaker surely knew so well personally, true motors of development and generous supporters of those who saw the same opportunities as they.

The words, the warning, of Gage Smith seemed to be suspended in space above his head. Jake Sullivan felt like Joe Btfsplk from one of his favorite comic strips of his youth, *Li'l Abner*, who had had a dark cloud hanging perpetually over him. Gage Smith was his dark cloud.

Whatever his reasons (and Jake understood perfectly well that misdoers did not want their deeds examined by auditors), Gage appeared unable or unwilling to grasp the severity of his demands—the near practical improbabilities of being able to categorically do what the worrisome emissary and his cohorts wanted to get done. This was the DOJ! One did not simply push a stop button. These were investigations that had been underway for years. These were seasoned investigators. Whomever you were, even if you were the bloody president, you did not simply tell DOJ to stop.

A false trail to misguide and dilute efforts was, Jake knew, the best anyone could hope for in the short term. Thereafter, if major new events happened that involved DOJ and competed with resources needed by Section T15-Z, then maybe, just maybe, he could make some more lasting adjustments that would severely weaken both Group 8 and D-2—possibly leading to their dissolution.

This was a best-case scenario. There were many more probable outcomes that would leave the threat of DOJ in place even if anemic.

Gage and all those looming behind him needed to understand.

There were no guarantees.

⚘⚘⚘⚘⚘⚘⚘

While hearing-room fights with legislators and heated squabbles over resources were part of the job, Rodney had no reason to believe his current congressional work would be challenged any more than previous commissions had been although the present assignment certainly was more challenging—much more challenging.

Rodney had his own misgivings.

They well could be mismatched.

The massive power and reach of DOJ notwithstanding, Section T15-Z was up against a truly never-seen-before adversary with immense power and savvy. To make matters much worse, it was not a manifest threat. It was not a Columbian drug cartel nor a Montana militia. It was an omnipresent yet rarely seen force which few in the political leadership acknowledged (at least in public) and even fewer in the citizenry knew existed.

Rodney had known from the open-air audacious actions of Delpro that these people felt themselves untouchable. He recalled how, not all that long ago, it had been the good guys who had been untouchable. He remembered having read how, in 1930, a *Chicago Tribune* reporter had dubbed Eliot Ness and his crew "the Untouchables" as they pursued Al Capone for two and a half years. Rodney and his team had been at it for far more than two and a half years and they certainly were not untouchable. Their work required significant political and fiscal support. They were vulnerable and they could fail.

Failure, however, was not part of Rodney's vocabulary.

The risks and the potential impendence of waning support were real and concerning issues. But the alternative was unthinkable. Day after day, Group 8 and D-2 built stronger and stronger cases, gathering more and more data on how pervasive and potent the unseen Domov had become.

He had to make sure Senator Sullivan understood.

Relaxing in a blue-and-white striped canvas *chaise lounge* in front of his villa with an icy Tom Collins in hand, Robin McCandless looked over at his younger brother who was equally engaged—the siblings' attention darting between an undulating blue-black sea and a still topaz sky dotted with snowy cumulus clouds. Between sips and an appreciation for another enjoyable late spring day, Robin was introspective—introspective yet wanting to share with his brother.

"Ya gotta wonder," he started.

"Hein?"

"Yeah, what if we'd never left here?"

"Oh."

"Yeah." Not waiting for, not really wanting nor anticipating Horace's inputs, Robin went on. "Think about it—maybe we'd be corn or barley farmers with a covey of grandchildren by now?"

"Hmm."

"But we left."

There was no reaction from Horace as he took a bigger than usual gulp from his sweating glass.

"And we did a helluva lotta stuff."

Another gulp.

"I know you have a lot still on your desk, so to speak, and that you've done major deals. But excuse me a second while I pat myself on the back—it seems few others would dare to do so. Delpro, and you were a critical part of it. It was one terrific operation!"

Horace gave a weak but heartfelt, "Yep."

"I know it's gone, and I know it probably had to go at some point—I'm just pissed it went the way it went. But what's done is done. Yet what really burns me is that we did so well and set so many precedents you'd think others'd appreciate the lessons I know we all learned—and the hard way."

"Course."

"It's all about connections and making tough decisions."

"Uh-huh."

"Ya gotta be smart of course and get all your ducks lined up—stuff most think they can do but, in fact, as we showed, stuff that really only a few can do well."

"Hmm."

"There's so much out there—so many opportunities. But ya gotta be careful—plan carefully. Ya know, ya gotta know what you're do'n—where you're go'n and how you're gonna get there."

Another big gulp.

"We're off the field now, or at least I am. That's fine. But I really wonder if these other guys who've picked up the flag will manage to keep it waving on that high hill they hope they occupy?"

The hollow clink of his ice cubes told Horace it was time to go inside for a refill.

At all Costs

VIANNEY Cisse was dead.

Within a fortnight Antoinette followed her beloved.

His passing had surprised his family but not his doctors. Her departure had shocked everyone.

Vianney had been a great success. Through his energy and innovation, he had created a family business, some would have called it an empire, that would ensure his sons were weatherly and powerful throughout their lives.

Antoinette, however, as was often the case with the strong female actors, had worked in the background. Though not in the limelight that had seemed to follow her husband, she had been the true counterbalance for the family, slowing the overzealous and cautioning the impulsive. She had been the unflappable wife and mother who had kept things steady and secure.

The French *Association des Anciens Combattants* offered the family a plot for Vianney in Paris' Père-Lachaise Cemetery, stressing that this was an exceptional and much-sought-after honor appropriate for an African who had helped free France (not to mention who had significant financial interests in the same country). With suitable deference, the family chose a simple burial in Man for *Monsieur et Madame*—a ceremony they felt reflected the values of the loving couple.

From a practical perspective, Luc and Marc had been running the family business for a number of years. Each had been indoctrinated by their father with a work ethic that clearly prioritized hands-on hard work as the key to success—no cushy skyscraper offices nor chauffeur-driven limousines for them. Nonetheless, each had taken time off to marry and establish a family; to the casual observer, this may have appeared to be more of a business decision than an emotional or social contract. After all, with the passing of time, succession needed to be assured. Luc now had two daughters and Marc one son.

The work continued.

It was full steam ahead—continued expansion of profits—continued growing footprint.

Everything was the same.

Everything was different.

One of the chief differences, though the Cisse Brothers were unaware, was that Domov found itself with potentially conjoint operations in one locale, and it was unclear if these operations would be parallel, overlapping, or intertwining. This was highly unusual. Orest and his top lieutenants tried to keep field-level activities hermetically sealed, solely overseen and operated by one arm of the hydra that was Domov. Contrary to this practice, West Africa was now seeing a convergence of action from different groups and different directions. This added significantly to the complexity.

Cisse enterprises were mainly connected in a rather limited way to the organization thanks to the early overtures of Sir Horace and then, through him, the closer ties with Chantal Silue. While the family business had flowered and grown, it remained a family business—even with the new ambition to make a mark in France. Domov's position had been very much in the background—most frequently totally unnoticed by the brothers. Domov was able to use and profit from the Cisse's efforts in a number of indirect ways that never surfaced. It was symbiosis at a distance.

With priority operations currently underway in Werst Africa, Chakir and Onyx Associates were effectively in the same playing field as the Cisse Family, but with much closer ties to the upper echelons of Domov. Orest decided that totally separate and unconnected maneuvering of two entities without some central coordination was too risky. They could quite simply stumble over each other with a faux pas leading to unwanted repercussions.

The *Maliar* decided he needed to pluck Sir Horace out of his beachside torpor and have the elder mediator tactfully make sure everyone was on the same page and that all communication channels were open. From that point, Chakir would be able to effectively get his assignment off the ground, working with, as necessary, the Cisses and Chantal.

Sir Horace, gruff curmudgeon that he was, had a unique skill set that allowed him to engage folks in subjects that could otherwise be thorny—doing so with a bucolic bonhomie that was very persuasive. He would be the right tool from the toolbox to scope out the terrain in Abidjan and assess how difficult it would be to get all the forces pulling or pushing in the same direction.

For his part, Sir Horace let his brother know how tired he was of being used and abused—secretly most gratified to be able to get back into the field with a meaningful task at hand. Back in Abidjan, back in a comfortable atmosphere and an ambiance that had been sorely lacking from his days on the Black Sea shore, Horace was in his element.

Sir Horace was not only in familiar territory geographically but also professionally. He knew how to reach out to people and help them share their story including how current events were affecting their work and play. Marc, Luc, and Chantal were all now old acquaintances and easily reachable for a cup of strong robusta coffee or a bottle of good *Ivoire* beer.

As the old messenger later reported back to the *Maliar*, the risk of "fuckups," as Horace dramatically called them, from the Ivorian residents was extremely low. Both the Cisses and Chantal were aware of Domov, yet practically speaking, only in the most general of ways—the organization pragmatically viewed as a silent partner and source of good market information. The brothers, while working hard to get a foothold in France, had already staked out their terrain and identified their interests. They were not looking for new investments and definitely not considering any move into the projects on the Cameroon-Nigeria border.

Chantal's zone of action was more fluid—changing with the political and financial winds. Nonetheless, she too had no intentions of going too far afield and had never run into any group called Onyx Associates.

In Horace's seasoned opinion, the Abidjan-based trio would not be muddying up the waters. They were staying in their lanes and offering modest benefits to the organization. However, as a sideline, the hardened veteran noted that the brother's forays into France could well ruffle feathers and put them at odds with some very powerful and nasty local forces that were ordinarily best left unprovoked.

Orest welcomed the report and sent word to Chakir to carry on without even a courtesy call to the other Abidjan-based actors.

The juggernaut, frequently surprisingly fleet of foot, gained momentum.

Chakir began planning in detail—sending people into the remote forested area that was the target of the road- and bridge-building activities. His mandate as the overseer *in situ* was to look at all options. For an entity like Domov, the indirect and invisible attributes of a project were often the most promising and the most challenging to line out.

The construction work itself offered potential profits. It was amazing how much revenue could be added by narrowing a road by two inches, using a quarter inch less asphalt, or inserting an additional if superfluous footing on a bridge. With some imagination and generous contributions to the family budgets of the highway department officials in the two countries, blueprints could easily be adjusted to add windfall benefits for the contracted company or companies.

However, in the bigger picture, these benefits were relatively small and short-lived. The real justification for such direct involvement by Domov, rather than using an innocuous small local company to extract the modest proceeds, was the longer-term gains in terms of putting in place trading channels—channels optimizing the already heavily-used riverine transport networks.

The Benue River, though seasonal in its upper reaches, was a major tributary of the massive Niger River System that led, when the rains permitted, to the important port of Garoua in northern Cameroon. Garoua was a transit point for all manner of contraband—much coming from Chad, Niger, and Central African Republic—including gemstones, arms, and people. The normal destination for downriver travel was Port Harcourt, Nigeria's fifth largest city, a petroleum center, and one of her major ports—also a city controlled by heavy-handed resident gangs along with very hungry and aggressive troupes of federal and local regulatory and policing services.

The town of Makurdi was located about 450 miles downstream of Garoua, downstream from the confluence of the north and south branches of the Benue River. Just upstream of Makurdi was the small community of Abinsi with less than four thousand inhabitants, sitting at the head of one of the few north-south roads heading into the forest zone. Leaving the riverbank, after sixty miles of very rough road, in the village of Ugabema, this tract joined the more travelled A-4—called by some a "highway." A little over one hundred miles further south on the A-4 was the town of Ikom. This government center in Cross River State was a scant fifteen miles on the N-6 to the northwest of Adjasso—the Nigerian town across the Cross River from Ekokku on the Cameroonian side of the border—the two villages the epicenters of the new construction projects and the hearts of the road and bridge work. This construction site was forty miles west of Mamfe, Cameroon while 150 miles north of Calabar, Nigeria, via Ikom. This lost-in-the-woods spot was the hub of the present consequential (by any standard) infrastructure projects and the gateway to areas that had heretofore been secluded lands with significant untapped natural and political riches.

Domov, through the eyes of Chakir, saw a chance to put in place a new set of pathways for their diverse business interests. They could divert river traffic at Abinsi and move it south as far as Calibar, adding new products or providing new services as they moved southward—including linking into the existing black-market traffic of petrol, ganja, and other materials dealt with through a number of parallel markets. A new hub in Calabar would allow them to avoid the congested and extortionate requirements of moving products through Port Harcourt. And, once in Calabar, the morass of mangrove canals allowed for relatively easy access to the Gulf of Guinea and the open Atlantic.

Chakir saw this as a private economic corridor (perhaps the first of several)—free of the formal and informal encumbrances and levies that plugged and shackled so many market channels and investment avenues. It was not, he had to be clear to his team, and would not become a major thoroughfare. It was, and would remain, in places scarcely more than a forest trace, but it could be a byway peopled by individuals and villages favorable to Domov—individuals and villages supported by Domov. As such, it could become an artery from the Atlantic into the heart of Africa with branches reaching the Volta and Congo River systems and ultimately much of the core of this massive continent.

To put in place such a conduit, not dissimilar from the cobweb of petroleum pipelines that crisscrossed the hinterland, was no small task. It required not only considerable financial resources—deep pockets—it also required a certain amount of physical reshaping of the terrain to accommodate the foreseen transit of goods—some fragile or even perishable.

The bridge and road projects provided the prescribed cover for Chakir to bring into the field a fleet of heavy machinery to, as necessary, change the landscape—all the while proclaiming this was part of the well-known Adjasso-Ekokku projects. If they later decided to enjoin these projects, they would have the considerable advantage of already having crews and equipment in place.

More pieces began falling into place.

⚘⚘⚘⚘⚘⚘⚘

While many eyes from the Domov mountain top were focused on Africa, the Mitchell family was gaining traction in North America. Although they had opted to implement a very different strategy—different structure and function—than Delpro, it was not, strictly speaking, true that Delpro did not impact on the newest iteration of international American criminal organizations.

Delpro had been very successful at operating in the full light of day—in full view. This was also the Mitchell's aim.

They had developed a trio of structures to house their—what they hoped would be—diverse and highly profitable operations. The real challenge now was to get the function down pat.

While there was no question that they were on what was commonly seen as "the wrong side of the law," they were not interested in what they considered as "hard" crime. It was generally accepted by all that such felonious acts as drugs, counterfeiting, prostitution, and the like were the domain of what was dubbed "organized crime." Whether undertaken by the ancestral highly-organized syndicates and mafia or the more frivolously-organized neighborhood and ethnic gangs, the Mitchells were perfectly content to leave these high-profile indignities to others (at least for the time being—this was not morality, this was practicality).

They needed to find their niche—a slot that was not fraught with risk and vulnerability. Not an easy task.

They had some examples from their early efforts in Pottsville, but these definitely needed to be reshaped and scaled up.

Their comparative advantage was that they were part of Domov (even if they themselves were not sure exactly which part). They were global and, if unwrapped, they were cyclopean.

With the consumer economy changing countrywide, they had a chance to link into the supply chains of the massive retail giants that were rapidly and indiscriminately replacing the old-time mom-and-pop shops that had once been the backbone of the supply chains from the village to the city. Small local retailers were being aggressively ousted by giant one-stop-shops that dotted the land—now virtually the same services and inventory from coast to coast. These behemoths consumed huge quantities of products—unable to scrupulously inspect and control what went into their customers' shopping carts.

This was an opportunity for the Mitchells.

With their financial and charitable structures, they were able to fund small factories, often operated by hanging-on former foreign students. These produced faux facsimiles of high-priced merchandise. This domestic supply was augmented by relatively large quantities of foreign-made products moved surreptitiously across a not-very-tight Canadian border (this another lesson learnt form Delpro).

In the aggregate, these items reflected the variety if not the volume of nearly the full inventory of the kaleidoscopic stocks of these gigantic super stores.

With these same channels, they were also able to help refugees enter the country through the back door and get what they professed to be a good job at some locations where the Mitchells had built larger facilities to supply even more contraband items to the greedy marketplace. They then further expanded their reach, helping these people in need get construction and service jobs. Of course, these new entries into the job market (controlled as it was) needed accommodation and this was again provided by the compassionate Mitchell group, adding to the group's profits.

It was an elaborate yet highly flexible operation. The Pottsville region remained comparatively small to avoid focusing undesirable publicity on the family's home-front. The Durango site, however, quickly grew into an epicenter that more than met the expectations of the Domov masters in Holwerd. They were once again an integral part of the American landscape. The Mitchells innovative businesses provided ample possibilities for other external Domov actors to enter the arena to the mutual benefit of all—or at least all those on the inside of the hydra that was Domov.

The *Maliar* felt things were moving a good direction and that he had a good grip on the reins of power.

Harold, for his part, was also feeling things were moving in a good direction.

Durango was very different from Pottsville.

As so much, it seemed, different but similar.

There was no comparing the physical environments. Vis-à-vis the Schuylkill River and seven hills that were key features of the Appalachian Pottsville, Durango sat grandly at the base of the San Juan Mountains with jagged fourteen-thousand-plus-foot snow-covered peaks accented by clear cerulean skies when seen from the banks of the Animas River that bisected the city.

However, like so many of its sibling cities, Durango had been established by the railroad companies as they strove to "open the west" (more, Harold had thought, to fill their bottomless pockets—the riches to be had in those days making him covetous). Like Pottsville, Durango was, or at least had been, a mining center. Initially, it had been the big silver mines in the San Juans. These were then more than complemented by scores of gold mines—the town becoming a smelting center for both precious metals. There had even been a romance with uranium including a local uranium mill from after the war until the early 60s. Unlike Pottsville, much of the previous mining activity had already transitioned into footprints visited by tourists and written about by historians and the local visitors' associations.

Mining and natural beauty aside, Durango was a very good place for the Mitchells to set up shop. As they had ample financial backing, Harold was able to invest in multiple sites under the cover story of these being the new expansion of an old-time eastern investment firm. He bought a rather modest yet sophisticated (with high-end security coverage) house on Lizard Head Drive, not far from Jenkins Ranch Park, on the northeast fringe of the city. Then, about three miles to the southwest, still on the east side of the river in downtown, not far from the long-established farmers' market, he leased a brick-fronted office that had previously been an accounting firm. Lastly, on the other side of the river, three miles to the north, where Main Avenue turned into Highway 550, he purchased land to build a mini storage. It was almost all there. S&J Logistics' western headquarters in downtown and Fig Leaf Storage on the road out of town.

This was all public facing.

The situation with Kindred Helping Hands Foundation was slightly different. Although the family's ties to this charitable group were not a closely kept secret, they did not want to shine too much light on their would-be philanthropy as it was still uncertain what role the Foundation would play in the overall functioning of the Mitchell operations. Harold waited until his second year before quietly purchasing a lot on East Second Street, just a block from the Catholic church (always a good look to have a foundation close to a house of worship). It was another year before, with little fanfare, Harold opened the offices of KHHF—as planned, only getting half a column on page five of *The Durango Herald*.

This was about the same time that the FLS facilities opened, with a similar design as the parent unit in Pennsylvania but four-times the size: two-thirds public mini storage and one-third commercial storage. Pending development of new market channels, initially Harold linked into a variety of Domov supply chains where he could obtain, through labyrinthine routes, a variety of agricultural inputs and food products (of perhaps questionable quality or uncertain purity). These were stocked in the commercial storage area and then distributed into wholesale and retail networks developed by some of the ex-foreign students putting down business roots in the southwest of the country.

The public mini storage did serve the community well. But it also served as drop-off points in for the distribution of a variety of products, including but not limited to those coming from the commercial warehouse—incoming and outbound networks compartmentalized and maintained by another subset of former students looking for their tangible benefits from the great society that served as their host (formally or not).

These relatively piece-meal distribution actions were all small-scale and disposable. If there were any issues or concerns, they were simply shutdown and disappeared. These activities did, however, complement larger commercial nets that were being built by S&J—structures that linked back to Pottsville and from there to the shrouded Domov amoeba.

Durango was open for business.

⚘⚘⚘⚘⚘⚘⚘

As things geared up in the foothills of The Rockies, activities for Kyrylo Rudenko were also expanding in Zhdanov (once again named Mariupol) well beyond Kafe Parus—much to his father's satisfaction.

Voldoymyr Rudenko saw his labors bearing fruit. The structures he had worked so hard to put in place were growing both in size and prominence. He was proud of the legacy he had been able to pass on to Kyrylo, and he was grateful for his links to Domov.

Although Voldoymyr had had no reason to know nor be involved, for some time Domov had been engaged through certain circuitous transnational pathways in activities in southern Mexico, especially Chiapas State. This out-of-the-way place had major resources including cacao and particularly coffee, resources with few checks and balances and those that were there were always negotiable. This was nearly an ideal setting for the organization to provide inputs and capture products—the inputs including labor that by any other name would be considered slavery.

This was a promising if volatile piece of the Domov mosaic.

However, even though war was good business, insurrections could cause disruptions that were not good for the bottom line. Chiapas had a long history of ethnic and cultural strife with many indigenous peoples being highly marginalized. The Fuerzas de Liberación Nacional (FLN) was a rebel band, a militia group that formed around these inequities. This group had been severely weakened with the storming of their training facilities at El Chilar Ranch. Nonetheless, the embers glowed red-hot, and when the governor of Chiapas increased oppression of indigenous people, the FLN jumped into a conflagration that became known as the Zapatista Uprising, the *Conflicto de Chiapas.* Violent descent changed from an inconvenience into a major impediment.

In normal, more peaceful times, Chiapas had become a thriving segment of the organization's global program. The valued internationally-traded commodities of cacao and coffee, the supply of inputs (including the human trafficking), the harvesting, transport, marketing and even banking of the receipts had all fit well within existing arrangements involving a variety of Domov silos—acting independently with central command and control only from Holwerd. It had worked. It had made good profits.

Unfortunately, the unruly civil unrest made things complicated and senior management did not like complications.

Domov agents had so far been able to walk a difficult line interlacing in different ways and at different levels both the state government and the insurrectionists. But the pendulum swung persistently, and the balance of power shifted from month to month. Chiapas was far from the seat of the federal government which already had a full calendar of burning issues without overextending themselves by going to the southern extremities of the vast country—they simply could not do much. The state resources were stretched and the reshaped and re-processed FLN was effectively able to establish a state within a state.

Domov was in a problematic position. Its seemingly self-sufficient components that oversaw the Chiapas program could not be seen as supporting rebels. At the same time, Domov could not maximize its presence without some arrangements with the rebels. It was a conundrum.

The solution could possibly be to make the FLN stronger and more capable of self-governance. If the freedom-fighters (as they saw themselves) could reach a point where they represented a realistic threat to national integrity, the federal government could find itself with no alternative but to forcefully intervene to find a durable longer-term solution—to re-establish stability.

This scheme focused on Kyrylo Rudenko as the potential catalyst to bring back the economic consistency that optimized profits. While going back to and adopting his father's first business arrangements, he was in the broadest sense expanding his part of the wider Domov empire, he had a high degree of plausible deniability. He was, after all, when objectively assessed, a very minor actor and not an integral component of any of the main silos forming the tentacles of the organization. Moreover, he already had struck arms deals with groups in the southern parts of the South American continent. He had the means to deliver extra support to the insurrectionists—support to be repaid with due consideration to the receipts coming from the cocoa and coffee harvests.

Kyrylo Rudenko could just possibly be the answer to the conundrum.

Kyrylo was ecstatic at the opportunity.

Orest was guardedly optimistic.

To make money (to gain power) you had to have money. There were no freebies.

It was ultimately a game of chance and often you had to go all in.

Domov had to leverage its resources to move ever-upward. This was not, of course, without risk.

There was the risk of financial failure. There was the risk of formal adjudication and potential incarceration. There was the risk of an overthrow by internal or external forces. If it materialized, this latter, and possibly all three threat categories, could ultimately result in the permanent departure of the current *Maliar*.

Guarded optimism was about as good as it got.

CHAPTER 8

GAINS AND LOSSES

"You only have to do a few things right in your life so long as you don't do too many things wrong."

—**Warren Buffett**

Don't Shake the Tree

TWENTY-FOUR hours after arriving at Félix Houphouët Boigny International Airport, Jan was still sucking in the much-appreciated tangy atmosphere of Abidjan. She had not realized how much she missed this drastic change from the totally different and somehow sterile aura of DC.

Jan was, according to those who knew her well, among the sharpest knives in the drawer. She was smart and, critically, she was practical. She knew enough to respect those who knew more than she. Whatever size her ego may have achieved, she did not let it get in the way of going to the right people, using the right tools, and adopting the right stuff to get the right information. She was wedded to doing a thorough job, achieving verifiable results, and reporting succinctly and correctly.

Sadly, Senator Sullivan had not realized these attributes—possibly he might not have even admired them had he known of their existence. He simply needed someone to create a diversion and a RPCV, from what little he knew, seemed a good choice as a distraction-maker.

In any case, high or low expectations of her boss aside, Jan knew she would give the assignment her best effort.

Before embarking on her return to West Africa, she had done her homework. She had done her own research and then reached out to the major newspapers including *The Washington Post*, *The New York Times*, and *The Daily News*. Her best lead had come from *The Daily News* who had put her in contact with Oriana Arquette.

Although Virginia businessmen's vague hopes of riches from African farms seemed far from the priorities of the vast majority of journalists to whom Jan had reached out, Oriana had been surprisingly open to discussion if overtly only modestly interested. After several lengthy phone calls, Oriana had invited Jan to come up to the city and Jan had promptly jumped on a train for the three-and-a-half-hour ride to Penn Station.

At the onset, Oriana had mostly reminisced about her African days, as she had called them, when they had chatted on the phone. However, once seated in a café on the corner of 7th Avenue and West 31st Street, less than a block from the station, Oriana had once again become the quintessential investigative reporter—offering some information but always trying to garner more.

"I'm sure you're excited to leave all this confusion and get back to the real world—with its own confusion, of course," Oriana said, gesturing to the throbbing throngs on the sidewalk outside the coffee shop's big plate glass windows, and only after each had sipped her redolent expresso.

"Well." Jan tried to smile diffidently, although she truly felt nearly intoxicated as she sensed she was on the cusp of something special. "As you've told me, you know Abidjan well and its *trottoirs* are certainly not less hectic nor cluttered than New York's."

"Indeed," the journalist responded with a somewhat wistful glance, "Abidjan is a big city and, in some ways, just another big city—but still, a wonderful place to go."

Jan tried to appear even more demure.

"Naturally, as an old Peace Corps hand, you probably know more than I do about navigating the byways and *maquis* of the city."

"Well." The staffer tried to hide a grin, "I am here, and I am going to Abidjan as a representative of Senator Jacob Sullivan and not as a RPCV going back to my roots."

"In fact." Oriana took another sip of the acrid drink, "that is why we're meeting—not to discuss Peace Corps, but to discuss the bridges the good Senator apparently wants to build."

"I guess they're bridges." Jan looked pensive. "But in any event, they are certainly services he wants to provide to his constituents—if they want to do business in West African, he wants to help. And then when he decides to help, he asks me to jump in the vanguard. This has led to you and your esteemed value as a resource in these efforts."

Kind of a strange way to say it, Oriana thought, but only interjected a single, "OK."

"At the beginning," Jan continued, "it seems kinda murky—what do these guys want? But I guess, in the end, it's pretty clear—they want money."

"As always."

"But Senator Sullivan doesn't want to just throw them a bone and move on. He wants—honestly, I'm not real sure why—to come up with some real options for these guys—real businesses that could be a partnership between Ivorians and Virginians."

"Nice idea."

"Nice or not, it's still mucky. I've talked to some of these back-home entrepreneurs, and they don't seem to have a clue about Africa, doing business in Africa, or even products that could be of interest that come from Africa—they don't have a inkling. Hard to figure out."

"Could be—or maybe no surprise there—you help me, I'll help you—reciprocity's been our political blueprint forever."

"Yeah." Jan drained her cup. "But it would be nice to have some proper guidance. As it is, the Senator wants us, me, to layout the options for these guys—supporters, I'd guess—and then they can decide if they like it or not. Lotta work just to be blown off but that's where we are."

"So, let me see," Oriana said, seeming to change gears, "your boss is proposing spending a small fortune to show to his buddies that he can get them info on Africa that they likely will not use—is that about it?"

"Don't know—could be."

"Well, as you note, these guys don't seem to be very focused other than maybe thinking about doing something in Africa—that's a pretty large landscape."

"Yep."

"Truthfully, I don't have much faith that this will lead to anything although I am a big fan of much more commerce with African businesses. Still, you have to do what you have to do, and I might as well try and see if my activities can be of any real help—if something does ever come from this, the paper would be happy to print a piece about international financial cooperation."

"Great," Jan said with less than great enthusiasm as Oriana's clear assessment seemed to have put a bit of a damper on her excitement.

"Anyway, I've been working with two ladies, Awa Konate and Mariama Mbaye. Awa is in Abidjan and will be able to help out with your assignment—she's got terrific resources and knows a lot about what's going on in the agriculture sector in Côte d'Ivoire. Mariama, as you can probably guess, is Sénégalese, but she is currently working out of here, studying shipping lanes along the West Coast and I am not sure exactly how you would get in touch with her on a regular basis, but I suspect you will not need to and Awa will be able to get you all the details you are needing at this stage to placate your boss and keep him from disappointing his supporters who are probably more ready to contribute to his re-election fund than to any farmers in West Africa."

That was it. Jan had what she needed. It seemed like this all could have been done over the phone and the trip totally unnecessary, but she liked trains.

Oriana had decided early on that she wanted to meet this Senate staffer face-to-face (knowing full well the trip from DC was gratuitous but a chance not only to see someone who could perhaps be an ally in the future but also a test of determination and perhaps patience—both key factors). She had also decided she would not share too much with the senator's representative. This Ivorian mission had all the markings of a boondoggle and there was no reason to open too many doors nor share too many secrets—even hypotheses. The foxy senator was most certainly just trying to put on an elaborate show to get some more contributions from possible big-bucks-donors who so far had been reluctant to ante-up the way the seasoned politician felt was needed for him to reciprocate as they most certainly felt was required.

Nonetheless, Oriana had been impressed with Jan: she was smart and motivated. There was a chance, likely a tiny chance, that this whole ill-conceived idea could metamorphose into something of true value. It was just possible, if things broke the right way, that the butterfly that emerged from the chrysalis, be it ever so mercenary in its concept, could have a positive impact. It was just possible that Jan could be the needed catalyst for the work with Awa and Mariama that was now approaching the doldrums. She had to keep an eye on Jan. Just maybe this idealistic Senate staffer could make a difference.

Now back in the tropics, Jan maintained her professional approach to the job at hand—the true end game still shrouded in fog.

Before reaching out to Awa, she spent a week getting up to speed about the goings-on in Côte d'Ivoire, visiting the Chambre Nationale d'Agriculture de Côte d'Ivoire, the Chambre de Commerce et d'Industrie de Côte d'Ivoire, the ministries of finance and agriculture, several local banks and NGOs, and even the Banque d'Afrique de l'Ouest de Développement—the BAOD.

Her newly-forged contacts at the BAOD provided a broader perspective for the whole of West Africa—adding some indications of pipeline plans for the entire region. The bank staff were particularly proud of the pending interstate infrastructure project joining Cameroon and Nigeria which they maintained had been on the drawing board for years. They applauded the recent efforts that effectively formalized and modernized major trading routes that had heretofore hit a zenith during the Biafran War. The bridge and related infrastructure, they maintained, would go a long way in bringing to fruition transcontinental communications and transportation, including linking with the PanAfrican Highway.

Once she had a good on-the-ground perspective of the chief actors and parts of the agricultural sector, she invited Awa for a coffee at the Hôtel Ivoire.

After a fortnight Jan was able to send Senator Sullivan an arrival report resplendent with photographs, references, and a special selection of local government documents that would be needed for any expatriate investment in the country with a special annex on BAOD activities including the flaunted investments in infrastructure in Nigeria and Cameroon—a bulky document reflecting extensive detailed background work but with the opportunities and way-forward sections still some ways off—these were early days. This was, in effect, a thorough introduction to Côte d'Ivoire (Jan thought to herself it was like those country profiles they gave to new Peace Corps Volunteers but much, much more, she trusted, exhaustive).

As they had all known from the initial data gathering before she had even left DC, nearly two-thirds of the surface of Côte d'Ivoire was farmland, nearly the same portion of their national income earned from agricultural products—coffee and cacao heading the list. Other important cash crops included oil palm, coconut, rubber, cotton, sugar cane, fruits (pineapples, mangos, papayas), and cashews. Major food crops for both local markets and export included a wide variety of produce from rice and maize to cassava and bananas along with soybeans and vegetables. The country's agricultural program was very active and very diverse. Where did Virginians fit in?

This was the question she posed in her report, shifting the onus back to DC and the Senator or his top advisors now needing to tell her where and how to concentrate on this much broader topic.

While she awaited guidance, she took a trip to the north of the country.

⚘⚘⚘⚘⚘⚘⚘

Senator Sullivan received Jan's report but first had to deal with much more pressing issues regarding this whole African investment fable. This was, after all, an effort to divagate from the subject of that pesty Rodney Mills and his crew. It was, he hoped, a pyrotechnic display to attract attention—like all pyrotechnics, something that would ultimately fizzle-out under its own weight. Nonetheless, for the moment, he had to find a way to get this Ivorian show on the agenda of his committee.

This committee, though it was not *sensu stricto* a true committee and more of an ad hoc group, as part of the Permanent Committee on Homeland Security and Government Affairs, under its Subcommittee on Emerging Threats and Spending Oversight, held budgetary authority over Mills and D-2. He had to carve out a place for his fable in this intricate and high-powered bureaucratic and legalistic formation. He had to have a new set of pressing activities that would require urgent funding that could compete with the ample resources already earmarked for funding D-2 and its aggressive big brother, Section T15-Z—urgent new actions that would hobble T15-Z for at least the foreseeable future.

It was an uphill battle, but he had his instructions.

Fortunately, his staff had a well-used skill set in make-believe—making carefully selected "facts" fit a predetermined situation. This was, in many ways, assuredly what politics was all about.

His team crafted a scenario where there was a growing and ominous external threat coming from African economic refugees—people who were fleeing their countries (what the less broadminded called "shit-hole nations") to try and find the pot of gold that had eluded them so far in their homeland. These disenfranchised and disillusioned individuals (the creators of the tale had decided against labeling those posing the made-up threat "bloodthirsty savages") were prime candidates, in Sullivan's vision of the looming problem, for terrorist recruiters—agents upon whom terrorist entities could call to do all manner of atrocities. These doubtless dangerous, forsaken individuals were, in the Sullivan story, furious that they had not been able to reap the benefits of the good life and were now ready, willing, and able to tear it all down so all would savor the desolate suffering that they saw as their daily existence.

To address this serious issue, Sullivan proposed immediate and significant economic stimulus to American companies to invest in Africa to provide better jobs and better working conditions (as, according to him, witnessed here at home—especially in Virginia) for locals, thereby making it no longer necessary for them to flee and become fodder for extremists. He even drafted (or his staff drafted) considered legislation that would curtail immigration (only for high-risk individuals, he assured all) and close loop-holes that heretofore made entry by refugees, in his words, a free pass. He wrapped up his package for the committee by generously offering his pilot work in Côte d'Ivoire as an example of things to come if the redirected resources and his prospective legislation were to get off the ground.

Jake Sullivan then prepared his own status report to Gage Smith—nothing in writing, naturally.

In some ways, Jake thought he might have been happier if he had had nothing to give to Gage Smith. If he had nothing to offer, he would be chastised but there would be no specific plans to tear apart—plans now already underway and plans, at this point, that could not, on Gage Smith's whim, be dramatically changed or sidetracked. The senator had cast the die and he now had to make the sale. He couldn't let this cretin upset his apple cart. Jan was in Abidjan. His staff had drafted the necessary documents to target financial support to potential economic refugees thereby preventing the inevitable terrorist threat. He had even had positive discussions accompanied by equally positive contributions to his war chest with prominent Virginian businessmen who truly were ready to drop millions on good-faith African investments. The train had left the station.

His concerns notwithstanding, the discussion—the presentation of the preliminary results—with Gage Smith had been ambivalent. The master's emissary hadn't criticized. He hadn't menaced or hollered. He really hadn't done anything. He had listened carefully then left with no reaction other than a, "I'll be getting back to you."

Jake Sullivan had seemingly been put on hold by his interlocutor. But, like it or not, the Senator still had to vigorously pursue the proposed legislation (even if a stage prop) and the funding reallocations (the insidious intent) he had already put forth. He had to convince his committee and he was almost there.

There was a lot of convincing going one in many quarters and at many levels of urgency. Marseilles was one such site. Les Caïds of Le Milieu had initially been more irritated than threatened by La Famille Ivoirienne—the bothersome brothers—and had tried to make them disappear through some rather tempered methods using their contacts at INTERPOL. The notion had been that the outsiders undertaking a variety of illicit, albeit mostly innocuous, activities including probable violations of immigration regulations, would be easily exposed to severe penalties if they did not go back from where they had come. Possibly a good idea in some cases, but not as regarded Marc and Luc Cisse. Although their spoor on French soil was still small (not considering Vianney's footsteps slogging through the war), the brothers had big plans and ample finances to back these up. Business had been very good.

Wisely fearing potential repercussions as newcomers and possibly vulnerable actors on a stage dominated by well-established backhanders, Marc and Luc had preemptively and with due diligence hired some very well-connected and very expensive Parisian lawyers to take up any and all legal challenges to their operations. Given the pedestrian nature of most of the easily discoverable offenses, it appeared likely few in law enforcement would have the appetite to go full-out over the long haul with skilled solicitors willing (as per their clients' orders) to spend years if necessary to resolve the tiniest points. Therefore, the Caïds' formal statutory approach, while it could conceivably have some impact over years, appeared impotent against the immediate Ivorian predicament. And, by the time any formal measures would have taken effect, the Africans would have grown much stronger, doubtless competing directly with Le Milieu in areas where they wanted absolutely no competition. It was troublesome.

Les Caïds needed to consider a more immediate and permanent remedy.

Harold was in his own way looking to remedy a number of issues—perhaps better put, to solidify actions such that they would not need remedies—prophylactic or otherwise. Just like the Cisse brothers or Jan and Jake, although he was unaware of the operations of these actors also struggling up parallel ladders to hoped-for success, Harold had activities that were beginning to take root—activities that were at the delicate budding stage where a hard shake could dislodge the bloom and even spoil the harvest. It was a time of prudence and patience.

His enterprises in Durango and beyond were incipient but doing well. He and his father had worked hard and apparently successfully to have nebulous (at best) links back to Pottsville. For all intents and purposes, he was, he hoped, the epitome of a young up-and-coming businessman—a start-up even if starting with a rather full dossier. To his neighbors, he was, if he had succeeded in painting the necessary portrait, a staunch member of the community and a hard-working nouveau entrepreneur.

In sculpting his image, he had followed his mother's wise advice. She had repeatedly said, "If you say it often enough, people will believe it."

Harold had made a big show, he trusted it was believable and believed.

He had taken a full-page ad out to announce the opening of Fig Leaf Storage. He had run new customer specials, offering senior and military discounts. Soon they were approaching seventy percent occupancy. It was working.

For S&J Logistics the pathway was somewhat more subdued. Harold started by reaching out to retirement homes, schools, health facilities, anywhere that prepared institutional meals. He distributed a brochure that showed how S&J had helped institutions along the East Coast make significant saving in their food purchases, offering the lucky residents of Durango and the surrounding counties an opportunity for similar benefits.

Then, once he had a core of clients and a portfolio of services (some real, others imagined), he opened a branch that targeted what he called "home and ranch supplies." Here there were items for the hobbyist and the small-scale farmer or horseman. This was an entry into the agricultural field that he hoped would expand to the farming and ranching community at large.

The Durango Herald wrote a story about the newcomer, "Young eastern merchant helps communities get a leg up."

It was working, his canard was taking hold.

However, what Harold knew, and the outside world did not, was that he was a young up-and-coming businessman, an eastern merchant, on a razor's edge. He had to develop a solid cadre of legitimate well-thought-of businesses into which he could slowly and meticulously integrate a variety of sordid (as some would undoubtedly see them, although he simply thought of them as more profitable) enterprises—some of which he did not, at least at this stage, fully grasp. He was, after all, a part of a vast web and there were still many secrets in Holwerd.

⚘⚘⚘⚘⚘⚘⚘

There were many layers of secrecy at Holwerd, but all curtains were pulled back for Orest. All curtains that is, except for the functioning of the watchers—the *obetovať*. From Orest's perspective, this was a known unknown. He could not, would not spend his time worrying about a midnight assassination because some unseen persons labeled the *obetovať* were unhappy with his work.

And, for the moment anyway, he was happy with his work.

Most of the routine actions were self-contained in their nearly hermetically sealed packaging—siloed, operating like, he hoped, perpetual motion machines—his direct inputs required rarely and only for the most crucial concerns. Domov was, after all, more than a company. It was a culture.

The founders had done well. The foundation was on bedrock. His energies chiefly needed to be focused on new components potentially to be added to the Domov web or special projects that would contribute to this now time-tested labyrinth.

Joe and Harold were getting traction in regaining the terrain lost with Robin McCandless' unceremonious departure. With any luck, they would build a program that would be even larger and stronger than that left in the ashes of Delpro.

Similarly, things were promising from the African project. Chakir was making real progress. When all was said and done, this was a small project, but it was both emblematic and possibly catalytic. It was, if successful, representative of how Domov leadership could configure discrete activities under a single seemingly independent operator delivering major actions that generated important profits. The project was also conceivably a starting point for a wide range of new investments—above and below board—that would be very beneficial to Domov.

Orest was happy but not complacent. He understood far too well how fragile the balance was—how tenuous any equilibrium could be at any point in time. The Domov tree had strong roots and a stout trunk—but its fruit was fragile—highly susceptible to the vagaries of society and the caprices of man.

Poison Fruit

RODNEY was not religious. He was neither a Bible-beater nor a Bible reader. Nonetheless, while he would not have recognized the passage in Matthew 7:18, he would have completely understood: "a good tree cannot bring forth evil fruit, neither can a corrupt tree bring forth good fruit."

He was aiming to unearth and destroy the corrupt tree that was Domov. This was not simply about justice served, it was about retribution. Hal would have had it no other way.

Although formally and ideally, he needed both the blessing and support of Jake Sullivan's committee just as much as he needed the frank collaboration of Felix Manchester and his Group 8 along with the broader structure of Section T15-Z, D-2 was a well-equipped, well-staffed crew with an outstanding track record. Rodney was neither hamstrung nor permanently put on hold due to the delays in getting the full endorsement of Sullivan's group. He had the mandate to fight crime, and he had no real barriers to doing his job—albeit the doing part was unquestionably more challenging when going it alone.

Rodney knew, unlike himself, Felix was a devout Christian. He would have immediately understood the verse from Matthew—undoubtedly knowing the full liturgical context. Rodney understood the leader of Group 8 would be less comfortable going ahead without all the necessary authorities and resources guaranteed by the complete backing of Sullivan et al. However, he also was reasonably confident that, being a professional, Felix would not oppose nor complicate Rodney starting off with D-2 pending the total mobilization of Section T15-Z under the renewed mandate awaited from Sullivan's committee.

Therefore, this was Rodney's next move. After all, who knew more about the subject than his team? No one. They had been the first to cross the threshold, and they should carry-on even if this meant moving ahead without the absolute imprimatur of all the interlinked government entities.

Rodney looked back to move forward.

The first real wealth of Domov-related information (although Domov was not even a known item at that time) had come from Hal and Eddie's foray, retracing Eddie's path with Delpro in Spain, Zambia, and Malawi. This had led to Hal's uncovering key pieces of the global puzzle that had been Delpro. Back in the States, they had continued to uncover bits and pieces with the additional help of Eddie's partner Lisa, a lawyer at DOJ. While each activity was insidious on its own, when the dots—even only those few they saw, and they knew there were still many more yet to discover—were connected, Delpro was revealed to be a cavernous and wildly corrupt organization.

With Hal's death—his unquestionable murder in his colleague and lover's view—Rodney had picked up the challenge and continued trying to add more pieces to the puzzle Hal had worked so hard in framing. Interactions with collaborators, possible accomplices, including the more compliant Charlie Stancik, Paula Patterson, and Peter Volman (some more conversant than others) had added significantly more valuable information.

Mr. Don Drumpfsh and Inter-Act in Kansas City had also, under duress, provided voluminous material about Delpro and its activities, both domestic and overseas. However, this had principally been documentation about Delpro's overt operations. Delpro had been audacious, doing much in plain view that others would only consider if hidden by impenetrable layers of circumscription and privacy. These were threads to follow, but threads that all too frequently led nowhere.

Most remained a Gordian knot.

Moreover, by the time Robin McCandless vanished in the mists of Chesapeake Bay, it was already clear that, as prodigious as Delpro had been, it was only a piece of an incredibly large global structure with pharaonic dimensions that was covered by a thick blanket of suppression, silence, and secrecy in an effort to remain unnoticed and unnoticeable.

By the time McCandless resurfaced in Romania, Rodney had just begun to lift a corner of the tightly woven Domov blanket. Recent revelations continued to raise the covering sheath ever so slowly though much remained in obscurity.

Still, the peek under the coverlet combined with all the material he had been able to accumulate with the help of his pivotal collaborators had provided unique insight into the invisible hydra that was Domov.

One of the many hurdles facing Rodney, one that had always been there, was finding an acceptable way to pursue his investigation on a transnational scale. Domov was global and he was officially a national investigator. This had been the reason for incorporating Group 8 under the umbrella of Section T15-Z—a cover for international operations. But he could not let administrative stalls set back all the work already done.

Surprisingly, the breakthrough when it came, came from Robin McCandless himself.

⚘⚘⚘⚘⚘⚘⚘

Robin McCandless was unaware of any assistance he may have provided Rodney—he certainly wouldn't have wanted to do so. However, Robin seemed unaware of nearly everything. He had been resting in his blue-and-white striped canvas chaise lounge in front of his villa with his younger brother when he got up to refresh his drink. After his first step toward the bar, his whole body had reportedly stiffened before crumpling to the ground. Robin McCandless had had a major stroke.

Rodney naturally had not been there when his nemesis had become comatose. He no longer had so much as one agent watching the villa. However, his team had good and on-going contacts with local authorities as well as a few carefully selected folks from among McCandless' neighbors who received a modest stipend to keep D-2 informed about the old man's status and the goings-on at the villa. These *in situ* informants proved invaluable.

McCandless had been taken to the local clinic by ambulance then, diagnosed with a severe stroke, immediately transferred to Heka Hospital, not far from Old Town in Constanța, thirty-five miles away. After several months with no improvement, McCandless had been moved to Porumbel Albastru (Blue Dove) long-term care center. This was a high-end private facility located in Constanța among the luxury tourist hotels off Bulevardul Mamaia on the small spit of land that separated Siutghiol Lagoon from the Black Sea.

An aging Sir Horace, now looking even more weathered and worn, worrying more and more about his own health prospects as well as his older brother's, stayed in the villa in Vama Veche, making weekly pilgrimages to Porumbel Albastru. At times accompanied by one of McCandless' many associates—after decades "in the business," McCandless had few friends but many contacts.

One of these contacts was Ralph Tave, entrepreneur, philanthropist, and Chairman of Cumberland Savings Bank in Lexington, Kentucky. Ralph Tave's grandfather had changed the family name from Tsvetayev when they had migrated from Leningrad as soon as the first rumblings of World War II could be felt. The family had settled in Pine Mountain in Harlan County where Ralph's grandfather had managed to find a job as a common laborer at JBW Coal, Inc.

In the postwar period the family had made an impressive jump from rural poverty to living in the posh neighborhood of Greenbrier in Lexington. Rumors were that this magical transformation had been more due to laundering funds from the homeland than from the sweat of the brow in a coal mine.

Whatever the story, Ralph Tave had inherited a considerable fortune and considerable influence from this late and beloved father. Ralph Tave had also been a business colleague of Robin McCandless. The details will likely never be known, but their relationship had been sufficiently important for Ralph to make the arduous trip to the Porumbel Albastru, apparently to see if he could still communicate with his old confederate if not old friend.

Given McCandless' importance, potentially still when comatose, with a reduction of stipends going to Vama Veche (Sir Horace not warranting, in the head of D-2's opinion, the same coverage as his big brother), Rodney had been able to arrange a small budget for a Constanța private investigator who regularly checked on McCandless' situation, reporting back to Rodney's team. The investigator, Mr. Barbaneagra (Rodney had been informed the surname translated as black beard—he had no idea if the gentleman ported a beard), among other tasks, had arrangements with Blue Dove staff to frequently check the ledger that recorded all visitors to patients. Ralph Tave's name had been part of Mr. Barbaneagra's periodic report.

This had flagged all of Ralph's interests known to D-2 including Cumberland Savings. Although any ties to S&J Logistics or Fig Leaf Storage were buried very, very deeply—basically, at this stage, beyond D-2's reach—the bank's books, nonetheless, raised eyebrows of the forensic accountants on the team who poured over those portions of the financial archives to which they could gain access. There was an inordinate amount of international activity for a small Kentucky institution—especially large amounts of capital moving back and forth between various funds and firms in Eastern Europe.

This was not the time to launch an in-depth exploration of the bank's practices and partners—stealth out-trumped thoroughness. Cumberland Savings gave Rodney the hook he needed to build a new and much-needed front for the war on Domov. Once the scope of Domov, if only gauged by its shadow, had been appreciated, Rodney knew for a fact what he had long expected. Actions in the US had been too important to stop with the departure of Robin McCandless. There had been and would be attempts, probably many, to re-establish Domov's presence—to harvest the profits the organization knew were only awaiting the grasp of its tentacles.

These renewed efforts on American shores would definitively remove any bureaucratic or legalistic obstacles for Rodney's engagement, even though the principal object was an international, really a global operation.

Rodney began plans for a two-pronged way forward. On the one hand, he would sanitize and generalize the information regarding Cumberland Savings in a status report for Jake Sullivan, removing specific details but highlighting the fact that no one should be having the delusion that, with the crumpling of Delpro, the threat of Domov was gone—hopefully further justifying the need to move quickly on getting Section T15-Z fully-funded and running smoothly. On the other hand, for in-house consumption, he would guide the D-2 crew as they prepared a much more detailed and focused assessment of the bank's activities, building out from this hub to other linked enterprises or individuals. This second prong would be fodder for his team. They would do what they did best and, by all available means, ferret out as many parts of the story as possible.

Rodney hoped these would be the first of many steps to overcome the growing inertia—to be the catalyst for needed action.

⚘⚘⚘⚘⚘⚘⚘

Prong two was crucial, but prong one had its own trajectory with much less influence possible from the leader to D-2.

The D-2 Team dove into Cumberland Savings. After following all too many buried leads and seeking all too many carefully concealed contacts, they began to uncover a much different picture of the financial institution. It was not unusual for a bank to be the owner of farms and farmland when the bank had to foreclose on these properties. However, this was a transitory situation. These assets would generally, as promptly as possible, be sold to more solvent investors. Not so with Cumberland Savings. The bank, through a series of clandestine intermediaries, was one of the biggest farmers in the area.

The chief commercial crops of Kentucky were corn, soy, and tobacco. Cumberland Savings was the ultimate owner, frequently passing through one or more shell companies, of no less than four score of farms ranging in size from less than one hundred acres to nearly one thousand acres. These were all listed as active farms, most producing one of the state's three principal crops. However, when D-2 agents visited a random sample of farms, they found no row crops. All operations visited were growing trees—Christmas trees, ornamental trees, or nut trees.

Farms with recorded harvests of soy, corn, and tobacco had no fields of soy, corn, or tobacco while they had acre upon acre of trees. Moreover, these same farms were not members of any agricultural association—not the soy board, nor the corn or burley tobacco growers. They were also not listed in the membership rolls of any of the various associations covering tree crops. The farms were registered and paid taxes but were totally isolated from the wider agricultural community.

Still, the department of agriculture reported sales of corn, soy, and tobacco through local marketing channels from all the farms identified as being part of the Cumberland Savings' cohort. Seemingly to validate this point, during site visits, agents located and photographed active grain and tobacco storage facilities on all the farms although their land-use was fully devoted to trees. These farms were apparently bringing in harvests from elsewhere, holding, then selling.

It was puzzling. To add to the perplexity, the tax submissions for these farms stipulated their income was totally from these brought-in harvests—although the returns did not cite these as coming from the outside, but simply reported these products as the sources of the farms' revenues. There were no financial records for the tree crops at farm level.

As the well-seasoned D-2 investigators continued unearthing more and more arrangements, they discovered that various farms within the broader Cumberland population of agricultural properties were clumped into management and marketing groups. There was a group for each category of silviculture—Christmas trees, ornamental plantings, and nuts.

It looked like each subset was autonomous (or gave the appearances of autonomy), each separate assembly leasing bank-held land from other farms ostensibly growing cereals or tobacco but in fact involved in the actual cultivation of tree crops. For example, those Cumberland farms actually growing Christmas trees were part of a collectivity where the silviculture group's management leased the bank's land and assumed all responsibilities for producing and selling the tree crop while, on paper, the farm sold foodstuffs (rather a different twist on sharecropping); these arrangements and the receipts from these leases, moreover, did not appear in these farms' official financial records.

It was like Two-card Monte. Farms growing trees were reportedly selling other products while seemingly unrelated commercial cash-crop farms were selling tree crops. Someone had gone to a tremendous amount of effort to make the simple complicated.

It was muddled (and undoubtedly intentionally so) at best.

At the very least, Cumberland Savings was likely liable for non-reporting of income from its family of farms. Then the management and marketing entities were also potentially in difficulty for misrepresentation and non-reporting of their financial status. These groups were officially non-profit growers' associations and not agri-businesses.

These facts notwithstanding, neither D-2 nor the broader Section T15-Z was interested in enforcing tax law. These irregularities (and worse) would be fully documented and filed. If other legal proceedings were ever launched against Cumberland Savings, the tax dossier would find its way into the hands of the IRS. For the moment, it was just additional background information used to paint a picture of Domov's fingerprints in the US—proof of the proverbial rotten apple that could spoil the barrel of fruit.

Rotten or not, Ralph Tave and Cumberland Savings were the freshest spore—an opportunity to make real progress on the tangled Domov saga. Rodney knew, ready or not, they had to move forward and snatch the chances Fate offered.

D-2 analysts scrubbed the crops brought-in from still unknown outside sources and that accounted for the vast majority of reported farm income. This started with both botanical and agronomic check-ups. Posing as food safety inspectors from the department of agriculture, D-2 staff had been able to get samples of the soy, corn, and tobacco being stored on the Cumberland farms. Genetic analyses of these plants showed they were from cultivars grown in Latin America and Africa—not the US. Then, yields were analyzed. Looking at the quantity of corn and soy sold off the farm and ostensibly harvested from the farm's fields in comparison to farm size, the reported sales would reflect harvests of 300 bushels per acre for corn and 200 bushels an acre for soy—two and three times the state average, respectively—hard-to-believe production. Finally, the same grain samples were used for chemical analyses to see if there were any fertilizer residues discernible—the tests indicating a fertilizer profile known for material produced by W. Bryandt Ltd.—Brazil's largest agrochemical producer and global exporter.

Conclusion: the farms were indeed funnels to US markets—channeling far more product than they would have been able to grow had they even been engaged in row-cropping.

These were uncontrolled surreptitious imports.

This determination, perhaps not surprising given the context, brought back clear recollections of the web of ag-related transnational companies that had been woven into the Delpro tapestry including Trusted Industrial Products, Poseidon Consignments, Ace Foods, Farm Services, and Western Farm Supply, along with two major US companies, Simpson Investments and General Industrial and Chemical Products. Behind many of these firms was the uncanny and the urbane Lusitano, Señor Tomas, and behind him there was always the seemingly omnipresent younger brother of Robin McCandless, Sir Horace Bartley.

If Rodney looked hard enough, there were signs of a resurrection of the Delpro ways. These had sadly included human trafficking. This offense had, after all, been the topic that had set off the Secretary of State during that benchmark meeting in Brentwood. Rodney had to mobilize teams to review the records, such as they were, yet again for any signs of illegal aliens and undocumented farm workers to see if they could uncover the footprints of those who had walked among the Delpro elite.

This required resources. Damn the Sullivan Committee. Rodney needed to be able to have a free hand!

Ralph Tave had unknowingly opened the door. The splash of effort concentrated on Cumberland Savings did not, however, mean this was the sole area of interest regarding Tave's activities. Rodney and his team took a long look at Tave and his broad portfolio of actions. In addition to his bank chairmanship, Tave was engaged in a variety of operations, the most prominent (or at least the ones that stood out the most) were his charitable foundation, Bootstraps Fund, aimed at alleviating rural poverty and his direct management of an agricultural engineering firm, Best Farm Design LLC—"BFD" to his friends. Those in the know said Tave focused on agriculture and farming families due to his peasant roots in eastern Europe (although the family had come from Leningrad which had had a population of over three million before the war—Tave's grandfather, according to historical data made available to D-2, having worked as a cooper before taking refuge in the US—hardly rural peasantry). This historical inconsistency, nonetheless, was not a reason in and of itself to personally prioritize Tave. Many immigrants embellished and modified their histories to make them, they hoped, more acceptable—more easily assimilated. Furthermore, as chairman, Tave was not necessarily coordinating or even privy to the unsavory and probably unlawful affairs of Cumberland Savings. He was a person of interest—a person to closely examine. The list of areas of interest was growing, and the resources were dwindling pending legislative approval. For the immediate, Rodney needed to focus on definite on-going illegal actions that seemed to fit within the Domov mold (probably linking at least thematically to Delpro) and then work back up the ladder to those who were guiding these enterprises. To move people of interest into the category of target required this bottom-up approach. It was a lot of work. There were a lot of people of interest.

⚘⚘⚘⚘⚘⚘⚘

While Rodney's team examined and re-examined transactions coming from the early investigation of Cumberland Savings, Joe and Harold had no idea how close they were to being unmasked. Luckily for them, they had very carefully covered their tracks and, probably more importantly, D-2 inspectors had found so much questionable material early on that they did not have the pressing need nor the time to dig more deeply.

While the Mitchells weren't immediately aware of the possible threats coming from their ties to Cumberland Savings, they knew and had always known that they were involved in a job the security of which was threatened by a potentially dangerous domino effect. One had to look no further than Delpro to see that once the pieces started falling the entire house of cards could crumple. The risk was continuously there. Nevertheless, one became inured to it while still trying not to become too habituated and nonchalant to the constant jeopardy—trying to always be on guard.

⚓⚓⚓⚓⚓⚓⚓

As Rodney's crew assembled and analyzed more and more material about Ralph Tave and Cumberland Savings, the leader of D-2 began to feel they were finally getting enough traction to have a real impact—enough traction whereby at least some in Domov would take note and appreciate their possible liability and culpability. This could really lead to somewhere—to something.

Then there was the Sullivan Committee and Rodney's relationships with Group 8 and the overall function of Section T15-Z—all arrangements he might have wished to avoid, confident that his own team had already proven their abilities in dealing with this matter themselves. Still, arrangements that were sadly an unavoidable political necessity. To move forward and attract the resources they required, they also required the shield of Section T15-Z and the collaboration of Group 8. It made things much more complicated, but it was necessary. Now, necessary or not, it was tied up by Jake Sullivan. Rodney was, to say the least, frustrated.

Manure or More

COINCIDENTALLY, the Honorable Jake Sullivan was frustrated. He was valiantly trying to spread his own story (some would later kindly call it spreading a bucket of manure, others, less kind, calling it a raft of shit). He started by taking a rather random poke at DOJs priorities in his attempts to deliver for Gage Smith. He started by attempting to pull attention (and funding) away from Section T15-Z by shining a light on what he imagined (or portrayed) as a major security crisis—foreign (and often non-Christian, to boot) hordes at the country's doorstep waiting the chance to bring forth all manner of chaos.

He recalled for his committee members, his proposed legislation, to provide immediate and significant economic stimulus to American companies to invest in Africa to provide better jobs and better working conditions, thereby keeping the horde at bay while, at the same time, tightening immigration regulations to assure the safety of folks at home.

He waved Janice Pittman's report in the air as though it had come from Mount Sinai. He proudly, with unbridled hubris, gave himself bountiful credit for his forward-thinking in already having staff in the region to make critical assessments. He professed his team leader's recent report made compelling arguments for all to see about the threat that was developing right under their noses.

Still massaging Jan's report, he then shifted gears and lauded what he dubbed on the spot the Nigeria-Cameroon Infrastructure Investment Project—the NCIIP—as an example of a macro initiative with deep positive repercussions. He noted it was, however, unfortunate that the US had not been in on such major development efforts from the onset. If his legislation were to pass, it was exactly this type of activity where American companies could do good, employing locals, and keeping the threats away from our hearths and kin.

With practiced flourish, the senator completed his diatribe, calling on his fellow senators and his much-respected committee members to support the legislation he had put forward and, pending its passage, to allocate resources through their committee to initial efforts to explore opportunities for American businessmen—the best in the world, of course.

He concluded by observing that, since he already had staff in place, the committee could in short order provide some much-needed financial assistance to this team's efforts, temporarily taking funds from those previously earmarked for supporting Section T15-Z; hypothesizing that, in reality, the money going to his staff in the field would be the same as money going to Section T15-Z. These public monies, he recollected, were critically held to ensure the security of the homeland while addressing emerging threats. Section T15-Z had, after all, been proposed as an umbrella regrouping D-2 and Group 8 for just this reason. This fact notwithstanding, the senator's team at present on the ground in West Africa would be another tactic to achieve the same goal—and a tactic with fewer complexities and a shorter timeline. It would be the right thing to do in the immediate for the committee to refocus resources from Section T15-Z to his staffers working out of Côte d'Ivoire. The committee could then, naturally, go back and seek additional urgent funding to be able to support Section T15-Z, allowing it to do its essential work and, at the same time, backstop the efforts currently underway in West Africa.

He once more, in closing, brandished Jan's report, announcing, "My staff are doing terrific things!"

⚘⚘⚘⚘⚘⚘⚘

While Senator Jake Sullivan and Mister Rodney Mills, Esquire struggled in the same arena, persistently pulling in opposite directions, the work of their respective teams continued, although at somewhat reduced levels of activity pending the resolution of the issues being put before Sullivan's committee.

Again, the preemptive D-2 team, searching for each morsel of scat that could be found along the trail, attempted to look everywhere for everything. This attentiveness paid off. They came across some leads that lead both back and forward.

Some years back, Rodney's earlier investigations via the BTF group into the wider network of Delpro had uncovered the gunrunning of Delpro associate Radutu Botezatu. Through truly impressive exploration starting with illegal weapons imported into Ecuador and Peru—Czech-manufactured Ceska Zbrojovka 88G assault rifles, Zbrojovka ZBII Falcon X anti-material rifles, and Ceska Zbrojovka 99W automatic pistols—agents had traced the transport of these arms to Alimento Atlântico vessels coming from the port of Faro in Portugal. They had then been able to follow the trail through the Mediterranean and into the Black Sea to Constanţa and onward into the heart of Romania to the ultimate exporter, Articole Sportive Moderne (Modern Sporting Goods), a Botezatu company.

Now the team had heard of Romanian arms—MD 98 machine pistols, Pistolul model 1998, also known as Dracula, and MD 63 assault rifles, Pistol Mitralieră model 1963/1965—that had been found in caches of the Militia 47 group in Idaho. From here, with great forensic work, they had been able to follow the weapons back to the FNL in Chiapas State, Mexico. Apparently, this rebel group was so well supplied with arms by outside supporters it was able to sell some of the surplus for needed cash—part of this surplus evidently ending up in Idaho.

Still following the trail upstream, they were able to again link the trans-Atlantic movement of these weapons to Alimento Atlântico and the port of Faro. However, from there, the pathway that had been used for the earlier arms shipments seemed to have been abandoned. Investigators raised serious questions. In the case of the earlier interrupted arms deal, Botezatu had taken great efforts to hide his exporting of Czeck-made weaponry. Would he now be so brazen as to identically repeat his previous arrangements and use Romanian weapons which were even closer links to home? Most felt this was unlikely. Most felt this more recent shipment was probably the work of another "businessman" exporting the items into Mexico.

The D-2 team report to Head of Operations Mills said, "Following the transnational channels, we can definitively state the weapons in the US originated from the other side of the Atlantic. The apparent demise of Delpro yet the use of pathways in common with earlier arms deals known to have involved Delpro indicates a possible set of common denominators that could bridge to Domov. Yet, the differences in weapon type and trans-European movement vary significantly, making us consider the possibility that these arms are coming from a different source—a source we have still to definitively identify."

Rodney summarized his colleague's work in a note to the Sullivan Committee, emphasizing the presence of highly dangerous illegal arms in the country—further substantiating the urgency with which the committee must act to quickly fully fund and activate Section T15-Z.

Rodney had recommended to Senator Sullivan that no immediate action be taken against the Idaho militia—now was not the right time. This was a unique opportunity to wait and watch (as D-2 did so well)—only rounding up the culprits when they had gleaned as much detail about their activities as possible. Before exposing themselves, it was critical that agents gave the Militia 47 members time to divulge their plans so that the agencies could better understand their targets and priorities—taking precautions as necessary.

Jake Sullivan, however, felt the time was right right now—right for him if not for agents looking to give the militia members enough rope to hang themselves. Sullivan went directly to the chair of the Permanent Committee on Homeland Security and Government Affairs and, indicating he had nearly singlehandedly uncovered a dire plot, handed over all the information on the smuggled weapons.

Federal marshals promptly confiscated the arms and arrested the militia members. Although the plans for the use of these weapons were never uncovered, Senator Sullivan got a feather in his cap and some dangerous armaments were taken out of the hands of dangerous people, but Section T15-Z was still not fully funded nor activated.

Jan was familiar with the French expression to "*péter plus haut que son cul*." Crudely, to act as though one was a big shit, more properly, to be arrogant or appear more important than you really were. When she had first heard this as a volunteer, it had been worth a giggle. Now, feeling almost as though she were whirling aimlessly around like one of those funny beetles in a fishpond, she wondered if it applied to her. Had it been arrogant of her to accept to come back to a region she so respected but, in all honesty, with which she had had only a fleeting relationship? Had it been foolish trying to be something she was not, to have agreed to do a job that seemed so great yet, at the same time, so unclear? Had it all been a mistake?

Jan had sent her first report to her boss confident that she had done, and done well, the necessary steps to establish the required contacts and foundation to begin vigorously identifying opportunities for Virginia investors. Nevertheless, her report had categorically stated that she needed the senator's go-ahead before she could do anything more.

That had been weeks ago.

No word from the Honorable Jake Sullivan as Jan felt herself unavoidably changing from the Congressional Staffer on a mission to the aimless tourist. At least, as far as she could tell, she was still being paid, but life in the Hôtel Ivoire was wearing very thin. To make matters worse, she was embarrassed to get back in touch with Awa. They had planned well together. They were ready to go. Awa had had a long phone call with Oriana and everything had been arranged. The only holdup, that Jan assured Awa was a mere formality that would be taken care of quickly, was Sullivan's green light.

Still nothing.

It was embarrassing.

It was frustrating.

Although Jan was nearly oblivious to any quagmires other than her own, she was not alone in feeling downhearted. Jake was feeling stymied, but it had nothing to do with Jan nor her assignment. Her report (which he'd never read) had become his talisman—really a stage prop just like her mission. He had no, nor had he ever had, any interest in helping Virginians invest in Africa. He certainly had no interest in helping Africans. He was the centerpiece of his interests, and these interests were now far too fluid. He needed to gain control.

He had hoped Gage Smith would have been happy with his efforts—he hoped Gage Smith would have communicated with his higher-ups that all was OK.

But he had no word.

Then that damned Rodney Mills had found these crumbs that he had blown up into national security concerns. All rubbish, but enough to get the members of the committee sidetracked and possibly ready to fully fund Section T15-Z.

It was a crock of shit.

Still, it was his crock, and he had to find the best way forward.

He had already gone all in with Jan. Maybe, in retrospect, his idea had been too harebrained—the idea to have American foreign investors suck up the dregs of those far-off befallen societies so that these same dregs did not turn into America-hating terrorists.

He had tried hard to make the sale, but his colleagues appeared far from sold on the theory.

Nonetheless, he had to double down—he could see no other choices.

He had one of his senior DC staffers read Jan's report and make some bland remarks while also drafting a cover letter for his signature not really apologizing but indirectly saying it was unfortunate there had been such a long gap between the reception of the report and his feedback.

The commented report complete with cover letter was sent (with a big red ink stamp saying it was "URGENT") to Ms. Janice Pittman in care of Consular Services, US Embassy, Abidjan. In the same big manila envelope was another letter addressed to the ambassador with a copy for Jan, saying the senator's staff member would be continuing her assignment in Côte d'Ivoire with an option to enlarge the effort to other areas of West Africa, asking the ambassador to assist in any way possible. Jan had the green light.

Jan almost greedily consumed the contents of the manila envelope with the bright red "URGENT" stamp on its face. She had been worried when the embassy contacted her to say there was an important communication from Senator Sullivan. This could be the formal end of all. In her present state of topsy-turviness, she thought she might welcome bad news as it would get her out of her frump and back to the US where she could look for another job—she was fed up. Then, when the taxi had dropped her back at the hotel and she had rushed to her room and torn open the envelope, she was satisfied. Everything, all the disgruntlement of past weeks, seemed to disappear as she saw the news that her work would continue and possibly expand. It was OK.

In her report, a key portion had been the recommendations for the next steps including working closely with Awa and, by remote control, Oriana. The senator apparently agreed with the liaison as he had given the go-ahead for all the recommended activities.

Jan called Awa and arranged to meet for a stimulating cup of robusta coffee and, at long last, a planning session to move forward.

They met at Le Numéro 69, a café not far from the Grand Marché de Treichville where the ambiance was superb.

"It's been a long time," Jan said, not really wanting to go into the embarrassing details of the long hiatus.

"*Dis donc*, don't tell me. I've been at this quite a while and things are either running hot or cold—there's no lukewarm comfort zone," Awa replied, trying to push away unnecessary chitchat about why things didn't go as they might have liked, and pushing the conversation to the core issues of now-now—Awa was always businesslike.

"So true," Jan acknowledged as she jumped into the work of the day. "Well, it seems the senator has approved our suggestions. There were really very few details from his side—just some minor comments and a few easy-to-answer questions. Overall, if I am interpreting things correctly, and I well may not be doing so, it seems we're cleared to do as we've proposed and even kick things up a notch if we want to. There seem to be no concerns about our working together, I'd guess they see the possible connection to Oriana and the paper as a plus that could give them needed publicity."

"That all seems good," Awa replied, it could have been a statement or a question.

"I think it is," Jan continued. "The senator seems to have shone a light on what he now calls the NCIIP—the pending project my contacts at the BAOD mentioned—so somehow we need to fold this into our work—he apparently sees this as a perfect example of projects that should be done by American businesses but projects where it looks like US interests may have been marginalized or at least not well consulted."

"With a formal clearance and possibly a mandate to go bigger," Awa inserted, now with growing signs of excitement, "we can, checking with Oriana first of course, bring in Mariama and see how her work to date may be incorporated into our work—she's been learning a lot about freight and logistics relating to transnational commerce and this would be an important part of a bigger picture."

"Definitely," Jan carried on, enjoying the discussion, "I think we can make a strong case for zooming out and adopting a scope that would be West African. And, looking back at the efficacy of my last effort, this time I think I'll send a letter to the senator thanking him for his comments and approval and informing him, in line with his suggestions, we've scaled up to a regional level. This way we'll go ahead straight-away and not wait for any feedback from DC. I'll also write to the ambassador, as I was copied on the Senator's letter to her, and advise that, in line with the senator's priorities, we've adopted a regional approach although we will continue to use Abidjan as our base of operations."

"Sounds good."

"Yep." Jan smiled to herself, she was learning (she hoped). "I'll additionally ask the ambassador if the US Information Service has any funds to help us as this is an activity that is trying to significantly increase the American presence in the region. We can even offer, if you can arrange it, to have the ambassador interviewed by phone by Oriana so that there can be an article in the paper about how the US embassy in Côte d'Ivoire is helping American businesses get established in West Africa."

"Sounds great."

"Once all that foundational stuff is done, we'll need to meet with Mariama. It'd really be excellent if we could as well find a way to get to the bridge site to see what's going on. Anyway, I'll go back to the BAOD and see if my contacts have any additional information on this subject since it seems close to the senator's heart. You can brief Oriana, and we'll see if she can get an interview for the ambassador."

"Fine."

From the onset, in his (totally affected) homey way, Senator Sullivan had stressed to Jan that this "African thing," as he called it, was a totally bare-bones activity—"just trying to help those folks back home." He often reiterated that he and Jan had to do everything on a shoestring. These were, as all knew, truly tough budgetary times.

However, the reality was that the anxious statesman was willing to move the goal posts as much as need be to get the desired positive reaction from Gage Smith and his cronies. If this meant spending money from other pots, so be it. He would go back to the committee and stress the urgency of protecting the homeland and how, given his deep commitment, he had been willing to temporarily use his own resources knowing full well the committee would cover these costs post factum if necessary.

This time, when he got an envelope through the pouch from Abidjan, he quickly passed it to the senior staffer he had designated as the focal point for his "African thing." He maintained he was far too busy to read all the correspondence himself, but he did now take the time and effort to go over the high points with his staffer and then advise as to how to promptly reply. It looked as though there was, at the end of the day, potentially a lot riding on this adventure in West Africa.

After he had been briefed about Jan's latest update, it was apparent the girl was taking the assignment seriously and actually garnering material and making contacts that could be beneficial if he could only lay the predicate here with his fellow committee members.

Therefore, through his underling, the good senator advised his representative in Côte d'Ivoire to move ahead quickly on her planned activities. He encouraged the work with that lady from *The Daily News*—both in the field and in regard to the possible interview for the ambassador—this was all good stuff. He said he would have another letter drafted for this same ambassador to ask her to support his work with some USIS funds (implying but not saying directly, funds he knew she had). Finally, pending additional local finances, Jan should open a foreign currency account at the local Standard Chartered (as he had been advised by aids) and he would assure some supplemental funds were sent her way since she was doing so much so well.

Who knew? Jake thought, maybe this would all work out?

Some time back, Jan would have been thrilled with the news from DC—both the fact that there had been a prompt response and the fact that there was now more money with which to work. Perhaps unhappily, she had learned her lesson about the ups and downs of this job—the hot and cold as Awa had called it. This was probably an up and there surely would be downs forthcoming.

Her pertinacious skepticism (or authenticity) aside, this was all positive. She and Awa would now be able to plan some things they could really do while reaching out to Mariama on what was looking like the logistics chapter of their work and, among other things, trying to organize the interview between the ambassador and Oriana assuming the efforts to secure some USIS funds were successful.

These plans, as they had already discussed, should now be able to include a visit to the well-touted (by the good Senator Sullivan) Nigeria-Cameroon Infrastructure Investment Project. This part was, needless to say, more easily agreed to than done. By design, these infrastructure development activities were taking place in a very remote area—this remoteness one of the selling points in terms of opening-up the economy.

While most of the work was designed to be undertaken from camps built in eastern Nigeria, at Awa's suggestion, it was much easier to access the site from the Cameroonian side.

Using the senator's new funding, leaving the ambassador's secretary to work out the interview arrangements with Oriana, and with the promise from the ambassador that there would be some USIS dollars forthcoming, Jan and Awa flew to Douala and took a bus to Limbé where they allowed themselves a twenty-four-hour break on the beach before heading due north to Mamfe in the four by four with driver they had hired. The 165-mile, five-hour trip crossed rubber, banana, and coffee plantations and dense natural forest as well as many a deep mud hole. In Mamfe, they were able to get two spartan but relatively clean rooms at the Presbyterian Mission. On the mission veranda after an equally spartan evening meal, feeling tired from the jostling of the travel but happy to be there, over cups of Nescafé in a country that produced top quality coffee, they strategized for the next day.

The principal Cameroonian site was Ekokku, an hour away to the west. They had not attempted to make any advance arrangements for their visit—they really didn't know who to contact and doubted they would receive a very open-armed reception if they did manage to get in touch with key actors. Naturally, anyone would want to know what they were doing, and they didn't have a good answer. The truth was they were scouting things out for Senator Sullivan (and for their own curiosity). The two ladies agreed their travel was not a junket for a change of pace from the routine of Abidjan. They agreed this was an important part of the overall assignment. They really had to see the place to understand the proposed project. Nonetheless, there were no assurances that they would be welcome. There was not even any assurance they would be able to see much—this was a densely forested area, isolated both physically and socially. So they finetuned their antennae to take in as much as possible from this remote ecosystem, not knowing exactly what information or observations would serve them best in the weeks to come.

The next day, after a surprisingly good breakfast, they put the driver's skills and the Land Rover's muscle to the test as they drove to the border. The road, if even worthy of the title, was more of a mud track through the Ejagham Forest Reserve—called by some the roughest road in the world. Officially it was part of the major N-6 roadway, but the reality was that parts were barely passable by anything with four wheels.

When they finally reached the small town (village really by any objective standard) of Ekokku, neither knew what to expect, but what they found was not what either might have possibly anticipated. There was practically nothing indicating any new construction nor any important project at hand. The town, snuggled up to Cross River, was bisected by the N-6, ending at a rather ramshackle border station on the east end of an equally ramshackle bridge. There was a police station a short distance from the border and a Presbyterian Mission further down the street—the two buildings appearing as bookends for the residential area where there were children, dogs, a market square, small off-licenses, and a chop house (restaurant). It was simply a typical rural hamlet with all the basic needs if none of the add-ons. There were no overt signs of the great NCIIP and no one with whom they spoke seemed to know anything about building a new bridge, upgrading roads, nor any sort of important civil works that were in the offing. It was as it always had been, just a blip on a 1,281-mile border.

Chakir Awal smiled to himself. One of his colleagues in the States had sent him a message asking about the Nigeria-Cameroon Infrastructure Investment Project that one Senator Sullivan was holding on-high as an example of the type of project the US needed to encourage—with US leadership, naturally.

Chakir had replied to his colleague that no such project existed. This was, strictly speaking, true. In spite of a lot of positive gossip, some possibly well-founded, presently there was no such active project as far as Chakir and his co-workers at Onyx Associates knew—and through the Domov network, they knew a lot.

Chakir knew the BAOD liked a project concept for extensive infrastructure investment targeting eastern Nigeria and western Cameroon—opening up some very remote areas for economic growth. However, this was, as of now, still a concept. Project ideas of this sort had been around for a long time. This was not new—not in content nor geographic focus. It was merely a recycled proposal that finally appeared to be gaining some much-needed traction from within the BAOD as well as from some major donors. But so far it was nothing more tangible than an idea.

This was the official line and the reply Chakir had offered to his state-side colleague. As always, the truth lay some distance from the official position. Chakir's confidential information was that the project was gaining considerable momentum and could be approved at any time. Some very powerful people had their eyes on some heretofore untapped and profitable resources. Therefore, with the right whispers in the right ears, it was, indeed, an imminent possibility for a funded project with an eight-figure budget to be launched in the very near future—a budget alone that made this appealing to Domov and that allowed Chakir to be Abidjan rather than Holwerd. There were multiple opportunities in the region, but a mega project provided not only a chance to be a bidder and potentially open a new line of profits, but it also offered a formal cover for Domov and its agents to go scurrying about the hinterland, whether planning infrastructure or dealing with other "family business."

In a best-case scenario, Chakir's efforts would lead to a much larger Domov presence and significant profits for the home office. In a worst-case scenario, there would be a much better picture of how Domov could position itself in West Africa for maximum advantage as well as an enhanced presence in the region to encourage and better benefit from parties like the Cisse brothers, Chantal Silue, and others.

Chakir had intentionally not made direct contact with these Domov associates. Following the strategy laid out by the *Maliar*, local counterparts had already been informed in one way or other about Onyx Associates by Sir Horace.

For the time being, he felt the best tactic was to still keep a low profile. Nonetheless, he had, through the intricate network woven into the Domov tapestry, using friends of friends, let those with Domov links know that high-level work planned for some time was now underway in the region—work that was built on the efforts of these allies and work that would ultimately be reflected in potentially impressive profits for these same allies.

Chakir laughed quietly to himself as he thought of his new role as a cheerleader building team spirit. Not really a typical Domov activity, it was all about messaging.

There was a subtle subtext to the cheerleading: "Don't shit where you eat." There could be unfortunate repercussions for associates if overzealousness led to any regrettable situations with local authorities or other unwanted factions. Discretion was essential—as always.

Jan and Awa were not privy to all the information that Chakir could access. Therefore, they were still surprised at the lack of any footprint to be found in Ekokku.

Back in Abidjan, they decided not to disclose the full level of nothingness they had recorded. Who knew, they countered, things could change tomorrow? So, they informally reported back to the ambassador that they had had a good trip and had spoken with a number of local residents who were all enthusiastic about the possibilities for a major new infrastructure project in their area. They then summarized the meeting with the ambassador in the format of a trip report to Senator Sullivan's office. They concluded their brief report stating, "NCIIP will certainly be welcome as this area is currently cut off from mainstream commerce and communications. As these isolated communities open up after NCIIP, there will be multiple opportunities for US firms."

Orest was keeping tabs from afar. He had confidence in Chakir. If things went well, it could be a boon for Domov and lead to a whole different form of organizational structure, at least in West Africa. If things did not go well, it was unlikely the status quo would be disrupted. And there was nothing wrong with the status quo.

Oriana had no knowledge of the *Maliar* nor that the person in this (maybe) august position was her father. If she had known, it would have been interesting.

Judgements

When Rodney had been very young, his mother used to read to him the stories of Robert Louis Stevenson (he remembered the musty aroma that seeped from the pages as his mother read through the well-worn leather-bound volumes she had inherited from her great aunt)—he'd loved those stories and those books. This developed into a life-long affection for Stevenson. He recalled one quote attributed to the author, "Don't judge each day by the harvest you reap, but by the seeds that you plant." He worried now about the seeds that he and his team had been able to plant. They needed to prepare the terrain for a major offensive through the combined resources of Section T15-Z. But they ended up like people impatiently waiting for the rain to fall—the rain in the form of action from the Sullivan Committee to open the channels for needed functional support. Nonetheless, they could not get sidetracked by the inaction of the committee. They had to focus. They could still do a lot.

There was a massive amount of data through which to sort. They had recovered great quantities of material from Delpro, especially from the offices overseen by Don Drumpfsh that had effectively become archives at Robin McCandless' behest. There were also a large number of documents and interview reports from a wide variety of individuals who had interacted with Delpro directly or indirectly. They had developed a database to be able to look for correlations between different topics and different individuals. With the revelations of Cumberland Savings and Ralph Tave, using this database, they spent significant blocks of time looking for relationships with past topics flagged as being Delpro-related. This paid off.

Two interesting relationships popped early in the analysis. Both Tave and the bank appeared to have had relationships with Arrow Head

Timber and Cattle Company in Oregon—a firm Eddie Hall had been able to link to Delpro. It also looked as if the Kentucky duo were tied to a fish processing plant located between Austin and Forth Worth, Texas—a plant that Charlie Stancik had helped supply through his work for Spot On in Costa Rica and an operation directly attached to Delpro.

It seemed Mr. Tave had been engaged in these two activities both financially through the bank and technically through his own engineering company which had had several lucrative contracts with each of the operations. There was a lot to distill.

While his team delved into the life and times of Ralph Tave in minute detail, Rodney first checked that Robin McCandless remained out of commission at the Porumbel Albastru, wanting to make sure this wizard of committing crimes in plain site would not resurface to further complicate his work. Once he was comfortable he would not have an unwanted visit from this infirm thaumaturge, he began his own assignment targeting Jake Sullivan.

It was becoming increasingly apparent that the senator was not just slow to start—not just deliberate and a stickler for procedure. From all current indications, he was intentionally raising concerns to try and delay or even derail the support and oversight intended for Section T15-Z. There had to be more to this than met the eye.

Rodney knew the background of the Virginia statesman. He knew Old Dominion's legislator's true backstory was quite different from the biography proffered to constituents with no shortage of historical hyperbole. This was, for the political class, more the rule than the exception. It certainly was not unusual nor, as a standalone issue, criminal. It wasn't the building of idols that was likely the culpable issue (if there was one and there probably was). Sullivan was a shrewd politician. He understood well the fable of his life would not pull him down. There was more.

D-2 had always been a powerful group in terms of its investigative access—it had had to be. Leveraging this power and applying the time-tested adage he'd seen proven correct so many times when working at the SEC, Rodney followed the money. The official line was that both branches of thc Sullivan family were monied with longstanding and influential noble ancestries. Rebecca Jameson Sullivan's claims to deep roots and even deeper pockets appeared to be factual—she was part of the old Virginia aristocracy. As Rodney knew, Jacob's claims to fame were far less factual. However, again, at face value, this didn't appear to be a major concern. His stated net worth, including that of his spouse, was just slightly over three million dollars—not a concerningly large fortune for a four-term senator. But Rodney could and did go much further down the tunnel that led to other layers of the senator's finances.

With practice and patience, he was able to make surprising if not unexpected discoveries.

There were multiple offshore accounts in Saint Kitts and Nevis, Belize, and the Cook Islands with assets totaling more than fifty million dollars as well as safety deposit boxes in Guernsey and Luxembourg. There was probably more but this was enough. There was too much subterfuge. Senator Jake Sullivan was definitely beholding to some group or groups for these riches. Logically, the types of folks using hidden foreign accounts were the types of folks who wanted to be invisible and just the types of folks D-2 was trying to lock-up. It wasn't a very big leap to conclude that Sullivan's efforts to stall and even divert support for Section T15-Z could well be intentional and aimed at aiding his behind-the-scenes bankrollers. Jake had apparently put himself on the auction-block and now it was time for payback.

There was more.

Rodney was able to access the senator's travel records during his congressional down time. This was a springboard to examining the legislator's wider travels.

On nearly an annual basis Jake Sullivan took a holiday with his family to the US Virgin Islands, renting a beachfront bungalow at Bordeaux Point, not far from Botany Bay. Most years, according to the records Rodney studied, the family rented the beach-house for two months. Rebecca, sometimes with the children, sometimes with other relatives or friends, would go early and get everything organized. Jake would then join his wife, not infrequently commuting (unceremoniously at tax-payer expense) back and forth from the island to his office in DC depending on the exigencies of the day.

This was all relatively common knowledge and used politically from time to time by the senator to uphold his support for more investments in Puerto Rico given his professed wide-ranging familiarity with the area.

Rodney was, however, able to plunge more deeply into Sullivan's holidays.

Most years, Jake (often with his wife but not always) would go from Bordeaux Point by boat or air to the French island of Guadeloupe—a mere 265 miles away (Saint Kitts and Nevis only 170 miles away). The immediate destination was Sainte-Rose, a half-an-hour drive from this

French island's largest city of Les Abymes. From here, there reportedly would be a chauffeur-driven vehicle waiting to take him to a secluded villa near Rifflet, another eight miles westerly on the extreme northwest tip of Guadeloupe Island.

This property was not only physically isolated, its ownership and even architecture were methodically entombed. It was only thanks to D-2's unrivaled investigative possibilities that Rodney was able to uncover the fact that this villa was one of many real estate investments belonging to Raymond Girard.

This name was familiar from Rodney's work under BTF when they had spotlighted Radutu Botezatu and through him had been able to uncover the apparently very important Easter weekend conclaves in the Făgăraş Mountains that assembled the ignoble quintet of Liu Li, Janco Momberg, Bohadan Kushnir, Sebastian Carvalho, and Girard. Raymond was unquestionably part of an inner circle with connections to Domov. In addition, Raymond was seemingly Jake's friend, associate, or benefactor (perhaps all three).

This was potentially grim. This was, if it all ultimately could be validated, a tangible thread tying Sullivan to Domov through Girard.

So far, this was all conjecture. Rodney had no hard proof. Nevertheless, practically this was actionable in terms of how the focal point for Section T15-Z strategized his next steps.

There was no need to bring Felix and Group 8 into this theorizing at this juncture.

Rodney decided to quietly and informally put together a small team composed of his two most seasoned forensic accountants, Ted Whether and Sara McNab—Ted and Sara both having worked with Hal. They knew their work and they were also the epitome of discretion. Together the trio would develop the best tactics for addressing the gentleman from Virginia.

⚘⚘⚘⚘⚘⚘⚘

Tactics were pivotal matters on several fronts. In two totally unrelated cases, entrepreneurs with loose Domov ties were learning the truth in the old saying, "don't poke the bear."

The Cisse brothers and Kyrylo Rudenko were both having to rethink their tactics for growth and expansion. The brothers had been at odds with Les Caïds since their unceremonious and uninvited insertion into Marseilles life. Similarly, Kyrylo had managed to get himself crosswise with the Solntsevskaya Bratva over arms sales to Muslim groups in Georgia. In each case the long-established syndicates wanted their undesirable new competitors to simply disappear. In both cases the competition was an irritation verging on becoming a real problem. In each case, the syndicates were proceeding cautiously. The French likely had no idea of the Cisse's links to Domov (and this may not have made any difference)—they knew they had to be careful with all interactions with African groups. The Cisses were certainly not alone. There were many so far unaffiliated and independent African groups operating on the margins of Les Caïds' affairs—the last thing the French syndicate wanted was for these foreign groups to coalesce into a common and powerful front. It was a touchy situation.

For the Bratva it was more clearcut. They had known the Rudenko family for years and had known of their ties to Domov. They had applied and wanted to continue to opt for the philosophy of "live and let live," but Kyrylo was pushing the limits. He had previously been focusing on, and should continue to focus on, far-off markets and not get into the Bratva's sandbox. A late-night visit to Kyrylo's home tried to underscore this point.

Similar situations but different reactions. The Cisses, with their strong legal foothold, doubled down and began expanding into a variety of black-market channels they could supply with products of African origin. Les Caïds took a breath and decided it was not (yet) the time for an outright confrontation.

Kyrylo Rudenko's roust from bed had had the desired impact. He decided to stay clear of any Eastern European and Central Asian interactions. As if a sign from the stars reinforcing this decision, he was unexpectedly contacted by a representative of Herramientas Agrícolas Especiales (Speciality Farm Tools) in Mérida, Yucatán, requesting a pro forma for a very large order of weaponry. Not only was the order very large, but the potential client was requesting generic arms. Kyrylo had the liberty to pick and choose from a wide variety of options from Eastern European manufacturers, supplying those where he had the largest margins. This new and immediate opportunity cushioned his gut reaction to go head-to-head with the Bratva—a possibility against which his father had strongly cautioned.

Tactics mattered.

⚘⚘⚘⚘⚘⚘⚘

There was a backstory to Kyrylo's new deal.

Herramientas Agrícolas Especiales was physically located in the small community of Tamanché, halfway between the city center of Mérida and the shores of the Gulf of Mexico (each about fifteen miles away). It was secure, secluded, and accessible to a variety of pathways for securing the raw materials required to fabricate and market the farm implements it proudly sold throughout southern Mexico. As many enterprises, it also did other things.

Herramientas Agrícolas Especiales was the Mexican affiliate of The Farmers' Home, a well-known agri-supply chain in the Midwest of the US with headquarters in Racine, Wisconsin, on Chatham Street, just a block from the shores of Lake Michigan. Lambert Richardson was the CEO and founder of The Farmers' Home.

Lambert was no longer a young man. He had been a colleague of Robin McCandless. They had cooperated on a number of activities, most involving the movement of varied merchandise between the US and Canada via Lake Michigan although some of the dubious material came directly from Atlantic sea routes through the Great Lakes-St. Lawrence River Waterway.

The products involved in this trade covered the gamut from one-off movement of items, probably specific misappropriated articles, to more regular consignments of everything from pharmaceuticals to hybrid corn seed. When McCandless and Delpro vanished, Lambert had thought this portion of his business had come to an end. However, he received a letter postmarked Amsterdam asking if he would be interested in continuing the arrangements on a case-by-case basis. He had agreed and there had been irregular but not infrequent transactions with communications always emanating from Amsterdam.

Still, these cloaked arrangements from afar were only a portion of Lambert's extracurricular activities. He had a wide variety of clients with a wide variety of interests. One of his contacts and a possible client was Mercer McMaster whom he had met at an annual meeting of the National Ag Suppliers Association. Mercer had a more modest chain of stores in the southeast with his offices in Savannah, Georgia. Lambert and Mercer had been in regular communication, just to chat or to try and resolve problems that were common to both areas such as supply chain glitches or burdensome new regulations. Both men considered themselves as freethinkers who felt less was more in terms of government involvement—or, for that matter, anyone else's involvement.

Lambert had been more curious than surprised when he had received a call from Mercer indicating his colleague from the Goober State would be passing through Chicago and would like to meet with him at the Marriott for a business lunch.

After a satisfactory if not spectacular meal, Mercer had stared at his Badger State lunch mate, "I've got a really big deal, Lambert—don't want to scare you off."

"Oh," the elder of the two had replied stoically, "don't scare that easy."

"OK. Don't want to get too far into the real nitty-gritty, but you may or may not know, I'm a member of the Southern Continentals."

"Never heard of 'em."

"Yeah. Not too well known and certainly not this far north of the Mason-Dixon line."

"Yep."

"Well, like our forebears who fought the Lobsterbacks in 1776, we're a group of patriotic Continental Soldiers fighting for our freedom—our culture."

"OK."

"Well, it's different up here. But back at home we got a lot of concerns. Won't go into it all but it's enough to say that this is serious, and we need to make damn sure folks know it's serious. This requires firepower."

"Lots go'n on."

"I know you might think this is not your fight, but it might be your business in a real dollars-and-cents way."

"Always interested in good business."

"One of my brothers had made contacts with the folks fighting a similar battle in Idaho. They needed their own firepower. They had had their own ties to a rebel group in Mexico and obtained some really impressive weapons from these guys—weapons originally coming from some supplier in Eastern Europe apparently. But the Feds found out and now our chums are locked up and the guns gone."

"We can't have this happen to us."

"I know you've some investments overseas and I thought you might be able to help out—there's be a big check in it for you."

That was it. Mercer wanted Lambert to become a gunrunner.

After they had said their goodbyes, on the drive back to Racine, Lambert had realized he was not opposed to gun-running. He was opposed to getting caught. He'd have to think about it.

The thinking had been done—the result had been the contact from Herramientas Agrícolas Especiales to Kyrylo Rudenko.

Lambert was reasonably sure there would be no major issues getting the arms into his facilities in Tamanché. Moving them north was the real problem. He decided the southern land border was too risky. He went back to his old ways when working with Delpro. He'd use the Great Lakes-St. Lawrence River Waterway. He moved ag supplies by freighters all the time. Guns mixed in with grass seed and weed killer shouldn't be a problem.

It was turning into a busy time.

Jan and Awa had expected things to peter out.

Just the opposite was happening—but not reportedly on-the-ground at the proposed NCIIP site.

Senator Sullivan had amped-up his rhetoric about the NCIIP in particular and investment in West Africa in general. He was making it a showcase topic—never missing a chance to tout it in the Senate or at political gatherings. It was now a subject inextricably tied to the lawmaker and one for which he was receiving considerable press coverage. The media was asking, "Will Jake Sullivan succeed in opening new frontiers?"

Jake immensely enjoyed the limelight—both for its own (political) sake and for the attention it showered on the topic that was such a priority for his unwelcome overseer Gage Smith. He had promised a diversion and he hoped he was delivering.

This senatorial enthusiasm translated into pressure on Jan to deliver so that Jake could continue delivering. Because Jake was somewhat a realist, he knew Jan needed backing in her work. The senator increased both his financial and political support to Jan's efforts. Now she had to produce—and quickly.

With the additional patronage from DC combined with the assistance from the Abidjan embassy, funding and political agency were no longer the critical limiting factors. It was time to go all in.

Jan arranged with the Embassy to do personal services contracts for Awa and Mariama, organizing for her Sénégalese colleague and New

York City graduate student to have an extended expense-paid stay in Abidjan. The trio then set about their work, no longer seeing NCIIP as the centerpiece but almost as an annex to a thorough assessment of investment opportunities for Virginians and Americans in general.

Africa had never been a mainstream investment destination for US entrepreneurs. There had always been a modest American presence, but the real external funding had been from the former colonial rulers—this rapidly being replaced by a Chinese domination. France, however, was still in a very powerful role in Côte d'Ivoire as well as across nearly all the francophone countries of the region.

Mariama had been doing double duty. Her project for her masters was an examination of the logistics of sea-lanes along the west coast of Africa, looking specifically into the best routes for freight bound for the US—a subject that was of interest both to the would-be investor and her back-home employer (from whom she had a short-term leave-of-absence but with whom she still had long-term bonds), Eastern Atlantic Imports.

She was looking at the movement of raw materials to the north and west—to Europe and North America. She was looking at the movement of both production inputs and finished products to the south and east, from Europe and North America. When she tried to chart it out on a map, it looked like chicken scratches—there were lines going everywhere. She decided she needed to start with one product and then build out. Her chosen opening commodity was Côte d'Ivoire's number two food crop, cassava (with complete agreement from Oriana—full circle back to the "manioc mess"); as her team and most knew, a major crop providing important harvests for both domestic use and export.

This had not been a difficult decision. It was common sense. Oriana had, of course, already done a great deal of journalistic work on the broader subject of trafficking agricultural products and arms around the Atlantic Basin. In this reporting Oriana had zoomed in on cassava as a suitable and traceable target since it was not grown in the temperate climates of North America and Europe, hence all supplies imported. Additionally, it was an important component of the agricultural programs of countries like Angola and Côte d'Ivoire where she felt possible extralegal trafficking lanes could be having real impact. In one way or another, Oriana had already documented and told a good part of the narrative. This was a solid foundation upon which to build.

Mariama, with Oriana's encouragement, hoped to dig even deeper into the work presently on the table, but looking through a different lens.

Oriana had been trying to highlight crime and corruption—to hinder the illegal flow of arms and other illegitimate products (animate and inanimate) by shining a bright light on the illicit pathways that brought these dangerous products into the arenas of common citizens. Mariama was concentrating not on the illegal merchandise per se but on the logistics of moving these products or any others from Africa to markets in the rest of the world, with a priority on passages to North America.

The starting points (or restarting points) were the acknowledged shared elements—the benchmarks—between Oriana's groundbreaking work and Mariama's new approach. Chief among these were Alimento Atlântico and the port of Faro. As they were working from Abidjan, it was also possible that Oriana's initial identification of Les Entreprises Cisse as a firm of interest could merit further examination.

Using the sturdy base of existing information, the trio began an analysis not dissimilar from that undertaken by Rodney when probing Ralph Tave and Cumberland Savings. As in that case, something jumped out. A company called Approvisionnement Alimentaire Européen had a profile very similar to Alimento Atlântico's—in this instance, the company operating out of a base at the Port of Sète, 125 miles due west of the Port of Marseilles. Documents of incorporation indicated the CEO of Approvisionnement Alimentaire Européen—called AAE by many—was Yves Noirot. AAE appeared to be an important actor in the export of agricultural products from Atlantic Seaboard ports in francophone countries ranging from Gabon to Morocco. Freight was transshipped through Sète for final destinations around the world. It was as though Approvisionnement Alimentaire Européen and Alimento Atlântico were siblings.

However, the Ivorian team could only go so far. It was well and good to cite AAE as a company to consider when US businessmen were looking how best to get merchandise to or from francophone countries (for better or worse was unclear). But this superficial citation did not get into the detailed data about the enterprise that the team were seeking for their current analyses—they were able to do little more than a rather simplistic inventory of freight providers.

For them to make, as apparently anticipated, clear recommendations to the senator who would, in turn, pass these on to wealthy American businessmen, they had to have a much more in-depth knowledge of the enterprises and actions they were proposing. However, they had few investigative assets—especially when operating on behalf of a US government official on foreign soil.

They reached out to Oriana, hoping through the paper she might be able to get more background material.

Oriana was unquestionably dedicated to the task and *The Daily News* had a trove of information resources. Nonetheless, she was unsure as to the appropriate action going forward. As more and more details came to light, it became increasingly likely that this analysis—this investigation—would be transnational if not trans-continental. There certainly seemed to be a scope that potentially exceeded the normal boundaries of investigative journalism.

Ultimately, it was Blake Samuelson who, reacting to his colleague's queries, recalled one Rodney Mills, some sort of federal agent who had had something to do with African matters, reaching out to the paper some time ago looking for background about a company called Delpro that had somehow been implicated in some arms sales involving a Portuguese sea freight company. If memory served, the company's name was Alimento Atlântico.

Things appeared to click into place—Oriana needed to talk with this federal agent.

Blake was able to make the critical introduction to Rodney.

⚓⚓⚓⚓⚓⚓⚓

As things potentially took on a very different configuration with possible links to federal agencies and agents, Oriana found herself uncertain for the first time in a long time. In various versions and iterations, the subject of misdeeds in Africa, especially regarding the agricultural sector, had been a battle she had been waging for years. However, she had always done it on her terms and in her own way. She had strenuously avoided the authorities—any authorities. She had been dedicated to thoroughly investigating and then carefully illuminating the human costs of bad and criminal acts.

She understood on the practical side why Jan had to reach a certain endpoint dictated by her boss. And she, along with Awa and Mariama, were now united with Jan. Everything had a cost.

Still, the cost of joining hands with the Feds was high. She was apprehensive.

She was also apprehensive because of her private life which, for the first time, was becoming more and more important to her all the while it was becoming more and more difficult to find private time.

Her relationship with David was strengthening and expanding. He was a great guy. She did not want to further jeopardize this partnership by adding additional work to her already overloaded schedule—a schedule that seemed to be pushing David out and risking their future together.

From the early days, in very general terms, she had spoken with her lover about her work and the objects of her journalistic efforts. However, she felt less was more. She didn't want to inundate him with pedantic minutiae. She wanted to be transparent but make sure he realized their relationship was a top priority. Still, up to now, she hadn't come forth about the letter addressed to his father she had unintentionally encountered, so there were some secrets hiding in the cracks of their liaison. These facts notwithstanding, and these included a rather incomplete (for whatever reason, she herself was not sure) recounting of her work with Jan, she felt she and David had a bond that allowed for (pretty) frank discussion and, in her own unfortunately rather obtuse way, she had tried to forewarn her beau that if her work took a new turn, as it just might, her time might even be less her own.

As usual, to her gratitude, albeit with a bit of surprise, David had said that whatever she needed to do was fine with him. He had known she bore many crosses when he had first met her (pun intended, he had added with a wink). In fact, this had been one of the many things that had attracted her to him, and he had known these could not simply be abandoned in the name of love. Nonetheless, this did not prevent them hopping into bed at that very moment.

So, for better or worse, Oriana prepared to meet Rodney.

For his part, Rodney could not recall if he had ever met Oriana. He felt he probably had read some of her bylines. If he had known her full biography, he would regret the two had not met sooner. As it was, he was still fixated on Ralph Tave. As it was, just as Raymond Girard was possibly a common denominator linking multiple malefactors, it appeared likely Alimento Atlântico was a similar common thread—a thread that looped through several arms sales as well as through a variety of activities coupled to various illegal acts. Now, looking for commercial conduits to move hoped-for products to and from West Africa and the Mid-Atlantic US, his dear friend Senator Sullivan and his African team accompanied by a rather well-known New York City journalist had uncovered other attributes for Alimento Atlântico along with ties to an apparently mirror-image French company, Approvisionnement Alimentaire Européen. It may have been too much to say the clouds were lifting, but there were now possibly certain recognizable shapes emerging from the fog.

Rodney arranged to meet with Oriana for lunch, choosing the upscale Grainerie Taverne in the city's Flatiron District (he was on an expense account).

⚓⚓⚓⚓⚓⚓⚓

Operating in totally different spheres, Harold was seeing the fruits of his labors. Things were really going quite well. All his Durango-based ventures were growing according to plan. He himself was no longer the newcomer but an established member of the community and a respected businessman on the board of the local chamber of commerce. A new and thriving status quo had been successfully established.

It was time to have a comprehensive strategizing session with Joe—something best done face-to-face. As one of their guiding principles was to keep the ties between Pennsylvania and Colorado as obscure as possible, Harold devised a hopefully nearly-risk-free formula for a sit-down with his adopted father. There would be a fundraiser for Kindred Helping Hands Foundation in Chicago. He would make sure many people were invited and that there were highly visible events with celebrities in attendance, good food on the table, and an open bar. That should provide a suitable smokescreen for the two *collaborateurs*—the father and son team—to meet in anonymity and security.

Harold wanted the charity event to go top-drawer. He chose as a venue the Hilton just across the street from Grant Park and Monroe Harbor. This was carefully calculated. As the fundraiser whirled forward with great hoopla, Joe and Harold would meet at Buckingham Fountain in the Park—out in the open where unwanted onlookers should be easy to recognize.

There were no hugs nor displays of emotion—it was simply two men sitting on a park bench having a rather impersonal chat.

"Welcome to Chicago," Harold started lamely, "hope all's fine at home."

"We're fine," Joe jumped in, not able to keep a smile off his face. "Your mom misses you as do your brother and sister—but we're all fine. And it seems you're fine too, off on your own on the slopes of the Rockies."

"Things have gone well so far—but don't want to get ahead of ourselves. S&J Logistics, Fig Leaf, as well as KHHF are all doing well as are the staff I've been able to discreetly recruit. We've started expanding in both the state and some neighboring areas, but I'm concerned that if we go too far too fast, we'll attract undesirable attention and raise troublesome questions."

"You're right. You probably do need to throttle back a bit. We don't want to be too showy. And, equally important, we need to coordinate with the overseers upstream to see how the input-output channels to Pottsville and Durango can be advantageously linked—or possibly, equally advantageously, totally separated. It's getting complex."

"Exactly, that's why we needed to talk."

"Agree totally. I suppose we'll be needing to do this on a regular basis."

"Huh?"

"Yeah. Alignment, or the intentional lack there-of, for our two operations is critical. For example, the big bosses have just sent me a very cryptic query about getting more directly involved in the 'labor issue' as they call it."

"No clue . . ."

"So far this hasn't come your way. But we've been providing some indirect and very hush-hush—even from your mom—she wouldn't like it—support to the movement of illegal laborers into, and at times, out of the country. We've managed so far to be pretty far removed from the real activities, just helping with some of the logistics—it's like a job S&K was built for." Joe tried to offer a half smile.

"OK."

"Well, this is all really mushrooming—hopefully not out of control. And it's now become the 'labor issue' where the higher-ups see there's a real chance to take a bigger bite of the apple—actually gaining some ground from the Latin syndicates who have been dominating this market for some time."

"OK."

"For example, the dairy industry out your way in the West—especially in Idaho—relies heavily on illegal aliens for their labor—claim they can't make it if they have to pay the official minimum wage. Pathways for these workers have typically come across the southern border, but this is currently heating up and has become a sensitive political firefight. Once new routes are open, the Latin groups may lose some of their comparative advantage, and our leadership feels there's an opening for us to really gobble up some valuable assets. Maybe having the workers come into the country via Canada or even directly along the eastern or western coastlines. They're looking at everything to see how they can have a bigger footprint."

"Hmm."

"Yeah, 'hmm.' Not sure where this is going but we're likely in it, one way or another. Up til now I've been able to keep all this at arm's length but don't know how long this will last. So far this has pretty much been an area where, although there's been a lot of investment in parallel labor supply for Europe for a long time, the US has been kinda a no-go zone. But as the bosses see things bend in the organization's favor, it's gonna be hard to put on the brakes. It could get messy."

"OK."

"Oh, and another thing. Again, possibly a concern but as of now too soon to tell from my seat."

"Sure."

"As you know, my intentions, I believe my marching orders, have been to re-energize the organization's presence in the US and maybe North America. With the dissolution of Delpro, I've always seen us as the next generation of organization operatives reclaiming our place in very lucrative markets."

"Exactly."

"Yeah. But the primary thing here is the assumption that with McCandless' departure and Delpro's seeming downfall, we were working with a clean sheet. However, it appears likely, based on the news I've been receiving, that there are shards of the old structures that are still alive and well in one way or another. For example, among others, the names of Lambert Richardson and Ralph Tave have, according to our chiefs, popped up recently. Ever hear of them?"

"Nope."

"Not sure what it means if anything. Of course, if you think about it, everything didn't just come to a screeching stop just because Robin McCandless left and declared Delpro dead. There was too much on the ground—too much going on. But we need to be aware and keep our eyes open. There are and will be remnants of all that Delpro did—McCandless and his group had their fingers into everything."

"Sure."

"Yep. Our—maybe their—the 'they' being our overlords—basic intention has always been to re-establish an active presence here—to regain the terrain we once had and regain the profits we are now lacking. Our—maybe their—thoughts were that we would rebuild a new and better organization—possibly benefiting some from the earlier efforts in terms of markets and contacts. I guess we didn't factor in the obvious—when McCandless left, nearly everyone else stayed and many of these folks kept on doing what they had been doing. This is probably fine. They—the hangers-on—will almost assuredly see the advantages of going back to the organization as they had likely done better with Delpro than without—that means better with Domov than without. Anyway, that's our hope and expectation. But we have to be aware that some of these folks who've stuck around have likely expanded as Delpro dissolved—they just might have aspirations for grander things to come for themselves and not be too open to, as they maybe could see it, another big dog coming in to gobble up their work. Who knows? We've just got to be prepared, that's all."

"Will do . . ."

"And, before I leave this, there's another side of the coin—of course. These hangers-on have been hanging around for a long time. All the while the Feds have been gearing up. I don't know—probably no one knows—how many of these older generation transgressors have come to the attention of this ever-tightening effort by the Feds to get a strangle hold on our operations. Going back to rekindle old relationships and markets could be dangerous if the Feds have made inroads. We need to be doubly alert."

"Sure thing."

"I know you'll do fine—you always have. You've done fine setting up this meeting. But we need to keep communicating. And it's not easy. I guess the most practical and lower-risk option is to keep doing as we're doing and meet face-to-face from time to time."

"Sure thing."

"Just remember, Harold, my boy, take it easy. It's a long fall if we start to stumble."

"Dad, we're on track. We've done a good job. I'm sure the leadership is smiling. Few could have done what you have done."

"Hope so, son."

It was almost one of those "your-ears-should-be-burning-because-they're-talking-about-you" moments. As the Abidjan ladies connected some of the dots between Alimento Atlântico and Approvisionnement Alimentaire Européen, *La Fleur de la Mer*, a 7,000 DWT vessel of the very same Approvisionnement Alimentaire Européen entered the Port of St. John's, New Brunswick, at the end of her transatlantic voyage from Sète. Prior to the record of this docking, there was a slight and rather dubious reference in the ship's log to her first putting into Glace Bay, Nova Scotia, to drop off a merchant seaman needing urgent care at the Cape Breton Regional Hospital, a dozen miles in the interior.

La Fleur was, surprisingly, carrying a shipment of Brazilian soybeans to a country that was a soy exporter. If queried, the ship's agents were advised to say that the cheaper product from South America would be used in animal feeds whereas the higher quality (so they said) Canadian harvest was going into foodstuffs for more direct human consumption. At least that was their story.

Brazilian soy was indeed offloaded in St. John's. What was not reported was that, in addition to an apparently ill seaman, at Grace Bay, by prearrangement, the vessel had offloaded more than forty illegal immigrants originally from the Balkans along with several hundred pounds of uncontrolled pharmaceuticals that had been fabricated at an unregistered plant in Pézenas, twenty miles to the northwest of Sète.

It was good business. The human cargo would end up as underpaid laborers on vegetable and fruit farms or in fish processing plants. The faux pharmaceuticals would enter Canadian supply chains targeting US clients trying to get cheaper medications north of the border. There were even a few meager profits from the sale of the soy.

Yves Noirot was a good organizer. And, if one knew the right threads to pull, one would discover all these arrangements almost invisibly linked to Raymond Girard. The business of doing business was good business—the business of doing clandestine business was even better business.

Orest wan't thinking about soy or any other type of cargo. He, trying to stay realistic and detached, was happy with the way things were going in the US and around the globe. There was money to be made, and they seemed to be making it. Their coffers, large as they were, had never been so full. Domov was definitely reaping what it had sewn—the decades of laying groundwork and finding key actors were paying off. There was an old Russian proverb, "every vegetable has its time." Domov was having its time.

CHAPTER 9

NO GUARANTEES

"We must expect reverses, even defeats. They are sent to teach us wisdom and prudence, to call forth greater energies, and to prevent our falling into greater disasters."

—**Robert E. Lee**

Judicial Policies

RODNEY knew Section T15-Z was officially seen as the forward phalanx in the US's efforts to battle global crime. The DOJ had a clear policy to engage in this battle against enemies both visible and invisible. The agency declared that:

> International criminal organizations represented a direct and escalating danger to the health, safety, and security of the American people in the homeland and abroad. These rapidly growing and increasingly influential organizations were actively involved, among others, in drug and weapons smuggling, illegal migration, human trafficking, money laundering, and illicit natural resource extraction. These flagitious structures with state-like powers that often-overshadowed international borders disrupted law enforcement, promoted violence, encouraged corruption, acted as proxies for contentious interventions, as well as directly or indirectly supported insurgents and terrorists.

It seemed apparent he was on the right side of the equation. His work should easily receive the full support of government. Yet he was still fighting day in and day out just to get his long-justified budget approved although he had fully briefed the Sullivan Committee on multiple occasions. Hal had warned him about the frustrations—at times the risks—in fighting bureaucracy, but, even to the veteran civil servant, this felt excessive.

The apparent stonewalling of the committee's backing of Section T15-Z was totally unknown to Jan and her confederates. She, and by default they, had their instructions from the boss—from Senator Sullivan. This was, at least from the view point of the seat of power (particularly as seen from First St. Southeast, Washington, DC 20004), all about helping Virginians (the unsaid last part of that aim being "helping Virginians make more money"). Now, with Oriana's important involvement, the aims had expanded. Nonetheless, Jan still felt this was not contrary to her core assignment as long as she could come up with a formula to help Sullivan's constituents.

Oriana had to focus. She needed all her discipline not to get sidetracked because it would be so easy to end up chasing butterflies.

Things were mixed-up (and mixed together). There was David. There was the paper. There was the crew in Côte d'Ivoire. Now there was Rodney. Yet, when you scraped it all off, she was Sophie's daughter. As her mother before her, she had core principles that were her essence. Like her mother, she hoped she was following in Julie-Victoire's footsteps—setting valuable precedents while doing all possible to promote justice and equity. It was no small task. As she had learned while recuperating in Abidjan, the trick was often to dissect the local conduits from the international engagements that were more likely acting with a much higher level of malfeasance. Whether in Congo, Burundi, Angola, or Guinea, she had attempted to shine a light on these far-reaching nefarious activities by looking first at the intercontinental trade routes that allowed the operators (both cloaked international controllers and high-rolling local entrepreneurs) to become so wealthy and powerful. This had not changed. She saw this as perfectly compatible with Jan's mandate—the two perspectives mutually reinforcing.

Rodney took the train up to the city the day before he was scheduled to have lunch with Oriana at the Grainerie Taverne. He, with exceptional extravagance (he reminded himself he was on an expense account), took a room at the plush Barbury Garden B&B on West 21st—just a ten-minute walk from the Taverne on East 20th and right next door to Theodore Roosevelt's birthplace. The B&B apparently named after Barbury Castle located in North Wessex Downs, dating back to the 6th century Saxon kingdom when Cyrnic of Wessex reigned—all this information highlighted on a shiny brass plaque on the wall next to the small and highly-polished oak reception counter (Rodney thinking that King Cyrnic must have been around over a thousand years before Teddy Roosevelt—then wondering why he had had that thought—the roots of history were deep and tangled).

The now battle-scarred agent tried to have a relaxing evening, pushing aside thoughts of Sullivan and Domov in favor of going to Broadway to see *Les Misérables*—perhaps thinking focusing on others' miseries would sooth his own. The next morning, after a surprisingly restful night, he had a superb breakfast in the Garden's garden before taking a long and leisurely walk up to the Empire State Building and back through Madison Square Park—all the while playing and replaying in his mind different strategies for the lunchtime discussions, unsure of what the outcome could and would be. It was unclear to him where Oriana fit in the mosaic that was becoming his life's work.

The lunch, much like the breakfast before it, turned out to be superb. Over hors d'oeuvres and impressive entrées of fish, the discussion, carefully chaperoned by Rodney, focused on Oriana—her growing up in France and her growing older in NYC. Then over coffee and crème brûlée, Rodney steered the conversation in a more focused direction.

"I understand," he said zeroing-in, "you've been looking at trade routes up and down the West Coast of Africa?"

"Indeed." She half-smiled as if embracing an old friend who may have changed in the ensuing years, "This has been one of my never-ending subjects going back to when I was recuperating in Abidjan. Given my field work, I became very interested in the channels for arms sales—both legal and illegal. As I explored and got major help from more knowledgeable colleagues, it became clear these weapons were just a portion—of course, a very important portion—of a large network of mostly illicit international trade that moved up and down the Atlantic, from Africa to Europe and then frequently onward across the Atlantic to North or South America."

"We've encountered such pathways ourselves," Rodney chimed in.

"Well," Oriana continued as though Rodney had said nothing, "as an outsider, the arms market was very hard to investigate. Mostly, I had to rely on second- and third-hand information—a lot of it more drama than fact. But, following other journalists' recommendations, I was able to document that the movement of agricultural products often seemed to mirror the traffic of arms.

"For example, the cassava trade, at least the intercontinental part of this trade, appeared to follow many of the same channels—I guess maybe because the cassava as flour is often used in fake medicines—illegal products moving along the same conduits."

"Yep, we've seen the same."

Not missing a beat in spite of Rodney's interjection, Oriana seemed to be gazing inward, almost in a recital. "I was able to garner the support of the paper and even bring on-board two African ladies—one a student here and another affiliated with a university in Abidjan—to look into this matter in more detail. We're pretty much still at it.

"Things took kinda a weird turn when Janice Pittman appeared on the scene in Abidjan. She's a staffer for Senator Jacob Sullivan and it seems the senator is trying to identify investment opportunities in West Africa for his constituents—or at least that's his story."

"I know Senator Sullivan," Rodney managed to say without wincing.

"Sure," Oriana said deflecting the comment, "guess he's pretty much a big-wig down your way. Never met the man, but it did turn out that our work in Abidjan and even the wider West Coast region does overlap with what Janice is tasked to do. From the paper's perspective, collaborating with a Senator's crew is a plus. And I've met the senator's lady. She seems OK—been in West Africa before, knows her way around, and willing to do what's necessary to get the job done."

"The senator's been widely flaunting his West African affairs—adventure I'd call it, but he calls it a pre-investment analysis."

"So I've heard. But I, and I guess we, tend to turn a blind eye to this political speak. We're pragmatic. With a senator involved, the embassy has now anted-up some additional funds as well as backup support. The paper is happy as can be—all this makes good copy. Drink the Kool-Aid or not, we've got good people on the ground, ample funds, and are able to get stuff done—some of it's what the good senator wants—maybe some of it's a little more outside his current thinking. But it's all good—or so it seems."

"I guess." Rodney sensed the pause this time was for his inputs. "We're all in the early stages. Still, it seems clear we are all working in the same direction—often with, or at least focusing on, the same individuals and groups. I'd suggest our policy be one of open communications. Make sense?"

"Suppose." Oriana seemed more guarded, "While I certainly know what my ladies and I have been hoping to do for some time, and I think I have a pretty good picture of what the Virginia lawmaker wants—at least on the surface—realizing he's assuredly got multiple agendas—I'm not really sure where you think you fit in?"

"Not really sure either," Rodney replied to the journalistic probe, trying to show more confidence than he felt. "To be honest, like yourself, but for even longer, we've been chasing these miscreants for years—folks that do all kinds of bad things and seem untouchable—generally invisible. I won't bore you with all the details now, but it started way back when I was at the SEC and we were investigating a US company called Delpro. Through a combination of luck and skill we uncovered lots and lots of things—even identified the key actor at the head of Delpro but also realized he was but a cog in the wheel and there were several layers above him hidden in fog and fiction. Nevertheless, we learned a lot and continued to build our case—our cases. This has now all moved into the DOJ under a special section that joins my former SEC group to another group that is more active internationally—my team initially targeting mostly US evil-doers.

"No need now to rehash too much—some I can't even mention as it's too sensitive or too uncertain. It suffices to say there are a lot of folks working on this from a variety of angles and a wide range of offices and agencies. Everyone's trying to connect the dots. But it's far from easy.

"Right now, the most important thing is to have a list of valuable contacts—you high on this list. If you're agreeable, we'll just make sure our phone lines are open, and we'll discuss more as we move forward along our separate paths?"

"I guess I'm OK with that," Oriana said almost hesitantly. "Since Blake Samuelson made the arrangements for us to meet, I have to assume the paper is on board. They obviously like to be able to write a story with the maximum largesse possible and bringing you guys into the tale is good for their business. But I don't share in the paper's profits, so I'm more concerned about what really gets done—what really gets done that matters. I guess agreeing to talk is fine and we'll just have to see how it all plays out."

"Sounds good."

With that, Oriana suggested they have, as she called it, a *pousse-café*, a digestif to top off an excellent meal before they each went their own way.

⚘⚘⚘⚘⚘⚘⚘

While Oriana and Rodney were considering arrangements for more open exchanges, others were wondering about possible policy changes that could impact them for the better or the worse. The Cisses were wondering how long Les Caïds of Le Milieu would continue with their rather "soft" countermeasures aimed at the French investments of Les Entreprises Cisse.

What the Cisses did not know was that things were not quite as "soft" as they might have imagined.

Les Caïds had their own impressive intelligence network. Since power was knowledge, they wanted to know as much as possible about the bothersome brothers from Côte d'Ivoire. They were able to trace a considerable amount of the unwanted duo's trading and transport back home to Sète and Approvisionnement Alimentaire Européen—AAE—with Yves Noirot. Once this thread had been isolated, it was a relatively easy matter to apply considerable pressure on Noirot. He should gently persuade the troublesome Africans to keep to their African trade routes—even if these transited through French ports. If this were accomplished, Les Caïds would offer protection for the Ivorian merchandise while in French harbors. If this did not happen, Monsieur Noirot's future in the shipping industry as well as the future of Ivorian products would be uncertain.

Yves Noirot was wondering how worried he should be.

Lambert Richardson, for his part, was wondering how shipping policies—even clandestine operations had their policies—would affect his bottom line in regard to on-going arrangements between Herramientas Agrícolas Especiales and Kyrylo Rudenko. While his client, Mercer McMaster, was, at least as he portrayed himself, a moralist (Lambert thought of him as more of a pecksniffian bigot), the Racine businessman was all about the bottom line—morality was not part of the equation. As he had seen demonstrated time and again through his interactions with Robin McCandless, high risk levels demanded high profit margins. Getting his consignment to Georgia was going to be costly and risky. The earnings had to be really significant.

About this same time Ralph Tave was wondering about tax policy and how to interpret a visit to his office by an IRS agent seeking innocently (as the agent underscored several times) additional information about Tave's foundation. The congenial taxman indicated this was simply routine—a few quick questions that were asked of nearly all foundations—neglecting to mention, of course, that he was actually an agent of D-2 and not the IRS.

As would be expected, unaware of the specific machinations underway across the Domov empire, but completely aware that these arrangements and schemes were part and parcel of daily business, Harold was totally occupied by trying to see how best to implement the policies he and his father had discussed. What was the best arrangement between Pottsville and Durango? How could, as his father had suggested, he throttle back a bit and still keep his forward momentum? All the businesses were doing well and growing. Yet things were changing quickly, and he didn't want to get so far ahead that he fell into the abyss—sometimes the world was flat.

⚘⚘⚘⚘⚘⚘⚘

With all the energy focused on approaches, arrangements, and protocols, it was not at all unexpected that BAOD policies affected the implementation of NCIIP. Development was complicated and often it was those who were ostensibly trying to do the development who made it unduly complex—at times, for their own interests. Big, transboundary projects were hard to monitor, offering opportunities for unofficial salary top-offs for those involved—from the day worker to the highest level of management. And the benefits were not limited to those directly engaged in the field. Project planners and oversight officers from the mother agency had a variety of opportunities to act as emissaries for important private sector interests or to simply pocket some crumbs from a well-fed budget.

It seemed NCIIP was going ahead, but slothfully at best. There was a necessary pre-implementation alignment of a wide mix of interests from both formal and informal actors. Groundbreaking would likely be months if not years away. These preliminary activities would tap into the same pot of funds that would ultimately supply the final project, thereby diminishing the resources for the main project but providing early "stipends" for a spectrum of appreciative and patient players in the interim.

Chakir knew the system even if he couldn't profess to really understand it. Yet for him NCIIP was both an objective and a guise to reshape important market channels in this portion of West Africa.

He began crafting his first of possibly several private economic corridors—Domov corridors. He carefully planned the diversion at Abinsi going south all the way to Calibar. He oversaw teams that mapped the best channels and elaborated a roster of potential collaborators from local villages along the way. He zoomed out to a wider view, imagining how this corridor could link to interior routes to Chad, Central African Republic, Niger, and perhaps parts of the unbelievably wealthy Congo basin. Possibly ironically, there was, in the furthest reaches of Chakir's spectrum thinking, a possibility that Calibar could become a backdoor into illicit and high-paying Western European markets, linking through Nigeria to the ancient Berber trade routes across the Sahara that were in use to this very day and then transiting into Europe from North Africa.

It was a lot, and it was definitely not trouble-free. Nonetheless, as per arrangements, others in Domov's vast sphere gave the work of Onyx Associates a broad berth, and they continued to have the needed support from the upper echelons of the organization.

Jan and her crew were not privy to the inner workings of BAOD nor the related tactical adjustments made by hopeful participants such as Chakir and Onyx. However, unlike many would-be bridge builders, she had been to Ekokku and seen what was, or more importantly, what wasn't on the ground. She fully appreciated that if this was to take off, it would be a long slog. Still, this reality notwithstanding, it truly didn't affect to any significant degree her assignment from the Senator.

As far as she could tell, for her boss, NCIIP was a sign board (or perhaps a metaphor), nothing more. It announced the possible type of business opportunities where American interests could and should be more invested—a tangible product of the Virginia politician's hoped-for policy of devoting energy to helping his folk make money (thereby, of course, banking votes for himself). Whether the actual project took off or not didn't greatly affect Sullivan's message. The totem—or a facsimile thereof—remained regardless if the bridge was or was not ever built.

In this light, NCIIP was peripheral to her job. Jan filed it in an easy-to-find place and went about mobilizing her team to continue to canvas the area for demonstrable openings for Virginian businessmen with a concentration on actions in the agricultural sector.

Part of this search for opportunities took the ladies of Abidjan back to the border area with Guinea—an area with bittersweet memories for Oriana. The turmoil continued in the three-country sub-region of the parrot's beak, encompassing heavily forested and diamond-rich lands claimed by each of the three competing countries. With rolling hotspots bringing brutal conflicts, there was a corresponding wave of refugees that seemed to be constantly on the move, sloshing from place to place—sometimes seeking shelter in the relative security of Côte d'Ivoire.

Not only was this flow of humanity a serious problem in and of itself, but it also impacted on the team's work in regard to assessing agricultural investing. One of the drawing points to funding labor-intensive businesses of the type often considered as start-ups along the West Coast was the cheap cost of labor (common labor frequently readily available for a few dollars a day with minimal if any fringe benefits). However, these sporadic inflows of refugees brought a ready if technically illegal source of even cheaper labor to the farms and fields in border areas—labor that in some cases was subsidized by disaster relief agencies that provided the basic amenities to those driven away from their homes by war (even if these same individuals were working on a nearby cacao or cassava farm).

Given this scenario, one might have thought that in Côte d'Ivoire, considering the nearly continuous disruption in neighboring countries, there would be a significant population of permanently displaced persons one way or another competing with local residents and working in agricultural operations across the country. While this pool of black-market labor definitely existed, it was, according to Mariama's estimates, considerably smaller than should have otherwise been expected.

While conventional wisdom was that those fleeing the conflicts tried to stay as close to home as possible, this did not seem to be the case for a significant number of those continuously harassed by the fighting of others. After years of bloodletting, this group apparently had decided it was time to go. Mariama and Awa were able to trace a pathway taken by many to leave the war-torn forests all together. The twenty-four hour plus trek took them from Nzérékoré in the sylvan southeast of Guinea to Kankan in the center of this country shaped like a crooked finger, and from there on to Boke in the littoral northwest—a total of 800 miles of challenging travel, at best. From here the travelers continued a short distance to the small coastal village of Victoria and by water, surrounded by mangrove forests, continued to their apparent final destination, Guinea Bissau.

At this juncture, Jan's crew needed more resources. They reached out to their emeritus member, Claudia De Angelis who had much more knowledge of the enshrouded Lusophone country first visited by explorers from Lisbon in the 1400s.

According to resident historians, the kingdom of Bissau was founded by the King of Quinara more than seven hundred years ago. However, over the ensuing centuries, more frequently than one would have chosen, Guinea Bissau had been considered practically a pariah—especially recently by many from West Africa including a number of high-level officers from the BAOD. Worries from those both outside and inside the self-proclaimed but poverty-ridden republic (vacillating between socialistic and fascist leanings) included recurrent violent political upheavals sometimes bordering on despotism as well as being labeled a major drug transit point for the movement of cocaine and other products from South America into European markets. To the objective observer, the country, slightly larger in surface area than the State of Maryland, had indeed been repeatedly plagued by disputes regarding its form of governance going back decades and decades, even before Portuguese colonial rule. In recent history these included repeated military coups accompanied by a political and social isolation that made monitoring activities in-country frequently difficult to impossible.

To many an onlooker, Guinea Bissau was a mystery, like a Japanese Himitsu-Bako puzzle box whose trigger could not be found.

Nonetheless, Claudia had the best chances of penetrating the curtain of shadows that all too often shielded the country. She had good contacts. Professor De Angelis was not only a former UN employee and Mariama's advisor, she was also an advisor to *Estudiantes por los Derechos de las Personas* (EDP—Students for People's Rights)—a group that worked on human rights issues around the world but with a focus on Columbia and an emphasis on calling attention to the ills befalling the larger population across the country due to the prolonged impacts of the all-powerful drug cartels. EDP did their best to document drug traffic to Bissau—information that was shared with Claudia De Angelis. Claudia could be a key to the puzzle. Arrangements could be made. Arrangements that would ultimately involve Oriana and Rodney.

⚘⚘⚘⚘⚘⚘⚘

In the background other arrangements, or, more correctly failed arrangements, were potentially laying the predicate for the unexpected connecting of some dots. SAMHAFRI—the Samantha and Hal's Friends

Foundation—was established by Eddie Hall and his partner Lisa in Samantha and Hal's memory, using part of the significant estate Eddie had inherited from his Uncle Hal. The foundation attempted to help refugees and other vulnerable people get adequately settled in the tangled and challenging ecosystem that was the United States.

Over the years since the deaths of his loved ones, Eddie had seen the once fledging foundation evolve into a mature and well-respected establishment with a full-time director overseeing a very competent staff and a host of beneficiaries. Nevertheless, co-founder Hall maintained a seat as Chairman of the Board of SAMHAFRI as it continued to grow both in terms of acclaim as well as finances. As Eddie saw it, part of his job was reaching out to other foundations to try and develop a cooperative unit where efficiencies were gained, and impacts maximized—this approach part of Eddie the surveyor's spatial vision of how things should work.

Hearing of the Arkansas-based Kindred Helping Hands Foundation (Eddie's foundation based in Oregon, therefore links to another geographic area would seem to offer advantages) that had a good public record in using a spinster's wealth to help the needy, Eddie decided it would be good to build a bridge with these charitable cousins to the east.

However, KHHF was not into bridge-building. Eddie's overtures were so rapidly and rudely rebuffed that he was immediately suspicious. Why would people helping people immediately avoid joining hands with other people helping people? There was, of course, competition among foundations for both financial support and the spotlight. Yet this rarely took the form of such an aggressive brush-off as he had received from KHHF. To say they had been churlish would be to rather severely under-report the degree of acrimony Eddie sensed as his efforts to join hands failed miserably.

Eddie still had a very close relationship with Rodney. In fact, when the lead DOJ agent would be overwhelmed with all the goings-on (and not goings-on) in DC, he would slip away for a quite weekend with Eddie and Lisa on the Oregon Coast where the loudest noise was not a pontificating politician but the crash of waves against ancient basalt.

On one such visit, as they watched the sea foam spiral into the air with the thunder of the surf, Eddie asked his sort-of-uncle, "Ever hear of a foundation called Kindred Helping Hands?"

"Nope," a rather blasé Rodney replied, not really wanting the conversation to go anywhere near work.

"Just curious," a seemingly stolid Eddie persisted. "These guys have a strange way of doing business—or at least a strange way of showing they care."

"Huh?"

"Yeah," Eddie said, trying to dig deeper, "from all the info I could get, they seemed like a good partner but when I tried to contact them, foundation to foundation, they unceremoniously drove me away without a word."

"Of course," Rodney said, attempting bravely to divert the exchanged, "they probably know what an asshole you can be and wanted nothing to do with you."

Ignoring Lisa's smile and Rodney's attempts to change direction, Eddie stubbornly continued, "Well and good. But there's a minimum of propriety—especially within the wider foundation family."

"Let me tell you." Rodney still tried to shift gears, "propriety doesn't exist today. Come back with me to DC and you'll see firsthand the bullshit that passes as civil discourse. Within an hour you'd be heading back west needing a big ol' hug from the lovely Lisa. Rudeness seems to be the new badge of honor—go figure."

While Lisa seemed to be enjoying immensely the banter, Eddie was undeterred in his efforts to get a serious answer or at least make a serious point. "Rude or not, something's not right. Know you've got your hands more than full and I'm not really asking for anything in particular. It's just that when one group is so outlandishly bad-mannered, it runs the risk of adversely affecting us all. So, if this group ever pops up on your radar, just remember my observations. Something smells and it's not the seaweed at low tide."

Rodney tried to look mildly interested for the benefit of his hosts who were as close to family as he now had, hoping the conversation was wrapping up while thinking to himself, smell or not, there's gotta be a really strong case before the feds'd jump in. DOJ doesn't typically have a policy of going after charitable foundations when there's so many felons to chase.

Fortunately, the gods changed the pace. The phone rang. Eddie's friends up the coast were calling. The smelt were running. It was time to go catch dinner.

Hidden Fees

You pay for what you get and Lambert was paying a lot—he hoped he'd be well compensated. He was worried about his bottom line. While, for his own protection, he was not directly involved in the on-the-ground preparations, his people had informed him they were expecting the arrival of the shipment in Tamanché any day now.

He would keep the cargo there for at least three months, Mercer's rushed schedule be damned. He had to make sure this consignment had not been flagged by anyone. He had too much at stake. There were good profits to be made, but not huge riches. He was already well-off. It was more the thrill of accomplishment at his age. He would test the system, and he would win against the odds. Still, there had to be a worthwhile payout.

He'd been at this too long to get into a hurry—careless inattentiveness to detail was a sure step towards the worst form of failure. Regardless of his client's crass impatience, he'd take his time and get the job done right.

Once the shipment had been frozen in his warehouse at Herramientas Agrícolas Especiales for long enough to be as certain as possible it was not the object of scrutiny by any unwanted actors, he'd get it back on the water. Using a discrete freight handler like Approvisionnement Alimentaire Européen, he'd move the shipment up the coast to the St. Lawrence and into the Great Lakes. The cargo would be off-loaded at the Port of Sarnia at the southern end of Lake Huron at the mouth of the St. Clair River. From here it would be repackaged by local Farmers' Home staff prior to being put on a much smaller vessel before crossing over into US waters and traversing the long axis of Lake Huron from south to north, moving into Lake Michigan and on to the final destination of Rowley's Bay in Liberty Grove, Wisconsin. At Liberty Grove, back in the day, he had had some shared facilities with a company called Spot On—one of Robin McCandless and Delpro's ventures, now defunct. But the old buildings were still there. The shipment would again remain in a storeroom that was part of these structures for a few weeks to let any dust settle before the last leg by truck to a Farmers' Home warehouse near Sturgeon Bay, forty miles to the south. Once carefully tucked-away in a secluded corner, the cargo would stay as long as necessary for him to formalize all the details with Mercer. Lots of pieces—lots of needed pieces.

⚘⚘⚘⚘⚘⚘⚘

As Lambert moved pawns about the map and Mercer grew increasingly testy, Yves Noirot was preparing to pay another sort of premium in kind. Les Caïds had been very clear; his future in Sète and the continued profitable operations of Approvisionnement Alimentaire Européen depended on doing them a favor—depended on getting the increasingly irritating Cisse brothers far away from any area where Le Milieu had activities. It was time for this stalemate to end. The Ivorians had to go.

To his credit, Yves was able to find a solution that showed both ingenuity and empathy although it used up no small part of his social capital. Noirot had been a supporter of France's renowned culinary industry for years—helping the masters of the kitchen procure equipment and supplies at special (a.k.a. duty-free, read as bootlegged) prices through his informal lines of commerce facilitated by his position at the Port of Sète and the vessels of Approvisionnement Alimentaire Européen. He had connections.

When he was contacted by one of his long-time clients to reverse the normal flow of scullery stocks and help him get several shipments into the US, he learned that the gentleman's nephew was starting a posh new bistro in Manhattan featuring all the French classics sought by the wealthy American epicurean restaurant-goer—the gentleman and his nephew not wanting to pay full price for the sizeable amount of equipment and supplies required to get such a venture going.

This spawned an idea. What about a "twofer?" While the city was the epitome of being swank and cosmopolitan, DC was very international with a growing African footprint. There could be a sort of annex to the city's French restaurant, an African-centric eatery for the international gourmand in DC. Simultaneously setting up the two new endeavors using Yves's informal channels and special pricing could be advantageous for all.

The French restaurateurs were fine with the proposal as long as they got a cut off the top of the DC action. A strong and perhaps slightly exaggerated pitch to Antoinette's niece, Minata, took some of the polish off Maquis Maman Afrique and made a new start-up in DC very appealing. From Minata to Antoinette, to Marc and Luc; the Cisses decided to relocate. It seemed like a win-win-win.

⚘⚘⚘⚘⚘⚘⚘

Chakir was also thinking about winning. He recalled the proverb from his homeland, "The wise buyer chooses the neighborhood before choosing the house." This applied to the widely proclaimed, but largely inactive NCIIP—still more of an idea than a project. However, the project was the house, and he had chosen well the neighborhood. There were already multiple advantages for Domov along the Nigerian-Cameroonian border. His energies had been well invested because a noteworthy Domov imprint was already developing along the road to Calabar.

⚘⚘⚘⚘⚘⚘⚘

While some things were growing in the forests along the Nigerian-Cameroonian frontier, NCIIP was still not among them. However, as surmised by Jan, this fact did not deter Senator Sullivan. He continued to use this multimillion-dollar development scheme, as he called it, as his ensign for the direction he wanted to push US investment strategies in Africa. In his words, "more dollars were popping up in the most unexpected places." "The profits," he said practically ad nauseam, "should be harvested by Americans (by Virginians he wanted to add but didn't)."

Initially Rodney was unsure about the senator's preoccupation with NCIIP. It seemed to be competing for his time while it was really a non-issue. It was easy to imagine he had another more convoluted agenda. Be that as it may, reaching out to Oriana who in turn discussed with her colleagues in Abidjan, as far as anyone knew, this was in fact what it seemed to be, a totem he was incessantly flagging to try and make space for more US money moving into and out of Africa—a significant portion of which, one way or another, was planned to land in Virginia. As Jan had already concluded, the realities on the ground were of little interest to the senator but his need for a flagship kept his team in place and this allowed the crew do concentrate on other topics which to them, and to Rodney, were of more substantive importance.

Rodney drew twin takeaways. On the one hand, if NCIIP hit a bad stretch in spite of current thoughts that it was gaining some traction, this could be a weak spot on the senator's agenda where he could be vulnerable to criticism for flaunting untenable projects. On the other hand, with Oriana backstopping a highly motivated and well-supported team in the field, in spite of NCIIP, there was an opportunity to gain a lot of needed but heretofore uncaptured information. The bottom line was that it could all be useful although, in the immediate, it did not help with his no-funding conundrum with the cantankerous Senator Sullivan. If he were to be able to solve his funding riddle, there undoubtedly would be a price to pay—he hoped it wouldn't be too high. Yet, as he knew perfectly well, the value of time was at a premium.

The Ivorian team was truly highly motivated. While the object of their attention was more times than not a moving target, now there was an expanding part for Claudia De Angelis. Through her various connections and with the help of EDP, she had been able to fine-tune some suppositions—strong theories that nonetheless still needed to be verified and documented.

It appeared much of the overseas contraband brought into Bissau came from the Columbian coastal community of Moñitos—called by many travel advisors "the best coastal tourist destination in northern Columbia." The interdicted merchandise came to this tourist hotspot from numerous inland supply centers. Once in Moñitos, the products would be consolidated and repackaged before being carried by small indistinguishable pleasure craft to waiting offshore freighters—freighters often from Alimento Atlântico. When these vessels offloaded their freight—large and small—in Bissau, they reportedly on-loaded a very different payload: people. At present, chief among these passengers (if one could use this word) were the individuals they had been monitoring, fleeing the parrot's beak and the bloodlust for diamonds. These refugees were then, in very harsh conditions, transported up the coast to Europe—apparently some carried as far as North America—a new version of the Middle Passage of the sixteenth through the nineteenth centuries.

Claudia's informants also identified a local Bissau resident, Señor Tomas Ferreira, as one of the key actors and investors in Alimento Atlântico. Señor Tomas, a close compatriot of several very high-level government functionaries, was reportedly the pivot point for most of these incoming and outgoing shipments—be they animal, vegetable, or mineral. However, Señor Tomas was not only deceptive, he was also nearly ethereal—never seen, at least in Bissau and undoubtedly other ports of call. Yet, as Rodney was to inform the group when he heard the news of Señor Tomas' involvement from Oriana, the illusory investor was visible and even at times prominent in his role as member of the board of several multinational corporations across the globe including two major US companies, Simpson Investments and General Industrial and Chemical Products.

While these new details were likely simple annotations in the notebooks of the Abidjan team—filling-in some blanks but not really prompting any action—for Rodney they were much more. Rodney's though-we've-never-met relationship with Señor Tomas went much further back to Delpro and the original investigation of Robin McCandless. In some perverted way, it was almost like finding someone from your high school class now lived next door—time for a reunion. Time to go back to the archives and the fading yearbook photos.

There was a still unclear yet, in Rodney's opinion, a highly probable connection between Señor Tomas Ferreira and Mr. Ralph Tave—good ol' boys in their own rights with deep roots that had run in the direction of Delpro and thereby Domov. Two material links in the chain (a proper G120 high-test trammel chain) that anchored a multiplicity of dissolute and illicit activities that continued to be ongoing in the US in spite of the widely purported downfall of Delpro.

This was also a chain that connected to Raymond Girard and his Guadeloupe villa near Rifflet—a chain that entangled the good Senator Jake Sullivan. Girard was another of those whose name had surfaced during the old days of the SEC investigation into Delpro and its associates. He was of the same ilk as Ferreira, one of the venerable headmen of Domov with a tenure going back years and a power base only rivaled by the senior-most Domov chiefs.

Unfortunately, while painting a picture from the past to the present was a useful tool to try and mitigate problems in the future, in today's fast-moving, highly-compartmentalized, and highly-computerized world, the door to the past, even the recent past, was all too frequently quickly slammed shut—critical and fundamental knowledge sealed in worn and dusty boxes in the attic, rarely found and even less often opened.

Rodney felt lucky in this regard. Although currently, especially at DOJ, there was pressure to focus on now and not to dwell on the past (interpreted by many as, "don't look back"), he was to a large extent working with the same core team he had had at the SEC. They not only had a history, they also knew the history of their subject matter. In the modern sphere of formal investigations, this was an incalculable advantage.

Rodney would perhaps have been surprised to learn that connections to the past were also a premium for Joe Mitchell. Joe loved his family, adored his wife, and was devoted to all three of his children. He was now comfortable in the US—comfortable in Pennsylvania—at home in Pottsville. But in those overly quiet hours before dawn when he would sometimes lie in bed next to Susan and wonder how and why he was where he was, he knew in his heart he was still Yosyp Myshchenko. His roots were still in Ukraine. His story was a Ukrainian story with a rich and powerful history.

Joe thought back to his discussions with his nephew-cum-son—really *his* son. Harold was special. Although a first generation native-born American, Harold seemed to have an almost inherent deep appreciation for his roots and his history—able to straddle the past and the present in, from Joe's perspective, a truly amazing way—much more adept at dealing with this duality than Joe himself.

In addition to his profound respect for and seeming understanding of his ancestors as well as his responsibility to uphold the heritage he had gained from them, Harold, as he grew and prospered in Durango, demonstrated a keen business acumen combined with what his adopted father could only think of as superb survival skills. As he had said in Chicago, things were going well, but they didn't want to fall off the cliff that carried them to the heights of success.

The heights were there, but in Joe's assessment, these heights were there for Harold. He had reached his plateau. His path from his birthplace had, in many ways, been as amazing as Harold's surprisingly deep attachment to this same fountainhead. It was unquestionable that Domov was doing all possible to expand its now diminished imprint in North America with the disastrous, in many ways, dissolution of Delpro.

However, it was equally unquestionable that it would be Harold or others who would pick up the *Maliar's* standard to lead this advancing new front in the battle for global domination.

For Joe, there was still a lot of work to get done. Yet the facts, the facts for which Joe was in many ways grateful, were that the beacon emanating from the *Maliar's* perch no longer burned incessantly on Pottsville—there was another epicenter for Domov in the foothills of the Rockies.

Far from the mountains, as Mercer McMaster monotonously worried Lambert Richardson about his shipment (Lambert assuring the impatient member of the Southern Continentals that these things took time), Ralph Tave was lamentably the object of a different sort of spotlight than the one Joe was now happily avoiding—Tave, unable to shed his own unappreciated prominence in the eyes of unwanted authorities, was nevertheless trying to make sure this light did not spill over to Joe Mitchell and his operations.

Ralph was guardedly optimistic. He felt his discoverable liabilities were limited.

It had been unfortunate that somehow, he had been spotted visiting Robin McCandless at Porumbel Albastru, but he had had no choice. After the move of the nerve center of Delpro from Crab Tree Lane to Candy Point, one of the last transactions Ralph had had with his long-time associate Robin McCandless had involved a shipment—a very large shipment—of brightly-painted and poorly-reconditioned farm machinery from India that Tave had hoped to sell as brand new to a just-opened Kentucky start-up. The items had reportedly arrived in the US, but Ralph had never received them, nor had he ever been given any indication as to their whereabouts. He needed to recover this consignment to either sell or make permanently disappear at the bottom of Cave Run Lake. Now he still had no clue about his machinery, but he had, in spite of all efforts to the contrary, unavoidably moved out of the shadows and was the subject of at least one cursory federal inspection if not the object of other more worrying and far-reaching investigations.

Yet, with luck (Ralph felt he had always been lucky) this would fizzle out as had previous less serious but nonetheless troublesome enquiries. He had received some cryptic communications from unknown yet credible individuals who indicated they too had been colleagues of Robin McCandless. According to these friends, apparently the authorities had some links tying Ralph to Arrow Head Timber and Cattle Company in Oregon and a fish processing plant in Texas. These were overgrown trails that would likely lead nowhere—it had been (by most standards) a long time ago. There were, in the view of these same sources, also some rumors connecting Ralph to Señor Tomas Ferreira and these potentially could be more bothersome if the snoops got any traction.

On the positive side, Tave seemed to have adequate deniability with regard to the anomalous agricultural activities of Cumberland Savings (what do all those politicians today do, they "take the 5th"). After all, he was only the chairman and did not have any responsibilities for the day-to-day investments and operations of Cumberland. While the bank was going to have a multitude of difficult questions to answer, Tave had taken all the necessary measures to be able to declare, "I have no knowledge of these matters" when questioned.

Tave had, for all that, through other unseen but to-be-believed contacts, been aware early-on of Cumberland's ties to S&J Logistics, Fig Leaf Storage, and KHHF. Fortunately, as in his own case, he had been (he hoped) able to bury the most disquieting aspects of Cumberland's links and partnerships so deeply they would never (he hoped) be unearthed.

Ralph Tave sold himself as one with the land, flaunting his fictitious peasant roots. Albeit much of this was hype, Tave was an agricultural engineer and a good one at that. If there was one thing he knew how to do, he knew how to bury things. When he hoped Cumberland's more disquieting relationships were buried, there was a very good chance these channels were hermetically sealed to the outside world.

But now the IRS was poking about his own life. On the surface, things were OK. His taxes were paid. His accountant had years of comprehensive records to share with any auditor. For his personal investments and income, Bootstraps and BFD had detailed and well-documented stories showing how a poor immigrant family had made good.

There was perhaps reason for optimism.

⚘⚘⚘⚘⚘⚘⚘

Gage Smith was many things, but he was not an optimist. He considered himself a realist. He was also a practitioner who had done a lot and seen a lot.

He remembered clearly first getting involved. He remembered how he had wondered how far it would go when, on an overly-theatrical call he had been asked to make to the senator, he had gruffly declared: "Jake, you've gone too far, my friend—really too far. There will be consequences."

The game had started.

Gage knew it was deadly serious, but it was also a game. There were teams and there were strategies for winning; using the best skills and tactics as well as the most brutal actions. It was all about winning regardless of how you played the game.

The game was ultra complex and global. It was everywhere and it was nowhere.

Gage liked games. He was a chess fan.

Gage felt he had at least a partial picture of the on-going developments and tried hard to keep his finger on the pulse of Rodney's work as well as he could—the DOJ investigation piece of the puzzle having been highlighted by the highest ranks of Domov for his particular attention. In many ways, he saw himself as the key man-on-the-ground.

Gage's connections to the Domov's inner circle were, given the circumstances, pretty good. So, he thought, was his general awareness of this massive organization's overall plan to keep getting bigger and better although he was not privy to the specifics (seeing the big picture was hard unless you sat at the top—the organization's apex was heavily shrouded and closely guarded, but over time Gage had had the occasional opportunity to see more—he had taken special efforts to study the few snippets that had crept into his path—all this only slightly lifting the dense veil of secrecy that had covered the utmost layers of the group for decades).

His ties to his overlords had generally been indirect although he had had occasion to communicate directly with the boss of bosses a few times when extremely urgent situations had arisen. Most often he communicated via sterile channels with the *Maliar's* entourage. Throughout, the persona of the King of the Hill remained an enigma (even though he was among the rare few who had actually talked with the *Maliar*), it was a position with which he was more than a little familiar and of which he was continuously in awe. The *Maliar's* nearly pure power was as intoxicating as it was frightening. As a pawn (he liked to think of himself more as a knight—but if he were honest, he knew this was probably not the case—life's a bitch) on the game board, he felt pride in his successes and trepidation for any missteps.

Gage still believed he was master of his destiny in spite of his embroilment in so many sticky wickets (as they had called them in London) through his affiliation with a major global criminal coalition.

Indeed, Gage felt these ties to Domov were his destiny.

Gage's internship at the beginning of his Domov work had, unbeknownst to either as they had never met, retraced many of the tracks traced by Charlie Stancik who had ended up being one of Robin McCandless' top aides—Gage not having the institutional bonds Charlie had had, always being more of a free agent. Somewhat after Charlie, but unknowingly following in his footsteps, Gage had worked with both Fredericks, Higgins, and Woods and J. P. Thorne LLC on a number of Delpro assignments before being again reassigned to London where he had heard of the reported death of McCandless due to an inexplicable boating accident on Chesapeake Bay.

Then he had been relocated back to the US.

But that all seemed like ancient history. His normal small-cog-in-a-big-wheel role had changed demonstrably when he had made that first call to Senator Jake Sullivan. Gage understood, almost intuitively, the critical role of political champions—whether the local Harlan County commissioner or a Senate chairman. Sullivan was more than a buffer—he was, or should have been, an active piece on the game board—maybe a rook.

Yet Gage was concerned the ever-ambitious and always-hungry senator had made one of those fearful missteps. He had, more-or-less in plain view, accepted the largesse of Mr. Raymond Girard and the hospitality of his Guadeloupe villa near Rifflet—maybe it was simply too tempting to be able to go back to DC and brag about your "fantastic Caribbean holidays." The senator and certainly his family had more than ample means to holiday wherever they chose with as much opulence and prestige-making fluff as could be desired. He did not need to accept gifts. Perhaps the temptation was too strong. Perhaps the habits were too hard to break. The "why" didn't matter now. To Gage's practiced eye, Jake Sullivan was vulnerable, and this was not a good thing for his boss in Holwerd.

He had dramatically warned the senator he had gone too far. Maybe he had?

Ironically, Senator Jake Sullivan was concerned he was not going far enough—nor fast enough. While he certainly did not see the whole picture—and knew he was really only reacting to a smidgen (as his mother-in-law would have called it) of a much larger production—he saw enough to know that Mr. Gage Smith represented people one should work with and not against. His political future and even his private livelihood could be immensely affected by those behind Smith—both for the better and the worse.

His efforts and his results through Jan's good services had managed to deflect some from the irritating and incessant Rodney Mills' persistent demands for more money—now-now, if you please. The loquacious lawmaker had, he thought, made a convincing argument to his subgroup of the Permanent Committee on Homeland Security and Government Affairs that funds were urgently needed to protect the homeland from the potential wave of economic refugees that could inflict all manner of ills from economic to national security problems. Given the necessary accountability to the taxpayer and the need for additional fiscal control demanded of legislators, it was clear that providing funds to this critical set of actions he proposed would unfortunately but unavoidably result in a reduction of funds available to competing recipients including Section T15-Z. Moreover, funding the needed refugee measures was only a bandaid for the imminent concerns. They needed to go to the root of the problem and do, as he had already outlined: quickly invest in the economic development of other regions of the world like Africa to ensure that locals found more economic advantage staying at home rather than making arduous trips to come to the US and worry America's already over-taxed citizens.

Jake felt—Jake was sure—he had made a strong case. That equally irritating and incessant Gage Smith should be happy.

As what he saw as vindication of his efforts, Senator Sullivan was visited by Ms. Loretta Williams, registered lobbyist for the Investment Defense Fund—IDF. Ms. Williams was, she informed the senator, not only an effective influencer, as she called herself (Jake unsure exactly who all she planned on influencing), but also his constituent as a voting lifelong resident of Petersburg, Virginia. And, she added with a beautiful smile, a very happy constituent as the senator was doing great work for the state.

Specifically, Loretta thanked the senator for his invaluable hard work and dedication to those pivotal issues that were also the aims of IDF:

helping the needy of the world by putting in place the means whereby the finely-tuned industrial and financial machinery of the United States could help others climb out of poverty and desolation. Senator Sullivan was their champion.

Ms. Williams did not come only with empty accolades. IDF had many very well-to-do and powerful members. As she understood the good senator already had some staff in the field to initiate his ever-so-important work, IDF was willing to work with existing regional economic communities to establish a specific trust that could be used by would-be entrepreneurs to establish local businesses. Moreover, to discuss in minute detail the workings of this trust, IDF was happy to invite the Honorable Mr. Sullivan and his family to an all-expenses-paid, ten-day trip to Geneva where IDF would engage the Ecumenical Humanitarian Trust—EHT—and the International Center for Democratic Ideals—ICDI—in the design of their new proposed project.

For Jake this was great news (not to mention a free holiday in one of the most expensive cities in the world). This was validation of his position and information he could take to his committee to further stress the point that they needed to act now on these matters even if this meant some regrettable negative short term (he stressed short term) impacts on the functions of some agencies and bureaus such as Section T15-Z.

What Senator Jake Sullivan did not know, of course, was that Loretta Williams was an associate of Gage Smith and that IDF was a carefully curated fictitious shell which had been set up by Chakir Awal before he had left Holwerd for Côte d'Ivoire. While IDF was a little more than a carcass with a nebulous institutional history as well as limited functionality, EHT and IDIC were firmly enmeshed in the tentacles of Domov. It was a small world.

Radutu Botezatu was less sure it was a small world in any positive sense, but felt his world was shrinking. Ironically, before the technology and communications revolution that computerized everything and made instantaneous information exchange a fact of life, it had been easier and more profitable to do business. In those days, if he had a product someone wanted, they would discuss the price and make the sale—full stop. People knew people and a handshake sealed the deal.

Today it was different. It was globalization. The marketplace was full and all interconnected—a customer would just as likely leave you in the dust when better arrangements were found, even if these were on the other side of the globe or with a never-seen supplier.

At the same time, the authorities and policing agencies were also connected. In the good old days, it was a lot easier to stay in the shadows—to grease the wheels when need-be. Today it was all about transparency—everyone looking over everyone else's shoulder. Today technology crept into the furthest corners. Today everybody had a camera, and anyone could spread the news far and wide as to where you were and what you were doing. As far as he was concerned, they should bring back the horse-and-buggy days.

Nevertheless, part of this worldwide connectivity was that Radutu Botezatu himself was more in the know about the goings-on not only in Eastern Europe, but damn near anywhere. Things were changing, He had heard how some of his brothers and sisters in Domov were meeting the changes. They were opting for new, less-intrusive ways to adapt to a new, perhaps more controlling world.

While he was wont to make any major adjustments just to keep up with the rigors of modernization, he almost unwillingly but unavoidably changed to necessarily evolve with an evolving world. Inside Domov, however, things were more enduring. He was still a seemingly valued mid-level actor—still organizing the (he thought) important Easter Weekend Conclaves in the Făgăraş Mountains. He was still part of the wider decision-making processes albeit all, as it should have been, still rotated around the judgments of the *Maliar*.

On the business front, there had been a lot of modifications (under the banner of modernization, he thought with a wince). Not too long ago, he had managed all transactions from the source to the final destination. Now this chain was cut up in smaller more localized pieces to reduce risk but also inevitably reducing oversight and profits. The same products were still moving but they were part of a much more varied market basket and they were moving through very circuitous, often nearly impossible to trace, pathways.

His world had been reshaped. Yet, true to his core philosophy, "in for a penny, in for a pound," he had already invested too much for too long. Just to keep up (with whom?), he was not going to alter his actions to the point where they became unrecognizable. He was too old to start over. His world was shirking but it was still his world, and he wanted it to play by his rules.

For his part, Orest knew it was a small world—this was, from his perspective, the foundation of his work. It was a small world controlled by Domov. This was not, naturally, the current version of the 1960s fears of global domination. Domov didn't dominate (at least directly). Domov did business. For these businesses to thrive and expand, Orest knew there was a premium on efficacy—all forms of efficacy. They had to be effective in covering their tracks—operating in the shadows. They had to be effective in their business ventures—profit was the sole measure. They had to be effective in their partnerships—those closest to you were all too often the ones who put the knife in your back. They had to be effective in building their teams—high-quality and efficient staff at all levels were essential. Finally, they had to be effective in their investments. While the bottom line was paramount, you had to spend money to get money, and often this meant enticing favors and facilitating action—money well spent was effective.

There were always inefficiencies. There were always problems. However, Orest now began to get an inkling of suspicion that multiple things were not really going as well as he had initially calculated—as he had hoped. He did have good people. They all had good and well-thought-out plans. They were all dedicated to the organization but equally to their own personal gains in wealth and power through the organization. This was as it should have been. This was as it had been envisioned.

Still, when it was all said and done, he had a degree of concern that was very atypical. His way of doing business had always been to plan as carefully as possible—meticulously (as his mentor had told him, "Measure twice, cut once")—and then let the others do the work. No one was a specialist nor an expert in everything. He had staff—excellent, highly-paid staff—who were authorities and leaders in a wide variety of disciplines. He had always believed in letting those in-the-know do the job. This still seemed the best tactic. His people had proven themselves many times over. Nevertheless, the worm of doubt was twisting in his stomach. Were they all on the right track? Did they need to go back and revisit their roots?

While the *Maliar* strategized as to how best to efficaciously plant the seeds for bigger and greater actions, the daughter he never knew was also strategizing—or more correctly reviewing her strategy. Her work had always been important—been at the epicenter of her daily routine. Now she felt her work was pushing David into the backroom while she entertained the crew from Abidjan in the living room. This had not been her plan. It had just happened, but it shouldn't have.

She needed to put a premium on her private life.

David was too important.

David was too good a person.

He encouraged her to focus on her intoxicating (for her) work as he knew this was her very essence. He said he understood. He was patient. He happily went to Penn Station every day for the commute to the Energy Elite offices in Elizabeth, New Jersey—every day giving her a hug, or if she were away, a call. When they were together, the passion still raged.

Nonetheless, she felt she was being unfair to David—unfair in several ways. She had never told him about reading the letter she never should have seen. She had never asked about Yosyp Myshchenko. She had never asked about Radutu Botezatu, though she and her team had researched the Romanian businessman as well as they could given the pall of darkness that seemed to wrap around any news concerning his enterprises or activities.

She should be more open with David.

She should put him first.

It had been (it was) unfair to become so engrossed in her work as to have little time for the man she loved. She felt she was pushing him away and that was the last thing she wanted to do. She needed to bring their relationship to the forefront. Their unique and deep love was a premium—a rare gift not to be squandered.

Rodney had no idea of Oriana's struggles when he called her for an update. He did know now, however, how valuable a source of information she was becoming. He too put a premium on something—on the growing volume of data collected by the Abidjan crew regarding Alimento Atlântico and Approvisionnement Alimentaire Européen as well as other eastern Atlantic Coast transporters—all this helping fill-in several blanks as did the crew's details about the merchandise moving up and down the coast including, sadly, trafficked people.

This information was invaluable.

With the ability to overlay a dusty chart of officially long-gone Delpro activities (yet, as Rodney was now aware, many not truly gone, simply repurposed) superimposed on a work-in-progress depiction of recent known Domov actions, Rodney and his team were able to get a better if still fuzzy picture of at least a representative sample of current events likely attributable to the global hydroid organization. Moreover, while the highest levels of Domov were still cloud-covered, the long-time and still-going operators like Radutu Botezatu, Raymond Girard, Tomas Ferreira, and other well-known actors from the Delpro days had laid a spoor that led from the past into the future—a spoor that provided relevant and recent insight into the structure and functions of the basilisk that was Domov.

It was, of course, a moving target. Rodney needed to refresh his information on a regular and increasingly frequent basis. Hence his call to Oriana.

"You keep sending good things my way, thanks," Rodney said.

"You're welcome, I guess," Oriana replied with a little less enthusiasm in her voice than normal. "It's always a challenge to know what to send on as there's so much and a lot could be and probably is a red herring."

"Just keep doing as you've been doing—more is better and we can cull things on my side."

"Fine. Just to give you a heads-up, we may be getting into diminishing returns."

"How's that?"

"As you know, much of the traction in terms of US support and financial resources has been a result of Jan and the fact she's Sullivan's staff and Sullivan is still beating the drum of NCIIP—now diluting it a bit with more general position about the need for Americans to invest more in Africa with US government facilitation.

"Finally, as all of us, he seems to see that NCIIP, if it ever happens, will take a long time—longer than he wants to deal with as his timeline is tied to the US election cycle. He needs things to tout now-now. And I think we've already provided him with quite a bit given that the average voter is not interested in too much detail; they tend to swallow his spin regardless of how it's presented—at least the dedicated supporters who are all-in for Jake. He likely feels he now has what he needs, and we've been there long enough—enough's been spent. We've been there in the flesh to provide an *acte de présence* as verification of the senator's efforts. Probably not much more showmanship required."

"Makes some sorta sense," Rodney interjected.

"So," she continued with the same cadence as if Rodney had said nothing, "I suspect that Jan's assignment will come to an end soon and this will severely affect our work. This is especially true since we've already done so much. We don't really know what all is missing—we don't know what we don't know—but the marginal costs are getting higher and higher. We've lately made a lot of progress with Professor De Angelis' inputs and still have some important tasks on our group calendar, but I am not sure how much longer we'll be at it."

"Understood," Rodney offered, and he really did understand. "We'll just have to take it a day at a time. We've already gained a great deal through your work, so we'll just wait and see how things roll out."

After the call, Oriana thought, Maybe now I can get my life in order?

After the call, Rodney thought, How will we be able to fill-in further curious blanks of the sort the Abidjan crew was so adept at untangling if this valuable resource is disbanded?

About the same time Oriana and Rodney were deep in thought, Joe was also thinking about the past and the future while returning in the present to Pottsville after having had one of his more or less regular meetings with Harold—this time in Denver (again, meeting in public in plain sight at a coffee shop off East 11th Avenue next to the Denver Botanic Gardens). All had gone well, and Joe was happy to be back in Pennsylvania, drawing nearer to the welcoming embrace of Susan who he knew anxiously awaited his return. As he reached home, his mind nostalgically flashed back to a time when the kids were running in the yard, running to greet him when he came home from work at the mine. That was long ago. Much had changed. He hoped Harold was up to the task—he had a big job ahead of him.

For Jake, it was all part of the job. The trip to Geneva, officially recorded as a trade mission, family included, had been enjoyed by all—at least he thought Loretta had enjoyed it too. Loretta Williams had proven herself to be the ever-pleasant guide, interpreter, and counsel. She organized outings for Rebecca and the kids. There had been concerts and plays. The food had been spectacular, and the accommodation lavish. It was, to top it all off, all on someone else's tab.

Of course, five-star tourism was a side event. The core of the trip was the consultation with IDF and the meetings they set up with EHF and ICDE. Overall, this alphabet soup of organizations assured the senator that their organizations were just what he needed to expand his program for encouraging more international US investment—not simply in Africa, but around the world.

This was just what Jake needed to hopefully tip the scales in terms of getting significant funding for these awaiting investment opportunities albeit, of course, at the expense of greater support for Section T15-Z.

However, as Jake knew all too well, there were no free lunches (nor free trips to Geneva). On the eve of their departure, Lorette had had a tête-à-tête with the senator in a secluded corner of a quiet bar across the street from the family's hotel.

"Hope you enjoyed your stay here, we certainly enjoyed having you."

"It's been grand." Jake hoped he wasn't coming across as too ostentatious. "My family will never forget this wonderful time, and I am most appreciative of the discussions with all the excellent folks you have managed to arrange."

"Well, we all have great expectations."

"As it should be."

"Indeed. Yet, Senator, I need to be candid."

"Of course."

"People here, once they are committed, they really don't like seeing things derailed."

"Naturally. Same back home"

"Yes. And people here do their homework."

"As well they should."

"Let me cut to the chase. Arrangements, beneficial to all, with groups like EHF and ICDE can be tied up with undue government red tape or oversight. This is in no one's interest."

"Understandably."

"So, people here are looking for some form of guarantee or commitment. A proclamation, for example, ideally from that committee you head-up, that they will support the arrangements both politically and financially."

"I'll do what I can."

"I know you will."

On the Swiss Air flight back to Dulles, watching the world below slip by from his plush first-class seat, Jake Sullivan, the astute politician, understood that once again pressure was being applied. Those applying the pressure were almost certainly running out of patience and who knew what they'd do when they felt the time had run out?

They wanted a proclamation. He would do what he could to get one.

Proclamations

THERE are claims of glory and claims of innocence. There are claims demanding payment. There are claims asserting resource rights and familial lineage. And there are claims proclaiming, "Trust me. I know what I am doing!"

Orest was most concerned by the latter. He understood all too well that most did not know what they did not know. Moreover, the impact of this phenomenon was a well-acknowledged dilemma of yet-to-be-determined magnitude. Of whatever scale, it was significant. Yet it was hard to build effective safeguards against ignorance.

Complete ignorance of Domov and its activities was an advantage. An incomplete or even an incorrect understanding of Domov and its investments could prove problematic. Much of Orest's work involved heading off problems before they arose. The easiest way was to keep as much of the population as possible ignorant of the very existence of Domov.

This, of course, had been one of the principal mandates of the position of *Maliar* since its conception. Orest, as others, took it very seriously. Secrecy and stealth were paramount. Any breach of the shroud was, therefore, very troubling.

In this instance, there were no discernible breaches—no holes in the fence to mend. But there was the worm of doubt that undulated and twisted in his gut. Something was not quite right. He knew what he was doing—or at least fervently believed so. The big question was those who overestimated their capabilities (or their thirst for power)—those who claimed all was fine when it was not.

⚓⚓⚓⚓⚓⚓⚓

While the man perched at the pinnacle of the organization began to sense previously unknown worries and doubts, unawares, others down the pecking order claimed with a clear conscious all was truly going well—things were bigger and better.

⚓⚓⚓⚓⚓⚓⚓

Probably one of the ones closest to the *Maliar*, Chakir Awal, was also feeling as though things were going pretty well. Although in the broader West African context, activities with Onyx Associates had yet to blossom into the basket full of hoped-for opportunities, and in spite of the fact that NCIIP was still, at best, on the drawing board, real tangible progress had been made in Nigeria—the Associates still occupied with excavating the groundwork upon which to form a unique and powerful lattice of local alliances. Through these efforts, Chakir and his colleagues had made significant advances in laying the foundations for a local network with a hub in Calabar. The pieces were all falling into place—not without, naturally, an ample dose of encouragement—what was locally referred to as *dash* or *baksheesh*. As they said, "Man wey naked no dey put hand for pocket (to accomplish some things certain pre-conditions are necessary)."

Then there was a glitch.

Everything from Adjasso-Ekokku to Calabar was practically arranged. The problem—and a big problem—came when they tried to build-in the link west to Port Harcourt and Warri—a link that was a high priority as it led to the heart of the country's petroleum industry.

Moving west out of Oron, across Cross River from Calabar, Chakir's staff on the ground began reaching out to community and traditional leaders, using the same tactics they had used when organizing the pathways from the north into Calabar They had only gone twenty-five miles when they reached the town of Eket (also called Idong Afianwe since there was another Eket in Switzerland). Here they had a head-on collision with the New Niger Delta Liberation Front (NNDLF).

NNDLF proclaimed their group, their home-grown camarilla, represented the marginalized delta and coastal communities that had been raped by the occident, their resources plundered, and their culture left in tatters. They advocated for secession. Their charismatic leader Joseph Togo had been killed by the military and his successor, Ebikake Dobra. Ebikake, ironically translated from Ijaw as "accept good things," and Dobra, meaning "man of peace," had moved the center of their operations from Delta State to Akwa Ibom State and Eket. Mr. Dobra did not welcome any outsiders—especially some unknown strangers who could not or would not say from whence they came and why they were there. For him it was extremely simple, the community should shut out the newcomers—even if they offered generous enticements. Dobra reminded his people how they had taken the poison fruit already and it had brought them no good. There was absolutely no reason to even talk with these outlanders.

When the Onyx team tried to insist and sweeten any offer, Dobra sealed the point by killing three of the seven-member team—allowing the others to flee into the bush. This was unheard of. This was unplanned. This was really a problem. Not only for the loss of life of good people but also for the fact that it couldn't be kept from the authorities. Sooner or later there would be some sort of follow-up by the military, and they would want to know why foreigners were trying to make deals with the good folks of Eket and got themselves killed in so doing.

For Chakir there was only one option: forget the east-west leg of their network for the time being. The north-south leg was sound and unaffected by any issues regarding NNDLF or repercussions of their savagery. They would put the finishing touches on their "northern business artery," as they called it, running from the coast and Calabar all the way up to Abinsi. Then they would return to Abidjan.

Much further west, in Côte d'Ivoire, Luc and Marc Cisse felt they had played their hand well. France had been an overreach. Their legal firewalls against the Les Caïds had made significant cuts into their profits, and those French hooligan longshoremen played rough. The shift to a DC concession had been a boon, not only to get out of the way of the threatening Caïds but also providing the much-coveted foothold in the US.

This necessary adjustment had also allowed the brothers to concentrate more effort on their activities closer to home—things had come full circle. While their investment portfolio was now highly diverse, they had decided to focus on agriculture—more precisely, thanks to their experiences in France, focus on high-demand tropical agricultural products that could be clandestinely inserted into European market channels. Of particular interest was coffee. There was an expanding demand for high quality coffee with what consumers now called "traceability"—basically, as far as the Cisses could determine, this was just merchandise that had a story attached to it. They were great story tellers.

If this was what customers claimed they wanted, this is what the sons of Vianney, an Ivorian farmer with a terrific story, would provide.

Kyrylo Rudenko, son of Voldoymyr (who also had a story to tell), was also committed to giving customers what they claimed they wanted. What they wanted opened up brand new opportunities for the Ukrainian exporter (as he saw himself). Up until now, there had been almost no market for Eastern European arms in the US. After all, the US was the major manufacturer—reportedly, as Kyrylo had read, the source of four in ten arms sold around the globe. A tiny speck on that portrait, he was now selling arms in the US.

As arms sales soared, as did armed conflicts (including an increasing number of well-armed run-of-the-mill criminals worldwide), and as economic inequities approached never-seen-before rifts between the haves and the have-nots, voluntary and involuntary human migration was growing nearly as fast as the arms' trade. An acknowledged significant portion of this human tide was comprised of lost souls captured in trafficking to fill needed but unwanted labor slots in food production, domestic cleaning, and a plethora of other activities where the local elite considered themselves above such menial and distasteful tasks.

Supplying warm bodies to do these unpleasant assignments had been one of Cynthia Owens' main preoccupations through Özgürlük. She had typically zeroed in on unwanted segments of Turkish society as well as unpopular segments of the populations of neighboring countries, thereby earning the protection of the Turkish government.

This had been good business for Cynthia since relocating from the US. It had also been good business for other segments of the Domov family where they were able to tap a labor pool (albeit conscripted labor) with a special and often unique skill set.

Then there was one of those much-regretted missteps. Özgürlük's staff had been informed of a large group of "candidates" for work in

Europe—the concocted Turkish NGO officially involved to handle the logistics to ostensibly help the group get formal UN refugee status. It had been reported that these targets were members of the much reviled and often feared Kurdish community—members of the hated PKK (Partiya Karkerên Kurdistanê—the Kurdistan Workers' Party)—one of the government intermediaries assisting in the venture remarking, "These depraved dogs can now be filth-eating workers for pestilent infidel Europeans—see how they like that."

However, after the group had been herded into containers and shipped to Greece, it became apparent there had been a horrible mistake. The jettisoned people had actually been clandestine members of the fierce OKK (Özel Kuvvetler Komutanlığı—the military's Special Forces Command) who were trying to infiltrate the Kurds.

The government was furious. Özgürlük was shut down with a deluge of negative publicity claiming the NGO had actually been a worthless husk covering for faithless individuals who did nothing but spout Communist propaganda. Cynthia Owens had vanished—most unsubstantiated reports indicating she had been able to flee or otherwise she would surely have been imprisoned or unceremoniously killed.

Whether intentionally leaked or the result of good police work, in one way or another, INTERPOL got word of the ill-fated adventures of Ms. Owens and her NGO and passed this on to Felix Manchester who, in turn, shared the welcome news with Group 8 and Rodney.

⚘⚘⚘⚘⚘⚘⚘

What was not news was that nature abhorred a vacuum. Although the Cisse Brothers had been a long way down the Domov echelons, their affiliations in the global marketplace were unquestionably known to Domov, even if by rather convoluted pathways. They may have been the base of the pyramid, but the actors occupying the base were of the utmost importance—they supported the apex—they were literally the building blocks of which the cenotaph was made.

When the Ivorians shifted out of Marseilles there was a hole—a hole much desired by Les Caïds—a hole where the Le Milieu could further reinforce their stranglehold on the multitude of illicit activities that were entangled into the daily life of the city and the port. Also, a hole that Domov would have liked to fill with an entity one way or another linked to their vast network—not letting the void pass to their long-time rivals.

Filling holes was an ongoing challenge for Orest. These holes lately seemed to be the home of the worm that was wiggling its way through his abdomen. While he realized the worm was his internalizing of the nervous ticks his stomach and intestines were making as they were seemly adapting to reflect heightening stress levels, a more clinical symptom of his growing anxiety was, for the first time ever, increasing blood pressure—this from a man who had been in tiptop shape his entire life. Now, added to all, there were possible health concerns—modest though they may be.

Unlike many, the *Maliar* did not have to worry about health insurance—not even about access to the best health practitioners. At Holwerd, among his entourage was a highly qualified medical technician who, prior to joining the organization, had served as an outstanding medic for the 45 Commando Royal Marines. Willy McNaught was both a talented and skillful corpsman. He was also very conscientious about health matters. He was all in favor of preemptive action—advising his boss it was time to see his doctor.

Orest's predecessor had arranged for a world-class doctor and a highly-qualified dentist to be on-call for him twenty-four seven—the doctor in Geneva and the dentist in Paris (always adopting the principle of seclusive deterrence—being a moving target in the shadows). Discretion was everything. These practitioners had just enough other patients to make sure their practices had all the appearances of normalcy. But there was no question. There was one principal patient: the *Maliar*.

Willy arranged for Orest to go promptly to Geneva for a thorough check-up and any necessary treatment.

There were institutional as well as individual checkups.

Under the prevailing circumstances, it was definitely not everyone across the vast Domov food chain who claimed things were hunky-dory or claimed to know the needful. It had always been a game of cat and mouse (the big question being who was the cat and who was the mouse)—the opposition being the authorities, whether the leadership of pre-WWI Ukrainian villages or modern-day international crime fighters. Once global in scope, the happenings in America had always been critical to the overall health of the organization. The departure of Robin McCandless and Delpro had been a shock for which they were still in some ways compensating. The dogged and amazingly effective actions of the US investigative agencies—chiefly those under Rodney Mills' guidance (a man on a mission and always someone to take very seriously)—were more than an inconvenience. They were a threat.

Many in the Domov flock (from Radutu Botezatu, Raymond Girard, Tomas Ferreira to Joe and Harold Mitchell), although only seeing a limited number of pieces of the jigsaw, were keenly aware of the growing threat to the organization's health as witnessed by the only-just-starting deep plunge into Ralph Tave's life and affairs. Word traveled fast through both formal and informal channels.

Domov as designed, more correctly put, as iteratively shaped by Andriy and Lehya, was not a club where members paid dues, an association with fees to join, nor even an enterprise where one purchased shares. Domov was a worldwide web where knowledge and strategy were transformed into wealth and power.

Kyrylo Rudenko, the Cisse brothers and many, many more in one way or another attached to this web operated their businesses, made their managerial decisions, and took home their profits (or losses). It was the coordinated and analytical knowledge of these business outcomes that allowed Domov to insert itself in a mutually beneficial manner—at times, or as necessary, using methods and practices that could be seen by some as illicit at the very least and brutal at the other end of the spectrum. Nevertheless, if Kyrylo moved merchandise to Mexico or Luc and Marc had regular shipments going to northern Italy, there were opportunities for the Organization to "top these off" for the benefit of all. Power was knowledge.

It was instinctively a two-way street. If it worked well, knowledge moved as easily from the bottom up as from the top down. Also, essential to success, this knowledge had to be balanced by ample supplies of anti-knowledge—what some recently began to call fake news. It was sleight of hand by master prestidigitators, seamlessly replacing fact with fiction, then using the fact adroitly to multiply many times over its impact.

However, to be effective, this knowledge (and anti-knowledge) had to move through hermetical conduits. Unsealing these buried passages was the ever-present threat—a threat growing through Rodney's Mills' ceaseless digging regardless of major barriers such as Jake Sullivan.

This potential vulnerability was acknowledged as a cost of doing business across the Domov system. Only the naive or those on the very lowest rungs of the organization's twisted ladder felt that things were great. There had always been and always would be risks and threats. However, at present, these seemed all the more manifest—all the more menacing to Domov's health. Regardless of how these circumstances affected others, for Orest it appeared these evolving facts raised his blood pressure.

⚘⚘⚘⚘⚘⚘⚘

While, at Willy McNaught's insistence, Orest went for a checkup, Mercer McMaster checked up with Lambert Richardson about his consignment. Fortunately, to take the pressure off them both, Lambert was able to set a date for delivery—getting money in the bank and Mercer off his back. The cargo had been moved from Rowley's Bay in Liberty Grove to the Farmers' Home warehouse south of Sturgeon Bay where it had stayed out of sight if not out of mind for several weeks to make sure it had left no trail for the curious to follow.

Lambert was now comfortable throwing his merchandise into the immense river of freight that ebbed and flowed across the country. He quite simply had gone to his shipping broker and put in a formal request for a free agent trucker to pick up the cargo for delivery to Savannah, Georgia—a trip of over 1,200 miles, practically due south.

Within forty-eight hours Rich McKnight knocked at the door of Lambert's office at Farmers' Home—his big red Mack in the parking lot. With no real delays, the paperwork was done, the freight on board (in multiple nondescript wooden crates addressed to Mr. Mercer McMaster with no return address), and the truck smoothly gliding down Highway 57 to Green Bay where he would hit Interstate 43 south.

Rich, by arrangements with Lambert, had planned two days for the trip—charging Farmers' Home for a full load so he would not have to stop en route to pick up any more freight since the crates only filled a fraction of the truck's impressive capacity. The Wisconsinite farm supplier seemed ready and able to pay a significant gratuity to get his consignment to its destination as quickly as possible, so it was to be as close to nonstop as possible, hopefully straight to the client's door.

On day two, now on Interstate 24 where it bounced back and forth along the Tennessee-Georgia Line, just outside Chattanooga, there was a roadblock manned by US Marshals. Two inmates had escaped from the medium-security Federal Correctional Institution in Memphis by slipping into the nearby Shelby Farm Park and then apparently following the Wolf River east, keeping to backroads and rural hamlets, the pair managed to make it into the Blue Ridge Mountains. There were reports they were trying to ultimately get to Atlanta. The duo had actually been the coordinators of an Atlanta-based band that preyed on the elderly—selling fake luxury vacations, fraudulent health and life insurance policies, and even pirated medical equipment. The latest rumors were that the twosome, tired and impatient to reach their destination, had highjacked a vehicle at gun point to make the final run to what they hoped would be a safe haven in sprawl of the Big Peach. The order, therefore, had gone out from the Marshals' office to search all vehicles heading into the metro Atlanta area.

Rich stopped beside the marshal with an up-raised hand, his truck letting out a big gasp of the air brakes as though welcoming the respite. The uniformed, clean-shaven officer queried unsmilingly, "Where ya from?"

"Got freight from Wisconsin going to Georgia—been on the road since yesterday. On I-65 since Indianapolis until I hit I-24 at Nashville—nuth'n but miles and miles of freeway I fear."

"Documents, please," he said, still without the slightest smile.

Rich handed the officer a binder with all he hoped was requested including certificate of insurance, motor carrier authority, truck and trailer registration, IFTA license, paper logs, annual safety inspection report, and bill of lading. While his colleagues questioned other drivers, Rich's marshal retreated with his spoils to a stool carefully positioned in the shade of a yellow poplar where he proceeded to peruse the binder page by page.

Returning to the Mack after a big swing from the thermos under his stool, the unsmiling officer handed back the binder. "At first glance, it's all OK on the paperwork side, at least for the truck and trailer. More complicated, always, for cargo. Let's have a look inside."

Rich descended from the cab, going to the rear of the truck to open the big sealed double doors for the marshal. The fit officer gracefully leapt onto the bed and began examining the crates that were securely fastened in the front portion of the trailer. "Not much written on these is there?"

"Nope."

"Did the consigner add anything?"

"Nope. Just what's on the bill of lading."

"And that's not much."

"Nope. But I just drive the rig. Don't ask questions as long as the papers are up to speed."

"Sure. But there are laws. Each of these items is required to have specific papers with the reference numbers indelibly written on the crates—we need, just to mention a few, the Importer Security Filing, the ISF, along with a handful of customs forms including the CBP 6059B, the CBP 7533, and the CBP 3461. Where are these?"

"OK. I get it. There's a bunch of stuff—important stuff—that's typically with the cargo and that clearly isn't here—maybe it's missing or maybe the shipper has it. I don't pack or load the boxes. I'm just a simple teamster—not a lawyer, heaven forbid," Rich said, trying to keep his rising temper under control as a flare-up would help no one.

"Understand. You're the driver. But we got rules. I gotta open at least one of these—maybe more. There's just nothing indicated on the outside—no docs taped or stapled to the side as there should have been. Should be more. I'll be right back—don't go anywhere."

The officer went back in the direction of the stool but then turned toward the tree where there was a duffle bag. Getting a pry-bar and screwdriver, he returned to the trailer. This time Rich got in with him.

With no more conversation, the marshal pried off three of the unfinished one by fours of which the selected crate was constructed, revealing a great heap of excelsior below. When this was scraped off, there was not only the fragrant aroma of fresh gun oil, but a clear view of the oiled weapons lined out in the bottom of the crate like a rasher of bacon.

At least the officer did not draw his sidearm. But he did frown more deeply, ordering Rich to get back to the rear of the truck and not, under any circumstances, leave.

This was the beginning of an experience Rich would never in his wildest dreams have thought he would have had and would have hoped he never would have had he known what it was all about.

Rich's truck was impounded, and he was placed under guard—fortunately at a cheap Chattanooga motel and not in the county jail. The authorities had agreed that on the surface it seemed as though Rich was an innocent victim and, as he professed, he was just a hardworking driver who somehow got bad cargo. This possibility notwithstanding, they did a thorough probe of any and all records for Mr. Richard Wayne McKnight including his parents Wyatt and Ida McKnight of Minot, North Dakota.

The search results came back as Rich had claimed. There was nothing in his nor his family's past to indicate any criminal, certainly not any gunrunning, history. He was released, as was his red Mack minus the cargo, with the understanding that he would make himself available for any subsequent questioning or testimony.

Rich needed a break. Unfortunately, it wasn't ice fishing season but maybe he could go and hang out at Uncle Warner's ranch.

⚓⚓⚓⚓⚓⚓⚓

As should be expected, the minute the US Marshal jumped down to the ground after opening that first crate of weapons, he was on the line with his colleagues in DC, demanding urgent investigations of both Mercer McMaster and Lambert Richardson as well as surveillance of both men.

Mercer's connections to the Southern Continentals' militia popped quickly. This in and of itself was ample justification in the Marshals' eyes for seeking an indictment on gun-running as well as more than enough reason to immediately arrest McMaster and the other leaders of the militia.

Lambert was another story. He maintained, like Rich, he was an innocent victim. Just a businessman who was handling some merchandise through his Mexican investments as part of one of his main jobs as a freight forwarder. This seemed to be borne out by the conclusion of their initial examination. The only links between the two men appeared to be through the National Ag Suppliers Association. Although McMaster's hard right politics were well known in Savannah and elsewhere, Richardson politically was a clean sheet—no activism, basically a middle-of-the-road Presbyterian registered Republican. The international nature of his businesses, moreover, made his explanation plausible. He did, and had for a long time, move a lot of freight—especially up the Atlantic Seaboard and inland through the Great Lakes.

It was, in fact, this latter point that was Lambert's downfall—but it took a while. His dossier belatedly arrived in the hands of D-2 and finally with Rodney Mills himself. A little light went off in Rodney's memory when he read about the shipping of items through the Great Lakes. Way back when, Rodney had been told by Charlie Stancik how young Charlie had started out working for a company called Spot On that, as it turned out, was part of the broader US Delpro network. With Spot On, Charlie had been involved in moving contraband between the US and

Canada—not big shipments of freight, but who was to say these had not happened too. They probably had.

Rodney had the archives reopened and assigned a team to go through any details linking Delpro to the movement of freight across the Great Lakes region; especially anything that could be tied to Liberty Grove or Sturgeon Bay where Farmers' Home apparently had bases. There it was, in some of the more banal documentation recovered from Don Drumpfsh. Lambert Richardson had received payments from Delpro. Then records of Fredericks, Higgins, and Woods, surreptitiously copied by Charlie, showed persistent relationships between Richardson and McCandless on a number of fronts. Lambert Richardson had been a Delpro operative and was likely still tied to Domov. He was no innocent victim. He was an important piece on the board—pawn or knight, time would tell.

⚘⚘⚘⚘⚘⚘⚘

Rodney was in some ways feeling a reprieve from Senator Sullivan's stonewalling. While the initial exploration into Ralph Tave's affairs had been undertaken by the IRS, this was the strategic first step in a detailed plan to uncover Tave's activities layer by layer. Now, joining Ralph was Lambert Richardson. Here the inquest was more in your face. They had the goods. Richardson had a long history with Delpro and by default with Domov. There was no reason to be coy. Rodney's colleagues took Richardson to facilities they had for just such occasions in the outskirts of Chicago. Here they would squeeze him until he was squeezed dry.

There was more. When Özgürlük had collapsed in Turkey, a vengeful government had leaked a myriad of details about how this group had functioned over the years including the trafficking channels for shackled labor into Europe and the Middle East—adding meticulous information about the most recent shipment of Kurds who weren't Kurds into Greece.

Using the recently disclosed material, INTERPOL with Group 8 technical support had been able to raid many of the facilities on this sort of new gnarled and reprehensible version of a reverse underground railway for slave labor—basically a chain of storage facilities for marketing human beings. More than a score of the units had been toppled with at least 120 people arrested. This was applauded across four continents as a coup for the good guys.

Furthermore, turning over the rotten foundations of these slave routes uncovered another subset of this commerce in human flesh: soldiers. With the growing number of hot aggressions and even wars going on at the same time as a (in some places) growing affluence in society, the citizenry of warring factions was often less and less interested in joining the fray themselves. As in the olden days of the US, they sought surrogate soldiers. In this case, even modest financial enticement combined with a brand spanking new uniform and weapon was sufficient to attract a variety of "volunteers" (really just another shade of economic refugee) to take up the cause for nationals who preferred to watch from the sidelines.

The newly-released material about Özgürlük showed not only its own network for supplying mercenaries but highlighted a number of sister parties who were in the same if not illegal at least noteworthy and tawdry business—all this welcome information for the INTERPOL and Group 8 databases.

In the aggregate, Rodney was able to loudly proclaim that, in spite of barriers (never mentioning Jake Sullivan by name), progress was being made.

Oriana was less sure about progress on any front. Had she known her father and had she known he was undergoing a comprehensive medical review, she might have been even more anxious. As it was, her unease was more about her future apart from her work (some might call it an obsession) on uncovering and denouncing through good journalism any and all draconian international criminal organizations and the suffering of throngs of hapless folks callously moved about the globe to serve the masters of industry.

She had, to her great satisfaction, carved out more time to focus more on David. They had rented a chalet for a week at Barnes Hole Beach, near Amagansett, 110 miles from downtown on the extreme east end of Long Island. It had been fantastic—and the beach had been fun too. It had been reminiscent of their ardent and lascivious trysts at the beginning of their now mature relationship. It had been emotionally and spiritually fulfilling and physically exhausting. For the first forty-eight hours, they barely left their bed—a big, sumptuous bed with a spectacular view of Napeague Bay.

As great as their getaway had been, Oriana had not taken the opportunity to bear her soul about her improper reading of David's family mail—this lack of complete candor, as she saw it, becoming her millstone. She had never mentioned Yosyp Myshchenko nor, in detail, any of her work with Rodney or the crew in Abidjan. David knew she still had deep roots in francophone Africa and had seen her articles in *The Daily News* on a variety of Afrocentric subjects ranging from human trafficking to cocoa farming. They never discussed the backstory of her columns, her new role as an important source of information for ongoing federal investigations, and certainly not, as she had only relatively recently learned from Rodney, the potential relationship of all this to a nearly invisible entity that was branded Domov (ironically, she herself not knowing the depth of this relationship). For David, his lover was simply an investigative journalist working on all sorts of wonderful stories.

Fortunately for both, Oriana's research had never led in the direction of Pottsville as she had been solely targeting international issues, these being her area of concentration as both a journalist and a concerned party. As she had told Rodney, she (and David) didn't know what she didn't know and liked it that way.

But secrets and ghosts aside, Oriana was happy, feeling she and David were as good as they had ever been. At the same time as she was seeing happiness looming on the horizon, it did not reach into all aspects of her life. Work was not progressing as quickly as she would have hoped. Sometimes it did not seem to progress at all. The activities with Jan et al had produced some good results. But they had also produced a lot of frustration. There had been some happy times but the intrigue and the challenges had been exasperating—all the more so given all the deplorable events they were documenting and the conscienceless individuals they were identifying.

The Abidjan crew with the backstopping of Professor De Angelis and Oriana herself had added a considerable volume of material to work she had started much earlier. They now knew much more about much more. But, in the end, nothing had really changed. The exploitation and the corruption continued seemingly unabated. Yes, Rodney and all the Feds were doing what they could—so were authorities around the world—but what would it accomplish? Would the bad guys disappear? Would the meek inherit the earth? Everyone knew the answer. You did what you could, but it was never enough. This, in and of itself, was reason for Oriana to feel saddened by the realities of day-to-day life. Nonetheless, she would soon be turning the page and delving into new nearer-at-hand concerns as she tried to build a home with David. Then, perhaps, she would be able to honestly claim she was making real progress. Maybe closing a blind eye—keeping one's naivety—was the best strategy after all? Just claim you knew nothing—it worked for so many.

Spreading the Word

GAGE Smith sometimes felt he was expected to work as a cross between a mafia enforcer and a missionary—always asking his clients to renew their pledges—suggesting they put-up or pay-up—whichever applied (those with weak hearts or weak knees need not apply).

Inasmuch as these "proselyting" assignments did apply to some of what Gage did, he was a force with which to reckon. Yet he did much more. He was a shrewd tactician and a critical thinker. He was a valued asset to the *Maliar* and the organization, but he was also a tool and the *Maliar's* philosophy had always been, "Find the right tool to get the job done right."

Gage thought of himself more as an instrument than a tool.

Some who knew him and a bit about what he did thought of him as a fisherman—hooking disciples for the organization. However, in this case, sometimes it was hard to tell who was fishing for whom.

In addition to his guidance of Senator Sullivan, Gage, in his current position along his tangled and varied life's path, was sort of an envoi from Holwerd for a number of the organization's projects in the New World even though he had only met Joe in the Făgăraş Mountains and had never met Harold. By design, Gage's work bypassed (with a wide margin) any and all local actors; his direct line of command was solely to one of the *Maliar's* top aids, the *Maliar* himself if so warranted.

Jake Sullivan was turning into a major effort. Despite Gage's personal attempts and the push by Loretta Williams with a very pricy junket to Geneva, things had not changed demonstrably. The *Maliar's* messenger had come as close to the lawmaker as he had with any other living soul outside the organization in regard to explaining in a very cursory yet hopefully meaningful way the structure and function of Domov. Sullivan had to know this was very serious stuff with very serious ramifications for both success and failure—the latter not at all welcomed nor expected.

From all indications, the Virginia senator understood.

Gage had been a devoted spectator as the senator had managed with varying degrees of success to defer and distract the needed support for Section T15-Z, and this action remained a high priority. However, much to the extreme frustration of Gage's bosses, both D-2 and Group 8 managed to plug along, making surprising progress in spite of severely diminished and delayed resources.

Sullivan's showy activities in West Africa had not proven to be a sufficient deflection. Ironically, according to reports Gage received, these may have actually rather backfired on the ground even if they had succeeded in waving new politically orientated flags in DC (pennants calling for new and stronger congressional support for more Afro-American business investment).

As part of the theatrics and a testament to the importance of this high-level legislative support, Jake Sullivan had had his own people studying the best opportunities for new trans-Atlantic enterprises. The senator's staffer in West Africa had proven herself to have been more than up to the job. But from what Gage could gather, not everything had gone to plan. The staffer had unexpectedly joined forces with a group of women who seemed hell-bent on putting their noses in others' business. They had not only begun painting, for the first time as far as Gage knew, an elaborate portrait of the organization's movement of merchandise up the African Coast—including that undertaken by some very distant partners—but the ladies had also, due to the good Senator's prodding, been very close to the early stages of the NCIIP where the organization had had hopes Chakir Awal (practically the *Maliar's* personal emissary) would have been able to make inroads (these now reportedly uncertain).

In short, the word Gage got from the organization's leadership was that the net results of the Sullivan Project were still to be fully assessed—the jury was out. Pending a verdict, the organization continued to invest heavily in the man's political career.

Now the stage had to be shared with a growing number of unfortunate actors in the US.

Gage had been asked (read as ordered) to follow the Ralph Tave drama very carefully. While the overseers seemed to feel Tave could sink or swim as he wished—effectively cutting him off from any exceptional support options other than assisting minimally if he decided to run for the hills—they were adamant that his affairs—any affairs that could be uncovered by any investigation—be cleansed of any possible links to Pottsville or the Mitchells. This was of the utmost importance. This was another of Gage's preeminent assignments.

Then there was Lambert Richardson. He was more of an anachronism—an old colleague of a now old and debilitated Robin McCandless who was presently fading away in a Romanian care facility for the doomed and the damned. The higher-ups were little concerned about Richardson's future other than ensuring that there were no tidbits that fell out of any close examination of his activities that could lead to negative repercussions.

Gage's plate was full, and this was likely not the end. He'd have liked it better if he had had fewer clients—fewer renewals.

Orest respected Gage's capabilities though he had only briefly met him on a few singular occasions (the guy had an impressive CV). The *Maliar* had confidence that Gage was doing a good job—as well as could be done without taking the risk of putting a much larger force in the field. It was time to do what he had frustratingly done so often—wait and see.

Waiting wasn't easy for anyone. It was, his doctor had told him, the stress of the job that had been pushing Orest into hypertension. He had, although he had been completely unaware, developed an irregular heartbeat in addition to the high blood pressure.

Over three days, Dr. Franz Schmidt—physician to the *Maliar*—had run a multitude of tests on his patient. He had overseen a broad spectrum of imaging as well as a stress test including cardiac telemetry. The synthesis of these results was that the organization's headman had the circulatory system of a man twenty years his senior—the job had or was in the process of destroying his health. He had been a prime specimen when he had come to Holwerd, the toll having been taken since then often hidden and difficult to gauge. But now it had reached a stage where it was unfortunately in full view. No news had been good news—now the news was not so good.

Someone who had been receiving no news was Sir Horace. He was disheartened. He was tired. He felt locked out. He tried to renew his contacts with old (both age-wise and long-time-workmate-wise) collaborators to no avail. Cynthia had stopped visiting. He had no word from the great grab-bag of activities he had initiated across the African Continent. Even his loquacious and I-thought-we-were-close colleague Chantal Silue was silent.

To add to his frustration, his big brother was still as vegetative as ever. No improvements, no changes.

Although he had returned to his roots, although he was living in a lovely seaside villa, and although he had no financial worries, life had lost its pizazz. He had always gallivanted into the furthest nooks and crannies. He had always vivaciously relished creating a unique persona for himself from shouting on high (in the coarsest barroom language) he was SIR Horace, to wearing a nearly clownish rainbow of clothing. Yet, alongside the curious exterior was a friendly interior that had managed to make and keep scores of relationships over the years—relationships that now seemed to be nothing more than ashes. He was now sessile. He was bored. He was frustrated.

Radutu Botezatu, Raymond Girard, Tomas Ferreira and numbers of other Domov affiliates, most of whom did not even know each other, were also frustrated. Via formal and informal channels alike, word, embellished or acerbic (no one knew), filtered through their ecospheres that there were concerns. Things, at least some things—maybe big things, maybe small things—were not going well. It seemed implausible that the behemothic organization that was Domov could have any significant concerns, but there it was—the rumor mill was vibrating with chatter of one or another sort of imbroglio.

Seasoned actors like Radutu Botezatu, Raymond Girard, and Tomas Ferreira were in a quandary. There had been palavers before—there had always been palavers. Was today any different? It seemed just maybe. Was it time to renew or rewrite their business charters or to shift focus? They all had day jobs, their public facing professions and occupations that they carried on on parallel tracts with their engagements with Domov. Was it time to go back and concentrate on their day jobs—time to try and become just ordinary folk? Should the Easter meeting be postponed?

In the absence of any concrete statements from Holwerd, most of the experienced operators decided to stay the course. This too would pass.

At the same time, Jake Sullivan wished the whole sordid business would pass. He was under growing pressure to renew and redouble his efforts to block Rodney Mills or lose a major portion of his political support (translated as money to campaign and top off his lavish expenses). Concurrently, he was under increasing pressure to quickly approve measures that would address critical homeland security issues by supporting those agents and agencies engaged in the fight against crime.

His sojourn into surveying and promoting West African business opportunities had turned into some sort of success—certainly there was renewed interest. But it had done little to, as he had hoped, overshadow Section T15-Z through the fabricated threat of new sources of terrorism from the African region.

He felt this whole affair was turning into a possible cluster-fuck. The DOJ guys were all-in—they'd been at this for a long time. They continually fought with Congress for their budgets and to be free of what they saw as excessive oversight. They had a history of aggressively making their case and bringing their cases to court. They won some and they lost some, but they did not shut down when they hit a pothole. The idea of one senator successfully halting a major ongoing DOJ investigation into a reportedly massive crime group was ludicrous. Senators Winterbottom and Brown were certainly not going to go out on any political limbs. In fact, as far as he knew, they had not even been contacted by Gage. It was all on him and still that gangster Gage pushed and pushed. The intimidating harrier from Domov refused to accept that there were limits—that only so much could be done.

"Only so much that could be done" was an argument that held no water for Orest and those involved in shepherding Domov at the highest levels. They lived in a binary world: there was the right result and the wrong result—nothing in between.

It had become clear that, while stopping Section T15-Z in its tracks was the desired outcome, there were no effective half-way measures. The DOJ agents had proven themselves dogged and resourceful—able to do a lot with practically no resources.

Still, this was no new news. Domov had always had a strong opposition—a number of enemies, large and small.

Orest thought of the organization as a pangolin—an anteater feeding on, yet continuously attacked by the small formic creatures. Not only, like the pangolin, was Domov endlessly bombarded by its prey, but both were solitary, nocturnal animals armored with heavy protective scales—the anteater's scales made of a hard fingernail-like material while the organization's tough protective layers were composed of lamina of flesh and bone fashioned from the actors on the Domov stage and a reliance on stealth, skill, and strategic partnerships (with an ample dose of ruthlessness as required).

Orest was convinced that Domov, like the pangolin, was up to the job in spite of all the challenges, in spite of being considered by many as an anachronism—the anteater endangered due to habitat destruction and poaching, the organization possibly endangered also due to changing environments and encroachment by competitors as well as by strengthened law enforcement agencies.

Orest recalled reading that pangolins were actually prehistoric—having been around roughly 80 million years. These amazing animals had proven themselves to be resilient—survivors. Domov, although it had a long history, was a much more recent addition to the global community. Nonetheless, the *Maliar* felt it was equally resilient—equally a survivor—the ceaseless attempts for its eradication notwithstanding.

⚓⚓⚓⚓⚓⚓⚓

Rodney, as would be expected, had no idea of how the opposition was feeling about his job and the potential threat of a full-strength Section T15-Z. He was, as usual, confident his opponents wished he would never have popped up on their radar. Shining light into the shadows was never welcomed by evildoers.

Zooming out to 30,000 feet, Rodney had to admit he was more satisfied than dissatisfied. Things could have, and at times had, gone much more poorly. In spite of the roadblocks being mounted by Sullivan, there was so much going on—the sheer magnitude of felonious activities was such that he and his team could not help but get traction somewhere, even without the needed congressional support.

Investigators at both D-2 and Group 8 continued to dig and then dug some more. Mercer McMaster was just a shiny penny on the sidewalk. Stopping illicit gun sales and getting gunrunners-cum-violent-militiamen in jail was good not only for the obvious direct impacts but also for the excellent PR it showered on both the public and private sectors—that penny tuning into real political capital. However, McMaster's arrest provided little in terms of new information about Domov.

Lambert Richardson was another story. He had deep roots. D-2 agents were able to unearth a detailed history going back to Delpro and even connecting to vanished Delpro collaborators Lieutenant Colonel Fritz Murphy, Dr. Christine Miller, Ms. Florence Gardner, Dr. Lance Newcastle, and Dr. Howard Dunford. While the missing, in effect Domov moles, had never been found, going back over their files in light of the current understanding of the functioning of both Delpro and Domov did point to other businesses and institutions entangled in this web. This look back tied to the present also confirmed Rodney's conclusion that Domov had not disappeared with Delpro and Robin McCandless. A noticeably scaled down, less coordinated version of Delpro without Delpro had been active throughout. Moreover, and more worrying, the activities of this cell or these cells seemed to have ticked up considerably in recent years. Domov had not left.

Ralph Tave's activities unwittingly provided even more information about this new version of Rodney's old nemesis. Agents explored, following exhaustively each fragment of information, scrutinizing the tiniest clues and past ties to McCandless as well as present work with the Bootstraps Fund and Best Farm Design LLC. These led to links to such now well-known actors as Radutu Botezatu, Raymond Girard, Tomas Ferreira. More, many more, pieces of the puzzle were falling into place.

A new concern began to seep onto the table. As the pieces fell into place and a clearer portrayal of the Domov theater emerged along with the identity of key actors, what was the next step? This information would, naturally, be shared with other investigative agencies worldwide, helping in the global battle. Some of the actors were in foreign lands outside the reach of DOJ, but what of those in the US? What of the Ralph Taves and the Lambert Richardsons?

If enough hard data could be collected, DOJ could convene a Grand Jury. The Attorney General could even consider appointing a special council. However, Domov's roots were old, tangled, and deep, reaching many powerful and hidden alcoves of government. If they so desired, congressional committees could create snag upon snag, holding up legal processes indefinitely if not ultimately having charges dismissed—even blaming the hardworking agents of Section T15-Z for wasting the voters' money and the lawmakers' valuable time.

Not knowing the best tactics to address this concern but feeling even more pressure to find a way to deal with Jake Sullivan, Rodney began to see how the increasingly precise portraits of Domov's US activities and Sullivan's connection to Raymond Girard and his Guadeloupe villa near Rifflet could best be leveraged to move his case forward.

At this point, there was indeed a case to be moved forward—forward on several fronts. For individuals like Tave and Richardson along with others—some known, others still to be uncovered—there was the real possibility of indictment.

For companies and institutions like Trusted Industrial Products, Poseidon Consignments, Ace Foods, Farm Services, Western Farm Supply, Simpson Investments, General Industrial and Chemical Products, and a potentially long list of other firms with ties to Delpro, post-Delpro activities, or Domov, there would be, at the very least, deep-diving IRS audits in their future. For offshore enterprises and operators, there would be a close follow-up by Group 8 along with joint investigations involving international agencies like INTERPOL.

It was a series of long and in many ways iterative processes. As soon as the curtains of obscurity were pulled back and the walls of silence pierced, in all likelihood some individuals would start telling their tales, incriminating themselves and others along the way.

With or without Senator Jacob Sullivan's backing, the processes would move forward—there was too much momentum building. Yet, the differences "with or without" were very significant. Without could be manifest as indifference or outright opposition. In the latter case, DOJ would likely still prevail—but slowly and at great cost, allowing many of the guilty parties to slip through the cracks. Expeditious and comprehensive actions were needed. The pressing question: Could these be provided?

All in Section T15-Z needed to renew and redouble their efforts to assure an answer of, "Yes." Rodney knew they were all up to the shifting demands of the job.

⚘⚘⚘⚘⚘⚘⚘

Gage's views of his job changed drastically from day to day. At this moment he felt like someone engaged in that hard-to-understand sixteenth century Scottish sport of curling; using his broom to sweep everything out of the way of the advancing twenty-kilo granite stone that was the key to victory. In this case, Gage was sweeping everything out of the way of investigators delving into Ralph Tave's affairs, making sure Tave's role at Cumberland Savings was seen as simply a cosmetic seat on the board and that he had no real position of importance with the bank. Gage had to, and apparently was succeeding at, burying any meaningful connections with the bank and thereby any trace continuing on to Pottsville or the Mitchells—this now his prime directive.

Domov leadership, rightly so in Gage's view, was not going to insert any new bodies into the field to fight the fires arising in North America. They had never been firefighters. If bad things happened, they burned to the ground and were rebuilt better. Gage was not there to stomp out fires but just to put up buffers, so they did not burn certain high value assets.

Investigations going back years, investigations having successfully unearthed a trove a data about Delpro and Robin McCandless, were not going to be easily derailed. They could possibly be slowed or redirected, but they would have their pound of flesh.

Domov—its staff and associates—had proven themselves to be very effective, very successful. But this relied completely on efficient covertness and anonymity; in an open arena they were no match for DOJ.

Resistant firewalls were needed to ensure the necessary invisibility and concealment of the Mitchells—the Domov actors with the direct lineage back to the homeland. These extraordinary protective measures, however, were not due to the family's heritage but rather due to the assessment by the *Maliar* that they were the best positioned to build a new empire once the current problems blew over—and they would blow over.

This exceptional protection was not afforded most of the operators—they were simply left to their own devices. Some were even given a push over the precipice. This latter tactic applied to the now used (the Virginia gentleman himself would surely say, "abused") Senator Sullivan. He had ultimately failed to achieve the goals established for him and he was expendable. It would be an easy matter for Gage to use the truthful (and regrettable) facts of the senator's vacationing in Guadeloupe at Raymond Girard's villa, add a few ribald embellishments, and, to avert

Gage's threatened scandalous exposure, the Senator would undoubtedly be willing to change careers as the necessary and unavoidable price of saving his marriage and his patrician status at home.

Gage proved himself again, this time as a skillful curler, sweeping clean the paths to Pottsville while sweeping Senator Jake Sullivan under the table.

⚘⚘⚘⚘⚘⚘⚘

Publicly, the Honorable Jacob Sullivan resigned his position as senator for the great state of Virginia due to health problems (privately there was a lot of kicking and screaming). While the governor of Virginia prepared a writ of election to fill the Senate vacancy, Jake and Rebecca Sullivan divided their assets between their dentist son and school-teacher daughter and retired to a seaside home at Pointe des Trios Vaches, three miles up the coast from the village of Anse-Bertrand, Guadeloupe. A Sullivan spokesperson informed the press that the senator's now delicate health required the more gentle climes of the Caribbean.

Gage had been a bit surprised by the choice for the Virginian's hideaway—at least he had chosen the other half of the bilobed island, away from Rifflet (the "island of Guadeloupe" actually the centerpiece of an archipelago of that name and the two lobes being the two major islands of Grande-Terre and Basse-Terre separated by the Rivière Salée—from the air the two nearly-connected nodes looking like the wings of a moth in flight).

Rodney was overjoyed with the good senator's departure, only wondering if his choice of refuge close to Raymond Girard's villa meant the fervent politician still was part of the network—a network that may have helped fund his costly relocation.

Rodney was also happy to note that Senator Winterbottom had been named to take over the leadership of the group that continued to be so critical to the future of Section T15-Z. He had always liked the Arizona lawmaker and thought they had a good relationship—certainly better than that with the now thankfully departed Virginia senator.

The possibilities of an improved environment for D-2 and Group 8 aside, one of the tangible impacts of Jake Sullivan's departure was the question about what would happen to Janice Pittman.

Jan took the news with aplomb. She had long since deviated considerably from the original mission laid out by her boss. She had established strong ties to Awa and Mariama as well as a good working rapport with Oriana. Jake Sullivan really didn't figure in her current priorities. Nonetheless, as long as she still had a staff position and was able to continue with her work in Abidjan, she was content to let the status quo run on until there was a new senator on seat.

Chakir was back in Holwerd—back in that part of the world where there seemed to be an algid gray shroud covering everything, blurring the horizon, making the land, the sea, and the sky appear as one. The dynamic yet fragrant high-energy byways under the sapphire-blue skies of the tropics with the heat that stuck to your skin like the dust hung on your clothes—all this was, at least for the time being, gone. There had been some successes but not the major breakthrough hoped for. The north-south channel to Calabar was established and already producing some traffic—products moving both up and down this twisting trace in the forest. Onyx Associates remained as a tax-paying business in Abidjan albeit in a hiatus—ready to be reactivated when needed. Hooks were also in place to grab onto any positive developments in the now much overdue NCIIP. Yet Chakir remained somehow sullen, things should have gone better.

All, including the *Maliar*, knew you harvested what you could. Every crop was not a bumper crop. In the final analysis, the results had been positive and Orest was satisfied, more so now that his close advisor was back at his side.

When everything was done behind closed doors—under the cover of chicanery—it could be hard to figure out how things were going. This had been a reality with which Joe had been struggling for a long time. Things seemed to be going well enough. Still there was an ever-present level of uncertainty.

They expanded S&J Logistics and Fig Leaf Storage through the relatively new western office run by Harold. Even Kindred Helping Hands Foundation now had a counterbalance to its Arkansas headquarters with a branch in Durango, but there was always that apprehension when someone knocked at the door. Who was on the other side?

The tapestry was complex. So far there had been no unwanted visitors to explore their liaison with Great Plains and Western Bank. However, word had filtered out that the same may not be true with regard to their links to Cumberland Savings. Ralph Tave had come under at least some level of government scrutiny, and this did not bode well. To add to the complications, KHHF had been contacted by a West Coast group called SAMHAFRI. This was likely just an innocent reaching out of one humanitarian organization to another. But who could be sure? Such innocuous probes could easily hit a tripwire that called attention to a carefully hidden charade or that prompted unwanted scrutiny of a buried riddle.

To add to the constant stress, Joe was uncomfortable with the current business trends. Knowing his roots, since the beginning, he had assumed he had some sort of "Robin Hood gene," most extralegal activities with which he was engaged being able to be rationalized by telling himself he was taking from the haves and helping the have-nots. He knew he was spinning a story for his personal justification, but it helped. Now, with what Harold had called the "labor issue," he was very uncomfortable. Most of those being trafficked—possibly with the exception of the rich politician or crook who was occasionally assisted in fleeing the country at great cost—the people being moved about—enslaved in many instances—were certainly not the haves. This, like jumping into the center of drug or arms sales, seemed to be crossing a line.

As the stress mounted, not wanting to burden Susan who was already overloaded, Joe did the unthinkable—he went to see his brother. Philip was now the Auxiliary Bishop to the Archbishop of the Ukrainian Catholic Archdiocese of Philadelphia at the Cathedral of the Immaculate Conception. They met at La Catedral Coffeehouse, about five blocks from the cathedral and ironically not far from the Vicariate of the Ukrainian Orthodox Church Kyivan Patriarchate in the US and Canada—Joe thinking in another world the Vicariate could have been part of Domov.

Over cups of strong Cezve coffee (appreciated in Ukraine since the time of the Ottoman Empire) the brothers conversed warmly as though they had just seen each other last week and not, as was the truth, that they had not seen each other for years—the conversation in English since, although Philip, in close contact with the large Ukrainian community in Philadelphia, could still handle even the slang of the Dnieper Valley, Joe had lost most of his native tongue through disuse.

"The whole family sends its regards—the kids're spread-out everywhere—Anna's a city manager in California, David works for a company in New Jersey and has a girlfriend in The city, and, you may have already heard, Harold is now working out West, in Durango, Colorado."

"Can't say I've been able to keep up with the goings-on of the family," Philip replied with such an inscrutable look that it was hard for his big brother to decide if he were sincerely indifferent or saddened by the news of how effectively detached his family had become.

"It's been a long time, ya know. Maybe you may find it hard to believe," the younger sibling continued, "but the work of God is tough and demanding—I'm really totally occupied with little time to sleep let alone think about the past—it's been enough just to try to handle the present and don't even mention the future. I've honestly not intended to neglect my heritage nor to cut any family ties—things just worked out differently than perhaps I had originally thought—our flock is surprisingly large and has diverse and often urgent needs."

"I'm sure," Joe replied with an equanimity that was more forced than natural, "and I am not here to talk about the past and only a little about the present. It is, indeed, the future where I feel I need your help and it is this that has pushed me to break the regrettably long yet unintentional separation that, from my side as well, has not been a result of any ill-feeling but solely because I too find myself much busier than I had even imagined."

"Fair enough," Philip said, and Joe nodded although he was not sure at all what was "fair."

"You know why we were sent here in the first place—I don't have to go over that old story. It suffices to say that things have gone to plan—probably several times over. We've done well, have been appreciated by the organization, and continue to see expanding business."

This time it was Phillip's turn not to completely know who the "we" were, but ignoring this possibly important element, he inserted, "While I'm well beyond and outside all that relates to the original 'family mission,' I'm glad you're happy with the way things turned out."

"Thanks, but it's not 'family business' that brings me here—at least not directly. It is, however, family."

Philip's expression showed a bit of consternation, but he nodded to his brother to go ahead.

"As you say, you're totally outside all that we're about. Still, you know our family affairs are not without risks—both internal and external.

I won't bother you with all the concerns, but I am sure you can recall enough of the stories of our youth about the travails of our ancestors who were smugglers and brigands in the Carpathian Mountains—well we're still in the same business with the same challenges. While it's become my life, I guess you're lucky to do what you do—far away in more ways than one and relatively stable if overextended."

Another nod from Philip, feeling nearly as though he were in the confessional.

"Anyway, the point is, as you can imagine, there's a lot of uncertainty. And what you may not know is that Harold is in this with me—in this all the way."

If he were shocked, Philip hid it well and after a suitable pause, Joe went on, "Sue is also aware of everything and even superficially engaged in some of our growing and increasingly varied activities. Crucially, Anna and David are entirely outside—as far as I know, they are completely untouched and have no idea about these ties to the organization and the old ways."

Philip offered a muffled, "Good."

"So, there it is," Joe continued, hoping he had been able to adequately simplify the complicated, "I wanted you to know, I wanted your blessing or your OK—I don't know. Anyway, I've left instruction with our attorney in Pottsville that if I'm gone—by gone I mean physically gone if I've been arrested or had to flee, as well as spiritually gone and in the ground—if you agree, you are to, in complete secrecy, receive the majority of our savings to be anonymously distributed through time to Anna and David. If Susan is not with me, she will have her own resources, but she too may need to distance herself from her children—we really don't know."

No reaction from Philip.

"I know, little brother, this is a huge imposition and undoubtedly something you would much rather not be tethered with . . . but I don't know what else to do. Sue, Harold, and I have made our choices and know the potential repercussions, but the other two kids are completely innocent and need to be protected and at the same time cared for. Please help."

"Yosyp, my brother, I will do all I can. You can have confidence in me. And please do believe in the future, God looks after us all."

The brothers renewed their faith in each other—wishing they had done so sooner.

⚘⚘⚘⚘⚘⚘⚘

While his birth father and the adopted father who had raised him were discussing in what was ironically nicknamed the City of Brotherly Love, Harold was also doing some spectrum thinking covering the past, present, and future. The expansion from Pottsville to Durango and then the transfer of the lead position to this western hub had all in one way or another been part of the original plan to reestablish a substantial footprint for the organization that was equal to or greater than that that had been there at the height of Delpro's reign. Obviously, years had transpired, and it was not simply a question of replicating Delpro. The new structure had to be shaped to correspond to the realities of the present and the opportunities of the future.

This footprint was multifaceted, the assortment of Mitchell enterprises naturally only one branch of the Domov hydra in North America. Other hydroid arms dealt with other isolated investments and other products—Harold aware of some and oblivious to others. However, to the extent any operations were transboundary, linking to the organization's global actions (the exception being some rather encapsulated Domov interventions which were limited to and embedded in North America outside Harold's scope), any movement of any merchandise (alive or dead) had to, in one way or another, enter Harold's world to deal with the thorny issue of US borders.

These were certainly more porous than the government portrayed. Nonetheless, there was a strong effort to control flow across the country's boundaries—these actions probably having more successes than failures. Without a doubt, the overwhelming presence of government agents and agencies at the southern border made this a high-risk overland crossing (there were tunnels, dune buggies, gliders, balloons and all manner of objects employed to try and leapfrog the physical border posts, but these had no guarantees of overcoming the substantial barriers). Often the best tactic seemed to be to try and cross elsewhere. The long eastern and western coastlines offered many opportunities while considerable effort was also focused on the border with Canada—5,525 miles long—the longest international border in the world.

Whatever strategies were chosen and plans put in place, clearly, by design, Durango was not a first stop for anyone making border crossings—on a south-north axis, Ciudad Juárez, Chihuahua, 800 miles to the south and Wild Horse, Alberta, a thousand miles to the north. Durango was about as close to the latitudinal center of the country as you could find.

Given this location, Harold had hoped that he would be relatively untouched by what he, as his father, saw as the undesirable but seemingly unavoidable trends to become more involved in the trafficking of arms, drugs, and people—areas where at most Domov had historically used disposable cut-outs and multiple layers of intermediaries, reducing the risk of direct involvement and the possibility of exposure in these highly sensitive areas while not unmasking the more critical components of the organization's network.

Harold realized his views were probably naive (wealth and power drove the process—certainly not any fuzzy ideas about moral versus amoral crimes). Yet, as the volume of these more tainted trades ratcheted up, there was no avoiding the ripples, sometimes the waves, that were generated. All manner of merchandise now occupied the spaces of FLS—some for hours, others for months. At the same time, S&J was increasingly contracted by Domov shell companies to arrange the movement of a great variety of ill-advised (in Harold's opinion) products—some so secretive that he was only aware of his staff handling unlabeled and tightly sealed packages and crates (no paperwork, no details). To even further complicate matters, KHHF was made more and more offers it could not refuse—shielded third parties proffering extremely well-funded "projects" to help the vulnerable—in reality most often covertly shepherding humans (generally undocumented conscripted labor with the occasional fleeing felon) from point A to point B.

Naive or not, pro or con, good or bad, ultimately it was a distinction without much of a difference—Harold knew that he like so many others were in Domov for the duration. He also knew that the organization was, comparatively speaking, not wholly totalitarian. Certainly, at his level, there were channels through which he could and did make his concerns and priorities known. He had had every reason to believe these issues were honestly received and reviewed in Holwerd. Then, regardless of his personal position, once the organization (as though it were a living thing and, in some ways, it almost appeared to be) had made its decision, it was automatically assumed all in the fold would matter-of-factly follow the pathways laid out from above.

The organization demanded fealty.

Strangely, Harold remembered a quotation his birth father had frequently cited when he, as he often had after the loss of his wife, made comparisons between the organization and the church—this before he left one for the other. The oft-used passage was Ephesians 2:19-21, "He did not make the Gentile a Jew. He took both of them as they became believers and made them into one brand new body, one that has never before been seen."

In those early days in Pottsville while a new normal was still being established (days now seeming long, long ago), Philip would tell his son, "It's not about being a Gentile or a Jew—although it well could have been—it's about being Orthodox or Catholic. And, in truth, spiritually it's not really about that either. It's about being faithful and having Faith or not. It's about choices."

Indeed, both the church and a global organized crime syndicate seemingly sought to create never-before-seen structures that enshrined the loyalty of their members while ensuring each followed the leadership of the elders ostensibly for the benefit of all. Unlike the church, the organization was agnostic in more ways than one. Not only was it indifferent as to one's faith and beliefs, but it was also indifferent as to one's ethnicity, nationality, sexual orientation, or favorite football team. The organization was all about results. Each piece on the board had expected functions and was presumed to deliver certain outputs—as long as this happened, nothing else really mattered.

Week by week, as Harold learned more—saw more (some of which he innately questioned)—he increasingly appreciated how complex Domov was and how it was certainly an organization that had "never been seen before." It was also clear that Domov had reached its current level of capaciousness and conquest by showing no quarter. Failure simply was not an option. Just like Philip's binary view of life with or without faith, the organization was equally myopic: succeed and stay, fail and go.

In spite of the required compliance and deference and even in light of the growing focus on those issues he considered questionable—or perhaps because of them—Harold reconfirmed, in effect renewed, his choices, determined to intensify his work and hopefully making both his fathers proud.

⚘⚘⚘⚘⚘⚘⚘

As Oriana successfully (she thought) intensified her own efforts to reinforce her oh-so-important relationship with David, still feeling she and David were as good as they had ever been, she was captivated by the news from Jan that her Senate-supported activities in West Africa would be winding down with the unanticipated departure of Senator Sullivan. There seemed to be a degree of equivocalness in Jan's interpretation of the next steps. Jan wanted to continue the work but, given the growing rift between what Senator Sullivan had wanted and what was actually happening on the ground, cutting congressional ties did not seem like such a bad thing (who knew what would be the priorities for the next senator from the state whose motto was *Sic semper tyrannis,* literally meaning "thus always to tyrants," practically considered as meaning "tyrants will be overthrown").

Oriana promised to look into options although any additional support through *The Daily News* appeared all but impossible. After she had confirmed the paper's inability (or unwillingness) to put any more resources into a pot they weren't really sure they had wanted in the first place, she made an exceptional call to Rodney under the overall umbrella of needing to catch up.

The journalist and the agent had what was probably seen by both as a useful discussion—each learning some and sharing some. When it came to the question of the Sullivan Committee and its well-publicized push-back against Section T15-Z while simultaneously pushing forward all sorts of rhetoric if not legislation calling for increased investment in West Africa, Rodney was vague about his view of the group now under Senator Winterbottom's leadership. Nonetheless, when the subject of the continued work of Oriana's team in West Africa came up, Rodney said he'd get back to her soon with some ideas.

Within a week Rodney had called Oriana with a tip. A well-funded West Coast foundation, SAMHAFRI, was interested in many of the same issues as Oriana's team in Abidjan. Rodney knew some folks at SAMHAFRI (to put it mildly) and thought there could be the basis for a long-term relationship if both sides were interested.

With Rodney as a bridge, Oriana was able to reach out to Eddie and explain the challenging work in which she and her colleagues were engaged—to which they were committed. For Eddie this was serendipity. This was the type of work which Samantha would have supported one hundred percent.

Over the ensuing years since a generous portion of his Uncle Hal Schleider's bequeathment had started SAMHAFRI, the foundation had done well on all fronts. Astute financial management had grown the foundation's assets many times over while its work on the ground had been successful in shining a light into knotty crevices where abuse and violation took place. Even though the foundation's work had initially targeted overseas human trafficking—aiming to go to the source—it was now broadening its scope to try and dig-out the destinations and end-users of this seemingly unstoppable flow of human misery. They were in the process of developing a network of civil society groups in the US who could help ferret out warning signals to alert authorities about possible cases of trafficked individuals finding themselves still in slave-like conditions but camouflaged in the midst of Middle America. However, at the same time, they remained ready to expand their international efforts, especially in Africa. With only the teeniest delay, the foundation was able to create a coordinating post for Jan in their just-set-up-for-this-purpose West Coast office in Abidjan as well as develop slots for Awa and Mariama (who had decided a shift to a new more beneficent employer would be an excellent move), with an ample stipend for Claudia De Angelis as an advisor. With amazing speed, Oriana's crew was still at work, now as part of the staff of SAMHAFRI. This was a true renewal. It was also a series of events that was most welcomed by Oriana. Not only did it appear to ensure the continuation their work in West Africa, but it shifted the overall oversight from her ill-defined position at *The Daily News* to the much more institutionalized work of SAMHAFRI—really, Oriana thought, passing from amateur status to that of professional. This boosting of stature added an element of increased seriousness while the revised operational structure ultimately gave Oriana more time to spend in other areas including her ménage—an added value for which she was very grateful.

Overall, Rodney may have been more satisfied than dissatisfied, but he was also concerned. For him, and probably for many others, it was far too simple to unintentionally turn fact into fiction—to mentally classify all that was going on as a good cops-and-robbers movie and not ongoing all-too-real brutal criminality. After all, their investigation, which felt as though it had been underway forever, was now an encyclopedia of people and places and a dictionary of acronyms and abbreviations. It was far too easy to impersonalize the interminable inquiry, to see it all as a phrenic puzzle in the abstract—a random assortment of stories and purported actions. But it was reality. It was dangerous. It was dire and dreadful. It damaged and destroyed peoples' lives. It dismantled any semblance of justice, driving forward corruption in its place. It was Domov.

Now there were powerful forces aligning against Domov.

The Congressional action under Senator Winterbottom's new leadership of the committee (still carrying its somewhat bureaucratic misnomer) was not only to finally validated the legal status of Section T15-Z while approving its significant funding, butt also, as part of the section's mandate, opening the door to major legal action. This was achieved not only through the application of the Racketeer Influenced and Corrupt Organizations (RICO) Act but also by having Domov officially declared a terrorist organization. Renewed and more in-depth testimony, especially from Felix Manchester and other colleagues at Group 8 who presented detailed analyses by INTERPOL and other global crime-fighting agencies, sketched new images ratcheting-up concerns and leading to superseding indictments for those already processed. Moreover, this fresh boost reinvigorated a call for updated action resulting in new subpoenas for the known malefactors at the end of the Delpro period heretofore having escaped justice, while adding new bad actors to the list as they were uncovered. This red flagging included both US and international bad actors, the acknowledged individuals ranging from Lambert Richardson, Mercer McMaster, and Ralph Tave to Raymond Girard, Tomas Ferreira, Radutu Botezatu, and even an enfeebled Robin McCandless with his little brother, Sir Horace Barthley. The net woven with Ann Winterbottom's full support was long and with a very fine mesh, permitting fewer and fewer escapees.

Orest enjoyed puzzles—you would have to be the *Maliar*. One of the many brainteasers that occupied his time at this moment was more of a leisure thought exercise than an operational decision. It was almost his form of spirituality. In those moments when he needed a diversion from the nuts and bolts of day-to-day oversight, he would wonder, "What is Domov?"

In many ways it was a puzzle.

Domov was as much as possible omnipresent. With him at the helm, the organization was surely active—hopefully very active—worldwide. Although there were many rungs in the ladder of responsibilities, this global enterprise was run from Holwerd—basically run from a cottage on the shores of the North Sea using the brainpower of a carefully-selected and highly-competent team along with pencil and paper. Although, much to the chagrin of some, computers were in the process of running everything, Domov was not computerized. From its origins, the organization's leadership had been technologically adverse—at least in terms of the communications and management technologies used for internal command and control. Phones could be tapped. Radio messages could be intercepted. Computers could be hacked. From the beginning, Domov operatives had shied away from modern conveniences in favor of keeping all the secrets in the heads of a few.

Recently Orest had seen a short public service film about NORAD, the North American Aerospace Defense Command, and the Cheyenne Mountain Complex bunker's command center—lauded for its state-of-the-art technology that covered North America with a canopy of protection against foreign attacks. From their fundamental philosophies of doing business to their positions on law and order, NORAD and Domov were about as far apart as one could get—polar opposites. Yet, from Orest's seat, both had massive power but one was based on the fickle whims of technology while the other was based on the oft-abused adage, "mind over matter" (Orest having read that this phrase dated to 1863 and the Scottish geologist Sir Charles Lyell's opinion that mankind would continue to increase its intellect and rely more and more on "improvable reason" to further expand the human mind's supremacy over matter—this theory only slightly older than Domov which in many ways was a manifestation of this principle).

The *Maliar* was still not sure if he was achieving any successes in the arena of mind over matter. However, if the matter piece of the maxim was held at least temporarily in abeyance, he was convinced that the key to success was the mind. Domov was able to intellectually analyze situations and act with an astonishing degree of alacrity and affect (and admittedly sometimes savagery)—others falling far behind. Plus, he was Domov. He was the *Kráľ Hory*. He was the King of the Hill.

CHAPTER 10

ENDS & BEGINNINGS

"I'm not upset that you lied to me, I'm upset that from now on I can't believe you."

—Friedrich Nietzsche

Beginning of the End or the End of the Beginning

In secondary school, Oriana had studied the eighteenth century French politician, Jean Anthelme Brillat-Savarin, who had said, "Tell me what you eat, and I will tell you what you are." She had thought it an interesting statement but would have rephrased it to, "tell me what you eat, and I'll tell you how you're doing." In her work she had seen far too many who could eat only what they could afford regardless of who they were—famine being a great equalizer. This was one of the foundational issues that had led her to invest so much effort in food and agriculture—these essential not only for survival but for society to thrive—most people in her adopted country having escaped the depravations of hunger experienced by the majority of the rest of the world including Western Europe after the war.

It was more than food for thought.

Among foods, however, as Oriana had long appreciated, cassava, or manioc, was one of the most versatile. Often identified as an omnipresent African staple, although reportedly originally imported from the Americas in the fifteen hundreds, cassava was an important ingredient in kitchens around the world ranging from Thailand to Ecuador. Still, in Africa cassava was a core part of the diet for millions of people. Local dishes were as varied as the landscape, including the boiled tuber, sauces made with the leaves (known through numerous names and preparations including the well-loved *Saka-Saka*), the tuber grated and fried into *gari* or milled into flour for meals like *fufu, Tuo zaafi*, and many others. The pasty dough could also be prepared into a sort of rubbery breadstick such as *Chikwangue* to be eaten as a snack or to accompany any number of delicious entrées.

Additionally, cassava had an abundance of commercial and industrial uses, including sweeteners, medicines, cosmetics, animal feeds, bakery additives, drinks, fabrics, biodegradable materials, adhesives, fuel, and others.

Cassava was a valuable crop.

Cassava was also a relatively easy crop to grow. You pushed a stick (a stem cutting) into the ground and as long and you didn't have it back-to-front, you'd generally get a harvestable product. For food use, the plant was frequently harvested after nine to twelve months while industrial users may choose to wait to harvest until after eighteen to twenty-four months when the tubers were more fibrous.

Cassava was often good business.

Cassava figured in a broad mix of Domov activities. Surreptitiously, as it did with many things, Domov was funding research into a litany of new cassava products including its use as a projectile from air-powered carbines and as a moulding material for the still nascent area of 3-D printing.

Given the diverse nature of cassava farming and processing, as all engaged in the value chain and all observing this same value chain now understood, the transnational trade in cassava offered advantages over and beyond the sales of the natural or processed products. This had been one of the main reasons for Oriana concentrating on this market early on—her work adding to that of Rodney who also recognized both the legal and the illicit dimensions of this trade.

The head of D-2, therefore, was not surprised but a little confused by what appeared to be déjà vu. A shipment of cassava flour had again been intercepted in the Brazilian port of Victoria (another reverse-osmosis arrangement from a market perspective as Brazil was the globe's number five mandioca—cassava—farmer with imports only possibly financially justified under the label of livestock products)—bulging sacks of the fine white flour covering a large stock of Romanian weapons. As before when at the SEC when Rodney had first received reports of similar arms smuggling, the shipment on an Alimento Atlântico vessel had come from the port of Faro. However, this time it had arrived in Faro from the Port of Sète via Approvisionnement Alimentaire Européen, which had also taken the shipment onboard in the Port of Cotonou—this not unusual since Benin is a neighbor to Nigeria, the world's number one cassava producer. In Sète, according to subsequent intelligence received from INTERPOL, the Approvisionnement Alimentaire Européen vessel had received a shipment from a local small Mediterranean shipper—this latter consignment traced to the Port of Constanța and ultimately the spoor leading back to Radutu Botezatu.

This last bit was what led to Rodney's confusion. Radutu Botezatu had had arms discovered in shipments through the Port of Victoria before. Would he repeat nearly the same thing given the risks?

These weapons had apparently been destined for the paramilitary *Colectivos* in Venezuela—a large shipment that undoubtedly brought top dollar. But was it worth the risk? If yes, what did this say about transatlantic arms trade?

While it was somewhat comforting to realize that most of the culpable actors were now known entities, these questions were worrying.

The Venezuela shipment had actually been arranged by Tomas Ferreira, he organizing the logistics, Yves Noirot supplying the transport to the port of Faro (their oft-used centralized point of departure), and Radutu Botezatu providing the merchandise. Accordingly, *sensu stricto*, unbeknownst to Rodney, this was not a rerun of earlier efforts as there was another agent charting the route. This was, rather, perhaps a case of too much sharing of responsibilities without clear (and historically correct) comprehensive coordination. It was, moreover, possibly emblematic of the solo type of actions engaged in by Domov actionaries but without the oversight of the organization—the "do it yourself" operations that were susceptible to this type of weakness.

Rodney had followed up the news of the interrupted arms shipment with a call to Mariama Mbaye. She continued to be the go-to person for information about the movements of cargo up and down Africa's West Coast—proving herself to be a tremendous asset to the work of SAMHAFRI. However, her current focus was on an apparent anomaly in her recent records. As had been documented from Guinea and nearly everywhere along the coast, the predominant movement of human cargo by sea-lanes was from south to north—people either voluntarily seeking (or involuntarily pushed into) livelihoods in Europe or occasionally continuing on to North America. It was curious, therefore, to uncover a countercurrent—an organized movement of people in the other direction.

There seemed to be a mini-migration of high-school-aged boys and young men from francophone countries—chiefly Côte d'Ivoire, Burkina Faso, and Mali—congregating at the Ghanian port of Takoradi. Initially, Mariama linked this to the rumors of the use of slave labor in the fishery of Ghana's Lake Volta, but it seemed unlikely the artisanal fishery could use a number of workers equal to the estimated flow into Takoradi. Furthermore, the rumors indicated the captive fisherfolk on the Lake were generally younger children more adept at working in the tight spaces of a dugout canoe.

As Mariama explored more, she was able to document that these illegal immigrants were simply transiting through Ghana, boarding small and medium-size fishing vessels flying the Costa Rican flag but apparently with Russian skippers. The entire operation seemed well choreographed.

There was more to uncover. Using the ever-present greed of medium-level port officials, Mariama was able provide the needed (albeit modest) supplemental financial compensation to the chronically underpaid civil servants in order to get the needed additional details of these vessels. They were all registered to the Costa Rican company Peces Tropicales Transamericanos. After a brief period in a Ghanaian port, the boats embarked on the 1,200-mile crossing of the Gulf of Guinea to Pointe Noire in the Republic of Congo, and the trail didn't end there. Relying on contacts through SAMHAFRI, Mariama was able to trace the movements of these groups inland as they took the nearly one-thousand-mile journey by battered and rickety river boats up the Congo and Ubangi Rivers to Bangui, the capital of the Central African Republic.

Migration into one of the world's poorest and most troubled countries was hard to rationalize until it became clear these were military recruits—budding mercenaries. For the equivalent of five dollars a day and a second-hand AK-47, they were willing to do the bidding of whomever paid and offered the spoils at the end of the day. While many of these would-be soldiers of fortune stayed in the strife-torn CAR, some continued on to other hotspots in neighboring Uganda or the Democratic Republic of Congo (this Congo-Kinshasa not to be confused with the across-the-river neighbor of Congo-Brazzaville). Most would never return home.

However, the river boats went both ways. Almost as though adhering to Newton's Third Law (for every action there is an equal and opposite reaction), when the vessels went back downstream, they had a new cargo of contraband and casualties. The very same battlegrounds that attracted the young militants sent thousands into the bush seeking refuge—no small number making their way to the shores of the Ubangi where shelter and even riches were promised for a sack of silver or whatever other goods the weary and fragile could manage to muster. At the same time, Central Africa was rich with diamonds and other precious stones—the boat crews took care to fill any unoccupied spaces or empty pockets with as much of value as possible before entering into the river's throbbing current.

The northward return leg by sea was nearly a rerun the southern passage, only bypassing Takoradi. The outgoing merchandise of whatever form was transferred to the ocean-going fishers at Pointe Noire and leapfrogged up the coast, this time all the way to the Moroccan Port of El Jadida—the port 275 miles to the southwest of Tangier on the N1 Coastal Highway, Tangier the most direct passage into Europe. At El Jadida the vessels also offloaded good catches of prime quality sardines to contribute to Morocco's renowned market and to provide excellent cover for their true mission.

Mariama furnished all this new information as a footnote on a brief to Rodney, focusing, as she imagined he wanted, on the better-known routes and shipments of their old friends Alimento Atlântico and Approvisionnement Alimentaire Européen.

As always, Rodney had found Mariama's work most illuminating. As Group 8's work had already uncovered in the post-Özgürlük investigations, the recruitment of youth into militia forces was, of course, not new. However, the organized structure of the networks that delivered the boy soldiers and picked-up other human cargo spoke to a high level of planning and oversight.

One particular piece of the brief that stood out was the note that the Costa-Rica-registered vessels were skippered by Russians. Rodney was able to query the records of Lloyds of London and reach out to other sources to take a longer look at these skippers and vessels.

Although formally part of the global Peces Tropicales Transamericanos fleet (which proved to be much larger than one might have initially thought), the vessels in question never left the Eastern Atlantic. In regard to their captains, it was not unusual that Mariama's informants had lumped them into the category of "Russian," in point of fact most were Ukrainian with only two native Russians listed in the fleet records.

The boats did not seem to have a local home harbor, their paperwork showing a base of the Port of Limon in Costa Rico. However, they had local agents in Calabar and Contonu in addition to Takoradi and El Jadida. Additionally, they were linked to a fish processing plant, GAMFISH, in Banjul—this plant, Rodney discovered, tied to a fisheries handling facility in Texas.

Rodney was impressed. As he zoomed out, it was all interrelated.

Orest had, as would be expected, a macro-level overview of the movement of commodities (living and otherwise) around the massive Domov web. However, on-the-ground details were at times sparse, especially when the activities were undertaken by operatives who were participating more in a role as themselves, private businessmen, than as agents of the organization (a mode of operations dating back to the organization's early days as the founders sought recipes to bring on-board independent-minded actors of long-standing). Yet this oft-used methodology notwithstanding, learning of the repeated interception (capture in his mind) of products on valued channels such as those recently and unilaterally used by Tomas Ferreira, Yves Noirot, and Radutu Botezatu was troubling.

From within and without there seemed to be growing disorder.

Was the *Maliar* slipping?

Orest undoubtedly did not think of himself in the specific imperial terms of the *Kráľ Hory*—the King of the Hill. After all, he smiled to himself, where was the hill? The Netherlands (Les Pays-Bas meaning "the lowlands") had few hills, certainly not along the North Sea seashore—the highest point, 1,059 feet in elevation, situated 240 miles away in the extreme south of the country, at the tricorner junction of the borders of the Netherlands with Belgium and Germany. Hill or no hill, he was sitting at the apex. He was the *Maliar*. He was responsible, and he was feeling older than his years.

Joe was not privy, of course, to the *Maliar's* thoughts. However, had he been, he would have understood. As he was driving through downtown Pottsville to pick up Susan at work—she was still nursing and her car was in the garage—as he drove to the Schuylkill Medical Center—what had been the Pottsville Hospital when Sue had started nursing—passing Saint Patrick's (where he was still a parishioner albeit with a very poor attendance record), he mused at how much things had changed and how much they were still the same. There was now all manner of new novelties he felt he scarcely understood. There were shops selling skateboards, speciality beers and coffee, along with exotically named things like Moo goo gai pan (what he used to call pork fried rice). However, behind it all there remained a handful of powerful coal companies that continued to fight the tides of the times and wax nostalgically for those days when coal had been king. Just like with Domov, what you saw could be misguiding—what you saw was all too often not what you got. Appearances were critical, but be careful when you peel back the facade. Pottsville may have appeared as a typical small town adapting to the ever-changing needs of the present. Yet it was likely Pottsville was still hemorrhaging as it had been for decades after the coal boom—there were no doctors to tell if the loss of blood would be fatal.

Was there an analogy between the coal companies and Domov—were both out of touch with the times? Were they both hemorrhaging?

It was complicated.

Joe too was feeling older than his years.

⚘⚘⚘⚘⚘⚘⚘

Harold would have understood at least some of his father's questions. The younger now leading Mitchell was feeling the pressure if not feeling older. They had wanted to gain traction and momentum. Mission accomplished. Things were moving quickly on several fronts—maybe too quickly.

S&J, FLS, and KHHF were all busy if not over-extended, each in their own, sometimes overlapping, sphere. Even though Harold had attempted to moderate the expansion of these operations, there was considerable external pressure—both from the clientele as the general public and from the clientele as, in any of a number of ways, Domov-connected.

To add to the smorgasbord that awaited his attention, he had been contacted by someone named Chakir who said he represented senior management, and he had some old files which he thought might interest Harold. It turned out these were updated lists of second-, third-, and fourth-tier parties and operatives who had been involved in one way or another with Delpro—senior management thinking it would be a good thing to fold as many of these individuals and firms as possible into the new and growing set of activities—tacitly stressing the need for effective inclusivity and coordination for Domov operations. Since the request was not discretionary, Harold put yet another set of activities into motion. He recruited a new team of would-be young residents, christening them the KHHF Outreach Unit. The official story was that the team was to explore those on the list provided as could-be donors to the foundation. The unit was to reach-out to each listed name to get a short biographical sketch and then to specifically determine if the interviewee knew of KHHF, for some reason if they had ever worked with a group named Delpro, and if they would like to be contacted about new opportunities. The results of the survey were to be passed to Harold who would decide about any follow-up.

The juggling continued.

For his part, Gage Smith did not like juggling. He wanted to concentrate on one thing, do it well, then move on. However, he worked at the pleasure of his boss or bosses and had to do what he had to do.

While the Sullivan issue seemed to have been put to rest, the work of and influence over the committee itself remained an open question. However, Gage's immediate priority, as per instructions, was to make sure the Cumberland Savings and Ralph Tave debacles did not have any knock-on effects. Tave was already under close scrutiny, probably close to being indicted. Whether he could save himself or not (or whether he deserved to be saved) remained to be seen. The first and easiest task was to get Cumberland Savings off the table, and this had been easier than one might have thought.

Gage had been able to plant a variety of fake but very professionally done information incriminating the bank and its officers. With impressive rapidity and efficiency, the local authorities had indicted the bank leaders and closed the institution—customers refunded in full for their investments even though, through regulator pressure, some of the monies to cover these large one-time payments had surprisingly come from heretofore undisclosed offshore accounts of the bank managers.

Cumberland Savings was no more and all possible links to the Mitchells seemed now to have vanished.

⚘⚘⚘⚘⚘⚘⚘

Rodney would have found it ironic if he had known that he was sharing similar sentiments with Harold Mitchell (although he had no idea who Harold Mitchell was). Following the ignominious departure of Jake Sullivan, action on all fronts had ramped up significantly. Section T15-Z was now fully functional. More and more offenders were identified and now feeling the weight of the complex cases that had been built diligently over the years. Many of the long known but heretofore untouchable key actors like the original Delpro moles along with Raymond Girard, Tomas Ferreira, Radutu Botezatu, and many others had now been red flagged and either faced justice or needed to run to the hills (if they had not already buried themselves in these very same hills). But, and it was a big BUT, there were so many more—still so many in the shadows with no red flag—not even a silhouette. There were still a lot of folks and institutions, still a lot of seemingly ordinary people, who were immersed fully or part-time in activities that were somehow tied to Domov. This was worrisome.

At the same time the cases against the known entities grew stronger and stronger, implicating others and illuminating previously unknown corrupt dealings. A good example was Ralph Tave. Mariama's latest brief had mentioned PTT: Peces Tropicales Transamericanos. Rodney recalled from his earlier work and the testimony of Charlie Stancik that this Costa Rican company had been involved through Delpro with a Texas fish processing factory—the factory also involved with Tave while PTT was tied to Tomas Ferreira—circles within circles. There were many threads upon which to pull.

Rodney and his team pulled on them all. Some were short, leading nowhere. Some were brittle with age and broke into tiny shards. Some, with delicate caresses backed up with needed bursts of power, were dissected from the wider tapestry. They were able to identify nearly a dozen disguised yet extensive passages ferrying illegal immigrants and contraband into Europe and North America. At this stage, once verified and documented, Section T15-Z handed over the actionable information to local authorities—domestic or international. If the cases went to trial, and most did, Section T15-Z had a group of lawyers who testified and worked with the relevant prosecutors.

To the satisfaction of all, it was working. The list of those convicted on Domov-related crimes was growing. However, reality continued to nag Rodney. Although still unable to concretely categorize or quantify

Domov and its impact, the one fact that had not changed for years was that this organization was huge, well-run, and more than up to the challenge provided by government agents of any service—the diverse legion of the cabal had been at it a long time and had highly honed skills. Could Section T15-Z realistically compete?

Whatever the true answer, Rodney knew the reply would be yes. They would, as they had always done, move ahead.

Rodney would have been pleasantly impressed if he had been aware of the repercussions the efforts of Section T15-Z were having in the field—it was not for naught that the organization had spent so much effort in trying to drive the DOJ crew down a dead-end street. Now, under orders from above, the old cadre of long-time Domov functionaries was being pushed further and further into the darkest shadows. Even those who were not already embroiled in some form of legal entanglement were ordered to stand down. For these once key actors, all threads to Domov would be cut for the foreseeable future. Gatherings like the Easter meetings in the Făgăraș Mountains were indefinitely suspended. Operators who were not at immediate risk of investigation or litigation should return fully to their civilian jobs. Those who were in more jeopardy should implement their long-standing emergency plans and go to ground. There was a general alert across the Domov empire.

As dire as this may have sounded to those few who saw the full scale of the warnings, this was not at all apocalyptic. It had happened before and would happen again. Domov was built for these threats. Domov was a multiform chameleon. Domov was an amoeba. When the external pressure built from whatever sources, Domov would briefly retrench and then reshape itself—never being out of business. Going back to the founders' original thoughts, this repurposing and reinventing was good for the long-term survivability of the organization. In relatively short order, it could completely change its superstructure, while the work on the ground, now painted a different color, continued. This fluidity had proven many times to be a successful tactic to counter overly aggressive law-enforcement or other inconveniences.

The repercussions of the now wide-spread anti-Domov actions were not evenly applied nor evenly felt. Grassroots proctors like the Cisses or Kyrylo Rudenko were aware of very little—almost as cut off as the soporose Robin McCandless. Tangential actors like Sir Horace or Chantal Silue sensed some changes, recognizing these more like a feral animal sensing the wind than by the results of direct activities. The less fortunate such as Lambert Richardson, Mercer McMaster, and Ralph Tave were talking to their lawyers while the entrenched entrepreneurs including Radutu Botezatu and Raymond Girard completely focused on their legitimate businesses as the more iniquitous actors in the mold of Tomas Ferreira or Yves Noirot faded even more into the woodwork. It was a reshuffling of the deck.

Gage Smith was not immune to this revamping. He was now to concentrate all his efforts and bring to bear all his skills to isolate the Mitchells from any ill-effects of the ongoing reorganization. Remaining in the twilight where he was so at home, undetected and undetectable, he was to buffer in all ways necessary the fledgling American program.

Oriana felt she too was experiencing some revamping (though, had she been privy to the wider landscape, her reconditioning would be nothing compared to what was going on under the tutelage of her unknown father). She was quite happy to move into a secondary role with the work of the ladies in Abidjan and more than pleased with the way the arrangements with SAMHAFRI were working out. However, as she should have known, it wasn't as though she had inherited a whole block of new time to spend with her dear David.

The African work, mostly due to her personal commitment rather than any professional obligations or official responsibilities, was still sucking up a considerable chunk of time as she, at the very least, attempted to keep up to speed with the work of her very driven and now highly effective colleagues. Then there was the paper. As, at least on paper, she had withdrawn considerably from her pervious Afrocentric work, Blake Samuelson had added a number of new items on her plate including (he considering it totally logical, after all, she was French) contributions to the food-and-beverage section with a focus on international restauranteurs starting up in the US—the first target preselected for Oriana's attention being a new African eatery in DC apparently run by Ivorians—right down her alley.

As she sipped her intense double espresso at an outside table in front of a small café on West 33rd Street, about halfway between Penn Station and Herald's Square, waiting to meet David as he returned from his daily pilgrimage to the Energy Elite offices in Elizabeth, New Jersey, Oriana watched the steam from her cup rise, climbing up the gritty facade of the Barclay's Bank high-rise. As her eyes followed the whiff of vapor above the cacophony of the sidewalk, the coffee-born mist seemed to be absorbed into the plumage of pigeons perched onto encrusted building windowsills, carefully watching for any crumbs left behind by café-goers. It seemed ironic. Here in one of the most renowned megalopolises in the world, as everywhere, there were always the scavengers waiting to see what could be taken—looking for the best opportunities at the least cost. The more things were different, the more they were the same.

Climax or Anticlimax

Joe had retired. Retirement was a benchmark for most coal workers and businessmen in Pottsville if not for most operators of Domov. He rationalized (using this argument to pre-clear his not-often-approved plans with upper management in Holwerd) that Harold had already taken over the reins and was now doing an excellent job. The tacit part of this decision was a declaration that Yosyp Myshchenko had done what he had been asked to do. The other unsaid part of this decision was that he was tired. It had been a long slog, but things had been accomplished. His children, both inside and outside the organization, were doing well. He and his wife were in relatively good health and wanted to enjoy some remaining years untethered—no longer needing to look over their shoulder and make sure the curtains were always closed.

Like many of their Pennsylvania confreres, they sold their home and business interests (at least the figureheads in Pottsville) and moved to Florida. Susan took a part-time job at a local hospital just to keep her hand in. Joe took up golf.

Orest and his lieutenants, of course, had been consulted before the decision on Joe's retirement had been finalized. Timing mattered. Where the senior Mitchell couple retired mattered. The whole thing mattered.

Exceptionally, Yosyp Myshchenko would be able to retire—to leave the organization. But it was conditional.

Overall, it was seen as a good move. Although Gage had assured all he had swept the ground clean and the Pottsville Mitchells were in no risk of getting looped into any investigation of Ralph Tave, Cumberland Savings, or other individuals or institutions that could tie them to the organization, one never knew. Moving away from the long-time base of Pottsville was a good strategic maneuver. On the more humane side, Joe had done a good job and was entitled to a respite.

Nonetheless, everything Domov-related had knock-on effects. Joe and Harold had been a team from the onset—a duo where the whole was greater than the individual parts in true Domov style. While Harold reassured all the upstream bosses that he could manage fine with his father's retirement (having wholeheartedly supported this honorable exit since it had first been mentioned), his hoped-for conclusion of an unencumbered status quo (if it ain't broke, don't fix it), however, was deemed uncertain given the rapid growth of what was now the entire network coordinated from Durango.

Orest felt they needed a backup. This was too much for one person, be he ever so capable. Thus, Joe's move was predicated on finding a senior person to work directly with Harold in Durango. This was not a debatable point.

The task of finding the right person for the job was assigned to Chakir who found Rubén di Paulo.

Rubén's roots were Columbian. The story was unclear, even to the superb researchers of Domov. Apparently, Rubén's father, Mateo, as a young man had been involved in the drug cartels until he met and ultimately married the beautiful Isabelle who wouldn't accept that her husband was a criminal. Isabelle's aristocratic family managed to arrange through still-to-be-identified means a job for Mateo at the US Embassy in Bogotá and then, with an amazingly quick turn-around, an unusual and hard-to-explain transfer to the US Embassy in La Paz, Bolivia. After five years in this capital reported to be the most altitudinous major city sitting at an elevation of twelve thousand feet on the Andes' Altiplano plateau, Isabelle and Mateo moved to Chicago. Confidantes of the couple indicated they never planned on starting a family, but within two years of settling on the shores of Lake Michigan, Rubén arrived.

The dismayed but proud parents had visions of their son becoming a doctor or perhaps a university professor. Yet, while Rubén proved himself to be a very adept student, he was quickly sucked up into the information technology wave that was bathing his generation. With good grades and demonstrable skills, he was able to get scholarships to carry him all the way through to a PhD at the University of Illinois at Chicago. Completing his studies with an impressive CV, Rubén had job offers from a number of Fortune 500 companies as well as several government agencies.

Nonetheless, despite these opportunities and his parents' warning not to drive away the golden goose that was on his doorstep, Rubén and a classmate from a wealthy Chicago family decided to strike out on their own and form an IT company: UMT—Upper Midwest Technologies.

With ample support from his partner's family, UMT grew quickly into a prominent IT firm with a focus on helping their clients not only have state-of-the-art information systems but also ensuring these clients had access to the quality of information for which they were willing to pay (and clients paid surprisingly large sums for information that was not really that hard to find).

Sadly, just as UMT was really establishing its place as a leader in the local IT community, Rubén's partner drowned in a boating accident on the lake. According to the company's terms of incorporation, if one of the parties was deceased, the company reverted wholly to the survivor. Rubén was now the sole owner of UMT.

It was about this same time that Rubén had been contacted by a certain Mister Gage Smith who was seeking information on a variety of cloaked subjects. This started a relationship that flourished through time and brought Rubén and UMT (admittedly, initially unknowingly) into the Domov web.

A decade and a half later, Rubén and UMT had been involved in an assortment of Domov-related actions—this time with full knowledge and forethought. Chakir had personally worked with Rubén on several occasions and found him to be a prime candidate to work beside Harold.

Before making Rubén an offer and finalizing Joe's separation, Chakir shared Rubén's biodata with Harold and the two met under the cover of a conference in Atlanta on supply chains in the twenty-first century—their individual meeting at the Waldorf Astoria, down Peachetree Road from The Whitely, the venue for the conference.

After brief and formal greetings, Chakir went straight to the point, "So, what do ya think about Rubén?"

"Well," Harold started, a bit too loudly, "let me first say I'm not real sure about this whole thing. Dad's been on the way out for some time, and I've really been running the entire show so I'm not sure why we need to take this step at this time?"

"We don't really need to go there, ya know. The *Maliar* has decided so we're just wasting time if we go back over this—the decision is made—it's only a question of who not if."

"Well, I just want to be on the record to say I have done this. I can do this. Bringing in someone new is full of risks and if things turn out badly, I want it to be clear where I stand—I've been doing this with no real problems and will continue to do this to the satisfaction of all."

"We all understand, and we all know you're doing a great job. We also know the uncertainties of bringing in any sort of outsider—certainly an outsider to this level of operations. But you must see, for your own benefit, not to mention that of the organization, we can't leave such a critical cluster of work as yours—really a continental hub—with no back-up and contingency planning—you need someone who can back you up and watch your back."

"Like I said, I'm on the record. I accept, even if begrudgingly, that the decision has been made and if it must happen, I see a lot of value to Rubén. On the public-facing side he will be very helpful attracting and supporting Latino clients—he is fully bilingual. This would also be a big plus regarding some of the growing areas of focus of our non-public-facing activities—activities I might add for another day's chat, with which I am none too keen—but we won't go there now. Back to Rubén. To add to the pluses, his IT skills would be a real advantage. So, unless he turns out to be a real asshole or something, it seems like you've done a good job finding someone if we really need to have someone."

That was that. Rubén moved to Durango as Joe and Susan moved to Manasota Key.

⚘⚘⚘⚘⚘⚘⚘

Orest viewed Joe's departure with mixed feelings, seeing it through multiple lenses. There was a bit of historical nostalgia. Joe was one of the Ukrainian-born old guard—a pioneer. His absence along with many of the old guards who had been adversely affected by recent events underscored the demand for new faces in Domo*v*. As a manifestly global giant, the core actors were changing in line with the increasingly worldly and hi-tech nature of the operations. This evolution was inevitable and probably positive, but it highlighted the changing times and the changing needs—Joe's retirement encapsulating all this in Orest's eyes.

These same eyes also saw a more pragmatic dimension to this departure. Joe was gone but still around. Was there a threat? He hoped not. The old "til death do us part" relationship between the organization and its soldiers was likely an anachronism. Nonetheless, when one left his corporal and clan (if Domov could still in any way be considered a clan) lives simultaneously there was a finality and a certainty.

As Orest wondered about the past and the future (jumping over the present), he inevitably circled back to his own future. At Willy McNaught's insistence, he made another visit to Franz Schmidt. Things—these being his heath—were not improving in spite of some medication and purported adjustments in lifestyle. To the contrary, Orest's health was declining more rapidly, Schmidt warning of serious problems if changes were not made soon. Exceptionally, it was time for Orest to make some personal decisions.

He shifted now to the present. What was the diagnosis here? While he had shepherded a major amplification of the organization, this had not been, naturally, trouble-free. While troubles were an acknowledged part of the job, the underlying assumption was that the negatives would be far outweighed by the positives. If this were not the case, then there were questions about the confidence the membership could have in his leadership. This was, in fact, the reason the functions of the *obetovať* had been built into Domov.

Ticking off the boxes, as he had done so often, there were negatives. Efforts through Gage Smith to sidetrack the US Senate Committee and the work of Section T15-Z had been terribly drawn-out and ultimately unsuccessful. This had not only added fuel to the work of his nemesis Rodney Mills, but it had taken off the board Jake Sullivan—a pliant politician who might have served future purposes.

All of this had been further mucked-up by the disastrous arms deal between Lambert Richardson and Mercer McMaster—a testament of why high-level command and control was essential to these delicate operations. Just when all efforts were focusing on wiping Delpro off memories and thoroughly sealing new activities from any external scrutiny, this highly-publicized gun-running catastrophe had pushed back progress on several fronts—adding to the risks that the new foothold they were trying to establish could be somehow affected.

These points all merged together when the subject of Delpro was breached. The old Delpro acts and actors had significantly faded but, of late, had resurfaced in the form of, among others, renewed legal actions even if some were done in absentia.

Delpro had had a much more expansive reach than most had realized—Robin McCandless had really done impressive work. With Robin's now seemingly permanent departure, it had been unrealistic to think that these stalwart "Delproians" would simply vanish or wait patiently for the parent organization to put in place a new structure. There had been far more threads left than Orest had appreciated—far too many loose ends for the keen eyes of Rodney Mills.

The missteps in the US had potentially had a critical effect on the building of the new program, but they had also had worldwide impacts. So many of those who, like Robin McCandless, had done their business in the full light of day, had now sadly been exposed. The organization had the built-in flexibility and adaptability to address the issues, but it would take time—time that would otherwise be devoted to garnering more power and wealth. This drop in receipts, so to speak, was an unpardonable sin.

Then there was an assortment of smaller issues that were not really that small and were like the straw that broke the camel's back. In the aggregate, things like their reduced presence in French ports and the inability to come to a meaningful agreement with Les Caïds of Le Milieu, the irritating work of unfriendly forces in West Africa, the loss (to who knew where) of Cynthia Owens and Özgürlük, and, of course, the never-ending competition with other Eastern European and global groups who wanted to dominate the stage in various areas of illicit trade, all these and more compounded and confounded Domov's efforts. All these reflected directly on Orest.

It was all disquieting.

Oriana had no clue as to her father's trials and tribulations. In fact, she was in the process of trying to put her troubles behind her. She was concentrating on her future—their future.

At this stage, she and David were a solid couple even without any formal vows, and this was the most important thing in her life.

She had decided to try and seal off her uneasiness about what to do about the misguided letter she had found among David's mail. She had shredded her notes and decided this, in the first instance, did not even regard her lover. Moreover, it was an old tale of no relevance to anyone now. She needed to simply forget it and ignore any flashbacks. It was as though it had never happened.

This jettisoning of what she knew full well could have been a possibly important piece of a puzzle did not affect her continued interest, albeit at a distance now, in the work of her colleagues in West Africa. She had (and was proud of it) deep connections to this region and was more than a little invested in the outcomes of these ladies' efforts although she was less and less directly involved on a regular basis.

With some redirection and reprioritization—basically an overhaul—of her days and months, Oriana found she had a very agreeable life which she most enjoyably shared with a most wonderful person. She was happy.

⚘⚘⚘⚘⚘⚘⚘

Jan's life was not full of hyperbolic good feeling, but she was at least satisfied enough with her present situation to stay in Abidjan as opposed to returning to DC. She felt she—really following the lead of Awa and Mariama—was doing good work.

With the Virginia governor's nomination of a replacement for the former Honorable Jacob Sullivan, the newly-seated gentleman—actually a gentlewoman—from Virginia had picked her staff and Jan no longer had ties with any US agency or institution (as expected, all links to the embassy had fallen off when Jan was no longer an official staffer) and this was just fine. The new arrangements with SAMHAFRI were excellent. All three women were paid more than they ever imagined they could be and, more importantly, they now had the support of a local office with staff and a budget and rapid-response links to the entire SAMHAFRI organization and network. It all exceeded her expectations—so maybe there were some hyperbolic good feelings.

The work with SAMHAFRI had widened the lens and they were looking in more places for more indications of abuse and illicit activities involving but not limited to human trafficking. The efforts in CAR were indicative of this new broader approach. There was definitely no shortage of subjects to investigate.

The Abidjan trio continued to liaise closely with Oriana. However, now this was more to brief her about the top-level activities as opposed to engage her directly in the sleuthing. Oriana also remained an important liaison—not only to the colleagues at Fordham but also to Rodney Mills whom they knew only by reputation but valued this direct line to a high-powered federal agency if needed.

It was all fine.

Yet, in those early morning hours as Jan lay in her bed waiting for the brilliant tropical sun to vault into the sky and the lonely neighborhood rooster to crow, before the volume of the *quartier's* ambient noise picked-up as neighboring households met the day, Jan would wonder if all she and her collaborators were doing was even leaving a discernible footprint. It was a game of whack-a-mole and it so often seemed the mole was winning.

Had Jan shared her thoughts with Rodney, he would have understood completely. The mole was winning. This wasn't pessimism, it was realism. This wasn't a reason to become despondent; it was a reason to become energized. This wasn't new. It was the way it had always been. The greedy, the power-hungry, and the unscrupulous—those for whom the ends totally justified the means, and the means were perpetually self-serving—had always been numerous. Without them, he wouldn't have had a job.

And he had a job—a big job.

He was loath to say things were going well. Nevertheless, the now Winterbottom Committee, to recast an old if ill-chosen term, was fully supporting Section T15-Z. D-2 and Group 8 were working smoothly together with much improved coordination with collaborating overseas agencies. The list of known and even indicted bad guys was growing. The end was unquestionably not in sight, but the picture was becoming clearer.

Gage Smith was all about clarity—at least his version of clarity. This involved making sure the messages he delivered were clear and well understood although the identity and even the affiliation of the messenger remained invariably shrouded—unknown.

Gage should've been, therefore, satisfied with the clarity of his new instructions. He was (once again) to relocate back to the UK. He had rendered several vital services in the US, but it was possible the shroud had slipped in the process, and they did not want to risk his identity being uncovered. Operating offshore would provide an added level of security as well as get him better situated to assist as necessary with other jeopardized operatives who were potentially getting closer to the spotlight as the global attack on Domov intensified.

In many ways, Gage was happy to have an out. He had aggressively followed his instructions and had hopefully accomplished what was intended. However, it was indeed prudent to put some distance between him and those with whom he had been so recently aggressively interacting.

He found a flat in Bisley, in Surrey, close enough to the M3 to get into the city if need be and far enough out of the city to be able to enjoy some peace and quiet. He liked the UK.

Harold liked Durango. Every day he marveled at how different it was from Pottsville—nearly polar opposites in many ways. Yet the job was still the job. With his father's retirement, the job had become much bigger. He was fine with all the changes and even found Rubén di Paulo to be an asset—quickly appreciating him as a valued and talented member of the team.

The original pieces of the Mitchell enterprises were maturing into operations with their own momentum and their qualified teams of staff. Perhaps ironically, it was the non-profit that was the most challenging. S&J Logistics along with Fig Leaf Storage continued along their bimodal paths—one lane, public facing, attracting a growing clientele and another, covered with layers of Domov secrecy, also flourishing as a sundry group of tangential actions overseen by the organization helped establish expanding ties with the new American operators. Crews and midlevel management were gaining experience and skill, customers were appreciating attention to detail, and business was good.

KHHF, however, had a more challenging and continuous balancing act. They still had to meet all the bureaucratic and social requirements of being an acknowledged charitable foundation, including having verifiable benefits for their targets of the poor and destitute. This was a major task in and of itself. Then, as the foundation was a critical intermediary in many of the less seemly activities including the clandestine movement of various groups of people for various reasons, the ability to meet the expectations of the organization while having a testable facade as a charity was a real juggling act.

They had come close to dropping all the juggled balls when SAMHAFRI had reached out so insistently and repeatedly. Ultimately, the same bland and hollow replies echoed over and over again had apparently made the point that KHHF was not interested in joining hands with anyone other than their impoverished beneficiaries.

So far so good.

The juggling, by all measures, was working on all fronts.

Harold would definitely not engage in any pompous and self-serving flattery nor any feel-good pat-yourself-on-the-back sentimentalism. The fact that things seemed to be moving forward well and at a good pace was, in his view, a warning he noted every day—the better they went, the worse they could get. Harold was a realist. He was always cautious and controlled—no over enthusiasm nor false expectations for the juggler with so many balls in the air. He understood all too well that, in point of fact, what the audience most wanted to see was that the juggler failed—the balls falling askew, crashing to the ground. He refused to give the audience this satisfaction.

Orest now instinctively juggled many things at once. This was the work of the *Maliar*, but each day it became more difficult. Each day the cautions of Franz Schmidt rang in his ears, competing with the sound of a clicking clock as it seemed, while his health declined, so too declined his scorecard as leader—there were more and more actions that could be viewed askance by others. For the first time, the possibility of being blackballed rose up as a real if unlikely possibility.

Things were not going well.

Orest began taking solitary walks in the nature preserve near the Cliffs of Wierum trying to assess the present and weigh the future. Although he had long minimized its role, the "board," the *obetovať* was a reality with which he needed to be prepared to contend.

How far should he go? In how much jeopardy should he put himself?

If he were forced to react to a judgment by the *obetovať* it could well mean not only the end of his leadership but the end of his life. The ultimate price was not out of the question when looking for punishment for failure (real or perceived).

Orest decided proactive was better than reactive.

There was an off-ramp, though one that had never been used.

He reached out to the *obetovať*. In the personal sections of *The Times* of London, *The New York Times*, the *Tokyo Yomiuri Shimbun*, and *Le Figaro* in Paris, he posted a short ad. To preempt the feared message of "Road blocked, classes at Svesa closed, please assist," Orest sent a simple and pre-selected message, "Classes at Svesa cancelled."

Not waiting for a reaction, Orest spent the next day arranging his overseas accounts. Then, carrying only a holdall with carefully selected items, he organized for a driver to drop him off near the port of Rotterdam under the pretext of needing to follow-up on some sensitive shipments. He immediately took a city taxi to the International Bus Station on Conradstraat where he bought a one-hundred-and-thirty US-dollar ticket for the 915-mile, twenty-five-plus-hour bus trip to Barcelona. The *Maliar*, now the ex-*Maliar*, had left Holwerd.

Postmortem

HAROLD was home early on Lizard Head Drive. This was very unusual. Typically work demanded a sunrise start and a wrap-up well after sunset. Maybe the addition of Rubén to the team was having tangible and beneficial effects.

He was just in the process of determining what wine to have with the exceptionally quiet evening at home when the doorbell rang. Answering the call, Harold found an erect, clean-shaven man of middle-age, above-average-height, sandy hair, and blue eyes on the stoop extending his right hand in an anticipated greeting.

"Mister Harold Mitchell," the bellringer began, with just a hint of an accent, "my name is Hans van den Berghe. I come from Holwerd."

"Please come in," the master of the house replied, trying to hide any dismay, "I was just opening a bottle of wine."

When both men were seated in Harold's comfortable salon, each with a glass of Château Pontette-Cannette Grand Cru Pauillac, Hans van den Berghe continued, "Sorry for the impromptu visit, Harold, if I may call you 'Harold?' I met your father years ago during a meeting in the Făgăraş Mountains, but I seriously doubt he ever mentioned me. Now, as I am sure you realized when I mentioned Holwerd, I am here in regard to the work of the *Maliar*."

This was a word Harold had only heard as a distant reference. The *Maliar* was almost like a historical figure such as William Shakespeare or Alexander the Great or General George Smith Patton—names heard and even valued without being personalized—more an institution than a human-being. He was unsure how to respond, offering only, "Yeah, 'Harold' is fine—please go on."

"Excellent," the man from the metaphorical hill took a deep breath. "You likely knew our—I say 'our' because, just as you, I am a part of the organization—*Maliar* was Orest Savchuk. I say 'was' because Orest has resigned. He has unexpectedly left not only Holwerd but the organization."

Hans paused for a reaction but there was none.

"At this stage, I am not at liberty to describe the process. And I am not sure I am even privy to the entire set of actions that have been and are being put in motion because of the unplanned vacancy at the top of the organization. I am a messenger and an agent, but I am not a decider. I am not even aware of the identities of those who do make such paramount decisions, but I can say that the decision has been taken."

Another pause with no reaction.

"Harold Mitchell, you have been nominated as the next *Maliar*."

This time there was an audible exhalation, almost a gasp.

"I should immediately add that this nomination can be respectfully declined if you so choose."

A nearly breathless Harold interjected simply, almost in a whisper, "Please go on."

"OK, but you've already received the bulk of my message." The Dutchman smiled and took a sip of wine before continuing, "still there is some background. As I am sure you are all too aware, the organization is concentrating heavily on re-establishing a significant presence here in North America. In addition to your personal qualifications which you have demonstrated so well over the years, having the new apex of the organization in North America is seen as an act that would underscore the priority given to these operations as well as show clearly that we are here to stay."

A glance at Harold indicated he was still absorbing what he had just heard.

"I know this is a lot." Hans seemed be to wrapping up. "So if you want some time, that's fine. Take as long as you need. This is obviously a communication we do not want to trust to anything except a direct face-to-face exchange, so I'll hang around until you've made your decision. I have a room in town as I don't want to put you out."

Harold seemed to shake himself like a cat getting up from a nap. "Hans, thanks. I can tell you now, I am honored to accept the nomination."

"This is wonderful news," the visitor said, seeming to conclude, "and I too am honored to have been part of the process. I must, however, inform you that, regardless of your immediate reaction, my instructions are to return to Holwerd as soon as I have your opening decision—which I now have. Lastly, I am instructed to advise you that I will be back in a fortnight to make real plans. The organization wanted to give you some days to let this opportunity sink in and allow you time to consider the implications—they called it 'a breather'— before we start putting more permanent changes in place. As I've said, with the commitment to expansion in North America, the organization hopes the new *Maliar's* base will be somewhere in this region. These are the details we will discuss when I return. So, thank you for the hospitality and I will see you soon unless we hear from you to the contrary."

It was done.

Harold did not reach out to Hans with the prearranged code, "cancel your travel plans." Harold did not change his mind. Harold was overwhelmed but Harold was now determined to be the *Maliar* (something, now a possibility, that had never entered his mind).

Harold did spend considerable time trying to assess the impact of this decision. He went through a myriad of mental gymnastics: what if this, what if that. But, in the end, he decided it was all about fate. This was his fate. He knew he could in no way imagine what the job of *Maliar* really entailed. He could not know what was in-store. The future was unrecognizable. It was his fate, and he would move forward.

It was, therefore, with an open mind and no regrets that he met Hans on his return trip. Once they had got settled again at the home on Lizard Head Drive and Harold had reconfirmed his acceptance of the position of *Maliar*, it probably should have been expected that Hans would have arrived with a draft game plan ready to go.

He had.

When Orest Savchuk had taken over for the deceased Taras Kuzmenko, the world at large and the world of Domov had been very different places. The shift from Bourg-en-Bresse to Holwerd had been the least of the challenges in the change of leadership. There had been some modest staff changes, but basically it was simply a question of renting properties and developing backstories for lives in the Netherlands as had been done for similar lives in France.

This transition was much different. Not only was the epicenter moving from one continent to another, but there was also a trove of documents and even a large quantity of IT and other tools in spite of the organization's distain for modern communications technologies. This involved a coordinated effort, and the crew from Holwerd had a plan.

Hans' great-grandfather had worked at Brand Brewery, an institution reportedly dating back to the thirteen hundreds and the oldest brewer in the Netherlands. Thus, he could honestly say that brewing beer was a family tradition.

With this in mind, the Holwerd staff had established BockBrew, an on-paper Dutch brewery with a long if totally concocted history.

The staff had then almost randomly picked the Pacific Northwest of the US as the best area for the center for the new *Maliar*—an area heretofore with little if any recent Domov activity (and only limited Delpro presence once-upon-a-time).

And there was a marriage. The Pacific Northwest had a burgeoning micro-brewery industry. Dutch BockBrew could slip in almost unnoticed but well-appreciated.

This was the prepackaging Hans brought for Harold's consideration—Harold now the new *Maliar* having the final say.

For lack of a better alternative, Harold was all in and Hans signaled to the team in Holwerd to send an exploratory group to find the right place and then organize the move with as little fanfare as possible.

A new cycle had begun.

Naturally, there were always cycles—there were always circles within circles. Yet, when it was all said and done, Rodney feared he was not far from where he had started. For Hal and for justice he had imagined that by this time things would have been signed, sealed, and delivered—due process and retribution achieved. This obviously was not the case.

To the objective observer, they were not far from where they had been when Robin McCandless had disappeared in the smoke of his vessel on Chesapeake Bay. Then as now the seriousness, the urgency, of the problem had been well understood even if the perpetrators and their organizations were often shrouded in the shadows.

Detailed and wide-reaching investigations had taken place. People had been indicted. Yet, the bad guys had continued to grow and flourish. Now, years later, Robin McCandless was out of the picture, but individuals likely much worse than he were center stage. Delpro had vanished and they now had a much clearer, if still heavily veiled, view of Domov—its reach, impact, and danger.

They had volumes of new and newly verified data on the litany of activities where Domov was directly or indirectly involved. But, in spite of it all, they were still apparently no closer to getting the leadership of the malefactors behind bars. They had been chasing their tail. They had tromped across a lot of ground in the process but were basically back where they had started. Or so it seemed.

On the positive side—perhaps—reports coming back from around the globe, especially through INTERPOL via Group 8, indicated numerous Domov and Domov-related activities had been interrupted if not halted. Though there had been few arrests, there seemed to have been considerable disruption.

Moreover, due to the shenanigans (as the Vice President had called them) of the Sullivan Committee and others, by Executive Order, Section T15-Z along with Group 8 and D-2 had been wiped off the roster—they simply ceased to exist, all replaced by SESB—Special Executive Security Branch—with direct funding through NSA and rather limited oversight from anywhere. It was a new packaging for an old job, but it included Rodney at the forefront and all the time-tested members of his crew as part of the new structure.

And not everything was back where it had started.

Actually, Rodney reminisced, several people who had been caught up in the web during previous lives or in earlier times had been able to divert their paths, not ending up chasing their tails. These folks, who had helped him build much of his original case against Delpro and McCandless, had somehow managed to sort through all the muck and muddle and find some level of normalcy. Maybe there was hope for them all?

His West Coast family, Eddie and Lisa, had become absorbed in the work of SAMHAFRI, even if doing so in their roles as overseers and not active on-the-ground players. What had started as a detached advocation had really become a vocation if not a passionate cause.

Similarly and surprisingly, Charlie Stancik and his long-time partner Jo McCormick, living not that far away from Eddie and Lisa, had reshaped what could have been a comfortable early retirement (with Rodney's go-ahead, Charlie, ever the businessman, had cut a very lucrative deal with DOJ for his testimony) into very engaged roles in a local community group aimed at improving needed services to isolated coastal dwellers—an assignment that, to their own surprise, had made good use of the skills they had honed so well, at least in Charlie's case, in the service of Robin McCandless and Delpro.

Perhaps equally surprising, given their proximity to each other and their potentially shared history—or at least parts of their histories—Eddie and Lisa and Charlie and Jo did not really see each other that often. They were certainly not mates albeit their tracks did cross, especially when working with Rodney or giving depositions to this or that committee or tribunal. Rodney had always felt they had too many common denominators to be friends. A respectable distance seemed to make for the soundest bonds.

The same scenario applied to Peter and Evelynn—a respectable distance with sporadic encounters relating to the prosecution of known rapscallions sustained loose ties to Rodney and the others for some sort of overarching common goal of redressing the injustices of Delpro and Domov. In the case of the latter couple, this close-at-a-distance phenomenon was the easiest to accomplish as Peter and Evelynn had, when the time had been right, moved from Cape Verde to Silves, Portugal (keeping to the lusophone culture), where they had an avocado farm—only coming back to the States when summoned by Rodney.

Among the group of once-young folk whose lives had been touched by Domov in one way or another, Paula seemed to have a present the least influenced by the past. She continued (at what some observers maintained was a "ripe old age") to work at the Center for Equitable Social Policies—CESP—living in the DC area and available when needed.

So many contrasting people and contrasting stories.

Rodney remembered interviewing Charlie, one of the first high-level insiders to really cooperate, who had actually intentionally chosen as a career path with a course leading directly to Delpro and so much more. During one of those first questioning periods, the introspective former operative had said, "It had been so good. It had been so bad."

Peter, however, a more unsuspecting mid-level insider, had not had Charlie's opportunities for advance planning nor weighing options—he had simply stumbled and then fallen into the waiting arms of Delpro. Yet, when he began assisting investigators and telling his tale, he felt even this arbitrary route had led to a strange mix of the good with the bad.

The other two members of the quartet who had been among his first witnesses presenting verifiable details about the multifaceted enterprise called Delpro that had ultimately led to the colossus that was Domov, two outsiders to these organizations, had had much more tangential if no less impactful relationships with these inimical enterprises—they seeing much less good mixed into the darkness and malevolence that generated so much wealth and power for those who continuously abused the system for their own interests.

Different views were sewn together by common threads of greed and wantonness demonstrated to varying degrees in various circumstances by a transnational syndicate that was always driven by a near manic need for more and more power.

These illicit actions were, as they had always been, the self-centered and pervasive misdeeds that provided the foundations of a case against skilled and stealthful adversaries.

Things may not have returned to where they had started but some things were pretty close. Perhaps, Rodney mused, it was all a question of finding new ways to do old things.

⚘⚘⚘⚘⚘⚘⚘

Harold was inundated with new ways and new things. Struggling ahead, during a rare respite, he smiled to himself as he listened to one of his new aides recount recent articles referring to growing skullduggery (the journalist's word) across the country that was, in the view of the writer, an omen of a return to the criminality of the 1930s. "If they only knew," the new *Maliar* thought. Actually, he continued his reflection, "If I had only known."

The transition of the organization's captaincy had been a massive endeavor. It had taken months. Thankfully, for Harold at least, through most of the initial period he had remained in the relative calm of Durango and attempted to continue with his old life as usual—to the outside world the same old, same old while internally he had worked hard on the handover to Rubén. Rubén needed to be brought in on the plans for the pending shift whereby his immediate boss became the big boss.

While a seamless transfer had been slowly taking place in the foothills of The Rockies, further west, on the crashing Oregon coastline where the much smaller coast range tumbled dramatically into the sea, the initial group called in by Hans had found a site for their micro-brewery: the small community of Heceta. This location had offered isolation and at the same time access to population centers and transport as well as communications hubs. It was ideal.

For Heceta the BockBrew brewery was not a prop. It had to be a real functioning operation that produced a high-quality product, even if in low volume—just enough to have adequate sales to justify the presence of the facility. Moreover, as a Dutch import, they had had to assemble all the needed hardware in Europe and then, after dealing with the formal customs' bureaucracy, ship this to the Pacific Coast of the US. All this had taken considerable time.

This had had, however, the advantage that, unlike in Bourg-en-Bresse and Holwerd where staff supporting the *Maliar's* headquarters had unavoidably been scattered hither and yon about the local communities with a variety of cover stories, here, with a functioning brewery as a nucleus, all staff could be linked to this centerpiece. Nevertheless, this scenario did require people who really knew how to make beer. Fortunately, Hans had trusted family members who had stayed in the business and were willing relocate for a handsome stipend.

Once BockBrew was up and running, it was time to find the locus for the *Maliar* himself. Five miles to the north of Heceta, on one of the tallest promontories that overlooked Cox Rock, a basalt islet a mile offshore jutting out of the frothy sea and home to a population of sea lions, they found a large and well-established homestead that was the perfect base for the new master of Domov—a location that also seemed to arouse inspirational thoughts among the staff.

Chakir, a fan of the 1971 film with Paul Newman and Henry Fonda, *Sometimes a Great Notion*, filmed further north along the Oregon Coast, exuberantly remarked that Harold may have been falling into the mold of Ken Kesey, the writer of the book upon which the film had been based, who was rumored to have had a reclusive hideaway somewhere near where the *Maliar* was soon to reside. Maybe this new ground would stimulate creativity—possibly even artistry.

Not to be sidelined, Hans, spying an ancient Indian Shell Mound offering the bleached and broken remains of seafood feasts of times gone by, more matter-of-factly felt he should remind his confederates that these old lands in the New World had seen many come and go and he hoped that, with all the planning and precautions, Domov would be here to stay.

The anecdotes of colleagues aside, setting up shop was a major undertaking.

Then, with the physical infrastructure and the staff in place, it was time for Harold to leave Durango and start the epic process of learning what he needed to know to don the mantel of *Maliar*. As with the move itself, this was no simple process. Even at the highest levels of the organization, there was compartmentalization. The *Maliar* alone held the keys to all the doors. A holistic briefing on the responsibilities and activities that were incumbent on the new leader could only be provided by a list of very high-level operatives, each describing in the minutest detail their own slice of the pie.

It was daunting. Harold could never have imagined the scope and breadth of Domov. He was astonished. He was intimidated. He was enthralled. He was energized. He was many things.

He was now the *Maliar*—the *Kráľ Hory*—the King of the Hill

⚘⚘⚘⚘⚘⚘⚘

Rodney had no idea his archrival was so close to home—really just a stone's throw from Eddie's house and those few roots he still had to the life of his dear departed Hal. Had Rodney realized how near his foe's command post was to his adopted family, he probably would have broken his stride.

Yet, in the absence of this revelation, it was steady-as-she-goes. In spite of all his skepticism, Rodney and his colleagues were indeed gaining momentum—most welcomely, the cadence of positive results finally ratcheting-up at an increasing rate. The legal and judicial systems were slow, but they did grind forward.

These advances had been greatly helped by the establishment of SESB. The core anti-Domov teams now had a solid mandate and solid funding. However, executive support alone was not adequate. They still needed the backing of Congress and here the Winterbottom Committee was proving to be very helpful, the Arizona senator herself a very open and convincing advocate.

The simple fact was, SESB had clout—considerably more than its predecessor. It was able to access previously inaccessible sources of information and build much more effective partnerships with its overseas partners. If there had ever been a chance to control or at least corral Domov, it was through the SESB.

Nevertheless, almost subconsciously, Rodney was forced to realize if not to accept that he would likely never see the downfall of Domov—an act he had so hoped to precipitate. Although his view of the totality of the organization was still far from complete (really just a peep show where his imagination with a good dose of common sense had to finalize the picture on the other side of the wall), each day and each week the glimpses he had of its operations expanded bit by bit. It was undeniable this cloaked hydra was engaged in so much misconduct—perhaps overly-dramatic to call it depravity—around the globe that it could probably be somehow linked to many of the major crimes worldwide. But it was also undeniable that whatever forces were mounted against it, the ever-changing amoeba would likely survive in one form or another.

The reality was hard to accept. Nonetheless, it shouldn't affect their efforts. Rodney and all in SESB needed to carry-on. They were making a difference.

Harold was thinking about differences—how different the position of the *Maliar* looked from the outside than from the inside. He had had no idea. The view from the top of the hill was nearly incomprehensible. The organization was truly everywhere and involved in everything—the coordination of this vast network now in his hands.

He was the steward of the seeds the organization planted across the planet.

This required not only actively jumping on a steep learning curve to be able to grasp the magnitude of these activities (most gratefully with the assistance of a very qualified crew around him—sharing their time between educating the new master and brewing complex BockBrew), but it also required a complete change in work style. In Durango he had been very much hands-on, examining all aspects down to the tiniest details. From the hilltop, it was impossible to micromanage—unrealistic to know more than the broadest outlines of the work underway given the huge volume of activities and enormous quantity of data that were filtered through the hilltop every minute of every day.

This was an adjustment he would gladly make. After seeing much more clearly the job at hand (he was still too new to fully grasp the entirety of the massive web that was the organization), he was committed to porting the mantle, to undertaking the responsibilities and obligations of the *Maliar* and, as a priority, determined to significantly increase the organization's footsteps on his home turf of the USA.

As Domov dug strong toeholds in the siltstone bluffs of the coast, this material thrown up from ancient seabeds during the Pleistocene—as though climbing these escarpments relentlessly if cautiously, an inch at a time—many of the spectators and actors waited, uncertain if there would be a third act or a curtain call. Many of the spectators and actors felt captivated to a greater or lesser degree by the growing forces that seemed to whirl around an energy source going back to Andriy and Lehya—by some means inextricably tying the past to the future, conveniently skipping over the present.

The spectators and actors, of course, continued to have their own stories.

Sophie Arquette received a card from Orest Savchuk postmarked Las Palmas de Gran Canaria simply saying, "Let's meet."

Oriana received her own card, hers postmarked Kirungu in the eastern DRC, the former colonial city of Baudouinville, from Awa and Mariama—her ladies had traveled down Lake Tanganyika to meet with Sister Sujitha who was working with local communities in the Marungu Highlands to try and counter human trafficking emanating from the activities of local warring factions. While Jan was further to the north, on the road from Lake Kivu to Kisangani, the former Stanleyville, which was reported to be a major byway to get human cargo down the river and to the Atlantic Coast—her crew closed their missive with, "wish you were here."

Horace Barthley and the comatose Robin McCandless received a picture postcard from Cynthia Owens saying, as could be seen from the picture, she was in Erbil, Kurdistan, and she hoped the brothers were doing well.

Raymond Girard received a note from Coastal Properties LLC in Fiji informing him that the owner had accepted his offer on the beachfront home in Naburenivalu.

Radutu Botezatu received a message from Bissau from Tomas Ferreira stating, "if you need a place to stay, I've plenty of room."

Joe Mitchell (a.k.a. Yosyp Myshchenko) got a hole-in-one at Oyster Creek Golf Country Club.

During an arms negotiation, Kyrylo Rudenko was killed by an overly anxious member of the Solntsevskaya Bratva.

The Cisses had expanded to a new restaurant in the city of Baltimore where, somehow tied to their eatery, they had a surprisingly high volume of imports coming through the Helen Delich Bentley Port—much of the ill-defined merchandise transiting immediately to private warehouses up the Patapsco River.

Chantal Silue received a memo from the Organization for Unity in Africa acknowledging her application for the post of Assistant Director of Economic Affairs and stating, at this stage, "no commitment either side."

Rich McKnight was ecstatic with his news: there had never been a better ice fishing season!

Shannon Baxter, Ex-Secretary of State, retired, received word from an old friend in Mozambique that "nothing's changed"—the human misery and human trafficking directly linked to international organizations, including those active in the US, was only increasing.

Senator Winterbottom was caught off-guard when she received a call with no caller ID. "Ann," the husky voice, almost a whisper, intoned, "you've gone too far, my dear—really too far. There will be consequences."

The new *Maliar,* too, was not immune. He received a postcard, forwarded by Rubén di Paulo from Durango, with a Trenton, New Jersey, postmark porting the short message: "Mark 8, Verse 36, 'For what shall it profit a man, if he gain the whole world, and suffer the loss of his soul?'"

Harold felt, in fact, very much in contact with his soul as he walked along the secluded sandy beaches, feeling the crashing waves sending little vibrating currents up his legs as his golden retriever, Jackson, perked up his ears at the reverberations of the surf, his nose held high, with apparent pleasure taking great draughts of the sea-scented air. This was pure nature and pure power. As foreseen, there was, the *Maliar* was sure, a pathway to supremacy for those with the courage and skill to take it.

We are thankful for the insight provided by Mr. Arthur C. Clarke in 1968 when, in *2001: A Space Odyssey*, he noted the Star Child's predicament: "For though he was master of the world, he was not quite sure what to do next. But he would think of something."

www.ingramcontent.com/pod-product-compliance
Lightning Source LLC
LaVergne TN
LVHW020522100826
845148LV00010B/1313